The Red Room

Kathleen Stewart was born in Sydney in 1958. She is the author of five books of fiction: *Nightflowers*, *Spilt Milk* (shortlisted for the 1995 NSW Premier's Literary Awards), *Louis: A Normal Novel*, *Victim Train*, and *Waiting Room*; and has published two collections of poetry: *Snow* (shortlisted for the 1994 Banjo Awards and the 1994 *Age* Book of the Year), and *The White Star*.

The Red Room

Kathleen Stewart

ALLEN & UNWIN

This edition published in 2000
First published in 1999

Copyright © Kathleen Stewart 1999

All rights reserved. No part of this book may be reproduced or transmitted in any form or by any means, electronic or mechanical, including photocopying, recording or by any information storage and retrieval system, without prior permission in writing from the publisher. *The Australian Copyright Act* 1968 (the Act) allows a maximum of one chapter or 10% of this book, whichever is the greater, to be photocopied by any educational institution for its educational purposes provided that the educational institution (or body that administers it) has given a remuneration notice to Copyright Agency Limited (CAL) under the Act.

Allen & Unwin
9 Atchison Street
St Leonards NSW 2065
Australia
Phone: (61 2) 8425 0100
Fax: (61 2) 9906 2218
E-mail: frontdesk@allen-unwin.com.au
Web: http://www.allen-unwin.com.au

National Library of Australia
Cataloguing-in-Publication entry:

Stewart, Kathleen, 1958– .
  The red room.

  ISBN 1 86508 313 5.

  I. Title.

A823.3

Set in Palatino by DOCUPRO, Sydney
Printed by Australian Print Group, Maryborough, Victoria

10 9 8 7 6 5 4 3 2 1

for Declan Cooney

Also by Kathleen Stewart

Fiction

Nightflowers
Spilt Milk
Louis: A Normal Novel
Victim Train
Waiting Room

Poetry

The White Star
Snow

I

1

WHEN MY FATHER DIED, I married a very thin man, a skeletal man. Perhaps I was trying to bed my father's bones, as Otto said?

The marriage was brief and mistaken—yet somehow revealing. But it was no use. When I'm with people, I may as well be on my own. That's how it is with me. And that's how it was with Sylvester.

Sylvester had penetrating, resentful, exhausted grey eyes, a mouth like a dehydrated plum and, above it, a sad little moustache like a piece of wrinkled twine. He looked as if he'd been badly dry-cleaned—shrunken here, stretched there—as if he'd never fit himself again.

I was seventeen. Sylvester lied and said that he was fifty-seven. Well, I believe that marriage is for life. But there are limits.

'Mother,' I said, the week after the wedding. 'What shall I do?'

'I don't know what you mean,' Elizabeth said.

'I may have been too hasty,' I said. 'He is old, his skin is like paper. His stomach groans and rumbles all night, and I cannot sleep.'

'Take a pill,' she said.

'Mother!' I cried. 'He is four times my age!'

'Heavens,' Elizabeth said. 'You always were a fussy child.'

Sylvester pouted when I left him, and sniffed, his mouth relaxing. (With relief? Or was he letting yet another belch escape, one final bubble of protest?)

And then, to cap things off, shortly after the tedious affair of the annulment, Sylvester died.

I perched on the astroturf by the side of his grave and tried to cry. But there was a cold empty place where my heart used to be. A dank dark place.

You can't get blood from a stone, I told myself. It took all I had to squeeze out the tears I laid on my father's coffin two years before.

And when I did cry, improbably, a little later, I felt that I cried more for my father than Sylvester—if you can measure such things.

Now it is just the two of us, I thought, then. Now both of them are hugging the worms. Now, it is just the two of us: beastly Beth and nasty Nora.

∞

'He was family,' Elizabeth said, when we were on our own again, after the funeral. 'Despite what you went and did.'

'And,' she went on, chomping on the words with evident relish, 'if you hadn't been the hasty sort, you'd have had a nice slice of his superannuation, and God knows what else.'

'But let it drop,' she said. 'You never listen to my advice.'

'I didn't marry him for his money,' I said.

'Is that so?' she said.

'Now don't start,' she said, raising a hand like a traffic warden. 'You're so argumentative. Pass me the sausage rolls. There. *There*. Under the lemon cheese pie.'

'They're gone,' I said, opening my arms wide in demonstration.

'Don't be ridiculous,' she snorted, elbowing me aside, and tipping her stocky body forward, into the frosty freezer. 'You are a preposterous, wicked liar, Eleanor.'

'Eleanora,' I said.

'Don't be silly,' she said.

She shuffled legs of lamb and tubs of icecream and plastic containers of frozen meals aside, then lifted herself upright, and slammed the lid closed.

'You've eaten them!' she cried, her eyes like hot blue marbles.

She glared at me, her eyes burning into mine, her jaw thrust out accusingly.

'Mother!' I protested. 'You know I don't eat meat.'

'Hff!' she muttered. 'Don't eat any vegetables either.'

She clutched my arm suddenly then, and stared at me with piteous eyes.

'Oh, but what shall I do now?' she cried imploringly. 'Sylvester was my dearest friend!'

'Oh, Mother, I *am* sorry,' I said.
And then the other mourners arrived.

It's always the same. We take the facts like a tablecloth, stretched tight between us, and we pull the cloth one way, and then the other. Elizabeth smooths the cloth, and rotates it on the table, saying: This is how it lays. I grab my end, brush off the crumbs, and straighten it again, and say: *This* is how it lays.

Of course, the surface of things must be kept smooth, so that life as we know it can go on. But below the surface, and below that—far below our everyday scuffles—is this terrible twisting and tugging.

And here we are, year after year, pitted against each other, bound by our horrible secret—the one subject, surely?, that cannot be twisted and turned around.

2

IT IS HARD, SOMETIMES, to see what is going on, what with the pattern of daily life, the obscuring web and weave of it: the homespun hook rug, for example, of the Bird family.

That was—that is—us, the Birds. Tweet, tweet. (Plenty of room for wit in that, but only from strangers. At home, in our little nest, we are frugal with our jokes.)

There we'd be. Me, chewing my pencil in my room, supposedly doing my homework—worrying about the growth-rate of my breasts. Elizabeth, my mother, in the kitchen—no doubt tossing off a prayer or two as she peeled the spuds. Ron, my father, in his favourite armchair, broiling in his own juices in front of the TV—resting up before the nightly after-dinner row.

Ron did his block daily. Recreationally, you might say. He ranted, and raved, and shook his tiny fists in the air. He beat me with his stick.

I learnt to avoid my father early on. As soon as I saw him begin to rake at his hair, like a B-movie lunatic, I ran up to cower in my room and say my prayers. In he'd thunder and chase me around, and thrash me wildly about the legs. Then peace, for the moment.

He behaved, I see in retrospect, as a *madman*. In fact, as several mad men. But not one word was ever said of this . . .

At other times, although he smiled tightly and said Pass the salt, he oozed controlled displeasure. The air in our house stank of it. (Oh, but the air in our house was so sweetened up with the artificial odour of piety—it was hard to tell whose air we breathed.)

'Ron,' said Elizabeth, archly, then. 'I sense ill-will! It isn't good for you to harbour grudges, dear.'
Sense? I'd think. It's tumbling out of him like bricks!
'Poor Ron,' she'd say.
'Now, Ron. Enough of your brooding!' she'd say.
Elizabeth withstood the mighty Ron—disarmed his rage with her wagging little finger.

And then. And then. And then Ron went to hospital to visit his brother, Richard—who was recovering after a triple by-pass—and had a massive heart attack and died. Right there in intensive care, while Richard stared whitely from his bed, across the mounds of get-well flowers.

'Ron's dead. A heart attack,' we said, lowering our eyes, waiting for condolences.

'You mean Richard, surely?' they said, one after the other, mortified at our grief-struck slip.

'No, *Ron*. Richard's in intensive care still,' we said. '*Ron's* dead. Ron Bird.'

'Oh!' they said, too stunned to offer sympathy. And the flowers, in the confusion, got sent to Richard, in the hospital.

It was odd, I thought. As if death had a very specific agenda: one heart, in this location. As if death had been standing there, determined to take a man.

∞

We mourned, Elizabeth and I, watching one another as if weighing the other's tears: regarding each other steadily across the breakfast table, stealing into each other's rooms at night to study the other's sleep.

I was numb, bereft, but not unhappy. I fixed the few flowers in thoughtful new arrangements.

Elizabeth glided around the house, cleaning—dressed all in black, demure as a novice—her eyes veiled, her mouth fixed into a strange new smile, a secrecy.

From time to time I stood in front of a mirror and tried to emulate this smile. I closed both lips firmly, slightly pursed them, then lengthened each corner into a thin line and lifted the ends—all the while holding them closely to my face, like the tips of a curled moustache.

It stood for pleasure, I decided.

Pleasure at bearing up so well after disaster? Or pleasure at a job well done?

After the funeral, I stood in front of the mirror, wearing Elizabeth's smile like a borrowed scarf, and I could not tell whose pleasure I had uncovered.

∞

Elizabeth—in the interests of truth, I would prefer to call my mother Elizabeth to her face, but this is not allowed. Elizabeth, my mother, took good care of me as a child. I am sure of it.

Her mouth tight, her eyes almost crossed with concentration, she washed every cranny of my body, twice a day—three times on Sundays. She has a genius, you could say, for cleanliness. (She and God—so close!)

Although I cannot remember clearly that far back, I can safely guess that my nappies were whitest white, incandescent flutterings on the washing line. I have a memory of softness, and the smell of sunlight . . .

That is my mother, I think—not this harsh-faced woman, arguing with me across the breakfast table, glancing sharply at my father's empty chair for confirmation that will never come now.

Admit it, I want to shout. Three was a crowd.

She fixes me with her round, angry, anxious, bright blue eyes. They protrude from her face, like eggs from boiling water.

My heart widens. You could drive a fleet of buses into the space. And then, flickering in the emptiness, the dampness that has become my heart, is a faint and luke-warm feeling: gratitude, with a small shawl of shame. Gratitude, that I do not look like her, squat and angry and tense—with mottled skin, and bulbous blue eyes, and ginger-grey steel wool hair.

I am tall, with big feet and green-blue eyes, and my hair is as red as the flame girl on the matchbox, and every inch of my skin is milky-white.

Well, all right. There are freckles on my milky skin. My eyes are queer. And if I don't wear my hair in a plait, it frizzes out.

All right, I am not good-looking. I stoop, no matter how many times Elizabeth snaps at me to straighten.

Why am I so tall—a giantess—though I stoop and stoop?

'Growth promotants,' Ron said darkly, more than once. 'Bully beef. You watch, your generation.'

Well, I suppose it's too late now. But now I don't eat meat.

Men whistle at me, though. Men notice my breasts. Ever since

I was twelve. 'Cover your chest, girl,' my mother hissed, still hisses.

That was when the trouble began. I was the trouble. Trouble was all around me, sprouting, with my indecent breasts.

3

I HAVE THIS RECURRING dream. The house is cut in two, moving slowly along the road on a trailer, like a derelict caravan—windows peeling back, walls oozing worms, paint falling off the doors, venetian blinds corded with live snakes.

And then the terrible thing happens. The terror that is *behind*. Like a dream opening onto another dream, the house cracks open further, and I see a pool of blackened water, and I am in it, and I am pulled into it, and I am drowning, and I look up and I see Ron, helping Elizabeth out. They have left me to die, I think. And I call out to them, and they do not turn to me, or answer.

Even now. Even now . . .

But some things never change. We squabble, we tug and pull.

'There is a lot of dirt and mess in this place,' Elizabeth said, this morning. 'And I am fighting it single-handed.'

'I did the floors yesterday,' I snapped. 'I did the skirting boards the day before.'

'Oh, really?' she sniffed. 'Last week, more like.'

She sighed, then rewarded herself with a small smile and added, 'Your father would do his block if he saw the state this house is in.'

Well, why should she and I change, just because everything else has?

'Ron didn't need an excuse to do his block,' I said, quite truthfully.

She gasped.

'I do not like your attitude, Eleanor,' she said. 'Apart from being surly and belligerent, completely uninterested and unwilling, most ungrateful and unco-operative, you seem to be developing into a nasty bit of work. You have a contentious reply to every remark I make. My reasonable requests for help are met with bitter complaints. Anything you *do* do is done reluctantly. And I am supposed to just leave you to it, am I? When you are totally unwilling to do any work, and you've got absolutely no initiative——'

'Mother——' I said.

'Not one more word of abuse from you, thank you,' she said.

'I——' I said.

'I, I, I,' she said. 'Selfish to the core! You just count your blessings. Go to your room, immediately!'

I turned, and left—went upstairs. Stomp. Stomp. Stomp.

It's always the same. I'll say: 'It's hot!' And she'll say, screwing her face up with disbelief: 'Hff! The weatherman said it was going to be cool today.' I'll say: 'I thought that film was rather boring.' And she'll say, regarding me with a pitying frown: 'Oh, dear me! You're getting things mixed up again, Ellen. It hasn't even been released yet.' I'll say: 'I'm feeling ill.' And she'll say, yawning: 'You're over-tired.' But if I say: 'Good heavens, I'm tired!' Then she'll say: 'Just as I expected, the way you carry on. You've caught yourself a touch of flu.'

Well, I think. Well!

Truth is subjective, and what do I know, anyway? Some people believe in parallel universes. But it irks me that I'm not allowed my truth.

When you have one truth, and everyone around you has another, that doesn't make you wrong, that doesn't make you mad. Does it? Not necessarily, does it?

I am not a crazy person, I tell myself. I'm a *truth-seeker*. (But don't think, because of that, that I'm the cruel, blunt type. I know when to close my mouth and turn away my eyes. I am not, despite Sylvester, always selfish and unkind.)

When the people (or person) around you flatly squash your truth, when they are so threatened by your truth that they shout and call you mad—then you know you're onto something. Don't you?

That's what *I* think, anyway.

Still, I never learn. I argue. I complain. I am just as much to blame as Mother for our awful altercations.

And I stay. There's no denying it. Like a snail in its shell, I stay.

∞

I thought I'd got away by marrying Sylvester. I thought I could get away!

A few months after Sylvester's funeral, I packed a small haversack and took a bus to Byron Bay. I found a room in a ramshackle house—not small, not large, with sand in the corners.

And then the letters started to arrive. Blue letters, in blue ink, on blue notepaper. Every morning there would be one, two, three letters slipped under my door. And, when I did not reply, there were telegrams.

Concern for my state of mind. Concern for my health. Concern for the desirability or otherwise of my associates. My associates! I was associating only with myself. When was it ever otherwise?

In the end I went back. I don't know why I went back. To stop the letters? To prove that I was safe and well? (Oh, but I was so lonely, don't forget. And Elizabeth was frantic at being left. She isn't young any more, and she wasn't young then, and . . .)

I went back, and felt very unwell indeed.

Elizabeth cooked us both invalid's meals: boiled eggs with toast soldiers, fish fingers with mushy peas, rice puddings, tuna casseroles, Welsh rarebit, and vanilla junkets, and I was ill for quite a while.

4

THERE WAS A TIME when it was just the two of us, grappling with the ghost of the third: Elizabeth, and our silent adjudicator, and me. There was a time when it was just us three.

Then Jasper arrived.

Jasper Pease was the boarder, evening things out to four. Five, if you count Sylvester's wan shadow. But I don't. Sylvester was an aberration, a misjudgment, a passing phase. As far as I'm concerned, Sylvester turned to dust—metaphorically speaking—as soon as the dirt filled in his grave. (I'm sorry. I know it's not charitable to think such thoughts. But Elizabeth was the one he should have married.)

Ron died. Sylvester died. I went away, and I came back. Time passed, and we went about our business. And then a notice was pinned up here and there—hand-copied, my mother having no faith in modern technology, especially since the business of the Turin shroud.

'There!' she said. 'Now we will just have to sit back and see if we are deluged with offers.'

And Jasper Pease, reading it at the local newsagent's, applied and was accepted, on account of his being the only serious applicant.

∞

I was in the garden when Jasper came. Not gardening, just standing in the lilies.

A quiet, mopy man was coming towards me, smiling lopsidedly, carrying a suitcase.

What colour were his eyes? They were sea-eyes: one moment blue, then blue-green-grey, then green.

He was tall. Not quite as tall as me. He was, perhaps, thirty-five years of age, with glistening fish-pale skin, and a flop of greased-back black-and-silver hair, the colour of blackfish scales. ('Niggers,' Ron used to call them, when he went fishing for them off the rocks at La Perouse.)

'He's very *suave*, isn't he?' said Elizabeth.

'Jasper,' my mother said delicately, the first night we sat down to dinner as a physical group of three.

He glanced up shyly as he slurped his soup. (Cream of pumpkin, with fresh ginger.)

'It would be better if you did not remove your shoes at table,' she said.

Involuntarily, I glanced down.

'I'll remember that, ma'am,' he said, and shuffled. 'Beg pardon, miss.'

But he hadn't! He hadn't removed his shoes at all.

Leaning closer, I noticed that his clothing oozed a fishy scent. And all that ma'am and miss! Where *had* he come from? Deep-frozen out of another age?

I helped Elizabeth carry out the soup bowls, to make way for the whole baked trout she'd stuffed in his honour.

'My, this is some spread!' cried Jasper Pease.

'Are you American, Jasper?' I said.

'Don't pry, Eleanor,' my mother hissed. Then coughed lightly, and laughed, and patted her mouth with her napkin.

'Eleanora,' I said automatically.

'My, that's a mighty pretty name,' said Jasper Pease.

He flicked his head back, and his silver-black hair fell into place.

'She's fanciful,' said Elizabeth.

'You like to go to films?' I said. He had to have picked it up from somewhere.

'No, ma'am. No, miss, I mean. Eleanora,' he said, dipping his head, then raising his flat face to show a sly, shy, sideways-slipping smile.

'You read a lot?' I persisted. 'Hemingway, or . . . or——'

'Let the poor man eat, Eleanor,' snapped my mother.

'And mighty fine food it is, too, ma'am,' said Jasper Pease, showing both rows of teeth.

He was like a dead man come to life, with all his animation off-centre, and all his inner wiring gone askew.

'Are you *Canadian?*' I asked, between main and dessert. (Mocha mousse, with swirls of chilled banana cream.)

At this he laughed quietly, and stared down at his empty plate.

5

THERE WAS SOMETHING STRANGELY familiar about Jasper Pease's eyes: sea-green, sea-blue, and then pond-dark, as if a veil had fallen over them.

I went to Lemonhurst Library, to borrow some books on iridology, and looked his Christian name up in a reference book. It means 'keeper of the treasure' in Persian, apparently. A variation on Gaspar—one of the Three Wise Men. Or were his parents keen on gem stones? Jasper: 'a cryptocrystalline variety of quartz'. A dark stone, I would think.

Names are funny things. I mean, Jasper *Pease*. Pease was not encouraging, not at all. Pass the peas please, Mr Pease. (And I bet Elizabeth imagines I'm going to marry him!)

Clack was my married name. Mrs Clack. I was pleased to divest myself of the name, along with the marriage. From Bird to Clack and back again. Maybe I married Sylvester because his surname made me giggle? Clack. Clickity-clack! Clack-clack. Mind you, the many-syllabled and sibilant Sylvester—with its suggestions of a silvery English glen—had its attractions. What a pity about the actual man. Oh, just don't *think* about it——

It's a funny thing with names, though. Why people name their offspring certain names, and what those names then mean to them, I mean.

I suspect Elizabeth and Marlene were named for Hollywood movie stars. Granny Brindle was always fond of the show-biz side of things.

Iris: that's one of those all-purpose plant names, inherited from some great-aunty. Josephine: an unromantic masculinisation of Grandad Brindle's eldest brother's name, who died at Gallipoli?

Darlene, however, was christened Dymphna. Which is horrible —Dymphna being the patron saint of the insane—although they couldn't have known she'd——

Actually, we're all crazy in my family. I mean, we're all *crazy*. Nothing certifiable, so far. But Darlene's the sort the others watch nervously at weddings and funerals. Darlene's the dippy sort that might do something.

Elizabeth keeps a sharp eye on Darlene, pulls her up on little things. Things I sometimes wonder if anyone else—anyone not in the family—would notice: Darlene getting a bit loud, her neck going mottled pink. Darlene getting her crazy-eye look. This particular laugh, where she brays and hoots, her whole body rocking while the rough notes rise higher and higher until even someone deaf and largely blind, like Miss Carew from next door, seems surprised.

Darlene is not a bad-looking woman, when she is quiet. She has protruding brown eyes, with exaggerated whites, like an anxious fox terrier. Her hair is auburn, with curls or waves, depending on the weather. She is thin, coltish, even at her age.

Her husband, Harry, is the most unimaginative man. Built like a boxer, sandy-haired and permanently sunburnt. I don't think he's even noticed Darlene is a little loopy. Probably just thinks she's feminine.

They have six almost identical sons, aged between six and seventeen, sized like those Russian dolls that fit into one another.

Harry and the boys are very sporty. They play, watch, read, think, and talk sport, while Darlene floats around sewing flounces on things and getting vaguer and vaguer. ('Still, she knows the wash cycle,' says Elizabeth.)

Marlene, by contrast, is a dynamo. A big bullocky overbearing strawberry-blonde, perched on a tiny pair of legs, endlessly striding. Her eyes—cobalt blue, and offended-looking at the best of times—bulge phenomenally when she is angry. She sweeps around, voicing opinions, bossing people about—but falls strangely silent in Elizabeth's presence, and defers to her in many things.

Frank, Marlene's husband, is a pleasant man, innocuous and entirely bald. He went grey, and then it all fell out when he was still in his twenties, Marlene says. ('Well, what a strain, living with Marlene,' says Elizabeth.)

Frank and Marlene have four children left. Joseph, the youngest, is confined to a wheelchair. Then there is a trainee priest. The other two are twins: boisterous individuals, who regard me with derision.

Marlene is Elizabeth's big sister. (Darlene is younger than them by twenty years: a change-of-life baby.) Older again, unmarried, but equally stubborn and bug-eyed, are Iris and Josephine.

Iris is seventy-three, and Josephine, a spry, arthritic seventy-five. They have pale-blue eyes and powdery white skin. Josephine is quite alarming, with her highly rouged cheeks, her kiss-curled grey hair, and her flour-white retreating chin; while dainty Iris—who has a loud and cranky voice, and flowing, frizzy silver hair she says was once like mine—patters innocuously about beside her.

Iris and Josephine live in Mortlake, the old family home. It is a mouldering terrace (fully detached), on the higher side of Lemonhurst, with an overgrown garden full of weeds and flowers that they ramble around in like a pair of perpetually startled geese.

On Ron's side there was only Richard of the by-pass, his wife, Brenda (pale, asthmatic, kindly Brenda—'A complete washout,' Elizabeth says), and their seven dull-eyed children—who we avoid now. Or perhaps it was they who withdrew from us, and with relief?

The family is . . . well, whoever Elizabeth says it is. Mostly, though, it is Elizabeth and her sisters.

(And me, of course. Of course, me.)

'Dymphna!' Elizabeth said, on the phone last night. 'She would have to be the scattiest individual on this earth. What a trial it is having to be responsible for another adult.'

'Put the silverside on the table will you Eleanora,' she called out to me. 'It's nicer with the chill off, I always think.'

'Oh, Marlene,' she said. 'When she gets an idea into her head there's no stopping her.'

'Yes, yes, I know,' she said.

'Well, I *did* have a word to Harry, after the second child. "Dymphna's not up to it," I said. "Can't you see she hasn't the brains of a sheep?" My dear! Not amused. "And I'm sure enough not stepping in to pick up where she leaves off, in terms of her caretaking responsibilities for those poor boys," I said. *Six* of them. I did warn the man. No restraint,' she said.

'Oh, I'm not talking about celibacy,' she said. 'Don't interrupt, Marlene. The rhythm method worked well enough for Ron and I.'

'I shall forget you said that!' she cried, and hung up.

She was standing by the hall table, her chest heaving, when I emerged from the kitchen where I'd been sorting out the condiments.

'Is Darlene having another baby?' I said.

'Dymphna!' she shouted. 'Dymphna!'

'No, she isn't,' she said, heaving a sigh. 'We can all breathe easy. We have that to be thankful for, at least.'

'No!' she chortled, then. 'Harry is no longer functioning in that department. It happens sometimes with age. God in his wisdom . . .'

And then Jasper appeared, his hair slicked across his forehead.

'Don't let me interrupt,' he said. 'I was only going to polish my shoes——'

'Oh, not at all,' said Elizabeth. 'We were just talking about my trouble-making little sister, who no doubt you will one day meet.'

'Little?' said Jasper.

'Yes, *somewhat* younger than I,' said Elizabeth archly, then bustled off humming to herself.

'And you,' said Jasper, staring at the woodwork, 'must be Cinderella.'

'Pardon?' I said.

But he continued to stare at nothing, smiling mysteriously.

'Dymphna,' Elizabeth said, returning with her feather duster, 'my youngest sister, is a burden we all share in the Brindle family.'

She flicked the duster over the phone, and its table, as if to erase them.

'Ah! Brindle,' Jasper said. 'What a charming name. I look forward to meeting this delicate creature.'

'Delicate? Dymphna!' roared Elizabeth, holding her duster upright as if it was a wand. 'Oh, no! Tough as a boot!'

'Touched, though,' she added, bulging her eyes significantly.

∞

Elizabeth makes a show of calling Darlene Dymphna. Why must she insist?

'You're always poking spiders with a stick, Ellen,' she tells me, warningly, when I ask such things. Or: 'Mind your own beeswax!' she'll say, her blue eyes sparkling.

Well, facts are facts, and lies are lies. And sometimes spiders *are* revealed when one uncovers something.

Is it wrong to want to know? I suppose God must think so, after what he did to Adam and Eve.

Anyway, my name—no matter what my mother says—is Eleanora. The emphasis is on the *third* syllable, but lightly. Is that so hard to remember?

6

WE LIVE—LIVE!—THE lot of us—in an unremarkable suburb. It is flat, with a slight hill. From the top of the hill you can see . . . roofs. Roofs of houses just like ours, pleasant enough houses in their way.

Sometimes, though, when it is not sunny, I look around and feel that we are drowning in a grey and soupy hell. I feel as if all the walls of the houses are groaning, are about to crack and spring open and release their screams. As if the roofs would lift off if they could, and a great moaning and wailing would emerge then. As if we are crouched in the very pit of hell.

Most people call it Lemonhurst. Hell, by any other name, I say, still smells as sweet.

All through my cramped, unnatural childhood—although I shook at night, although I could not sleep—I accepted that I was going to go to hell one day. (How many times did Sister Theophane tell me, 'You are going to roast in hell, girlie,' before she flexed her cane? It never crossed my mind a nun might lie. They *knew* these things. Didn't they?) Well! It's one thing to spend the afterlife in hell, but quite another to live there all your life!

(Of course, I'm only joking, book. It's only Lemonhurst, only Glass Street. *Hell* is something far more endless, far more ghastly.)

And what do we do in hell? We put the kettle on for another pot of tea. We prattle and potter about.

What is most awful about this hell called Lemonhurst is the cheerfulness. People struggle to show that they are not in pain. They grin, they grimace, they smile. They smile until I can see the skeletons behind their skin.

Some days around here it is filthy hot—as hot as hell is

supposed to be. The ladies' perms flatten then, or frizz. The men's skin melts onto their steering wheels as they speed away.

It is forever the 1950s around here: men work, and earn, and women tend the home, and breed, and mind the frightened children. That the men had any part in the procreation is belied by their reluctance to handle their offspring, by their eyes, by their absence.

There are no sea breezes, no refreshing puffs of wind, such as others are said to enjoy, living in the coastal suburbs.

The bearded sky belts down. Dogs go by. Pitbulls on leads, alsatians with withered haunches. Dobermen, rottweilers. The dogs of hell . . .

Of course, I can't say this to anyone, or they would think me mad. Or else insulting.

And, God knows, we do not welcome insult in our family.

7

I'VE WRITTEN A FEW sections in you, book, each night this week before I went to sleep, to bring things up to date. It's Friday now, and I am so looking forward to the weekend, when I can write in you almost any time I please.

For Jasper's delight, this evening, Elizabeth prepared a roasted leg of lamb—garnished with little bouquets of herbs, and larded with garlic and rosemary.

'None for her,' she said, as Jasper paused showily with the carving knife in mid-air.

'Are you vegetarian, Eleanora?' he said.

'I eat fish,' I said. 'No flesh, no fowl, and nothing with hooves.'

'Nothing of the devil,' he said quietly, smiling.

'What the devil, indeed!' said Elizabeth, mishearing. 'She's the dickens to please, Jasper. Now, there are the potatoes, of course, and the greens——'

Greens. There is a rota for vegetables in our house. Brussel sprouts, broccoli, peas—several sorts—then beans, ditto, runner, long, etc. Spinach, silver beet. Zucchini, asparagus. No green repeated two days running.

'I shall have vegetables with a little extra of the cheese sauce,' I said firmly.

'I don't know,' said Elizabeth. 'Really, I don't.'

'I am not anaemic,' I said. 'Do I look anaemic?'

There was silence.

'I'm not,' I said, and set about eating my dish of vegetables.

'I can't really see my way clear to cooking two dinners,' said Elizabeth apologetically, to Jasper.

'I am quite all right, Mother,' I said. 'And have been, for years.'

'Well,' she said, sounding dubious.

'I grew up on beef,' she said, and looked at me.

'You did, too,' she said defiantly.

'She did, too,' she said, leaning towards Jasper—as if translating.

'All these eccentric notions,' she said, and sighed.

Jasper gave her a lopsided grin, and stuffed his mouth full of meat.

'I do find all this talk of special diets rather unsavoury, when so many have none,' said Elizabeth, looking modestly to one side. 'Don't you, Mr Pease?'

'Jasper, please call me Jasper, Mrs Bird,' he cried.

'And you must call me Elizabeth,' she said, improbably.

'Oh, no, ma'am,' he said. 'I couldn't do that.'

'As you wish,' she said, and sighed again.

'My, oh, my! This lamb is cooked to perfection, Mrs Bird!' cried Jasper, saving the show.

'Why, thank you, Jasper! It gives me so much pleasure to see someone with a healthy appetite! *So* refreshing, isn't it, Ellen?' said Elizabeth.

No comment.

∞

Almost all our conversations occur at the table, Jasper Pease being as accomplished at whisking himself out of the house at other times as any man I've ever known.

Jasper, from nowhere, disappears each morning straight after breakfast, and is never back till seven-thirty in the evening.

Dinner at eight makes my mother's stomach rumble, but she is determined to do the polite thing, to do it right.

We all are. Somehow, everything hinges on this.

Yes, ma'am. No, miss. The only time, so far, I saw him falter and blink was in that minute before we bowed our heads in prayer.

Ah-ha! I thought. Got you, Jasp. Got you, there. You spy!

Just that quiver, just that moment. (Although, really, when I think about it, I can't say what it means.)

The rest of the time, he keeps on smiling—shyly, sideways, or else his too-big, too-tense grin.

Something about that grin . . .

He leaps up and down to help, and is led back to his place at the dining table by Elizabeth's remonstrations.

'Not after your hard day,' she says. 'Your hard day's work, Jasper.'

Doing what? Now that's the question.

Most nights, after dinner, Jasper tries to do the dishes, and gets in everybody's way—all the while, with his android's animation—deferring to my mother, nodding, smiling, half-showing his strange, flat, sombre face.

Excuse me, Jasper, what hollow of hell are you from? I want to say. What brings you here, to our shady little Hades?

But nothing, as usual. As usual, I say nothing.

Although I know he has come to do me down. Although I know he will be the death of me.

Through deep dark waters, he has come to bury me . . .

But that's just being silly, isn't it?

8

I AM SO SCARED of eternity, book. That is the fundamental truth about me. I am scared of the nuns in business suits who run things, the priests with their well-coiffed hair. I am scared of cars and trains and planes and public transport. The dark, heights, elevators, malice. At the base of this, at the very root, is a wheeling terror of eternity.

Eternity: the *other* world, the endless world—both apparent and obscured by this world, but inherent in it. Eternity: the formless land, wherein my soul shall dwell, for ever and ever and ever.

I imagine my existence in the afterlife as an infinite freefall through outer space: fast, faster, faster. And the end of this endlessness? There is no end. World without end, forever. That is my personal hell.

I have come from there, I think, and that is where I shall return. There is no wiping away what I have done.

At night, when I cannot sleep, I imagine other hells. I imagine the eternal life as eternal death. A blank blankness. A depthless, smothering black sack. Annihilation of form, but not of consciousness. The dark as heavy as damp earth. The only sound, of breathing.

Then again, sometimes I think it will be merely grey, this other world—a lake of endless loneliness and sorrow. And I will walk there, forever, will wade by its shores, forever, alone and weeping.

There is no God in my eternity. There is no godly presence. Only the brushing of wings and a quiet laughter.

And then, at other times, I imagine an eternity of fire and pain. A flaming sea, that opens after endless falling, that burns and sears and fries. And high, high above, peering down—Sister Theophane, clapping her cane against her palm, approving, as I fry.

I imagine a universe of fear, endlessly swallowing itself.

At times I wish to die, to free myself from this fear of death, to free myself from this fear. At times I wish to stab myself in the breast, to release myself from this earthly hell-world, where everything seems wrong and back-to-front. At times, I plan to get in first, to launch myself into the terror.

Am I mad to think like this? Am I crazy?

When I think of craziness, I think of Americans with their checked clothes and their station wagons and their hair that looks like a wig and their presidents who look like papier-mâché puppets. (To think these people rule the modern world! And before them, the English—an equally silly lot—sitting on their horses in red outfits, chasing foxes and whacking balls, and waving their handkerchiefs at the royals. Do the royals fear eternity? Does *Charles?*)

It is there, always there—eternity—a film on top of things, a shadow behind things, an undercurrent.

But *things* . . .

Our lives, our little activities, this earth . . .

It's all ephemera, isn't it?

9

EVERYTHING I WRITE DOWN here is true, book. But later, when I look at it, I think: Is my life like that? Can this be so?

Elizabeth is not above saying, when I disagree with her point of view—that is, frequently: 'Your vision is askew, I'm afraid, dear Eleanor.' (It serves, perhaps, as a calming mantra?)

This morning, for instance, I remarked on her becoming brand new blouse—pink, with white-pearl buttons.

'I gave this blouse to you last year but, as is your little way, you didn't wear it,' she sighed, 'so I am getting some use out of it.'

'Oh, Mother!' I said. 'I can't believe that's true. I love the things you sew for me.'

'Well!' she said. 'That's the first I've heard of it.'

'Now, now,' she said. 'Enough of the carry on. This is the blouse I made for you, a special gift, but if you don't want to recognise it, then that's that.'

'Still,' she said, pausing delicately—never one to miss a chance. 'Your vision *is* quite askew at times. I think you must admit it, Ellen, dear.'

'Pardon?' I said, to get her goat.

'I said your vision is askew,' she repeated slowly, as if I was daft.

'Oh,' I said, 'I thought you were talking to someone else.'

Ellen! Eleanor!

Of course I knew who she meant, but I said it anyway. Petty, I know. But petty, also, not to say my name. To tell me, over and over, that I am something other . . . Oh, hush, be done with it! I tell you, book, we are both equally strange and stubborn.

'I read recently, Mother, that pink is the navy blue of India. Isn't that amazing? I'd like,' I said then, to change the subject, 'to go to India one day.'

Well, I would. I am very fond of elephants.

'Ha!' she said. 'You couldn't travel alone.'

'It wouldn't pay for you to be a loner,' she said. 'It would intensify your . . . peculiarities.'

'Those who dangle on the edges of the flock get picked off by wolves,' she said. 'You mind that well.'

'I am not a child,' I said. 'I have experience of the world, you'd be surprised, and men.'

'Ha!' she said. 'That's a good one. Tell that to the marines. You've got a short memory, Eleanor.'

'I remember *everything*,' I said, and stared right back.

'Sugar!' she cried, having knocked her cup of tea off the kitchen counter.

'Shit, I think you mean,' I said daringly.

'What did you say?' she said, astounded. The fur above her lips quivered with excitement, and her round blue eyes began to stream with light.

'*What* did you just say?' she said, enunciating carefully.

'You heard me,' I said. Well, whispered.

'The insolence!' she cried.

She clamped her mouth shut. She glared at me, deep into my eyes, and she grimaced at the state of my soul—and I was caught, like a worm on a hook, all the coldness in me, all the emptiness and wrongness, all the dirt and evil, all about to rise to the surface.

I tried to swallow without making a lewd noise.

And Elizabeth looked at me. She lowered her bucket, crank after crank, into my well.

Her mouth was folded into a prim, kindly smile. Her lips were rigid with Christian determination. And she was wearing her mother-mask, her motherly concern pinned on like a brooch.

You are no more a mother to me than the next person, I thought, performing acts of duty, of kindness.

'Oh, girl . . . Dear me . . . Thank the Lord the nuns caught you, before the rot set in,' she said, at last, sighing, and she turned to mop up her tea.

Go away, I wanted to shout. You are not my mother. No-one is.

But who, if she's not my mother, is she? And who, if she's not my mother, am I?

10

WITH A NEW MAN to please, the evening meals are becoming increasingly elaborate, and more time-consuming in preparation at every level.

There is the rifling through of cook books; the shopping for delicate herbs and spices, and special cuts of lamb and beef; the hours of marination and simmering; then the serving of many courses; the washing up of all the extra pots and pans; the putting away—and the starting all over again.

Not forgetting the ritual cooked breakfast which compulsorily begins our day: Elizabeth, Jasper, and me. (Do I mean me, or do I mean I? What does it matter, when neither of us seem to exist?)

'Could you, please, if it is not too great a bother, dear, bring me this and that from Lemonhurst while you're up there?' Elizabeth said, this morning, after Jasper had whisked himself off to wherever.

She handed me a list that would take an hour, at least, to fill.

'Oh, all right,' I said ungraciously.

'Do I smell a burning martyr?' she said.

'No, Mother, don't be silly,' I said. 'Of course, I'll do it. I'll do it after work.'

'Do it in your lunch break,' she said. 'I'll need the lamb in the oven by five-thirty.'

'Oh . . .' I said. For I had only half an hour.

'I really am enjoying all this lovely food, aren't you?' she said. 'After all our privations.'

'Yes, Mother,' I said.

'Of course,' she sighed, 'it takes an effort from all of us. A small commitment to a happy home.'

'Jasper could put a bit more effort in,' I said.

'He's a busy, busy man,' she muttered. 'He's clean, tidy, and *so* polite. Leaves the bathroom in a pristine condition. And Marlene thinks him quite the dish!'

'Though, I do wish he'd go to bed at a reasonable hour,' she added.

She sighed between her teeth as she folded and put away the laundered table napkins.

'Have you ever wondered what he does?' I said.

'I expect that's his business,' Elizabeth said indignantly.

'You don't think . . . ?' I said.

'What *are* you talking about?' she snapped.

The silence swirled about us, menacing.

'I bet he's an undertaker,' I said brightly, then. 'That would explain the way he pongs.'

Elizabeth gaped at my bad manners.

'Well!' she said, narrowing her eyes. 'Regardless. It's good to see someone else actually doing some work.'

I let her have her little way. It makes her feel important.

But *how* could anyone disregard his odour?

There is something of the swamp, an ooze of eel, that permeates any room where he has been. That air of unwashed sock, which Elizabeth herself had mentioned. And dampness, all manner of dampness rising from his clothes . . .

∞

'You know,' said Elizabeth, this evening, sniffing suspiciously as we did the dishes. (The meal was a great success, of course. Turkey, stuffed with sprigs of tarragon, thyme, and rosemary. Homemade cranberry sauce. I had the vegetables, again.) 'I think we might have a bit of rising damp to contend with.'

'Oh, Mother!' I said. 'Don't be silly! It's only the lodger.'

How she stared.

11

I DO WORK, YOU know, book. I work in a photographic studio. Otto Horsefield is my boss. I do errands. I answer his phone. I assist. In a multitude of ways.

Otto does quality shots. Catalogues for supermarkets, mostly. Kitten calendars for chemists. (Nothing porny.) I work six hours a day, ten till half past four. As much as Otto needs me. Sometimes I help out in the darkroom, when he does his black-and-white. I enter his accounts and print them out. I position the backdrops. I hold the shims. I angle the lights.

When there is nothing more to be done and Otto is off, clicking his camera, and seeing things that I can't see, I study the models. I watch them pout and turn their heads and move their hands lovingly. Their heads sway on their necks. 'A little more delight,' says Otto. 'Lovely!'

I could be a model, with my height. But Otto doesn't ask me. Otto is gay.

'I would never allow a child of mine to work for a homo-*sexual*,' Elizabeth said, when I mentioned this, making the word sound like a disease.

Of course, she'd vetted him, before I took the job.

'Charming,' she'd said. 'Old world.'

'But, Mother,' I said. 'Otto *is*——'

'Nonsense!' she said. 'The man's a little thin, is all.'

'Is he one of us?' she said later, as we set the table.

'Well . . .' I said. 'He went to a Marist Brothers' school.'

'Excellent!' she said. 'They know how to bring out the best in a boy. At least, they did in the old days.'

'You know,' she said, as we spooned down our cream of celery soup, 'I think he's rather taken with you. Don't slurp, Ellen! You shouldn't let a silly thing like a small advancement in age faze you. What am I saying? How could I forget our Sylvester! But then, of course, the marriage was never consummated, was it, dearest?'

'No, Mother,' I said.

'There!' she said happily. 'You really can't pretend a greater knowledge in such matters, can you?'

'No, Mother,' I said flatly. 'And, of course, your nursing training.'

'Exactly,' she said. 'I know about these things. Homo-*sexuality* is not as prevalent as the media would like you to believe. I think, if you don't mind my saying, dear, you are a little *afraid* of men. Mmm? Could that be the case?'

'I'm not afraid of Otto Horsefield,' I said. 'He's a very nice man.'

'Just what I was saying,' she said. 'We are agreed.'

'But,' she said. 'Allow me to surmise. He does not attend Mass, does he?'

'I think . . . No,' I said.

'I thought as much,' she sighed. 'Now if you could only persuade him to come to St Clare's. I would be so happy. Because, you know, there *really* are only two sorts of Catholics. People talk about being lapsed, and it sounds so innocuous, doesn't it? But any Catholic who is not attending Mass regularly and partaking of the Blessed Sacrament is not lapsing, he is *falling*.'

'Yes, Mother,' I said, wiping my mouth. 'But Otto . . . I don't think Otto really minds.'

She stared at me aghast, her mouth forming a little square of horror.

∞

Well, time passed. The leaves yellowed. And Elizabeth kept on at me about Otto. Relentlessly.

'Your nice Mr Horsefield hasn't asked you out yet, has he?' she said lightly, over the cherry pastry. 'Well, that's an older man for you, isn't it? They've learnt a little patience.'

'But really, Eleanor, you might wear stockings to work,' she said. 'You look so unfinished, dear.'

'Yes, Mother,' I said.

'However,' I added modestly, 'you must remember I am Otto's assistant, not one of the models.'

'Phh!' she said. 'I don't think there's much chance of anyone mistaking that.'

Meaning?

'I could model,' I said to Otto, the next day. 'Couldn't I?' Trying not to sound too plaintive.

'Ye-e-s,' Otto said. 'But not for me, El. Not for the catalogues, anyway.'

'Why not?' I said.

'Don't be silly,' he said.

'No, tell me,' I persisted.

'Is it my eye? Is it off-putting?' I said.

'Don't be a wally, El,' he said.

'Then why?' I said. 'Am I *homely*?'

'Homely!' he said. 'My work is all about the home. Provisions. Services. Mundanities. The things these interior decor types leave out, but nonetheless——'

'Otto?' I said.

'You don't look regular enough,' he said finally.

'Don't look regular?' I said. '*Regular*?'

'That's not an insult,' he said hastily.

'Well, it's hardly a compliment,' I said.

'Quiet now,' he said. 'The girl from the agency should be here any minute. We don't want to hurt her feelings.'

And, sure enough, she had wide blue eyes, set apart in her head like pale blue buttons, exactly spaced, doll-like.

I *think* I know what Otto meant.

12

WORKING FOR OTTO IS never dull. For instance, once the agency sent this girl along for the meatpackers' calendar.

She was tall and beautiful, really beautiful. But totally the wrong sort: lanky, all bone, and no apparent breasts. Although it's not a nude calendar, at all, the meatpackers' girl should be robust. She should have breasts that really hit you in the eye. Not that Otto isn't a genius with the camera.

'Don't worry,' she said. 'I shape up.'

She reached into her bag and extracted two clear peach-coloured lumps and shoved them down her shirt and fiddled about.

She turned her back on us and shuffled her breasts about some more, then whirled around, arms crossed, and said, 'Voilà! What do you think?'

I have to admit it was amazing.

'Good,' Otto said. 'Very good. Ah . . . Lesley. Did you bring something gingham? Top half only. We'll only be shooting the top.'

'What about this little number?' she said, unzipping her hanger-bag.

'Great,' said Otto. 'Super.'

'You want to feel them?' she said, turning to me. 'I got them mail order.'

'Later?' I said. I felt a blush rise up my neck.

'Well, yeah. I don't mean now. We're working, aren't we, honey?' she said, winking at Otto.

But afterwards I could only look. Pale, fleshy, translucent—like preserved jellyfish.

'They live in a box,' Lesley said, scooping them up and putting them away. 'My little pets. Neat, huh? I don't want any of that napalm manufacturer's shit floating around *my* body.'

'She was interesting,' I said to Otto after she'd gone.

'Tits in a box!' he said, chuckling to himself. 'Have tits, will travel.'

'Probably didn't want that stuff in her, leaking, like she said,' I said.

'Oh, don't believe that pretty speech,' he said. 'She's as plastic as they come.'

'Otto!' I said. 'I thought she was really sweet.'

'You should see her early work,' he said, half-laughing.

'I've got to hand it to her, though,' he said. 'A real nice presentation. Classy, opting for the little tits.'

'They were fake?' I said. 'Her real breasts were *fake*?'

'Uh-huh,' he said.

'How do you know?' I said.

'I know,' he said. 'Believe me.'

'Oh, I do,' I said. 'I mean—well, I do.'

'Frankenstein's monsters,' he murmured vaguely.

'What?' I said.

'We're creating Frankenstein's monsters,' Otto said. 'You wait. It's the obsession of the age.'

'Doll-people,' he said morosely.

'I *hate* dolls,' I said.

'That's the spirit, darl,' he said, and clapped me on the back.

'Why can't people just accept they way they are?' Otto said—a tall, thin, balding man, with angular shoulders poking through his clothes, and a small pot belly.

'Heh?' he said, peering at me. His eyes were anxious, brown, with rings of navy, and hung with sad grey flannel bags. 'Bang on a bit of makeup.'

'Of course,' he added. 'Only on special occasions.'

All the rest of the day, I thought about Lesley, and all the doll-people, with their silicone breasts and their collagen lips and their botox vaccine faces.

There were stacks of magazines at Otto's, with stories about these operations—as if they were paper patterns you could copy! As if it was just revamping some old dress! Fat sucked out and injected somewhere else. Ribs removed for a nipped-in waist. Some of their eyes so stitched up they couldn't even close them. There were pictures, also. Horrible pictures.

'Look!' I said to Otto, holding one up, later.

'What?' he drawled.

He was pottering away in the corner, dusting his lenses.

'Look what they've done to her waist,' I said.

'Oh, yes,' he said. 'Who eats the spare ribs, that's what I want to know.'

'Otto!' I cried. 'You're so disgusting.'

'Well, yes,' he said, and went back to his lenses.

'Otto?' I said.

'Hmm,' he said.

'This Lesley,' I said. 'She——'

'She's a him,' he snorted.

'No!' I said. '*No*. You can't be serious?'

'I don't believe it!' I said.

'You ought to get out more,' Otto said, and winked.

'Really?' I said.

'Go to the movies, even,' he said.

Otto is such fun!

'No, I mean that——' I said.

'Lesley, my dear, was born plain Gregory Dorkins,' he said. 'Greg, for short. I knew him back in Ballarat.'

'Golly!' I said.

'Honey,' he said. 'The things that I could tell you . . . No. You don't want to know about those things.'

∞

That evening, I told Elizabeth about Lesley being Greg. Or was it Greg who was Lesley? One inside the other, neatly. Or perhaps it wasn't neat at all.

In reverie, Elizabeth's eyes soften and brighten, and become quite childlike. It is then that it becomes clear how large and well-shaped they are—although they protrude from their sockets alarmingly, like blueberry jellies stuffed into too small bowls—and of what a cloud-free and bright sky-blue.

That night, however, as she listened, she held a wide-eyed, dubious, and arrogant stare. I was familiar with that stare. Idiot! it said. Idiot! I cursed myself for mentioning sexual matters.

Her eyes were slightly glazed, her chin lifted, her mouth curled upon itself as if upon some bitter lozenge.

'Otto,' I said, and faltered, for her face was very frightening.

It was then, in the moment of weighing, judging, and condemning, that Elizabeth's face fell together. That it became itself.

Her blue eyes blared above disgust-shrivelled lips. Her ginger hair stood out, as if it would break free from its perm. Her whole face seemed to flame with indignation.

'Don't be silly,' she said, finally—swinging around and staring at me, her lips compressed with contempt. 'What utter, utter nonsense! I don't believe a word of it.'

'That's what I said,' I said, relieved. 'More or less.'

But she *meant* it.

'What absolute *bilge* you talk, Eleanor. How could a man look that much like a woman, close up?' she said, glaring. 'They'd never get away with it.'

'It's true,' I said. 'The eye can be tricked. Why Otto . . . There are cosmetic surgeons——'

'I wouldn't let them rearrange a hair on my head,' she cried defiantly.

As if they were out there in the bushes.

'I don't believe it,' she said, clanging the lid onto the salmon casserole. 'It's just ridiculous.'

'You are the most aggravatingly silly child!' she said.

'Imagine!' she said. 'Imagine your Mr Horsefield employing such a creature. I don't think so. He's older and wiser, dear, and not as fanciful as you.'

Something snapped. Something dreadful in me snapped and took control.

'Yes, I was lying, Mother,' I said, my voice high and rushed. 'I always lie. Always. I'm such a tease, I am. I just can't help myself. I'm so sorry, Mother. Sorry! Really! I can't tell you how many times I've had to confess my lies.'

And she stared at me, little computations clicking across her eyes. She stared at me, as if she believed me, finally.

'A lie of that sort reveals a very wicked imagination, Ellen,' she said quietly.

'We'll say no more about it,' she said. 'Of course, I can't remove the memory from my brain.'

Then there was silence, chilly and frightening.

'I've peeled the potatoes,' I said. 'Shall I scrub some sweet potatoes, too?'

She nodded, sighed, then said, her voice pinched: 'It's true that there *are* such creatures. I have seen them, by the side of the road. Near the city. I think you know the place I mean.'

I nodded and sighed, also.

Of course I know about Kings Cross! I may be a virgin but I'm not a fool. I saw it on television. Well, that was years ago, but I don't expect it's changed.

'I doubt very much,' she said tightly, 'that such individuals are allowed into places of proper business. I think you are mistaken.'

I shrugged and stared at the potatoes.

'Have it your own way, then,' she snapped. 'You always do. But rest assured I do not believe this pernicious nonsense of yours.'

'Furthermore, I do *not* believe,' she said, her voice rising, 'these stories about them having their male members removed. It's disgusting, and preposterous! How,' she finished triumphantly, 'would they urinate?'

'So many lies, spread about,' I said.

'Yes,' she said, eyeing me suspiciously.

13

'AND HOW HAVE YOU been occupied today, Mrs Bird?' Jasper said tonight, when he had run out of compliments, for the time. 'Something amusing, I hope?'

'Oh,' she sighed. 'Just another day of being a housewife, I'm afraid, Jasper.'

What an understatement!

This afternoon I came home from work and discovered that Elizabeth had not only rearranged my room, but also had thrown away many of my favourite things.

'Goodness!' she said, perkily, when I complained. 'What a sook you are, Ellen!'

'You just count your blessings, young lady,' she said, closing the door briskly. 'Next time I'll charge an hourly rate!'

'Now,' she said, as we went downstairs to cook the evening meal, 'don't you dare start in on me. It's ridiculous to harp on and on about a few old worn-out things.'

'Your room's a pig sty!' she added. 'I haven't even scratched the surface.'

'But, Mother, it's *my*——' I said.

'It's no good your sulking at me,' she said.

'But, Mother——' I said.

'Stop your haggling!' she said, flushing furiously. 'You're *so* insistent!'

'I've given them your unwanted clothing, by the way, Ellen,' she said. 'Those unsuitable frocks you clearly bought on a whim last week and hid in the back of your closet——'

'Oh, Mother!' I cried.

'Hush,' she said. 'Not now, if you please. You really are the most objectionable child.'

I felt as I often did: suddenly diminished, in her presence.

'But, Mother——' I said.

'Stop your infernal haggling,' she snapped. 'If you can't button up, you can go to your precious room, immediately!'

'Yes,' she said through her teeth. 'I thought that would set you right.'

'Who'd want to spend any time in there, even after all my efforts? The neglect! The filth!' she cried. 'Nothing about this house matters to you any more, Ellen. You're totally lazy and disinterested. Thank God I have Jasper to help me out!'

'He is so industrious and reliable,' she said, for the hundredth time. 'While *you* put all your energy into being difficult.'

Difficult! I was compliant to the point of paralysis!

'Jasper is a creep,' I said.

'That's very rude!' she said. 'I hope you realise you're being perfectly vile, Eleanor.'

'My goodness!' she spluttered. 'What did I do to deserve this? You and Dymphna are both so difficult to deal with. I've spent my *entire* life dealing with difficult females!'

'You hate us!' I cried. 'You hate us both!'

'Oh, Eleanor,' she said sadly. 'More of your fanciful fabrications, I'm afraid.'

Filth? Neglect? A bit of dust.

Well, dust. It's so perennial—like sin. It cannot be wiped away entirely. It soils. Gets into nooks and crannies. Has a tendency to recur . . .

But back to dinner—the focal point, after all, of our entire lives.

'Ah, Mrs Bird,' Jasper said, wagging his finger. 'You don't fool me. These culinary perfections! This divine lemon and white-chocolate sherry-cream trifle!'

'Many people do have a penchant for my little desserts, Jasper,' she said, inclining her head, glowing with a modest pride.

'And you, Eleanora?' he oozed.

'Well, the usual,' I said. 'We're rather busy at the moment——'

'Ellen's little hobby!' cried Elizabeth, laughing mirthlessly.

'Actually, Jasper,' she said. 'I worked *unceasingly* all day, sorting linen and much needed apparel for the St Vincent de Paul.'

'How charming,' said Jasper. 'We do so need the poor.'

Elizabeth overlooked that, somehow. Or did I imagine it? Or misconstrue——

'Your neighbours are putting in some trees, I see,' said Jasper then, grinning and baring his teeth.

'Who?' said Elizabeth sharply.

'The Snowballs,' I said. 'Gum trees. By the letterbox.'

'Oh,' she said. 'The *Snowballs*. Well. Typical.'

'New arrivals,' she explained to Jasper. 'Planting those monstrosities . . . Not that I'm not always the good neighbour,' she added hastily. 'Always ready with a smile and a nod and a wave. Perfectly willing to lend a cup of sugar or a helping hand . . . though thankfully no-one asks me.'

'Ha ha!' cried Jasper.

'The Snowballs are always braying on and on about the value of their property. Well!' she said. 'Our house is *far* more delightful and our garden is so fresh and green, isn't it? Gum trees! I shouldn't be surprised if next thing they rip their lawn up and put in native ground cover!'

'Your garden is, indeed, remarkably pleasant,' said Jasper. 'So lush! So verdant!'

'Yes,' she sighed. 'A little overgrown, it's true. It's so easy to cut the lawns, but no-one ever does it. So every so often I call in a little man.'

'There is no-one to help me, or to take an interest in the place,' she said sadly. 'Not since Ronald passed away.'

Over and over she said this. As if I was not a person! As if I never did a thing! (Of course, a *man* is different, I suppose?)

'I'm sure, in an emergency . . .' she said. 'Well, it *is* a family matter. I shouldn't like to involve the neighbours.'

'Ellen, I'm afraid, is not a willing helper. The garden,' she said weakly. 'I despair . . .'

'Oh, Mother——' I said.

'I shall take over the grasses,' said Jasper, his sunken chest swelling with sudden pride.

'Oh, Jasper!' Elizabeth cried. 'I would be so obliged.'

'My pleasure,' he said. 'Entirely.'

'Oh, you dear kind man!' she cried. 'If you would . . .'

Oh, God. The pair of them. It's more than I can stand.

Well, neither of us are gardeners. Everything I touch turns brown and dies. I should note that dig at me about the mowing was quite unnecessary, as Elizabeth can't even start the wretched rusty thing.

'I would like some assistance in the kitchen, Eleanor,' she said then.

'No, thank you, Jasper,' she said. 'I'm sure the two of us can get things spick and span.'

'You put your feet up, so to speak,' she simpered.

'You're all heart, Mrs Bird,' he said. 'All heart.'

See! she said to me with her eyes, when she joined me at the sink.

'He works so hard! Poor fellow,' she said.

'I work hard, and I do the dishes,' I said.

'Oh, Ellen,' she cried, 'you are a daft and silly girl.'

'Now, quiet, and let's get on with it,' she said. 'I'm totally frazzled in this heat.'

Though not a speck of sunlight ever entered the house.

14

IN MY BEDROOM, THE disarray is very ordered. (Ron *would* have a fit if he saw the amount of junk that I've got stacked in here.) There are queues of collections: over there my china and my watercolour kit, down the line embroidery, tapestry, cross-stitch, and on to pencils and pens, papers and assorted books.

Shoved in the back of my clothes' cupboard is my first communion doll, a red-haired Barbie-clone dressed by Elizabeth in an exact replica of my first communion frock—or was it the other way around? Bet Barbie refused to swallow her wafer.

On the day of my wedding to Sylvester, I was the bride doll, cheeks flushing furiously beneath my veil. I was wearing Elizabeth's wedding dress, recut and taken in, shapeless and shimmering, my stockinged legs protruding from the too-short skirt like long beige beans.

Later on, standing by the graves of Ron, and then Sylvester, with my plastic tears, it crossed my mind that no-one had ever marketed a Funeral Barbie: black A-line shift, little black headscarf, Jacquie O sunglasses . . .

On the bed, as I write this, there are two white sheets, two pillows in white pillowcases, a peach-pink blanket, the coverlet (blossom-pink), and me.

We are all here.

The queues of stuff sit still. Only the windows and I are moving. The windows are rattling in the wind in time to my breath.

And the clock. The clock is moving rather loudly.

What else is there to record?

Round to the left, umbrellas. Vertical clothes in the wardrobe:

a rainbow of pastel blouses that Elizabeth has made for me. My raincoat. My navy winter coat. My Fletcher Jones' skirts: black, navy, and charcoal grey. Horizontal piles in the cupboard by the door: jumpers—pastel, underwear—white, hosiery—beige. Shoes under the bed with the excess baggage (one tiny suitcase, barely used).

But it's all excess baggage, isn't it? Everything except the soul. Oh, the soul . . .

Since I was a small girl, I've believed that other people could look into my eyes and see the state of my soul. This is what I was taught, this is what I believe: God slips a soul inside each of us, as we are conceived, and then he waits to see what a mess we will make of it.

Now that I am older, and can supposedly think for myself, I still expect others to look beyond my outer appearance, to see my soul, and to *recognise* me. And I am constantly disappointed.

Now that I am older, and have had more time to think, I still cannot say for sure where my soul is located. I only know that it must be white to be acceptable to God, and mine is not.

I think of my soul, floating disconsolately up and down my torso, seeking a resting place. It is oval in shape, I imagine. Of course, it may be square. It may be lodged, hat-like, against my brain. (Is it translucent? Or opaque? Or both?—like the leg of a thick white pair of tights, stretched and held up to the light.)

∞

It was at St Ursula's, the local convent school (where I studied from the age of five until the day I turned fifteen, and promptly left) that I learnt about the soul.

The nuns at St Ursula's were housewives of the soul, flying upon any speck. We were caned, slapped, and beaten across the legs with whatever came to hand—pointers, T-squares, the wooden handles of a feather duster—all for the whitening of our souls. I told Elizabeth of these punishments and received that look: How improbable, it said.

I understand they banned these things long ago at public schools—but publics were poorly educated, and unfortunate, Elizabeth told me.

Well. I find it useful to consider that, in the sight of God, all men are born equal. (And when God says men, he means *women* too.) Just shows how incomprehensibly different God's vision is from ours.

At school, I learnt about the saints and martyrs, and the beauty of suffering. I learnt about the value of an early painful death, and the certainty of hell for girls such as I—who whispered in the stairwell, and drew coloured pictures on their rulers, and forgot to bring their bloomers for P.E. Girls, indeed, who did not contribute much vitality to the annual sports day. And I learnt about the soul, and the thousand ways to sully it.

How white was my soul, back then? Grey-white and nubbled, like a pair of old underpants? Or sheet-white, the colour of worn flannelette, well-washed, and only tinged about the edges with signs of wear?

I went quickly about my business, eyes lowered, for fear of giving myself away. There was always a nun—at the top of a landing, in the dark of a corridor—waiting, watching, impatiently tapping with her stick on the palm of her hand. It was just so . . . dark, at St Ursula's.

Every Sunday morning, for as long as I can remember, my family went to early Mass at our local church, St Clare's. There, Father Flannery was blandly uninterested in our souls. We were a congealed blob before him, almost witless—a baby, to whom he fed pacifying stories of Christ, and little tasteless wafers. Not once did he look into our eyes.

In the confessional at St Clare's, the grille that separated us, sinner from priest, and gave an illusion of anonymity, was made of some bronze-coloured metal that sparkled when I narrowed my eyes and moved my head from side to side.

'Forgive me Father, for I have sinned,' I murmured, waving my head, clasping and unclasping my hands.

Back and forth, back and forth, the murmured rituals. But nothing was solved or salved by doing this.

St Clare's is lined with modern wood and filled with light. A long tall building that looks as if it was carved from porridge. Nothing evil, its pale bricks declare, can ever enter. St Ursula's, on the other hand, was like a cave. In the gloomy chapel, surrounded by nuns with warning faces, I stared fiercely at the floor, or at my knees, head resting on the wooden pew in front. I lifted my eyes to the shining altar in fake supplication. I shuffled through my missal, impatient for the hymns. I cocked my ears to old Father Dougherty's faint but threatening lisp. The ancient priest's face was a halo, a faceless blur, as distant as the Pope's.

Every week, desperate to please or appease, I coughed up half a dozen lies to this priest, also (confession, twice a week, made demands on my resources): I was unhelpful at home. I did not make my bed. I stole ninety-five cents. I lied.

'Any impure thoughts?' Father Dougherty asked, momentarily gaining life. He was an old man behind a dusty partition, an old man with translucent ears.

'No,' I lied.

'Say ten Our Fathers and three Hail Marys,' Father Dougherty said, week after week, slamming the partition closed, sighing.

How could I tell him the truth? That every moment of my existence was riddled with sin.

Every thought, every word, every minor deed was an occasion for sin. Oh, how I shamed myself! But never did I imagine how ghastly my sins would be.

∞

Some people take Catholicism on voluntarily: for them it is a lacy structure, easy to wear, light as a golden mantilla.

I inherited my faith, and it brought—it brings me—no comfort. For me, the frocked priests and the black-robed nuns were the bell-ringers of my terrible doom. *Hell*, they said, *hell*. For ever and ever.

15

RON AND LIZ WERE old when they had me. ('Old enough to know better,' Ron used to say.) Before I came along and spoiled the fun, they used to travel, all over the world. Every chance they had, they saved towards another holiday, and everywhere they went—every city, town, or village—they souvenired another doll.

Can you imagine what it is like to know that you, by your very being, are a complete imposition? I came to this conclusion at an early age, but kept the knowledge to myself. My parents would have done better to stick with their collection of dolls—Brazil, Holland, Japan; Wales, Tahiti, Scotland—all in their little costumes, in their dust-free cases.

Ron liked a bit of order. He kept the glass doors of the cabinets shining, the shelves polished, and every doll in its proper place. They were my tiny torturers, all through my childhood. My thousand miniature rivals. My diminutive superiors, so perfectly neat and quiet.

I learnt early on that I, too, must be a quiet and undemanding doll—a doll, brought home, then shelved. A doll, indeed, never removed from its box. (Kept for display purposes? Or too tiresome to dispose of, once purchased?)

While Ron and Elizabeth were off on their jaunts, souveniring dolls, I stayed with Richard and Brenda: Ron's brother and his wife. Brenda was a tall thin woman with tiny dark eyes and a puff of pinkish hair. Richard was like Ron, though broader in the chest, feisty and eager-looking. Richard had his heart, and Brenda had her asthma. She was always pale and out of breath. I remember her long thin fingers, cool and damp as they smoothed my hair. Her tiny eyes, studying mine.

Did she see the bruises that Ron left? Kids fall over, don't they . . .

The travels and the dolls led one into the other. No-one could talk of the travels without being led into the doll-room—and the dolls then led to talk of other travels, on and on.

Liz and Ron, and their bloody doll-room. They were only really happy when they were playing with their dolls: rearranging their hair and fluffing out their skirts, and brushing them down with tiny brushes. There were country dolls and custom dolls—all painstakingly explained to the rare visitor. (Seldom second visits.)

All through my childhood and into my teens I witnessed the blink of the visitor, the wetting of lips, and then the dutiful following back, hunched with apprehension. And then, some hours later, they would emerge: Ron and Liz giddy with joy, their ashen visitor visibly shaken.

They could talk themselves dry, but only within the parameters of other places (caught in memory in a snapshot series of anecdotes, and symbolised by the gaily-clothed dolls). As if a colourful life could only be lived in another faraway place, in any other place . . . Well.

The dolls were *life*, book. Bought, and understood. Controllable.

The dolls were memory in 3-D, and silent. They couldn't open their mouths and say: It wasn't like that!

The dolls were . . . companions? *Friends*?

After Ron died, Elizabeth shut and locked the doll-room. Did she slip in there when she was in the house alone, and weep and sigh? Did she brush their curls and plait their tiny braids? Perhaps, while I was out, she stayed in there for hours. How would I know? Sometimes I crept home early, hoping to surprise her.

But then, perhaps the travels were really only Ron's, for the stories as well as the dolls were closed away after his death—as, earlier on, so many of their trips had been locked away into impossibility by my tedious birth.

Now her round was family, church, garden, home—and not much garden. And, if someone said in conversation: 'You've been there, haven't you, Elizabeth?' She'd reply, dully: 'Oh, yes.' And that was that.

It was all put away, like so many piles of old newspapers, like Ron's clothing and possessions—which were not thrown away, but relegated to the attic, after his death.

Perhaps it wasn't the same, without Ron? Perhaps the dolls had lost their lustre, finally. Perhaps Elizabeth had only ever been a sympathetic accomplice, fired by Ron's fervour? Or was it with a sense of preserving the sanctity of memory that she closed the doll-room and hid away its key, and locked away her store of stories?

It felt strange to think of them, the little army, neat in their rows, waiting for no-one, umbrellaed in their cabinets—dust falling like slow-motion rain.

One day, in the future (when Elizabeth has died, of course. You must not think I am insensitive, book, despite Sylvester), I will set a match to them.

Oh, happy day! I can almost hear the plastic crackling, see their tiny faces sighing in the heat, hear the shriek of their melting eyes . . .

16

AFTER THE LAWN-MOWER conversation, Jasper became a furiously attentive odd-jobs man. On the weekends, he never seemed to leave the house. Every time I glanced out of my window, he was clipping a hedge or painting a window trim, looking up. Was he *watching* me?

If he'd come to arrest us, why didn't he do it? Or was he biding his time, hoping we'd break? Oh, I don't know——

It all seems so unlikely, written here. But *something* . . .

∞

'Oh, Jasper! The eaves!' Elizabeth cried, this morning—thrusting a cup of tea at him as he passed through the kitchen. 'So nice and thoughtful.'

'Well, of course, we'll soon be joining you, making the place pleasant,' she said. 'Chores, chores, chores!'

'Mrs Garlic held us up this morning, just as we were returning home from Mass,' Elizabeth confided, by way of excuse.

'Our neighbour,' she said, leaning conspiratorially closer to Jasper. 'One of our many ghastly neighbours.'

'The nuisance!' she said. 'The time-waster! You'd think she'd see that I'm too busy to stand around talking. Oh, no! She's a real pain in the neck, that one! Never takes a hint. *And* I suspect she was inebriated.'

'Well, it's not for nothing that I have always had an aversion to Protestants,' she informed Jasper. 'And then, to cap things off, we were joined by that fool from over the road.'

'Art Snowball?' Jasper said.

'The one and only,' said Elizabeth. 'He with his ghastly gum trees, shedding their dull-leafed litter up and down the street! Eucalypts, indeed.'

'But that silly twit, Mrs Garlic,' she cried, 'seems utterly enamoured—of him, and with his wretched bogus *native* garden. Well, she would, wouldn't she, being one of those conservation ratbag nuisances. Did she gush! Really, there's nothing as disgusting as an inebriated woman.'

'"What do you think of my garden, Mrs Bird?" Snowball asked, the idiot. "It does not meet with my complete approval," I replied. Well! That was putting it mildly. But I am notoriously polite,' Elizabeth said. 'And then, just as I thought I was going to go screaming mad standing in that murderous heat, listening to the pair of them wittering on, along comes Rosaleen Rivers to put in her two bob's worth.'

'How terribly trying,' Jasper sympathised.

'That Garlic creature seems to be quite unbalanced,' she added. 'In fact, they seem to be quite an unbalanced family. Her sole interest is macramé. Have you seen those things she's got dangling from her verandah? Macramé . . . And, of course, the drink.'

'Drinking horrifies Ellen and I,' she said, blinking rapidly—her eyes intensely blue and bugging out.

'Speaking of wretched time-wasters, quick, Dymphna is coming!' Elizabeth cried, and we all ducked down. 'And—I don't believe it!—she's brought that smelly dog!'

Elizabeth was inclined to hide—indeed, was well-known amongst her visitors for doing this.

'Dogs are very dirty animals,' she muttered, 'always filthy around the crotch.'

'Of course, the poor dear means no harm,' she whispered loudly to Jasper. 'On the other hand, she does nothing helpful either.'

'Oh, my godfather,' Elizabeth hissed, as Darlene pounded at the door.

Darlene never took a hint. She thumped and thumped, until Elizabeth went out to her.

'Dymphna!' she cried. 'What a surprise! Won't you come in for a cup of tea? Leave little Freddie outside, will you? I don't want to have to redo the carpets.'

'This is Jasper Pease, Dymphna,' Elizabeth said grandly. 'Our lodger. Jasper, this is my little sister, Dymphna.'

'Darlene,' Darlene said, shaking his hand limply, and peering up at him with her bulging red-rimmed eyes.

'Charmed, utterly charmed,' said Jasper.

Darlene gave me a loopy grin, and winked—or did her eye twitch?

'Do have one of my famous Anzac biscuits,' said Elizabeth.

'I'm on a diet,' said Darlene vaguely, taking several.

'Delicious!' said Elizabeth, chewing with enthusiasm.

Jasper soon excused himself and returned to his painting, while I refreshed the pot of tea.

∞

'The silly twit!' said Elizabeth, later. 'Without notice, as usual.'

'Still, the poor dear,' she sighed. 'She is such a source of worry to me, Jasper.'

Jasper nodded attentively.

'Of course,' she added, 'I do what I can . . . One does, doesn't one? At least she has me to come to.'

'I'm sure the warmth and kindness you provide, along with your delicious teas, make a real difference,' said Jasper, batting his lashes at her.

'How sweet you are, Jasper!' Elizabeth cried.

'A lifeline,' I said dryly.

'Yes, yes,' she said, gazing over at the manger scene on the mantelpiece.

In our house, every surface has a doily with a little holy statue on it. Every wall has a crucifix, or a reproduction of a saint, or a set of praying hands.

By the dining table there is a giant painting of the Sacred Heart of Jesus—which is what finally put me off my meat. In the kitchen there are prayer tiles in a border around the workspace. Something to meditate on, while at the sink. Even in the bathroom there's a crucifix: made of silvery metal, with signs of rust about Our Saviour's feet.

For as long as I can remember, all year round, the manger, with Baby Jesus, sat on top of the TV. These days, it sits year-round (for ready reflection) on the mantelpiece.

All year round, there were palm leaves, dried and dusty, left over from Palm Sunday, stuffed decoratively behind the clock-radio, and some beside the toaster that gave off a whiff of green when it reached its highest heat. They are in handy reach now, artfully fashioned into crosses, and pinned to the noticeboard beside the fridge.

And, should one feel in need of it, still, there is always the reassuring plastic font of holy water by the front door, blessed and reblessed by Father Flynn (our parish priest).

'Yes,' Elizabeth sighed, 'I think you're right. There is just something about our home that soothes the troubled mind.'

'Ah, Mrs Bird! It must be all the love expressed in it!' said Jasper brightly.

17

MONDAY! WHAT A RELIEF to go to work!

There are our neighbours, Harry and Ethel Jumper, scrubbing their driveway, again. Does it help them to feel they are cleansing themselves of hidden sins?

Well, we all have our secrets, don't we?

Mrs Rivers down the road, up at dawn hosing her guilt away. Art Snowball, who runs and runs. Mr Garlic, who cannot get his car clean.

The Jumpers, particularly, have a mania for order. Witness the vicious pruning of their frangipanni trees. Well, I suppose now that their children have grown up and moved away there is no-one left to deform. Or are the clubbed trees an artistic expression of their inner beings?

Harry and Ethel's interior lives, I surmise, are filled with rampant disorder: pools of bile and unacknowledged vitriol, raging fear, and malignant discontent. And the guilt. The guilt. It weighs us all down, doesn't it? I can't understand why they don't just concrete over their lawn.

'Hello, Harry! Hello, Ethel!' I cry.

They ignore me. Harry and Ethel have ignored Elizabeth and me since Ron died—and contaminated us, perhaps, with joint widowhood. (Or was it the time they pruned our fruit trees as we slept, and then denied it?)

'Pleasant day,' I cry, and carry on walking to the bus stop.

It is most definitely not. A wind is whipping up, tossing leaves and twigs into the paths and gutters, and messing things up. The sky is dark, and full of threatening clouds.

Lemonhurst, it's the devil's own suburb, I always say.

I sit in the shelter, and wait for redemption by bus, and ignore the peculiar looks I get for writing in you, book.

The monstrous clouds, now, moving fast, seem to miniaturise the scene below them. The street, and the blocks of flats surrounding it, appear toy-like. The plane trees that line Glass Street are momentarily shrub-sized, and the big council-lopped whatsit tree that fills with birds at twilight looks like a potted jade plant. And then the sky is still, for just one moment, and everything returns to its normal size.

A few more people join me in the shelter. They smile, wince, click their tongues, and sigh heavily.

Moving towards us now, dark grey and smoking—as if the underlip of hell had been stretched up high—is a gigantic cloud, miles wide. Above, is a broiling mass of cloud of paler grey—all of it moving, like a mighty tidal wave, to cover Lemonhurst.

What a relief it will be when the storm breaks! When the gathering clouds of the tribulation are mightily massed, and the winds begin to blow—what a blessed relief!

How it will rip and splinter when the time comes! And our hearts will be torn from our flesh, and our ribs will be roasted, and the air itself will be flame . . .

And then . . . And then . . . And then the air will be filled with water, and there will be no escape. Oh——

18

I WAS RETURNING MY teacup to the kitchen earlier this evening when I overheard Elizabeth talking to one of her sisters. Marlene, I soon deduced, from the tenor of the conversation. I would not have lingered but——

'Oh, *her*,' said Elizabeth. 'Yes.'

'Very trying,' she said.

'Yes,' she said, brightening. 'They were impressed. I think the curried-egg sandwiches were magnificent, if I do say so myself.'

'Yes,' she said. 'Yes. Quite.'

'Oh,' she said, 'a shambles! I don't know how anyone can live in such disorder. Yes. Yes. She's still a little girl in so many ways——'

Well. Obviously, she was discussing Darlene, I thought. Because Darlene was a bit strange, and juvenile.

'She's becoming quite a problem,' Elizabeth sighed. 'Yes. *Very* taciturn. She simply takes no interest——'

Which was a bit unfair, I thought, given Darlene's attention span. That of a gnat.

'I know!' she said. 'I *know*, Marlene. It's all a matter of complete indifference to her: the church, the flower arranging, the choir. Oh, yes! Anything to do with the household——'

'Absolutely,' she said. 'Most unsatisfactory.'

Poor Darlene! I thought.

'She'd rather lie around reading,' sneered Elizabeth.

At this, I started. Darlene never—no-one in our family, except for me—ever reads. Do they?

'It seems to me,' she said then, 'that Ellen is quite deliberately making a rotten hash-up of her life.'

I felt my face and neck flush, as it used to when I was a child. I remembered the smallness, the sadness, the defiant heat and shame.

It's one thing, in private, to my face. But behind my back and——

'Yes,' she said. 'Exactly. And insisting on remaining involved in that silly little part-time job of hers.'

'Exactly!' she said. 'And *he's* supposedly so brilliant!'

'Precisely!' she said. 'The Mall!'

'Oh,' she sighed. 'If I bring it up the little ninny goes into one of her cranky states. More moods than a——'

'Yes,' she said. 'Yes, I suppose.'

There followed a series of murmurings and gasps.

'Oh, really!' she said. 'That wretched girl! She was the very worst of the deplorable gaggle that Ellen insisted on associating with in her youth.'

'Yes, I *do* despair,' she said, after listening for an unusual length of time.

'And they'll be marrying at St Clare's? Oh?' she said. 'I see. Goodness.'

'Do *you* know of anyone who might be a possibility for Ellen, who is in dire need of a male companion, as you know?' said Elizabeth, then, sighing.

'Our Jasper? Yes, I thought they might find a little interest in each other, too,' she said. 'Such a charming, serviceable young man!'

'Oh, no, she's taken quite a set against him. Can't imagine why,' she said, sounding not altogether unpleased.

'Yes,' she said. 'He *does* adore my puddings!'

'Well, dear,' she said. 'Must fly. I've another little job to finish.'

'Eleanor!' she called, coming into the kitchen—as if she knew that I was there, and listening.

'Well, for goodness sake!' she snapped. 'Don't just stand about aimlessly!'

I rinsed my teacup hastily.

'Jane O'Shea is getting married,' she said sweetly. 'How about that?'

'Pity the poor groom,' I said.

'You're tongue is getting acid, dear,' she said. 'She's marrying Jim Dooley's nephew——'

'What do you care?' I cried. 'You hated her. You wouldn't let her come around. You wouldn't even let me speak to her——'

'There's no need to have a hissy fit!' she said, staring hard at me.

'Will you please stop shuffling about, Eleanor?' she cried. 'You look as daft as Dymphna!'

'Oh, dear,' she sighed, turning away, and rustling about amongst the forks and knives. 'Your friends were all so *strange*. Such sullen, unfriendly, pallid types. I surmised, no doubt correctly, that they were all on drugs. You'll understand, when . . .'

'Oh,' she sighed again, as if it was all too much to bear.

I suppose she means marriage and children, and all the things so far from me that constitute a normal life. (Well. How can I understand? Perhaps I am unfair . . .)

'What were you saying about Otto?' I said, when the silence had become too heavy around us.

'Oh, nothing,' she said. 'I don't know what you mean.'

'And what were you doing listening in?' she said. 'As if you've got nothing better to do! Your room, for one, is in a deplorable state.'

'I don't know why you don't like Otto,' I said.

'Don't take that bold tone with me, young lady!' she said.

'It's not *I* who dislike him,' she said. 'I'm only thinking of your future.'

'We all think that that stupid photo work is pretty silly,' she said.

'We?' I said.

'Your *family*,' she said.

'It's obvious you would rather be with that ridiculous little man than with your family!' she cried.

'It's my job!' I said. 'I suppose you'd rather I was unemployed?'

'I'll tell you what. We're all pretty fed up with your aggressive attitude and your know-all remarks,' she said.

'Jane O'Shea was never on drugs,' I said. 'She was nice! I don't suppose she'll invite me to the wedding.'

'Oh, don't start!' she cried. 'You're forever dredging up the past. Jasper will be home soon and you've done nothing towards his dinner.'

'It's my dinner, too,' I said stupidly.

'Well?' she said, and gave me a stare.

'Why doesn't he do something towards *my* dinner,' I said. 'Why should I be running around after him?'

'Oh, don't be ridiculous, Eleanor,' she said. 'He's our lodger! Besides, he works so hard, poor fellow.'

'You don't even know doing what!' I said.

'Yes,' she said thinly, 'but I can tell the difference between an industrious type and a bone-idle person.'

On and on. Tug, pull. Always the same.

19

I SPENT TODAY CATCHING up on the accounts: Entering and printing out invoices. Folding them neatly into their envelopes. Sending them out to meet their fate.

At two-thirty, I decided to ask him.

'Otto?' I said.

'Hmm?' he said.

I paused. Breathed. Waited.

'Doesn't matter,' I said.

∞

I do not understand people. They do not make themselves clear.

Ron disliked us both. We enraged him. And yet he stayed with us for all those years. Was it merely the net of matrimony? The frown of the Church?

And Elizabeth dislikes me—hates me, *despises* me?—I sometimes think. Hates me sometimes, I suppose I mean. (Not all the time. Surely?) It is mean of me to think so, but I think it, sometimes. Is it my lack of get up and go? Or is it because I remind her so of poor Darlene?

Otto likes me. I know he likes me, but he likes to take a swipe at me, now and then. Is it because he's jealous that I'm the girl?

Sylvester. Oh, Sylvester liked me well enough, at first. His whole face crumpled with his smile. But he wanted—what? A nurse?

Pasty Jasper remains a mystery.

No, I cannot say I understand a single person. Not even myself.

I——

Well. Every so often I halt for a second and get the strangest sensation, and realise that I don't know what I'm doing.

Of course. It is true. I don't know what I'm doing. I don't know what I'm doing *here*. Does anyone?

I worry then that I will carry on blindly, and not know. And never know.

I worry that I am some sort of zombie, endlessly questioning and defending what are in fact mechanical actions and reactions.

If only I could simplify my position. If only——

If only I could forget. But these engulfing nightmares, the awful jumble in my brain. And eyes—and eyes, everywhere.

And people, half-glimpsed, then pulling out of sight—I swear it . . .

∞

I have my theories about Jasper. I watch and I occasionally follow him. And when I turn my face aside and suddenly back, I find that he is watching me—all sly and shy, a touch of derision in the corners of his lopsided, grinning mouth.

And then, tonight, out of the blue, I thought: If I sit still and silent long enough, if Jasper is who I think he is, if he performs his mission well—then I shall be freed, soon, from my mantle of guilt.

Because, any minute, any minute now, Elizabeth—or I (what does it matter now?)—will break.

Any minute now, I swear, I will.

Because the doubts, you know, because the fear.

I know he has come to spy on me. I know he has come to do me in.

He was sent, I know, to take me into darkness.

I consider the possibility that I am mad. Consider, discount, consider, discount. And so I set it all down here. Let *you* decide, book.

20

LIES LEAD TO MADNESS. Do you believe me when I say that? Do you think maybe I'm lying to you? Ha! Why lie to yourself? Because, my dear, the truth is painful. *Because the truth is painful.*

You know, don't you, book. You know. Faithfully, I write in you. And you know more than I do.

And I know where Jasper works! (Not that I've told Elizabeth, of course.) Jasper works at the Registry of Births, Deaths and Marriages. I know this because I followed him there.

Oh, what a relief! What a blessed, blessed relief! Jasper is a clerk! (Although it could be an under-cover front . . . Now, that's really being silly.)

Every morning for a week I followed him to Haymarket, to the building that houses the Registry. And then, one day, after nipping off early from work, I came back and I waited outside for him, and then I followed him again.

For hours, he walked aimlessly around the city's parks and public squares, apparently studying the flower beds and monuments. For hours and hours we walked, into the start of the clammy evening, and then I followed him home again.

Of course, I thought, he could be merely lurking—knowing I was onto him.

Well! Clients, form-lodgers, and miscellaneous searchers, all came and went from the Registry. But Jasper works there. I know this for certain, because yesterday I followed him in!

I readjusted my headscarf and sunglasses, and my bulky thrift-shop frock. I reapplied my smear of lipstick—how strange it felt! I straightened my shoulders, bent my knees, and puffed out my cheeks, and then I walked into the room where queues ten-deep had formed.

I stood at the end of a queue and slowly scanned the room—and then I saw him, pale and cool behind his half-glass.

I watched him operate for a while.

He glanced at me. Or, at least, appeared to. How I froze!

Did I imagine that? I thought. His damp eyes on me . . .

I shuddered, and stared boldly back at him. But he ignored me. (*If* he'd recognised me.) Carried on, blank-faced.

And then I left, and caught the bus to work, stripping off my masterful disguise—leaving only a trace of lipstick. A stain, as if I'd sucked some lurid-coloured fruit.

Jasper is a clerk! That's all!

Jasper is a clerk, there, where all the secret information is kept. The old marriage certificates, from the days when marriage was a career move. All sorts of paper documents—kept in cavernous underground storerooms housing drawer after drawer? And microfiche, I suppose. And all the information fed into the computer's bulbous brain: secret birthdays, and shed names, and unsuitable marriages, shelved alongside birth after birth, and death after death.

I wonder what secrets the files in the Registry hold: about, for example, Sylvester and me?

∞

'How's work?' I said, archly, at the dinner table tonight.

Elizabeth's eyes glared. Her mouth smirked silkily. She thrust more brussel sprouts at him.

'Oh, you know how it is,' Jasper replied, flicking back a strand of well-oiled hair. (I stared at his face—he seemed to be growing sideburns.) 'Another lousy dollar. And just as darned well tomorrow is another day, if you'll excuse my French!'

Elizabeth tittered appreciatively.

'And how was your day, Eleanora?' he elided smoothly. 'Hard at your . . . studies?'

For a moment my heart leapt and thudded against my chest, like a bullfrog desperate to escape.

'Ellen is taking some Time Out,' said Elizabeth, pleased with her grasp of the language. 'She is resting. Although she reads a great deal.'

'Next year,' she said, wearing the expression she usually

reserved for presenting a tray of her best-baked scones, 'she'll be returning to the university, of course. She's going to be a doctor!'

Elizabeth frequently enquires after, even applies for, other jobs for me. But this last leap of the imagination was too much.

'You know I never even sat the HSC, Mother,' I said, my voice level.

Elizabeth thrust more salmon and potato pie at Jasper: diversionary tactics.

'I'm thinking of doing a correspondence course in taxidermy, though,' I said.

I stood up, excused myself, and ran upstairs.

In the bathroom mirror my face was flushed. Red spots had appeared at the base of my neck.

I touched my face in the mirror, and was surprised to see my mirror hand meet mirror flesh . . .

Had he seen me?

What did he see, anyway—from behind the screen of his corny manners—with his cold, glazed eyes?

I went back down and resumed my place. They were still discussing my fantasy career.

'Mother,' I hissed. 'It's been years since I studied anything, and you know how that went. Besides, I like working with Otto.'

'Otto?' Jasper said, swallowing a mouthful of pie.

'Otto Horsefield. He's a photographer. Up at the Mall,' I said.

'Oh, nice,' he said non-committaly.

'You'd like university too,' Elizabeth said.

'There's nothing wrong with having low ambition,' I said, looking to Jasper for support. Surely he could not consider his clerical work ambitious?

'I'm not sure I agree,' he said smoothly, wiping his lips with his napkin and gazing from one to the other of us, so that we did not know to whom he had spoken.

'Dessert?' said Elizabeth.

That old stand-by.

'Peach sorbet,' she announced. 'With sugared yoghurt.'

'How exquisite!' cried Jasper. 'No-one could ever accuse you of having low ambitions in the kitchen, Mrs Bird.'

'Not when I have an appreciative audience,' she said.

'I can't tell you how long it's been,' she sighed.

'Oh, really, Mother,' I said, annoyed. 'It's not that long. What about——'

'Ellen,' she snapped. 'Stop gabbling and come and help me with the plates.'

21

THIS MORNING, JASPER HAVING gone to his glass cubicle, Elizabeth said: 'You *could* be a doctor, if you only stopped this nonsense.'

'I could be a fireman too,' I said.

But I have never had a desire to be anything, or anyone, except myself. This I didn't bother saying.

Elizabeth was a nurse, before she married Ron. And Ron was a rather good cabinet-maker. None of our furniture is shop bought. And I keep you, book, in the inlaid cedar box Ron hand-tooled for my tenth birthday.

A printer, a draper, a cabinet-maker . . .

It is true I have no trade.

'You can't remember being young, can you?' I said to Elizabeth. I gave her a withering look, stuck my breasts out, and flounced off to do my job.

It's a job, that's all. I'm not *it*. How awful to be nothing but your job.

Anyway, a doctor! I can't think of anything worse. Bad breath, and gangrenous limbs, and other people's colds and problems in an endless stream.

But a doctor has power over people. Is that the appeal? He sees them naked. He weights the scales in favour of life or death . . .

For Elizabeth, God is the great doctor of all souls, the specialist of the afterlife. I would think stitching up smelly human bodies would pale in comparison with such translucent surgery.

Why does she urge me to compete with God—over and over?

And why does she taunt me with my failure to finish high school?

It is true: I am not a successful person, or a powerful one. Well! And what of it? I do not want—I never wanted—to be either.

Elizabeth, note, did not go back to nursing after marrying Ron—despite the admonishments regarding *my* lack of thrusting career. But she is more, much more, than housewife, mother, landlady, and widow of Ron Bird. (Surprisingly, the insurance company paid up. We did all right on this and the superannuation for a while, then something or other about interest rates, etc. Hence, Jasper Pease.)

Ron's death money, now supplemented by the lodger, leaves Elizabeth free to work full-time at her calling: watcher of men, weigher of evil, apportioner of all blame.

She watches me, always watches me. With her basilisk eyes, she takes a scraping of my soul's cells every time I enter or leave the room.

She does not trust me. How she watches me! Her eyes, delving into my skin, warning me: *Keep quiet.*

They all watch me. (Are they all in on it? Could they possibly be?) A whole cauldron of disapproving women . . . Though Iris, now and then, gives me a conspiratorial wink.

Well, so she should. She *is* my godmother.

22

I COULDN'T HELP MYSELF. Yesterday I went back into the Registry.

I stood in the queue that had formed at Jasper's window, and waited patiently.

I was clutching a sheaf of papers, to look the part, and had hidden my hair beneath another ugly scarf. My lips were crimson, and shiny as a motor car! ($3.95 at Clarry the Chemist's, in Lemonhurst Mall.)

Shopping for my disguises in the opportunity shop near the Mall has added spice to my lunchtime duties. It strikes me that there are whole new lives in there, that can be purchased for ten or twenty dollars, all the way down to shoes . . .

When I reached the window, I leant close and spoke to the clerk behind it.

'That man who's usually here? Tall, dark, rather debonair,' I said, trying not to smirk. 'Where is he?'

'What, Pantihose? It's his flexiday, isn't it?' said the thin boy behind the glass, turning to his work-mates on either side—a stocky dark woman and a crumpled, pimpled-faced man—for confirmation.

'Yeah, Thursdays,' said the woman.

'What, Pantihose?' said the crumpled man. 'Flexi. Yeah.'

'That's what we call him,' the thin boy said, and waited for me to ask why.

'Why do you call him Pantihose?' I said.

'Nearest thing to a cunt,' he whispered, and they all fell about laughing.

'I'll put that in my report,' I said.

I whisked myself away, flicking one look back at their frightened faces behind the glass.

∞

Today I went to Sylvester's grave. I waited till the maintenance fellow had finished buzzing around beside me with a lawn trimmer, then I apologised. I apologised for my part in our marital discord. (I guess it was the shock. Nothing could have prepared me for the sight of that man's body.)

Then I went a few aisles up and stood beside Ron's grave. Checked the turf to see that nothing else had altered. Nothing had changed. All grass-blades in place. (He hadn't got out, I mean. Something I sometimes worry about.)

Then I went back to Sylvester's and retracted a few apologies. It takes two to tango, I said. You should never have lied to me about your age—and all the rest of it.

Then I went back to Ron's, and I told him all about Jasper, and how creepy he was. About Jasper and Elizabeth . . . Back and forth, from one grave to the other. And then there was nothing left to say.

I went home and had dinner, and watched the two of them parading their individual weirdness in front of each other—as if it was the latest in chic normality.

'Mrs Bird that was magnificent!' Jasper cried.

(Osso bucco. I had the cheese, *again*.)

'Why, a dish like that would give a dead man an appetite!' he cried.

I gave him a look.

'Beg pardon,' he said, crimsoning.

'Oh, not at all,' she said, smiling with all her teeth. 'I came to terms with Ron's death years ago.'

'One moves on, you know,' she said, the merry widow.

It was bad enough before, when it was just Elizabeth and me. But now . . . Now her voice was rising in a sort of triumph of hysteria, and her eyes were boiling blue, and bugging out, latched onto him—the lodger!—while he lowered his head with faked humility and shook it back and forth and tutted his tongue from time to time, obligingly.

Why don't you go to bed with him? I thought spitefully. Go on. What's stopping you, Mother? The Pope? Or your varicose veins?

The thought of Elizabeth and Jasper cavorting killed the remainder of my appetite.

'Who's for pie?' Elizabeth said. 'It's blackberry!'

'No, thanks,' I said. 'Mother.'

All this baking to impress that water rat!

'Yum, yum,' said Jasper ingratiatingly. 'That makes another slice for me!'

They grinned at one another like a pair of Mormons.

While Elizabeth was out fixing the custard, Jasper turned to me and said coldly, 'Girl came into my office yesterday. Wanted to know where I was.'

'Oh,' I said. 'Got a crush on you, has she? That's nice.'

'Thought it might have been you,' he said.

'Did you?' I said. 'No chance.'

Then Elizabeth came in—her hands ten times their normal size in a pair of oven mitts that were fashioned in the shape of lobsters—carrying the steaming pie.

We both stood up and began flinging things about the table to make room for the dish.

'You might fetch the custard jug, Jasper,' she said.

'Not a problem, ma'am,' he said, smooth as grease.

'Oh, do sit down, Eleanor,' she said. 'It's all under control.'

They ate their desserts—Jasper all polite smiles and murmurs, his cold sea-coloured eyes on mine now and then.

And then the nightly tussle over who would do the dishes. Jasper, as usual, graceful in defeat.

'Sometimes, dear,' Elizabeth said, passing me the tea-towel, 'you look so prim, you make me feel like I'm a teenager.'

'Oh, Mother!' I said. 'How sweet.'

We worked on in silence for a while.

'I couldn't ask for a better tenant,' said Elizabeth suddenly.

'Not even Jesus Christ himself?' I quipped, wiping a plate.

Elizabeth clicked her tongue and rolled her eyes.

'Well, he's got to stay somewhere when he hits town for the second coming,' I said. 'Doesn't he?'

'That's not a subject for jokes,' she said sternly.

Still, I could swear I saw something speculative glittering in her eyes.

23

AS I WALK THROUGH the streets of Helltown, all the dogs bark and snarl like wolves—even the little yap dogs.

'Don't do that to me, don't do it,' warned our neighbour, Mrs Rivers, this morning.

Her little white pekinese continued to slather and growl.

'Now stop that nonsense and go inside, Samantha,' she ordered.

'Stop it!' she shouted shrilly. 'Or I'll kick your head fair off your shoulders.'

But it continued to fling itself uselessly against the wire mesh of the gate, yipping and growling, until I passed out of sight.

The cats stroke themselves against the fences and hiss, and the dogs pull on their chains and fling themselves against their confines and howl, as I go by. (Piebald cats, their hackles raised, and black runts with truncated legs—demon corgis, and dachshunds with mange; and horrendous crossbreeds—poodle-alsatian, rottweiler-chihuahua—all snarling and baring their rotted teeth.)

Lemonhurst! Hell by any other name would smell as rank. Little Hell, I suppose it is, with its sprinklers perpetually running. Practice for Big Hell. The theme park that goes on for all eternity . . .

At the bus stop this morning, the other inhabitants stood close to me—too close for comfort, as if seeking comfort.

They were silent. (What we must communicate is too awful for any words, I think.)

Their close presence in the heat, the silence beside me, the unsaid between us . . .

However, rescue was at hand. Soon the bus would come flying

down the hill, and suck us into its coolness, and rest us for a time in its separate seats.

Only this, too, is an instrument of Little Hell. This bus, this *hell-bus*, with its fixed driver pressing on, flinging his vehicle around the curves, left, right, left, right, and up and down the hills—loading it ever tighter, ever closer, until we begin the final climb—crammed so tightly we barely dare breathe, for fear the weight of our breath combined will be the final straw that tears the bus backwards, hurtling backwards down the cliff-like hill.

I got off, in exhausted disbelief, at Lemonhurst Mall, along with most of the other passengers. A few bleak faces sailed on, heading to the city with its streaming population.

Lemonhurst Mall is smaller, quieter, more deadly than the city centre. There are more shoppers laden with prams and strollers and straying toddlers, moving like incredibly slow street-sweepers along the paved walkways. There is less to buy.

The shoppers' faces are sour with disappointment. They move so slowly, scanning for whatever it is that they can't have—it makes me think that they have never ventured into the city, where they would be mown down, moving at such a stolid pace.

The city is fast, and far away. We, in Lemonhurst, are in the mere provinces of hell, I think.

I planned to pass this on to Otto, when I finally steered my way through to his studio. But forgot, for I was late and knew I must make up an interesting apology or he would sulk.

Later, at lunchtime, I remembered, but he merely stared at me when I told him, so I shut up.

24

'AND YOU, MRS BIRD? What will you do today?' said Jasper, this morning.

He was all dressed and ready for a lovely bout of gardening.

'Oh, I shall clear up down at St Clare's,' she said. 'You know me. Always tidying up! Someone has to make the place look pleasant.'

The pale carved stone crosses on either end of St Clare's stand out high above the rooftops of Lemonhurst. It is a long narrow church, running the length of one block. That means it could fit three blocks of flats inside it, each three storeys high. Now, if each building had six flats, that would mean housing for eighteen families, or seventy-two street children, battered women, or homeless men. Or, to look at it another way, it could be sold and the funds distributed. The land is obviously worth a bit. It always is, isn't it? Nothing if not good with the eyes for a spot of real estate, the Church—full of gamblers and speculators. (Commandment number one: Position, position.)

But the poor are never satisfied, Elizabeth says. They would reproduce new versions of themselves. And they would have nowhere proper to worship. And the Pope, without his gold and his robes, would command no more respect than the local greengrocer. Well. I often wonder: Are these good enough reasons?

St Clare's is where we scuttle to on Sunday mornings and Holy Days of Obligation, and every other excuse.

Sunday, as you can imagine, is a big day for the women in our family. (The men, as from most things, are mysteriously exempt.) We all troop down to St Clare's together, arriving early to bag the family pew. Not that it has our name on it, engraved on a little plaque—but woe betide the fool who sits in it! Not that this happens often, anyway, as the church is large, and the faithful few.

But don't we all love a priest!

It is hard to say who is the greatest frock-chaser in our family. Marlene is perennially baking treats for Father Flynn. Always keen to whip up a hearty casserole for a wan wintery evening—although Mrs Grieves, his housekeeper, is quite up to the cooking, as he often tells us, with a kindly wink. Desiccated Josephine is eager to organise and even call the bingo, should a jovial masculine presence be temporarily unavailable. Ancient Iris, though all but returning to dust as she walks, provides the flowers for the church, rising before dawn to see each bloom is best displayed. And even Darlene—'Although she's barely able to brush her own hair,' as Elizabeth says—is always ready with a tray of lurid stick-jaw toffees for the parish fete.

Of course, none of them can match Elizabeth's culinary excursions. Elizabeth is also the queen in matters of household piety: votive candles, icons, drawers of holy medals and cards, and hideous little relics. To top this off, she is the loudest soprano in the parish choir—not that there is great competition.

Father Flynn is our current parish priest. He is a sad-eyed and waxen-faced man of middle years. Father Flannery, his predecessor, was more of a friend of the family. Afternoon sherry pow-wows. Lengthy consultations in the confessional, from which we emerged with dignity—patience being the reward of patience for those next in the queue. Natty little home masses. Blessings for every room. On occasion, he accompanied us on holidays—our own private family retreats! While Father Flynn is disinclined to visit his parishioners—unless they are ill, or old, or poor, or lonely. 'Not a patch on Father Flannery,' is Elizabeth's verdict. Well. I must agree.

Most apparently, his sermons are very dull. They are full of lengthy comments in parenthesis, weird tangents, and tragically unrelated anecdotes. His notes are worthy, and cohesive, I'm sure—if he could just *stick* to them. But his parishioners seem to baffle him. Seeing us in front of him, he begins to blanch, and then he abandons his notes and starts to panic. Poor old Father Flynn! He flounders his way, start to finish, never seeming to realise that the dumb-struck looks are mostly due to deafness and near-senility.

Towards the end of the sermon, he waves his arms about and says, 'So you see . . .' helplessly, a dozen or so times, gazing imploringly at his little flock. And of course nobody sees at all.

We really may as well be just a mob of sheep. But Father Flynn plunges on (no doubt praying all the while for guidance which never comes, or which he in turn misinterprets or mishears), and finishes each sermon in a lather, sweating his way to the end of every Mass, his forehead furrowed with a sense of failure.

And so it goes, week after week, Holy Day after Holy Day, Sunday after Sunday.

'I thought Mrs Black had taken over the flowers this week?' I said.

'Stupid novices!' said Elizabeth. 'More trouble than they're worth. That Candice Black is a total nong—she's a convert, say no more. "Keep your eye on that one, Iris," I said. Well! Iris rang me yesterday in a dreadful state . . .'

'Dear, dear,' said Jasper, always at the ready.

'These people do just the basic flower arranging, Jasper,' Elizabeth explained. 'They *think* the flowers are done, but there is no charm about the way the church looks. No charm whatsoever.'

'The worst part,' she cried, 'is that I'll have to go over it all with her. And she's a very dull woman, is Mrs Black.'

'Just a day of work and more work,' she sighed.

'Isn't it always the way?' sighed Jasper.

'Such an unfortunate name, too,' Elizabeth muttered, 'in view of the current fashionable sympathy for Aborigines.'

'But don't get me wrong, Jasper!' she cried. 'The congregation are by and large all very nice people. You would feel most at home.'

'That's very kind of you, Mrs Bird,' said Jasper.

'Elizabeth, please!' she cried. 'We're not formal around here, are we, Ellen?'

'No, Mother,' I said.

I excused myself, and went out to the kitchen to prepare the pot of tea.

'I'm afraid she's becoming something of a spinster aunt,' said Elizabeth, quite audibly.

'Ah, dear,' said Jasper.

'It's difficult for me to discuss it with her,' she hissed. 'I do feel there is some odd hostility around the subject. But, sadly, it is undeniable that Ellen is without a boyfriend at the present moment. And for quite some time, actually.'

'Dear, dear,' said Jasper. 'What a shame. Such an attractive young woman.'

'Mmm,' said Elizabeth.

'She *can* be so delightful,' she said, as I returned.

'I've brought some sponge fingers for morning tea,' I said, proudly. 'They are the latest things, from Italy.'

Elizabeth clucked her tongue, and winked at Jasper.

'You're still a little girl over sweeties, aren't you, dear?' she said.

I coloured, and laid the teapot out for her to pour.

Jasper smirked at me, then gazed adoringly at Elizabeth. The whey-faced oily thing!

'Eleanor!' she said suddenly, staring at me with exaggeratedly widened eyes. 'What on *earth* is that you're wearing?'

'Nothing unusual,' I said.

'Nothing unusual!' she said.

'She's so eccentric, isn't she?' she said to Jasper in a loud aside.

Jasper tipped his head back to laugh. I noticed that his lips were flecked with spittle. His laughing eyes were green and bright as emeralds.

I sat there stubbornly, taking the full measure of Elizabeth's disapproval of my outfit.

'I think you have omitted, Ellen,' she said, with prim thin lips and downcast outraged eyes.

'I've only taken the hem up half an inch or so!' I finally cried.

'Well, I wouldn't want to expose myself so obviously,' she said.

'I think she's showing off for you, Jasper!' she said, and giggled girlishly.

Jasper snickered, and they exchanged a glance, and then Elizabeth started laughing.

At that point, I excused myself, and stood up to leave the table.

'Jasper,' she said, 'before we head off to our toils, why don't we take a stroll around the garden?'

'What a smashing idea, Mrs Bird,' said Jasper.

And they left the room together.

A stroll? She never walks!

25

I DON'T KNOW WHAT Elizabeth's game is. Is she winning him over, to our side . . . In case? Or——

We watch each other surreptitiously, these days. We watch him watching us . . .

She scanned me this evening when I got home from work late.

Well. I don't know what I can do about my moods. All day, foreboding hung about me.

It is so . . . diffuse now. It is everywhere about me.

Poor Otto. He tried. He cracked some dreadful jokes!

'What is the matter with you?' Elizabeth said, finally, slapping down her wash-cloth.

'Oh—— nothing,' I said.

'You look so . . . Why are you looking like that?' she said, annoyed.

All frozen-faced.

'Nerves,' I said, trying to shrug it off—peeling another potato.

Because the dark, you know. The terrible falling . . .

'Nerves!' she said. 'Pure self-indulgence.'

She began to rattle about in the sink.

'I know it's silly of me,' I said. 'I just feel. I feel just . . .'

She stared disdainfully down the length of her nose.

'Sometimes I feel so afraid,' I finished, mumbling. 'Mother, you won't——'

'Fear is faith in evil,' she said dismissively. 'Although, of course, that Mall is not a place I would necessarily want to spend much time in, with that loutish element hanging about.'

Then Jasper came home, and we had to pack away our troubles.

∞

After serving the apple crumble, Elizabeth let off a little steam, treating Jasper to a surprising litany of Ron's sins. Over dinner! Surprising, because she had suppressed or denied all knowledge of them when he was alive, and seemed set on doing so forever after. Surprising, because such uncharitableness was in itself a sin.

'Dear Lord!' she said. 'I could have fallen down dead and *he* wouldn't have noticed, would've walked straight over me.'

Jasper tutted and shook his head sympathetically.

He listened to it all solemnly—nodding his head or shaking it slowly from time to time—his gaze lowered, occasionally allowing a sigh or an 'Oh, ma'am!' to escape his empathically puckered mouth.

'Not the most sensitive of souls, behind closed doors,' she said. 'Saved the toothpaste and smiles for strangers.'

'Mother!' I said, pleading with my eyes.

What would she tell him next? What would she——

'It was different for you,' she snapped. 'You were his daughter, his only child.'

Jasper nodded wisely here.

Good old Jasp. He lapped it all up. Nodding and sighing and licking his lips, and smiling in all the right places.

'You didn't have to *live* with him,' she added meaningfully.

'Oh, Mother!' I said, embarrassed. 'Must you——'

'That's enough, Ellen,' she said crisply.

'Indian giver,' I muttered.

'Pardon?' she said.

'What's the use of giving someone a name and taking it back again?' I said, knowing it was pointless.

'I——' she said.

'Father chose it!' I cried. 'And you resent it!'

'How wrong you are,' she said smugly.

'It's only a name,' Elizabeth said. 'Ellen is so difficult! Please excuse her outburst.'

And Jasper nodded and smiled like a gormless hayseed.

'Every night,' she sighed, taking another tack, 'I prayed for him.'

'I still do,' she whispered sweetly, her eyes half-filling with tears.

'God rest his soul,' she said demurely, rising. 'Quince pie, anyone?'

Her performance was extraordinary—with Jasper egging her on with his understanding, as if he was her acting coach.

It was ridiculous. I mean, Ron! Inclined to rant. Sour. A poisoner of atmospheres. A little Hitler.

An everyday man, in other words. A husband, a father. *A good provider.*

All right, he beat me with his stick. The stick he kept expressly for the purpose—just like the nuns did theirs. (I expect he was thrashed heartily by the brothers. Not that that's any excuse.)

All right, one time he went too far and broke my jaw . . .

But there were happy days, book! Good times to balance the bad: all the holidays they took together, leaving me behind with Aunty Brenda and Uncle Rick.

They were happy, weren't they? Wasn't that the point?

And what about the bloody dolls? I wanted to shout. Don't talk about him as if you had nothing.

What about the dolls, Mother? I shrieked to myself—as I had on many of these nights since Jasper came to grace our house—meanwhile rising to clear the table and ready it for the next course: berry pie with cream, rhubarb with custard, peaches and apricot fool, or foamy lemon delight.

Ever since Jasper moved in, and proved such a greaser at the dinner table, I was always waiting, always half-expecting to see Elizabeth pat her lips with her napkin, rise, and say, like in the old days: 'Would you like to see my dolls, now? I have quite a collection.' And then that familiar, self-deprecating titter, her eyes all moist and excited.

There was Jasper. So polite, so primed. A captive audience, indeed. (Perhaps that is all she ever wanted? A captive audience . . .) An audience for her delicately dollopped out litany of suffering and superiority, her conversation garnished now with sprigs of Ron's misdemeanours and maladjustments.

This was *Ron* she was undressing. Ron Bird. My father!

Why did she feel this need to confess his sins? And why to this slimy stranger? And why in front of me?

Why, after all those years when she said nothing?

I sat, and I listened, and I watched, astonished, as I was made her confidante-by-proxy. Sitting at the table, bound by table rules—too stunned, or too stupid, to say anything back.

There was nothing I could say. I should have said something——

My words were sucked into a vacuum as they left my lips—as if *I* was the ghost at the table.

26

LAST NIGHT, I WAS awakened suddenly. It was after midnight, pitch dark, the air thick with expirations. I was startled awake by—by what? A click?

I lay there in the dark, my heart thumping. Down below, somewhere down below, someone—who?—was creeping about.

And then I heard it. The sound of a key turning in a lock. The door—not groaning, not sliding, but yawning open. And then a footfall.

Silence. Another footfall. The click of the light switch. A laugh. A sort of sigh. And then a muffled explosion of laughter.

It was Jasper. Jasper, in the doll-room.

Where had he found the key?

He stayed—five, ten minutes? And then he moved to the door. I waited for the sound of the lock, and then his feet on the three creaking stairs as he returned to his room.

He didn't know it, but he was the first visitor ever to spend under an hour in there.

∞

Breakfast today began as the usual strained affair.

'Where are you from again, Jasper?' I said, while salting my eggs. 'Was it——'

'North,' he butted in. 'Up north.'

'The northern states?' I said.

'Good heavens, Eleanor!' said Elizabeth. 'Don't be pushy.'

'Oh, I don't mean to pry,' I said.

'Not at all,' said Jasper. 'It's just . . .' He glanced up at Elizabeth then quickly down again, with a fluttering movement of his lashes. 'It's just a little painful.'

'Don't think of it!' cried Elizabeth, placing her hand on his wrist, which lay pale and exposed on the table.

'You're with us now,' she murmured.

Jasper smiled gratefully. He turned to me, his mouth stiffening, a hint of spite lighting up his eyes.

I wanted to shout: Don't you see it, Mother! I thought you saw everything.

But Elizabeth was smiling hugely back at him.

'I'm a loner, too, in many ways,' she said.

Having spent not more than three days truly alone in all her life!

'When Ellen, finally—though frankly I am starting to worry for her—marries, and settles herself down with her own little family, I plan to resume my travels,' she said.

First I'd heard of it.

'Travels?' said Jasper politely—pretending he had not seen the dolls, the *evidence*.

I watched his face. I scanned his mouth for traces of derision. He was, if anything, smoother, more solicitous.

Elizabeth glowed as she passed the sugar, the salt, the replica orange juice.

'Oh, yes!' she cried. 'I was a great traveller in my youth, Jasper. From the steps of the Inca temples to the Great Pyramid at Cairo!'

'How marvellously interesting!' said Jasper.

'Yes,' she said, folding her napkin. 'Yes, it was. I used to so enjoy regaling my visitors with exciting anecdotes gleaned from my many journeys . . .'

'Not now,' she said sadly. 'Not now.'

'Perhaps, later?' Jasper said.

'Ah, yes,' she said, her eyes gleaming.

Something bothered me. I glanced over at Jasper's flickering lowered eyes.

He stretched, and patted his belly, and wiped his mouth, as usual. Then, he turned his head and blinked at me slowly, twice. Just like a doll.

I stared at him. Squinted. Was I imagining it?

'Ellen,' my mother said tightly.

'Ellen!' she repeated.

I was staring at him, thinking.

'If thine eye offend thee, pluck it out!' he said.

But not in the tone of a priest.

'Oh, Jasper!' Elizabeth cried. 'I didn't know you read the Scriptures! Isn't that lovely, Ellen?'

'Yes,' I snapped.

'She certainly has her little ways!' Elizabeth said.

My own mother. My own mother flirting with the lodger and refusing to recognise my name!

Sometimes I think she's not my mother at all. Sometimes I think I'm not her child. Sometimes I think I'm just some bit of modelled plastic from the doll-room, come alive!

'Have you travelled much, Eleanora?' Jasper asked politely then, although his eyes were slightly glazed.

'I've been to Byron Bay,' I said. 'It was lovely. I took a coach——'

'Ridiculous idea!' said Elizabeth. 'Sitting in some dreadful little room, wasting time, neglecting your own home and me.'

'Eight weeks of utter silence!' she cried, staring hard at Jasper, who murmured sympathetically.

'Six,' I muttered.

'But let us not trouble ourselves with the past! Let us be grateful for the present, and what we do have. Every day, Jasper,' she said fervently, 'I thank God for bringing you to us.'

'Yes, indeed,' said Jasper. 'That was a mighty fortuitous move. They do say, don't they, Mrs Bird, that God moves in mysterious ways?'

'Yes, Jasper,' she said, and sighed heavily. 'Indeed, He does. Sometimes I like to think that God brought you to us, to take Ron's place. In our hearts, dear Jasper.'

'Thank you, ma'am,' he said, bending his head. 'I'm truly touched.'

'Excuse me,' I said. 'I have to clear up.'

Throw up, more like it.

Later, standing at the kitchen window with Elizabeth—watching his pale and sloping figure move down the path, behind the hedge, then slide away—I commented on Jasper's newfound interest in God.

'Perhaps we should invite him to St Clare's with us?' I said.

Jasper—although he lowered his eyelids and looked respectful during grace—had not as yet accompanied us to Mass. Despite his weird Bible quote. Despite a little homely piety thrown in now and then, to pepper his mealtime conversations.

'Give him time,' said Elizabeth, her eyes quite peculiar, as if reminiscing.

'These things cannot be forced,' she said. Which caused me to do a double take.

'He has the Christ-spirit in him,' she said dreamily. 'I'm sure, if the calling was there, he'd make a leader among priests.'

'But, I suspect,' she added, her eyes fixed, gleaming, on the table, 'that God has other plans for Jasper.'

'He's probably gay, anyway,' I said, for no particular reason.

She glared furiously at me then, as if I'd committed blasphemy.

27

MONDAY, AT LAST! I thought the weekend would never end.

All day, today, Otto was talking about sperm. Apparently a man—an English tourist, typical—was fined this week for donating more than the legal limit, whatever that is. He'd donated two thousand three hundred times. Two thousand, three hundred!

'You're only allowed to donate *two* thousand times on a tourist visa?' quipped Otto.

'Think of the impoverished quality of the two thousandth squirt!' he cried.

'Oh, don't, Otto,' I begged. 'I'm going to lose my breakfast.'

'Breakfast,' he said. 'How quaint.'

'Scrambled eggs,' I said. 'Lots of toast.'

'Ugh,' he groaned. 'We'll speak no more about these things.'

'Well, I'm all for law and order, as you know,' he said, a minute later. 'But I can't help thinking, what a waste of a nice light lunch.'

'Otto, don't!' I cried. Although I wasn't quite sure what he meant.

'With the donor laws supposedly requiring complete anonymity,' he went on, 'think of the inbreeding in fifteen, twenty years time.'

'My God, Eleanora!' he cried. 'It's probably already started . . . How long have they been doing this diabolic sort of thing?'

'I don't know,' I said. 'Ages. Simply ages, I think. We'll end up a nation of corgi-loving horses!'

'I won't hear a word against my beloved royal family,' Otto sniped.

'Just imagine, though,' said Otto. 'You're sitting on your couch——'

'Who, me?' I said.

'Not you, *one*,' he said. 'Do you even have a couch, El?'

'Not one we sit on,' I said.

'Right,' he said. 'You're on the Ikea couch, the two ruggies are amusing themselves out in the yard, and you're having a squint at "Oprah" and a well-earned puff on a Winnie Blue . . .'

'And?' I said.

'In walks your husband, father of said ruggies. And, suddenly . . . Is it the light? Your sadly too infrequent state of total relax? Whatever. Hello, you think. How very bloody peculiar. He looks just like me, with a moustache!'

'Oh, Otto!' I said.

That was something I could never express to Elizabeth: it was fun working for Otto.

He was my *friend*.

And God knows I was not overburdened with those.

Meanwhile Odile, the hand-model, blinked slowly, her glossed lips—even though they weren't to be in frame—held open in a pout, wide enough to slot a matchbox between them.

28

'AND YOUR MOTHER? YOUR father, Mrs Bird?' said Jasper delicately this evening. 'They are——?'

Dead, I thought. You know they're dead. Don't tell me you haven't looked us up, Jasper. Don't tell me you don't know everything they've got on us, in there.

Before, there were the Birds, senior (Mavis and Albert), and the Brindles, Elizabeth's parents (Mary and Pat), and several elder aunts and great aunts, and old Pop, who was nearly ninety. They all drowned, over twenty years ago, when the boat hired for Marlene and Frank's eldest daughter's wedding capsized and sank in Sydney Harbour.

Ron and Elizabeth and I stayed ashore that day, pleading seasickness. And Harry and Darlene and the boys were off on a skiing holiday. ('In their defence, it *was* a hasty wedding,' says Elizabeth now.) It was just as well, as none of us could swim.

The bride, Bridget, sank without a trace. She was a big girl, made bigger by her wedding gown. Her husband died clutching her, they say. The tiny flower girl drowned, and the three young smiling bridesmaids. And poor Pop, strapped into his chair on account of his tendency to fall forward. And most of the older generation—too feeble to swim to shore—weighed down by wedding clothes and age, and stuffed to the gills with wedding cake.

Twenty-seven of the wedding party drowned. The rest swam clear, and lay on the shore wet and panting, at the feet of alarmed sunbathers.

By the time Ron and Elizabeth and I scrambled around the cove to them, it was nearly over. Iris and Josephine (who had insisted on wearing life jackets once the boat had left the wharf), were still bobbing about paddling ineffectually. We watched as Uncle Frank (who had proved heroic and clear-headed, shouting instructions to the others) dragged his youngest, Joseph, in by the neck, then collapsed. They both had to be resuscitated. (That was how Joseph became an invalid. He was in the water too long, they vaguely told me. And now his legs and arms have to be rearranged for him. Among other things.)

Since then, there's not been so much as a family picnic by a pond. Everyone is afraid of their memories, I suppose. (Actually, I think we're all half-mad—weighed down by our clinging dead, and hampered by our lingering ghosts.)

After that, I never learnt to swim, although I was sent to classes every summer. If I was an anxious child before the drownings, then after I was excessively afraid. At night I lay awake, too terrified to sleep, while my room filled with water in the dark, and memories, and worse imaginings.

I wept for them: trapped Bridget, wrapped in her yards of wedding finery like a shroud. The children, terrified. Pop, in his chair, slipping, skidding, falling—plunging backwards into the water as the boat rocked and tipped and pulled itself under. I felt myself going under, with them.

Once or twice I woke up screaming, and ran out to my parents (who were watching television), and was met with indifference and sent back to my bed—which seemed to me a watery grave.

And if my staring eyes, my pallor, or the way I startled easily were noticed, it was with derision and disbelief.

'Queer,' Ron would say.

'A most peculiar child,' Elizabeth agreed.

'Not *my* side of the family,' he'd say.

'Well,' she'd reply. 'Don't blame me!'

What they made of the tragedy I don't know. Did they feel lucky? Or ashamed that they'd survived it? Did they come to believe, as I did, that it was only a matter of time before the mistake of their exclusion was rectified?

Oh! This sounds so self-piteous——

I still think of the wedding party, one moment being photographed, then swallowed so abruptly by the dark green water. Their lives swallowed. Their unheard screams . . .

'Just as well we stuck to our guns,' Elizabeth was saying, her teeth gritted. 'I *knew* it. I had a *sense*. There was a cloud around the whole occasion. "A boat!" I said. "You must be joking, Marlene." "Frank's got his heart set on it," she said. "It's not Frank's wedding," I said pertinently. "He's paying for it," she said.

Well! It sunk didn't it. What a fiasco! What a frightful shambles!' Elizabeth cried. 'Oh, how *distressing* it all was.'

'We were the only family sensible enough to boycott the occasion—Ron, Ellen, and myself. Dymphna's skiing trip was pure coincidence. Or otherwise, as I like to think. God knows she hasn't the wits to swim her way out of a paddling pool,' Elizabeth said. 'She'd have ended up like poor young Joseph, propped up like a nong at home, day in, day out.'

'Joseph?' said Jasper delicately.

'Marlene's eldest boy,' Elizabeth said. 'Quite spasticated.'

'How awful, for your sister——' said Jasper.

'Yes,' said Elizabeth listlessly.

'——losing her daughter in that way,' he finished.

('The sea has taken my baby!' Marlene screamed at the memorial service held for Bridget. But otherwise and ever since she has appeared stoic—a family trait.)

'Oh,' said Elizabeth. 'What can anyone *do* anyhow? Dead is dead, after all. At least, I suppose, she has got Joseph.'

'And Frank, and Patrick, and the twins!' I said.

'He, at any rate,' she went on, ignoring me, 'will never leave her.'

'He'll never leave home?' Jasper said mildly, glancing over at me.

'Oh, never!' said Elizabeth.

'Ah,' he said, as if he understood.

Suddenly I thought, bizarrely: She wishes *I* was like Joseph! An invalid, and paralysed. Bound to her, boundlessly disappointing. Good old what's her name, guaranteed to never fail to disappoint.

Oh, this is madness! Isn't it?

'Just because one is a cripple,' said Elizabeth suddenly, 'is no excuse for allowing oneself to become a fat lazy slob, and dressing like a scruffy low-life.'

'No chance of Eleanora getting like that!' said Jasper.

'Which is how we like it,' said Elizabeth briskly.

29

THIS MORNING I SAID pointedly to Elizabeth: 'What do you know of Jasper's background?'

She gave me one of her incredulous, disgusted looks.

'Well . . .' I said. 'He asks so many questions, and answers very few.'

'I never pry,' she snorted. 'A man, after all, has a right to his past.'

'Oh?' I said. 'Does a woman have a right to her present, then?'

'I don't know what you're talking about,' she snapped.

'No, I don't suppose you do,' I said.

'You won't get far in this world if you go around talking in riddles,' she said.

'No,' I said. 'I don't suppose I will.'

'I quite expected that!' she said, her blue eyes flashing. 'Infernal girl!'

'I wonder, dear,' she said then, sighing, and changing tack, 'if you will ever stop all this lackadaisical nonsense and forge a career for yourself?'

For myself?

'Unlikely,' I said, although my heart was beating hard.

'Your attitude does not please me, Eleanor!' she cried, and stomped out of the room.

Go far . . .

Go where? Does she think God put us here to further our *careers*?

If life is a race—— If life is a swimming carnival, then I am always on the sidelines, refusing to change into my costume. If life is a test . . . then I shall fail.

I fear life. *I fear it.* It makes no sense to me. And, if I am unable to withstand the tests of this world, then how can I possibly make it in the next?

Oh, life. That holds so many deaths.

Many-faced, ever-lurking death . . .

So much is frightening, I find. This world. The other world in it. Eternity—inside the world we live in—invisible, yet present, like a hand within a glove.

Every day—as I run my mother's errands, and potter about with Otto—so much of life is frightening.

Every night I lie here, worrying, waiting. Waiting for discovery, or for God's terrible judgement.

There is such a terrible strain in waiting for something when you not only don't know when it will come, but what it is.

∞

Some nights I wake up clutching the edges of the bed, and the bed is rocking, rocking, and I am lowering in it in the dark, and the dark is all about me thick as blood and like a sea, and I think: I am in my coffin, descending, and I scrabble at my bedclothes, then: No, I am in a boat and I am sinking! I am drowning, *drowning* . . . I claw at the water, but I cannot rise to the surface and it is so thick I do not know if I am drowning in water, or blood, or earth, or is it air about me?, until at last I wake for certain.

I cannot let my eyes close then, or try to sleep, for when I do I slip back into it: the watery dark, my death.

It is strange. I dream of death. I wake in the pit of night in the dark of my room and I can *smell* death all around me. And yet I never dream of fiery hell.

It is so ghastly, here in my mind, sometimes I wonder if I might not be better off dead, and *there*. Can it be so much worse?

What form do we take there? If it is true that we are resurrected in our bodies, then can flesh so endlessly burn and burn?

Perhaps only old and wicked nuns still burn in hell . . .

I lie awake and think of hell for hours. Hell is other people, someone said. Well, I don't know. Sometimes I think that consciousness is hell.

Some nights I lie awake so long I run out of things to think. It is three, four in the morning, the dark like a blindfold on my open eyes. I am blank and still as a sheet of paper. How will I ever sleep again? I wonder.

Of course, in the end, I slide gradually into sleep. And when I wake up I don't know where I have been at all.

Only you, book, save me from myself. Without you to hear my side, I could not endure this . . . this farce.

So, what is this I'm setting down? My version of events? A litany of blame? The evidence? My *confession*?

God knows, I scrape my conscience clean each night. But still I come away laden with fear and doubt. Still I wake up, fearful and uncertain.

And still—let me write it here at last—still I cannot say, for sure, who killed him.

30

THE BUS GOES LIKE this: left, right, left, right, left, right, left, right. It twists and turns for miles, all the way into town. Here it comes now! Hurtling down the hill towards me, a fierce descending demon.

The bus stops. I board. Take my favourite seat. Open the window to release some noxious perfume. The demon folds its wings and assumes a bland expression—and it is the familiar slow-poke bus again, decelerating to turn yet another corner, while all on board purse their lips and exhale with irritation.

It is grey. The air stirs, transparent, grey over grey, flecked with clouds like shreds of marmalade suspended in a jar.

We trundle on, through endless patches of Lemonhurst.

Thank heavens I have you with me, or I would not last the journey! You are my solace, book. You are the one who listens to me.

A woman heaves her body up the steps, fumbles for her card, shoves it into the green machine, then bashes her way down the aisle to sit beside me.

I attract women. Large women, particularly. Men prefer to sit where they can quietly eye my body. Women appreciate the room left by my slender, thoughtfully-positioned form.

'I'm late,' she says.

I smile.

'Mother will give me hell,' she says.

Jesus, I think. At your age!

Mind you, I'm not so young myself. And despite my petty triumphs, still I scurry around, trying to pacify Mother.

God! I think. A lifetime of this to look forward to!

The women in our family live on and on. The men die off too soon. (Preferring eternal damnation to being with us?) Or disappoint, like Frank and Harry. Or slip away, like Iris's foreign beau.

Men are born difficult, and only manage to survive because of us, Elizabeth says. 'Street angels, house devils,' she calls them. 'You wouldn't believe!' she cries. And then she unfurls the litany of their sins—sins of omission, sins of commission—tallying the daily total.

She'll be wanting to be here for as long as possible. She'll be wanting to see every detail of the hash I make of my life. She'll be wanting to witness the next papal induction, and then the next—the very last . . .

'We can't forget them, the old ones,' the woman says, interrupting my thoughts. 'Not after all the work they did for us when we was babies, wiping our bums.'

She sizes me up with a glance.

'You'll think different when you've had a few of your own,' she says.

She hauls herself out at the next stop. A man gets on, flashes me a quick look, then sits in the seat across the aisle, where he can study my legs.

I am often surprised, when I consider the effect I have on men, why Otto never asks me to pose for his catalogues: My hand resting suggestively on a fridge. Or all of me, breasts pleasantly angled, beside some trays of mince . . .

All right, my eyes are queer. But there are camera tricks to get around any little problem.

Not regular, indeed! Can it be that Otto *sees* me?

The man across the aisle is drooling! Clearly he cannot see my temper, handed down, or absorbed from Ron and Liz. Clearly, he cannot see, sitting straight across from me like that, my soul. My filthy soul.

I have a strange effect on men. Tantalising and elusive. They look, but they never touch.

In fact, if you don't count the silly boys I've danced with at the church social—which you can't count as serious contenders—I've not been touched by anyone, except my parents and our family doctor and Father Flynn shaking hands after Mass, and Father Dougherty on Ash Wednesday, and Sylvester—although I'd rather not remember him.

And . . . and . . .

31

BEST TO GET IT over with. The freak-show aspect of our lives. What am I saying? It's all a circus, isn't it?

All right, there *were* some men in Circle once. But that was long ago. And——

Well, the Circle. Where do I begin? How *could* something so simple become so complicated?

All right. Well.

The Circle proper started out several years ago, with Elizabeth and her four sisters, and Mildred Cleghorn, a neighbour, and a couple of ladies from the St Clare's choir, Margaret O'Boyle and Mavis Purley—and myself, as an unwilling ring-in.

We met once a fortnight, on a Wednesday evening. We said the rosary and the Litany of Our Lady, and organised a few novenae for parish hard-ups and world disasters.

We were an innocent, if somewhat maliciously righteous, little group. We did a spot of sewing as we talked, and were inclined to comment on neighbourhood affairs, rather than world politics. We were so Catholic, it never occurred to us to discuss Catholicism, let alone to criticise the Church. Our most common occupations were handicrafts—knitting, sewing, crochet, tapestry, and the odd bit of quilt- or lacework—and copious decades of the rosary.

It was, I suppose, a pleasant enough way to pass an evening. And certainly it advanced my cross-stitch.

Afterwards, we drank coffee from sophisticated little cups with golden rims. Elizabeth and I brought out the supper we'd prepared: egg and cress sandwiches (crustless), red onion tartlets, cheese and asparagus twists—that sort of thing.

Then Marlene and Darlene and Mildred Cleghorn scoffed some

sherry. Elizabeth said, 'Just the one,' and managed several. And then—without the dutiful interspersion of prayers, which took up so much of the early part of the meeting—the group got down to some real gossiping.

At ten-thirty, we broke up, and I washed the supper things—while Elizabeth retired tipsily to bed, and the others returned to their homes, red-cheeked and virtuous.

∞

It was when Raymund Allan joined the Circle, two and a half years ago, that things began to change.

Raymund Allan was an enigma. He joined first the congregation of St Clare's and then its tiny choir and then, shortly after, began showing an insistent interest in attending Circle meetings. We were flattered, but did not know, at first, what to make of him.

Men were not officially barred from Circle. It had always been considered by us—and no doubt many others, Frank and Harry topping the list—to be not quite the sort of social experience a man would be interested in.

But Raymund Allan was *very* interested.

Raymund Allan was tall and wiry, and terribly emaciated, with a long straggling ginger beard, and sharp pale eyes that flashed about a room then seemed to fix on you—as if he had some particular personal message he wished to meaningfully impart with them.

What disarming eyes! So pale and cold-coloured. Candle-grey. I shivered when I felt them watching me.

Looking at him, I was reminded of Sylvester, and my marriage, which had come more and more to seem like an unpleasant dream. Because of this I shuddered slightly, or jumped a little in my skin, at the sight of Raymund Allan. No doubt this is why he continued to look at me longer than most—and strangely, with a smile flitting into his pale grey eyes and out again. At least, that is what I told myself. What other interest could he have had in me? (His glance was chaste, unlike Sylvester's.)

It was clear from the start that Raymund Allan was a man with much on his mind, and much that he wanted to say. It was odd, then, to observe him meekly standing with the choir, opening and closing his mouth, singing on demand. He had a large voice—a bass baritone, Elizabeth assured me. It was deep and resonant, and easily heard from amongst the quavering would-be sopranos, the floundering contraltos, and the two clapped-out tenors that made up the choir on a good day. (Vocally, Raymund and Elizabeth were quite a team.)

He was thin-faced and fair-skinned, inclined to ruddiness as he sang or as his thoughts exerted themselves, and somewhat wizened in appearance about the cheeks. (He was not an alluring-looking man at all.) I suppose that sort of thing is to be expected, as he was somewhere in his sixties. After a certain amount of time, we start to rot . . .

He dressed in a modest enough fashion, in dark almost priestly suits. Yet, despite his shrivelled stature, he was imposing in his bearing—tilting his thin face upward and looking down the length of his long, crooked nose. With his lips compressed thinly, his face reddening, and the beard and the remains of his ginger hair frizzing about his face like an aureole and glinting in the candle and stained-glass light of St Clare's, he looked like an Old Testament prophet.

And his pale, strange eyes! Fixing, then boring into one poor wavering chorister, then flying off onto another. Scanning the room, as if he was searching—decidedly searching. As if he knew what he wanted, and would find it, and would not rest until he found what, or who, it was that he desired. (Not that I ever imagined it was *desire*, as such. I had so little experience of these things.)

For the choir members, and the greater parish of St Clare's—a handful of down-at-heel men and doddering powdered ladies, with Elizabeth and her familial entourage providing the youth and vigour—Raymund Allan was a talisman.

For myself—sullen and haunting the corners, and singing along with the rest of the congregation in a slightly flat voice—he was a horrible reminder. A sort of stand-in for Sylvester's ghost.

Any minute, I thought—*I felt certain*—he will come to me with a message from beyond the grave.

32

HAVING A MAN IN Circle altered the nature of the meeting. People said things they didn't mean. And suppressed other things.

Raymund became our leader. This change occurred slowly—imperceptibly, at first—and then became quite clear. Raymund was the leader, and Elizabeth didn't mind. That in itself was odd.

Then one night, as we sat sewing—Raymund Allan calmly darning a pair of argyle socks—the conversation was steered onto Vatican II, and the ensuing loss of the Latin Mass.

'Goodness!' said Margaret O'Boyle. 'We're really getting political!'

It was not the sort of thing that we discussed, formerly. It was not the sort of thing that any of us would have even mentioned, really.

I had never heard a Latin Mass, but I sympathised with the disappointment at its demise that the older members expressed that night.

The Circle stayed late, reminiscing. The tone was careful. No-one wanted to complain. But, oh, what raptures of memories were evoked!

And then . . . And then . . .

And then things became a touch heretical.

Next thing you know, we were down in our cellar, celebrating the ancient Mass, with Raymund Allan robed up, and Elizabeth dressed as his aged and bad-tempered altar boy, swinging a fragrant censer.

Latin Mass became a weekly event, replacing the prayers and stitchery of the Circle. Latin Mass, in our cellar. Latin Mass, with Raymund Allan acting priest.

Everyone was sworn to secrecy. (Raymund Allan insisted on it.) But somehow word got out, and the Circle began to slowly swell.

There was the family still, of course: Elizabeth and her sisters and myself. Mildred Cleghorn from down the road. Mavis Purley, faintly bearded, and Margaret O'Boyle, with her plush plum lips. Mary-Rose O'Brien, and gossiping Gladys Gilmour. Bernadette West, soon followed by her husband Bernard. Then Jim and Irene Dooley, and Timmy and Helen Brennan.

And soon there were twenty of us, female and male, crammed into the cellar, gazing earnestly at the pomp and mystery of the Mass according to Raymund Allan, eagerly enunciating our Latin responses, and belting out the old but not forgotten hymns, with Elizabeth wheezing away on a tiny pedal organ.

∞

When Ron died, a vacuum was created. Years passed, and nobody came to fill it. Raymund was the man in our lives—after Ron and Sylvester, and before Jasper—and Elizabeth adored him.

She spent much of her time sewing him vestments, and running up shiny coverings for the altar that they'd built together out of our dismantled backyard barbecue.

How her eyes shone at the mention of him!

I suspect that Raymund—or Brother Raymund, as we began to call him (Father seeming to us, despite our far-gone state, to be encroaching on forbidden turf)—was something of a ladies' man, with some added extra that drew the men.

Nothing was too outlandish for him. Every week there were new and daring variations, accepted with barely a murmur. He won his way in everything, by autosuggestion or mesmerism—or else, as Elizabeth preferred, some holy gift.

Indeed, Raymund Allan had Elizabeth entirely under his thumb—along with the rest of the Circle, the choir of St Clare's, and fully half its tiny congregation.

I resisted Raymund Allan and his Latin Mass, at first, while all the while he studied me with his disconcerting pale gaze.

'This Latin Mass business,' I said to Elizabeth one morning, over breakfast. 'I don't know, Mother . . .'

She stared at me, raising her eyebrows.

'I really don't know how we got ourselves caught up in it,' I said carefully. 'Although, it's very interesting . . .'

She gave a delicate little yawn—as if under the strain of having to endure something very boring.

'Mother?' I said. 'Are you listening? I think, perhaps, we've gone too far.'

'Nonsense,' she said crisply, rising.

'God called us,' she said.

I groaned, tipping my head forward, letting my hair fall about my face.

'Pull yourself together, girl!' she cried. 'Will you get your head off the table and, for mercy's sake, brush that hair! Your appearance mirrors your appalling attitude, Ellen. What would anyone think, walking in and seeing you like this?'

'They can think what they like,' I said. 'Presumably.'

Or could they? There were strange tensions manipulating all of us.

'Who would visit at this hour, anyway?' I said.

Elizabeth clicked her tongue. She sighed and sucked her teeth.

'More times than once,' she said, 'I've asked God what he thought he was doing, sending me a changeling.'

'Oh,' I said, blinking.

'That's right! A changeling!' she cried, her eyes alight. 'Because you certainly don't get your pig-headedness from Ron or I.'

'Perhaps I'm not your daughter,' I said, to punish her.

'Oh,' she cried, turning her face aside. 'Do you think I will ever forget the pain?'

We sat in silence for a while, staring at the cooling toast.

'Oh, Ellen. Don't make a spectacle of yourself! I never meant *literally* a changeling,' she sighed.

'I am not a peasant!' she said. 'You silly nit. I only meant that it seemed to me that the devil had entered you, that the devil had marked you for his own. Well! He may as well have put one of his own in your place and spirited you away, you see.'

'Fine difference,' I said.

'I pray for you, Ellen,' she went on. 'You do know that, don't you, dear? Night and day. I pray and pray, and I practise the patience of a saint. And will you work with me? No. You will not. You take my helping hand and you push it away, Ellen, and I really don't——'

'Eleanora,' I said.

'You see?' she said.

33

BROTHER RAYMUND SOON BECAME a frequent dinner guest. Friday and Saturday nights were his regulars. And most Tuesday evenings he came round to choose and discuss the order of the hymns for the following night's Mass. Then Elizabeth would serve a light but tasty meal.

Brother Raymund was against all forms of physical pleasure—but he ate his dinner up, and chewed appreciatively.

After dinner, I went to my room. They stayed on, talking, their voices a steady murmur. I don't know what they talked about. God, I suppose. The liturgical language. I don't know.

The first evening that Brother Raymund came to dinner, they had cold pork, and *tongue*—with a salad of artichoke hearts, green peppers, and English spinach. The tongue lay lewdly on its plate, placed directly in front of my setting.

'Is there any of the tuna left?' I said, in a strained high voice.

Elizabeth shook her head, not altogether sadly.

'No?' I said. 'I shall just have the salad and some cheese then.'

'Pff!' said Elizabeth. 'No iron in your blood, but—count your blessings—you'll have nice strong bones, won't you, Eleanor?'

'Do you not eat meat?' said Brother Raymund politely.

'Only seafood,' I said. 'Fish, and so on.'

'Prawns?' he said.

I nodded.

'Oysters?' he said doggedly—as if he really cared to know.

'Seafood,' I said, to head him off.

He was leading to something. They always did, the flesh eaters.

'And lobster, of course,' he smirked. 'But they have little legs, don't they? As do prawns. And such piquant faces, with their big sad eyes.'

'Yes, but terribly cold blood,' I said, in a rush.

'Ah,' he said, smiling at Elizabeth, 'then you'd be partial to a little reptile, too, then? Snake? Or toad?'

Elizabeth cackled musically.

'Quite!' she said. 'Quite!'

'One *needs* a little flesh, doesn't one?' said Elizabeth. 'And I enjoy it. And why not? I think most normal people do.'

'We all have our ways,' I said, blushing.

'Indeed,' said Elizabeth. 'I trust you won't reject my chestnut puree?'

'Imported,' she said importantly. 'From Fortnum and Masons.'

I ate several sour and mushy spoonfuls with feigned relish, just to please her—she was so proud of it.

'Lovely,' said Brother Raymund, flicking back a wisp of beard, that was trailing on his plate. 'The English do know how to eat, don't they?'

After dinner, I excused myself. I did the washing up, and then made my way upstairs. On the landing, I paused and listened.

'Do you know of anyone who might be an interest for Ellen?' said Elizabeth to this old man.

In all seriousness.

34

I SUPPOSE . . . NO, NO suppose. What Brother Raymund *did* was put the mystery back into the Mass. There was a sense of ectoplasmic possibility hovering over his raised host. Even I could feel it.

At first it was just the Latin Mass. (The old ones loved it. Belching discreetly into lavender-scented handkerchiefs, they warbled their responses, voices quavering along to Elizabeth's lead during the well-remembered hymns.)

The Latin Mass was something entirely unexpected. Suddenly, the vague passes over the altar that I'd seen made sense. 'Holy, holy, holy,' sang Brother Raymund—and it *was* holy.

The air was filled with swoon-inducing scents. We chanted our mysterious responses. And the darkness of the cellar was like the hush of night, lit only by the altar candles.

Brother Raymund gave us the full mystery of the Mass. And then he added . . . little details.

I think my favourite of these introduced rituals was the solemn anointing with scented oils. This small ceremony preceded the start of the Mass proper. As he anointed our foreheads, one by one, Brother Raymund recited an ad hoc litany: 'Holy of Holies, Temple of Temples, Sanctum of Sanctums.' Repetitions that were made mysterious by repetition, that seemed to redefine the words: the words opening out from each other into unfamiliar shadings of themselves.

It was all to do with the idea of our bodies as pure and sacred vessels. (Nothing new there—I learnt that from the nuns, who purified my vessel with their beatings.) Still, I was taken in by the rituals, and the secrecy, along with the rest of them. I, too, took part, and shared in the delights.

And Brother Raymund, unlike Father Flynn, span a good sermon.

He went on and on about purity: purity of bodily flesh, the purity of the Virgin. The necessity for purifying our temples in readiness for the Great Purification—his term for a coming Apocalypse.

In this century, he told us, the order of the seasons and the laws of the elements were being overturned.

In our lifetime, eternal chaos would begin its reign, he said.

And we believed him. Sitting silently in the darkness of the cellar, we believed him.

Again and again, he reminded us of the glorious purity of the Baby Jesus—born of a Virgin who was conceived without the stain of Original Sin—and the innocence and bodily purity of little children.

'Be thee as little children, my dear brothers and sisters in Christ,' he said.

Our naked bodies were mysteries, he said. Holy, he said. *Holy!* We must keep them pure, we must purify them. He warned us not to eat red meat; tomatoes, chilli, red peppers; baked beans, spaghetti bolognaise, tomato sauce. Anything red was forbidden. Even the altar wine that he consecrated was white.

'Body and blood of Christ,' he said.

Who were we to argue? (Although I thought the meat rule was rather rich, after all his teasing.)

As Catholics—even as Christians—we were getting further and further into something we didn't fully understand.

Elizabeth didn't seem to care what strange things Brother Raymund said. He was her holy man.

I knew what we were doing, what he was telling us and teaching us, was wrong. I knew that. Intrinsically. But it was interesting.

And every Wednesday, I was down in the cellar, kneeling and standing, and chanting and singing, and yabbering away with the rest of them.

Instead of going over the same old boring Gospels, Brother Raymund talked seemingly at random—but without the woolly-headedness of Father Flynn.

He asked us questions, and left us pondering, long after his sermon and the majestic Latin Mass were finished: Is God dead? Is the devil in control? Has God given up on us? What happens to us, if this is the case? How can we, in this situation, still save our souls? These, and other questions, he set turning over and over in our minds.

'What if the next Pope was the Antichrist?' he thundered. 'Would anyone even notice?'

∞

The dietary requirements were fun at first. Elizabeth cooked white sauces, cheese and mushroom dishes, and fish and other seafood. After Brother Raymund's rulings were enforced, I gained several pounds.

And then there were more baroque additions. Brother Raymund's already titillating sermons were interrupted by trance states and visions, which perked things up even further.

'So long as you, my followers, are true to God, and follow strictly the diet I have set down for you—at His command—then you shall know no death,' he said, during one of these trances.

'Yes, my friends,' he intoned, 'I speak of the resurrection of the body.'

'If any one of us dies,' he said, 'in a pure state, he——'

'Or she,' hissed Marlene.

'——will reappear like Christ, three days after death,' he said solemnly, 'and remain like Christ for forty days.'

'Hear ye the Word,' he shouted, and abruptly came to, resuming the Mass.

Well, what the point of that was, I could not say. Still, it was impressive.

Elizabeth went through the pantry, the next day, chucking out any lingering shades of red.

35

SOON THERE WERE FORTY of us squeezed into the cellar. Then Brother Raymund started some serious prophesying.

His eyes rolled slowly up into the back of his head, until only the whites were showing.

'Disgusting,' muttered Josephine.

Then he spoke, shooting her first a baleful glance.

On and on he went about the blood of the Pope and his cardinals. The blood of the Pope staining the Vatican red . . . The blood of the *Popes*. Not just this Pope, but the next, and the next . . .

When Iris sat up and quaked at this—not at the actual prophecy, note, but at the act of prophesying—quoting numerous verses from the Bible, Brother Raymund quoted other verses back at her, then said: 'Besides, it's nonsense to suggest I'm foretelling the future. I'm merely remembering backwards.'

That shut her up. And no-one else was game enough to question him.

'It's all very interesting,' I said to Elizabeth, afterwards. 'But who tells him these things?'

'God,' she said abruptly.

'Can't argue with God,' I said.

She stared at me—eyes fixed, like a statue.

∞

Brother Raymund told us that we must fast on Sundays, abstain from sex wherever possible, and avoid all procreation. I said that

that shouldn't be a problem. I mean, most of them were so old. And I was . . .

Elizabeth was not impressed. But then Brother Raymund said that *he* would be fasting, as he was our leader, on Mondays as well as Sundays. 'Oh, my poor man! Come early to dinner Tuesday,' Elizabeth cried. 'You'll be absolutely famished!' At this, he gazed at her with his pale grey eyes, and merely smiled mildly.

'All day Sunday,' she muttered, for some time after that edict—but she blindly followed it.

We must cut up all credit cards and bankcards, Brother Raymund instructed. Everything bore, apparently, the mark of the Beast.

'Not the ATM cards, too?' wailed Mildred Cleghorn. 'No-one takes a cheque these days, especially not the supermarkets.'

'"A woman must be a learner, listening quietly and with due submission,"' Brother Raymund quoted.

'Offer it up to purgatory, Mildred,' said Iris acidly.

Brother Raymund warned us not to watch TV.

'That hissing beast,' he called it. 'That evil eye.'

'Think about it,' he said, 'as watching *you*.'

'See,' he said, 'it blinking rapidly.'

'Ah,' we said.

'The devil,' he said, 'peers out at you when you are in a mind-numbed state in front of your TVs.'

'He enters,' he said chillingly, 'your brains. He takes up lodging there, for free. But not so free, after all . . . Oh, the cost of his cartage!'

'Get rid of them,' he said. 'Get rid of them! Take them to the tip. Don't sell them, lest you sully your soul with another man's damnation.'

'Radios, newspapers, all these devil-machines must go,' he said. 'Out with them, onto the scrap heap. Or consider yourselves on the eternal scrap heap.'

'I think that's going a *little* far, don't you?' said Mavis Purley afterwards, when Brother Raymund and the bulk of the flabbergasted congregation had gone home.

'Not at all!' cried Elizabeth.

'I bet he owns a second-hand electrical goods outlet,' said Bernard West, who was rather rowdy.

'Brother Raymund,' fluted Elizabeth, 'is an incorruptible man. An eminent divine, in my humble opinion.'

'She's right,' said Marlene and Darlene and Mildred Cleghorn.

'Although I don't know how I'm going to persuade Bob,' added Mildred.

'Just move it to a less prominent place to start with,' suggested Iris.

'That's not what he said,' said Josephine.

'We're getting rid of ours,' said Elizabeth firmly.

'The clock-radio, too?' I said. 'How will we hold up the palm leaves?'

'Very funny, Eleanor,' she said.

'I'm not having an instrument of the devil in my house,' she said.

'We may as well throw the palm leaves out, too, then,' I said.

'As you wish,' she said. 'I don't want any arguments.'

'You two girls!' said Iris. 'Bicker, bicker, bicker.'

Brother Raymund also told us that once we had attained a higher level of enlightenment, through diet and through fasting from the twentieth century (no radio, no TV), we would understand that Jesus's parables were prophecies. He would show us how to truly understand them.

All of this scriptural input was quite mind-boggling, I thought. He even quoted from the Old Testament. ('The Old Testament!' scoffed Iris.)

Brother Raymund also said: 'Now is for the living.'

Well, I could agree with that. But how to act on it?

36

ONE PARTICULAR EVENING, BROTHER Raymund brought in a new altar cloth, laying it on the altar in place of the previous one, which Elizabeth herself had made. The cloth was purple and gold, and lovingly hand-stitched by Margie Gray—a queer doll-eyed woman, with long spidery lower lashes. (Would anyone wear false eyelashes *below* their eyes?)

'That scheming *bitch*!' Elizabeth spat—after Brother Raymund and the rest of the congregation had departed. It was the crudest word in her vocabulary, and rarely wasted.

Suddenly, strangely, I had the conviction that we were all bitches to her, all competing to win—what? The approval of Brother Raymund and Father Flynn—a couple of old fellows in frocks? (Or was she thinking more of the great draped one up in the sky?)

How would she handle sharing space in the afterlife with Mother Teresa? I wondered. With Mary Magdalene, and Mary and Martha, and the Blessed Virgin? Heaven must be getting quite crowded with all the saintly types. (Thank God I don't have that to worry about, myself.)

'It's only an altar cloth,' I said placatingly.

'It is not,' she snapped. 'It's the principle. I am adamant that I will not accept any favours from that unspeakable creature.'

'And what about that casserole she brought last week, the lemon chicken. Lemon chicken!' she shrieked. 'Brother Raymund raved on and on about her putrid lemon chicken—it made me think my culinary exertions were simply not up to scratch.'

'But, Mother,' I cried, 'you are an excellent——'

'Oh!' she wailed. 'That frightful creature! That simpering smile.

The fresh wave and set. The eagerness. Don't tell me you haven't noticed her overbearing eagerness?'

'I can't believe Brother Raymund could be taken in by a cheap little nonentity like her,' she said. 'We all know Margie Gray is a conniving little schemer.'

Poor Mother. I would never have guessed that she could be so jealous. And I know how shamefully one can burn with jealousy. I remember my childhood's thousand plastic rivals . . .

'He's probably just being charitable,' I said.

'Pig's arse,' she snarled, then blushed and turned away, and took some time to recompose herself over by the sink.

'Hypocrisy and manipulation I will not tolerate,' Elizabeth said, then, in a fluting voice, while folding a damp tea-towel into pointlessly smaller squares. 'From now on that awful little woman is barred from my house, and from all further meetings and holy celebrations held here.'

'Herewith,' I said.

'What?' she said, narrowing her eyes.

'From this day forth,' I said.

'Yes!' she cried. '*Precisely.*'

∞

The following day, she thrashed through her housework.

'How was your day, Mother?' I said.

'Must you?' she snapped. 'A series of devastating disasters, actually.'

Turned out a cup got broken and the cake she'd made for Brother Raymund had refused to rise.

Her face was still sharp and pinched as she prepared the evening meal—softening only to greet Brother Raymund, who had got home from his work and showered and come over to our house. (He ate so often with us, he may as well have lived with us, I often thought.)

'A difficult week, dearest Elizabeth?' he said, in his oozing solicitous way. 'I noticed your preoccupation during Mass last night.'

'It's nothing. Really. These things are sent to try us,' she said, with a defiant snap of her head.

'Well! Make yourself useful, Ellen!' she cried, staring hard at me, her blue eyes ruthless.

'She has none of my co-operative traits,' she muttered under her breath to Brother Raymund.

I hovered by the kitchen door and listened, as the kettle boiled.

'Really, I have been working so tirelessly, that is all,' said Elizabeth sweetly. 'All sorts of spring-cleaning chores, even though it's only autumn!'

'Good, good,' he said soothingly. 'No little crises of faith, then?'

'Oh, Raymund, no!' she cried. 'Thank heavens I have *you*, Raymund. What would I ever do without you? The only sensible man in the entire parish!'

∞

I never saw Margie Gray at a Circle Mass again—although she still attended St Clare's, slipping into her seat with a stubborn face.

As we all did. Attend St Clare's, I mean.

No-one abandoned the regular Mass. That would have implied a terrible sin.

I wonder how Elizabeth dealt with her jealousy? Buried it? I doubt that she took it up with Brother Raymund—who had, naturally, his own version of the Sacrament of Penance. (Something else that I resisted, initially.)

Did she confess her hatreds or her desires to Father Flynn? I doubt it. Not in their entirety.

How could she now? How could any of us? (Although, of course, I had always lied.)

It was a difficult situation, in the end, with Brother Raymund, the lay priest, the *fake* priest—although, with a sort of mass delusion, we expunged this obvious factor from our minds—commanding more respect than Father Flynn.

37

UNDER BROTHER RAYMUND, WE took Holy Communion in the old manner. He hand-fed each one of us tiny bread wafers—made by Mavis Purley—and then we sipped white wine from a silver chalice. (I avoided this part, occasionally miming the swallowing of a mouthful.) And then we chanted, as one:
'The body of Christ.'
'The body of Christ.'
'The blood of Christ.'
'The blood of Christ.'
'The body of Christ.'
'The body of Christ.'
On and on, until we were dizzy and almost delirious.

Then one Wednesday, over the coffee and sherry we served after—the only reminder of Circle days—Brother Raymund announced that he had an innovative treat in mind for the next week's Mass. We would have meatcakes in place of the holy wafers.

'*Meat*cakes!' I cried, aghast.

'But bread is traditional, Brother Raymund,' Iris said sweetly. 'You must concur with that?'

'Meat is more authentic, though, isn't it?' said Mildred Cleghorn.

Iris flung her a glance.

'We are trying to reach the true spirit of Christ,' said Brother Raymund. 'We are reaching back through the obfuscations of the Church, and trying to find the central core of Christ's desires for us. Body and blood, He said.'

'Ah,' said Iris.

'Our wine is white,' said Brother Raymund. 'Representing the purity of Christ's blood.'

'Just give it to me, red or white,' said Bernard West mock-raucously.

'It should really be blue,' said Darlene wistfully, 'ideally.'

And everyone cocked their eyes at her.

'The white wine, of itself, breaks with tradition,' continued Brother Raymund.

'The wafer,' he said, 'is only a recent fabrication. Bread, small cakes, something you could really chew—that is what is meant, sister.'

'It will be white meat, won't it?' said Marlene nervously. 'I mean, it's guaranteed pure?'

'Naturally,' said Brother Raymund.

'Well!' she said. 'I think it's a nice idea.'

'So long as we don't have to drink any real blood, ha ha ha,' said Jim Dooley, the butcher.

'But you could supply, hey, Jim?' said Brother Raymund cheerily.

'No worries,' said Jim. 'I'd give you a discount.'

'See me before next Mass,' said Brother Raymund.

Much hearty laughter . . .

And so it was that the following week, during Communion, we were presented with a platter heaped with tiny lightly browned cakes of meat—they looked like hostess tuna patties.

Normally, the atmosphere remained sternly formal during Mass, of course—but quiet chat broke out then as each member was fed their cake, in turn, and ate it.

'Delicious,' they said, one by one. 'What's in them?'

'Ah! My special recipe,' said Brother Raymund.

'It's the secret herbs and spices,' winked Timothy Brennan.

'Pork?' said Elizabeth curiously. 'Or chicken?'

'White meat,' nodded Brother Raymund. 'Of course.'

One by one they swallowed their meatcakes, then sipped from the chalice—which Elizabeth, as altar boy, took care to wipe after each mouthful was taken.

Brother Raymund and Elizabeth reached me and stopped, each thrusting their offerings towards me.

'You know I'm a vegetarian,' I said.

'But this is Mass,' said Elizabeth. 'It's different.'

'I can't eat it,' I said.

'It's only tiny!' cried Mildred Cleghorn. 'A bit of meat that size won't count.'

'Look,' I said. 'I know you don't understand, but it's a big deal to me. I don't eat meat. Ever.'

'That's what you think,' sniggered Elizabeth.

'What?' I said.

'Only teasing,' she said. 'Dear.'

'Dear,' she said. 'Everyone's waiting.'

'Oh, God,' I sighed.

'Eleanor! Blasphemy! Here, of all places!' said Elizabeth.

'Do not trouble yourself, sister,' said Brother Raymund.

I looked up at him gratefully, but he was staring at her.

'Eleanora?' he said. 'And you refuse our sacred wine, also, I notice. You refuse the body and blood of our Lord Jesus Christ, who died for you, that you might be saved——'

'Wine gives me asthma,' I said.

'Oh, for pity's sake!' cried Marlene. 'What a fuss about nothing. Can we get on with this?'

'Oh, all right!' I cried. 'Give me the wafer.'

I took it and ate it—sweet white meat, formed into a dollar-sized patty.

'There, that wasn't so bad, was it?' simpered Marlene.

'Now the wine,' said Brother Raymund.

'I shall take a small amount,' I said. 'Next time, could you consecrate some water while you're at it?'

'Of course,' he said sourly, smiling.

'I've heard quite enough about her digestion for one day,' said Bernadette West.

I turned, frowning slightly, but the old woman's face was beaming beatific forgiveness at me.

I grimaced back.

'Let us pray,' said Brother Raymund, and Elizabeth swung her incense and rang her bells.

And I repressed a belch—redolent with the aftertaste of sweet burnt flesh.

38

'I'M NOT GOING DOWN there again,' I said to Elizabeth, the following Wednesday.

'Don't be ridiculous,' she said. 'Of course you're coming.'

'It's *wrong*,' I said. 'It smells down there.'

'Smells?' she said. 'Oh, it's a little mousey, I suppose. A little close . . .'

'Perhaps some tiny rodent has died there, at some time,' she said blithely. 'So typical of you to focus on the negative. A tiny whiff! Why, no-one else complains! I swing that censer, here, there, everywhere!' she cried. 'I find it most atmospheric, and I'm not alone in that, I'll have you know——'

'You can't make me,' I said defiantly.

She gasped.

'The lip!' she said.

Her eyes bulged, then narrowed.

'You!' she said. 'You don't know which side your bread's been buttered on. Well, I'll tell you, Eleanor. It's both sides. Both sides, my girl.'

'Now,' she said, 'let me finish. You, Eleanor, have the sort of freedom to come and go that Josephine and Iris and Marlene and Dymphna and I only dreamt of. You've got a pretty little income, from your dead-end job, and very few household expenses.'

'But, Mother,' I said. 'I'm happy to——'

'Will you stop interrupting me!' she cried. 'You are an unruly child!'

'Can you imagine it,' she said rhetorically, 'once upon a time a young person would never dream of working and living in the family home without paying full board! But don't think I'm complaining.'

(It is not that I don't offer, book. I do, I *do*.)

'You've been given a good education,' she went on, 'and it goes without saying you've *wasted* it. Now, don't you argue. And furthermore, no-one has pressured you to take on an apprenticeship, or a course of study, that you weren't partial to, have they, Eleanor?'

'Do you think I wanted to be a nurse?' she cried. 'And are you grateful? No, indeed. You sit there with your lip extended, making the house unpleasant.'

'This rudeness, I tell you, has got to stop,' she shouted. 'This surly sullenness. Why, even Brother Raymund has mentioned your moods to me! And of course it's all *through* the family what a burden you've become.'

On and on she went.

'It's never been my intention to shame you, Mother,' I said, my cheeks flaming.

'Shame!' Elizabeth shook her head, her jowls wobbling sadly. 'It's you that ought to be ashamed. Do you know what Brother Raymund said the other day?'

'Something incomprehensible but clever-sounding, I expect,' I said.

'How dare you!' she roared.

'I——' I said.

'Brother Raymund,' she hissed, 'is a highly evolved soul. We cannot expect to understand him. We must merely reflect in gratitude at how blest we are to have him in our midst.'

'What's the good of learning something you can't understand?' I blurted.

She stared at me—her mouth hung open in a terrible square.

'Oh, all right, I'll come to the bloody Mass. Okay?' I said.

'Oh, merciful God! Save her from her own wickedness!' she cried. 'Of all the blasphemies . . .'

'I'll come, okay? Isn't that what you want?' I said.

'It's not about my wants or needs,' she said. 'It's *your* immortal soul I'm bent on saving. Do you think I could live with myself in the hereafter if I didn't try my utmost with you, Eleanor?'

'It's Eleanora,' I snapped.

'What a fuss about a name,' she scoffed.

'It's *my* name,' I said.

'You just can't resist a chance to take a jab at me,' she sniffed.

'Oh, don't start, don't start now,' she said. 'Not now, with

Marlene due to arrive any second and the others shortly after. Though there's no proper time for your ugly ways, you know.'

'Get to your room and change,' she said, 'and do something about your attitude while you're at it, or I swear I'll come and soap the devil out of you.'

And so I went upstairs and washed my face and pulled my hair back and changed my clothes.

'Here I am,' I said, a short while after, presenting myself to the early arrivals who had gathered in the living room.

'Ooh, dear,' whispered Josephine. 'That's a little too much cleavage for this occasion, isn't it?'

'Only if you're staring down my shirt,' I said. 'Besides, it isn't a real Mass. It's just pretend.'

At this they all looked horrified.

'It is a very sacred Mass indeed,' said Brother Raymund unctuously.

'Eleanor, the soap, the soap,' said Elizabeth, who was coming up the cellar stairs, already in her robes.

I nodded meekly, and did up another button—and we all filed out of the room, following Brother Raymund and Elizabeth down into the cellar.

39

BROTHER RAYMUND WASN'T ALWAYS on her side, you know. Not that I wanted him on my side. He sent shivers down my spine, with those queer grey eyes—like frozen milk, or dirty ice . . .

One day, though, he arrived early for dinner, and joined me at the gate to our house, where I was sitting on a stone.

'What is the matter, Eleanora?' he said, sitting down beside me.

I said nothing—merely stared awkwardly at the ground.

'The loss of a life is sad, tragic,' he said evenly. 'The loss of a life while still living it, Eleanora, is also sad, and tragic.'

'Forgive me for intruding,' he said. 'But I have noticed. You live—endure, rather—as if life was an endless sentence, not a gift. Why?'

I had nothing I wanted to say to him.

'What is it, Eleanora?' he said. 'There is something eating terribly at your heart.'

'I am afraid,' I said, before I knew what I was doing. 'So afraid.'

'Ah,' he said, slowly. 'I see.'

'There is much to fear, isn't there?' he said.

'It's the devil's world, isn't it?' he said.

'"When *he* tells a lie he is speaking his own language, for he is a liar and the father of lies. But I speak the truth and therefore you do not believe me." John 8:42,' he said.

'Oh, yes,' he said. 'I can feel your fear. But, Eleanora, there is something beyond the fear——'

'I know. Eternity,' I said hollowly. 'That's what I'm scared of——'

'Beyond eternity,' he said.

At this I listened very closely.

'Behind, above, and beyond everything,' Raymund Allan said, 'is the great Universal Oneness, the Divine Spirit of Unending Love, the Power of Love, the Principality. The Principality of Light!'

'The darkness,' he said. 'Now here you must leap with me—the darkness, my dear, is in fact light.'

'This makes all fear unnecessary,' he said. 'Do you understand?'

'What about hell?' I said.

'There is no hell, Eleanora,' he said gently. 'No hell, no purgatory, no waiting for judgement. Only shades of bliss.'

'Oh,' I said.

'Indeed, *Oh*,' he said.

40

SOME MONTHS LATER, THE cellar packed to full capacity, Brother Raymund went into a trance. He nodded to himself for several minutes, then came out of his trance, smiling palely. Then he began to speak:

'In 1999, in the month of June, Europe will be consumed by fire, and all of Asia submerged by flood,' he said laconically. 'Earthquakes all down both coasts of the Americas. New Zealand, well!' he clicked his tongue. 'And the eastern coast of our country will be hit by an enormous tidal wave.'

We all gaped.

The cellar erupted in cries and exclamations.

'Ladies!' he said. 'Sir.'

There was only old Bernard West with us now, staring with his mouth open. Jim Dooley and Timothy Brennan had decamped several weeks before, without elaborate explanation.

'Before the great waves,' Brother Raymund continued, 'there will be a cracking. Then fire.'

'Mother of Mary!' said Margaret O'Boyle.

'The Reds?' said Bernard West hopefully. 'The bloody bomb?'

'Rebellion,' said Brother Raymund opaquely.

'First fire,' he said, eyeing me, 'then flood.'

'You said——' I said.

'Metaphorically speaking,' he said.

'Tsunami,' he added kindly. 'That's Japanese for tidal wave. The waters will cover everything we now know.'

'Any questions?' he said briskly.

'Well,' said Mildred Cleghorn. 'The water. How long will it take to subside?'

'Oh, don't worry about the water,' he said. 'You'll all be selling up and moving out well before then.'

'Selling up?' squawked Iris.

'It won't subside,' Brother Raymund said gently. 'It will engulf.'

'This, all of this,' he waved his arms about the cellar, 'from the tip of Queensland to the tail of Tasmania, under water.'

We all shuddered.

'You will sell your houses and move to Katoomba in the first three months of that year,' he said.

'If not before,' he added ominously.

'The fulfilment is at hand,' he said. He stared at me, his eyes pale and assessing. 'And what I say to you, I say unto all: Watch. Then flee to the mountains!'

'I suppose you'll be arranging the sales?' said Bernard West.

Elizabeth levelled him with a glance.

'Katoomba?' she said, delicately. 'In 1999?'

'It's high,' said Mildred Cleghorn. 'I'll give you that.'

'Precisely,' said Brother Raymund.

'A little cold,' said Marlene. 'In winter. For the old people, I mean.'

'Well, stay and drown,' Brother Raymund said snidely, then folded his hands and lowered his eyes.

Marlene stared dead ahead, and everyone who knew remembered Bridget, and the rest . . .

'St Paul,' Brother Raymund announced, 'in his letter to the Thessalonians wrote "never treat the gift of prophecy with contempt".'

'"He that prophesieth edifieth the church." Corinthians 14:4,' said Brother Raymund.

'14:4?' said Iris.

He smiled to himself briefly, then looked up again.

'I have come here,' he said. 'I have travelled from far away, at great expense to myself, to pass on this news. To save a few true believers.'

'Oh, don't think we aren't grateful, Brother!' cried Marlene. 'It's just——'

'Just——' said Elizabeth.

'It's just so sudden,' said Iris sadly. Her unfocused pale-blue eyes wafted across my face. 'I've only just got the garden how I really like it . . .'

'They've got lovely gardens, up at Leura,' said Margaret O'Boyle. 'I'm sure——'

'Oh, it's a way's off!' said Josephine. 'Isn't it?'

'The end of time as we know it waits for no man,' chided Brother Raymund.

'We will survive?' said Helen Brennan anxiously.

'We,' said Brother Raymund, 'a select band of people of great faith and purity of purpose, shall lead the way into the new millennium.'

'And the water,' said Mildred Cleghorn, waving vaguely with her hands.

'So high!' he cried, leaping. 'Not even the roof of the tallest tower will be left showing.'

'Oh!' she gasped.

'I've never liked water,' muttered Josephine.

'Well,' said Mary-Rose O'Brien, clapping her hands. 'We shall have to set to, preserving, and buying tins, and so on.'

'They have shops in Katoomba,' said Darlene brightly.

And everybody looked at her.

'Should we tell the world?' said Marlene.

'No,' sighed Brother Raymund.

'The greater Church, surely?' she said.

'No, sister,' said Brother Raymund.

'May I tell my nephew?' said Irene Dooley plaintively.

Brother Raymund stared at her.

'Well, what about Jim?' she said indignantly. 'He used to be a member. Till his work got the better of him.'

'The hours, you know . . .' she finished vaguely.

'My children,' he said. 'You cannot argue with the facts: humanity needs a good prune. Dead wood must go. God, in His Divine Wisdom, has so ordained it. And He has instructed me to tell it so to you: the Great Purification is imminent. Ignore my words at your own peril. However, and mark this well, for I will say it only once. Only true believers will be saved.'

'But——' said Irene Dooley.

'Brother Raymund is giving us our *lives*,' said Elizabeth.

'Wouldn't it be more Christian to stay and sacrifice ourselves?' I said.

'Poof!' said Bernard West crankily. 'I don't think I fancy living in a depopulated world for all eternity with *that* one.'

'Take no notice, dear,' said Bernadette, smiling wildly. 'It's his hiatus hernia.'

'What about Timothy?' cried Helen Brennan.

'Yes!' cried a chorus of anxious wives.

'You may, if you must,' sighed Brother Raymond, 'take your husbands.'

'Well, how are they going to sell up if they don't tell them?' said Bernard West. 'Whose names are on the deeds, heh?'

'You may tell your families,' said Brother Raymund. 'But do not despair if many elect to disbelieve the truth.'

'What about St John? What about Revelations?' quavered Iris, who had actually read the Bible.

'John lived in a small world,' Brother Raymund said mildly. 'His revelations were of localised events. The Americas, Australia, England, France, indeed Germany. What could he know of such things?'

'Greenland,' piped Bernard West. 'The Bahamas, Papua New——'

'There will be,' Brother Raymund coughed delicately, 'atomic problems in Europe. Europe will cease to exist.'

'But Australia?' cried Mavis Purley.

'Sadly, much of the population will be erased,' said Brother Raymund. 'However, Australia will prevail, and our little flock with it. The meek shall indeed inherit the earth.'

'Brother, you speak of wondrous things!' cried Elizabeth.

'What?' she cried, then. '*What*?'

For Irene Dooley in particular was regarding her sourly.

'Everybody dead,' Irene said. 'What sort of a world is that?'

Nobody answered.

'We could dive. Afterwards, you know, and retrieve all the gold and jewellery,' said Darlene, filling the silence.

'Very useful,' said Marlene dryly.

'So,' said Josephine tentatively. 'Are you going to stay, Iris? I'd hate to leave Mortlake. But even so . . . It's not as if . . .'

'Drown?' said Iris. 'Oh, no, I don't want to drown. Besides, the mountains will make a change.'

∞

'Excellent news,' said Elizabeth, afterwards, as we were washing and drying the coffee cups.

'You know, if we sell now and buy up there we can probably afford to get two houses,' she said. 'And there will be a severe lack of available housing, won't there?'

'Of course, I would prefer to spend my last years in more sophisticated company,' she murmured. 'But so it is . . .'

'Not exactly a surprise,' I said.

'How so?' Elizabeth said, her eyes popping, her hands suddenly still in the sink.

'Has . . . ?' she started, and thought better of it.

She was always watching me and Brother Raymund—watching with a glittering jealous eye.

'Well, it stands to reason,' I said blithely, 'that these sorts of prophecies should include the happy news that everyone but you, the chosen few, will soon be dead.'

'Always something negative to say,' she said.

'So, dear. Are you planning to come with us?' she said, as she pulled out the plug.

I listened to the water rushing headlong down the drain, and shivered.

'You know I can't swim,' I said.

41

AND THEN, ONE WEDNESDAY evening—not many months after his great prophecy—Brother Raymund did not appear to celebrate the Latin Mass.

The week before had had to be cancelled, owing to illness in the family. And now the Circle were all gathered, restlessly waiting—almost frantic, after such a lapse, to re-engage in the complex and soothing rituals.

At eight forty-five, in groups of two and three, the congregation began to depart, muttering—leaving a dozen faithful sitting mournfully in Elizabeth's dining room, while she prepared pot after pot of tea.

At nine o'clock, two policemen came, instead.

Bernard West took charge.

'What seems to be the problem, officers?' he said.

'Your Father Flanagan . . . Sorry,' the younger of the policemen said, flipping through his notebook.

'Flynn, I think you'll find,' said Elizabeth, returning.

'Yeah, Father Flynn of St Clare's,' said the policeman, jabbing his finger at his notebook. 'Said a Mr Raymund Allan might be staying at this address. With a Mrs Birdy?'

'I am Mrs Bird. Alas, he is not staying here, with me,' said Elizabeth.

'With us,' I said.

'I haven't seen him,' she said, glaring at me, 'since, oh, shortly over a week ago. It is really very perturbing and out of character. A most reliable man! Have you——?'

'Not here then, right,' said the older, bald policeman. He made a motion as if to leave, then hesitated. 'Nothing to worry about, then. I'm sorry to disturb your party.'

Still, he stayed, and flicked his glance around the table.

'But what has *happened* to him?' cried Elizabeth.

'He's scarpered,' the young policeman said, and scratched his thin moustache. 'Scarpered owing two months' rent.'

Elizabeth gasped, and stared bug-eyed at him.

'He's gone!' she cried. 'Like that!'

'Don't you find that just a little worrying?' Iris said.

'Oh, his landlady's pretty worried,' the young policeman said, and winked at me.

'I never thought of him as a man who roomed,' Marlene mused.

'No,' said Mavis Purley. 'Nor I.'

'A man's got to live somewhere,' said Mildred Cleghorn magnanimously.

'Even so,' said Marlene.

'Well, thank you for your time,' said the bald policeman.

'But surely you're taking this disappearance seriously?' cried Elizabeth.

'Oh, we are, we are,' he said.

'But he hasn't actually done anything, has he?' said Bernard West. 'I mean, he could be planning to send a cheque.'

The two policemen exchanged wry looks.

'Well, he's disappeared!' cried Elizabeth. 'Isn't that enough?'

'Left town suddenly? Oh, he always does that,' said the older man.

'Indeed!' said Iris. 'Like some will-o'-the-wisp!'

'Yeah,' said his partner. 'Good old Ray. His usual trick.'

'You know him!' cried Marlene.

'Well acquainted,' said the bald man.

'Mr Allan is a well-known charlatan,' he said, smiling gently at each and every one of us.

From the room at large came an audible gasp.

'Oh . . . dear,' said Elizabeth icily.

'He didn't get any money off you, did he?' said the bald man.

'No! No, of course not,' said Elizabeth, her voice tight and frosty.

'No, he bloody didn't!' roared Bernard West, while his wife tugged at his elbow.

'But what does he do?' said Mildred Cleghorn. 'I can't imagine him doing anything wrong. In fact, I think you've got the wrong man's records out, because Brother Raymund is a very nice man. A gentleman.'

'Brother, is it?' the bald man said, smiling.

'I——' she said, flustered.

'Got you involved in his Church, did he?' he said.

The young policeman smiled and fingered his moustache.

'We prayed together, yes,' said Elizabeth, with tremendous dignity.

'Yes, yes. He's harmless enough, isn't he? It's not extortion, is it? A bit of prayer among like-minded folk,' the bald man said, and winked.

Were these *real* police?

'What could we book him under? Impersonating a priest? But it's all private, isn't it?' he said. 'And you're all adults, more or less. All in on it. Am I right?'

At this Elizabeth scowled and bugged her eyes, and Marlene's cheeks and Mavis Purley's withered neck turned crimson.

'That's his game,' his partner said. 'Goes around the country, impersonating a member of the clergy. Hoodwinks groups of Catholics, like yourselves. Bit of a laugh, really. Got him once, down in Bowral, for making off with the collection plate.'

Again the room was filled with gasps and sighs.

'The filthy beggar!' cried Bernard West.

'But why, why, *why*?' Mildred Cleghorn cried. 'Why would anyone do anything so mean and evil-minded?'

'Brought up by Christian Brothers?' shrugged the young policeman, and smiled at me, and held my eye.

Long seconds passed.

'Steady on, Bryce,' said his partner.

'How can you say such an awful thing, even in jest?' snapped Elizabeth, through lips of string.

'Because *I* was, madam,' the young policeman said dryly, and they left.

∞

'I think *he* was impersonating a police officer,' said Mary-Rose O'Brien huffily.

We all sat slumped around the table.

'Our Raymund,' moaned Josephine.

'Religious deception,' said Marlene. 'Of the cruellest kind.'

'Unbelievable,' said Mavis Purley.

'Good riddance to him,' said Margaret O'Boyle, pouting massively.

'No harm done,' Bernadette West said. 'Is there?'

'What a bunch of fools he must have thought us!' said Marlene bitterly, steaming from the room to get more sherry.

'Perhaps they are mistaken,' said Josephine.

'Another Brother Raymund,' said Darlene.

And everyone, as usual, simply stared.

'All over the countryside, making fools of good Catholics!' cried Marlene. 'It's disgraceful.'

'That it is,' Iris said, and sighed.

'I'm not going down *there* again,' said Mildred Cleghorn.

'Nor I,' said Iris.

'Me neither,' I said—too quickly or too loudly, for Elizabeth glared.

'So, are we selling up?' I said. 'Are we moving to Katoomba now? In 1999?'

'That charlatan,' said Marlene. 'To think——'

'Probably worked in real estate, not coffins,' said Iris.

'I didn't know he worked in coffins,' said Mary-Rose O'Brien.

'Wholesale,' said Elizabeth. 'A tad removed, you know.'

'Oh,' said Mary-Rose. 'Still . . .'

'Kept a lot of things very bloody quiet!' shouted Bernard West.

'Don't strain yourself,' said Bernadette.

'And I've done so much knitting already,' said Darlene.

'Mother?' I said. 'Are we——'

'Over my dead body,' Elizabeth said.

42

WELL, HE DID NOT come back. There was general disappointment and dismay in the Circle, and also at St Clare's.

The choir sounded thin, Elizabeth complained. But several husbands began attending Sunday Mass again, and Father Flynn seemed, almost imperceptibly, relieved—although I doubt he knew more than a minuscule fraction of the extent of Raymund Allan's domain.

After Brother Raymund left, we never held another Latin Mass. Who was there to celebrate it? What was there to celebrate, it was felt, without Brother Raymund? Indeed, who was Brother Raymund, after all, if he was not himself? We never mentioned it, or him, again.

We never held another Circle meeting of any sort in the cellar, either. Our dining room was quite able to accommodate the diminishing group as the newer members began, in clumps, to peel away. (Only the persuasive force of Brother Raymund could keep them there, it was generally felt. And no-one else wanted them, really.)

The Circle met, once again, each Wednesday evening. More modestly attended at first—and then quite sparsely. And then every other week, as it had in the beginning.

Soon there were only the originals left: Elizabeth and Marlene and Darlene and Iris and Josephine, and myself. Mildred Cleghorn. And Margaret O'Boyle and Mavis Purley. No men. And a comfortable size.

A routine was settled on: prayers, the rosary, some meditations—led by Elizabeth again—with pauses for parish gossip and exchanges of recipes.

We cunningly suppressed all memory of heretical practices, all heresies.

A few TV sets were repurchased—or dragged out of storage, in Mildred Cleghorn's case.

One by one, the women of the Circle got out their musty sewing, and blew the dust off their tapestries and their embroidery. (I was surprised to see how far I'd actually gotten with my cross-stitch . . .) We set about our work, our eyes shining with industry. Our eyes as shiny as our rosary beads.

Once a fortnight, then, we got together, and did our handwork, and said our prayers, and drank coffee from Elizabeth's tiny gold-edged cups—some scoffed a glass or two of cheap sweet sherry.

Soon the dangerous Masses were forgotten.

And a sort of peace came down on us. A grace, Brother Raymund would have said.

∞

Elizabeth and I burnt the altar cloths, and the vestments that had used to hang in our hall closet: Raymund's mock-priestly garments, and Elizabeth's now-pitiful altar robes.

We also burnt the candles and the incense in the incinerator. A great stench was released into the neighbourhood, drawing worried glances from Harry Jumper. Then Ethel Jumper's gorgon-like face pressed up against the fence, and shouted: 'My bloody washing. You've gone and ruined my bloody washing with your filthy smoke!'

Elizabeth sold—I believe—the chalice, the altar candlesticks, and the other vessels used for Mass. Or otherwise disposed of them. Even the altar was dismantled, brick by brick. And it was over.

And Elizabeth and I commenced to eat foods of all colours—although I still held back from pork and lamb and fowl and beef.

∞

First, there was Ron. Then there was Sylvester. And then there was Raymund. These were the men in our lives . . .

And then Jasper came to us.

Jasper Pease, with his sly smile and his strange manners and his winning ways. His masculine presence blessing our table. His unearthly exhalations wafting through our house.

On Circle nights, Jasper's usual practice was to slip out for a walk after an early dinner, or else to disappear upstairs. Reading, I suppose—or going through my things.

We always ate early, and lightly, on these Wednesdays. By eight o'clock—our usual starting time for dinner, since being joined by Jasper Pease—we had finished our meal, washed up, wiped and reclothed the table, and prepared the tray of cups and glasses for our after-Circle supper.

We had washed our hands and faces and brushed our hair and were waiting, needlework at the ready, for our guests.

When I say we, I mean Elizabeth and I. Jasper remained evasive.

'Are you sure, Jasper?' Elizabeth would say.

'Obliged, ma'am,' he'd say. 'But I must refrain.'

Never offering any explanation. (Most amazingly, never being pressed for one.)

'The night air, so invigorating,' he'd say, before bolting down our driveway. And he would not return till after we had gone to bed and sleep.

Occasionally, yawning, he would say: 'I must retire early, I'm afraid, ladies.'

'But, please,' he'd say, 'don't tone down your gaieties for me. There's nothing more refreshing than a prayer meeting!'

'Indeed,' said Elizabeth, invariably. Smiling, then looking a little downcast as he mounted the stairs, away. As if she always half-expected him to relent and join us.

But he never did. And she never pushed him. Oddly.

When I asked Elizabeth whether she minded much about Jasper not, at the very least, joining Circle, she glared at me and narrowed her lips.

'I expect,' she said frostily, 'he has other things to do.'

'Indeed,' I said.

'What?' she said.

'I agreed with you,' I said.

'Mm,' she said, staring at me. 'It's your tone.'

∞

There, book, that about sums up the Circle. That wasn't so hard, was it?

(Last month I completed a chair cover, and now I'm doing some embroidered handkerchiefs.)

43

AFTER A NICE DAY'S work, I wait for eternity at the bus stop in Lemonhurst Mall, a cold wind making snakes of my hair. A miserable group waits with me. Their faces haggard, their heads craning, they stare as if God himself was about to appear from around the corner.

On the other side of the highway are the old shops (an actual scent of mothballs in the air): Lemonhurst Florist, Lemonhurst Newsagency, Marie of Lemonhurst Ladies' Fashions, Lemonhurst Valet Service Dry Cleaners, Lemonhurst Fruit and Veg, free delivery.

There is the bank, that frightened me as a child with its respectable air. Just a red brick building, I see now.

This side of the highway is the Mall, with its shops stacked together like children's blocks, and its pastel plastic fittings, and the syrupy lull of its muzak, and half the shoppers already on Prozac—or one of its relatives.

I sit on in the bus shelter, that provides no shelter, wind and grit stinging my eyes. In ones and twos and groups of squalling threes, shoppers and workers and drifters of all ages cluster round. I close my eyes and press back into the shelterless shelter.

The bus comes, and I board, take my seat—leaving behind a surly mass who will wait and wait, eyes stung by grit and wind, for the next—and I sway left, right, left, right, with the others.

I look at them. (I am rude that way.)

I look at them and try to fathom their pasts and their futures. A few glance up, annoyed, furtive, interested, bland. Or frightened? I study their faces for clues.

Oh, the sad faces on that bus! The faces hanging from the skulls, slack with exhaustion and defeat. Oh, the eyes, the eyes!

What sadnesses they carry! (They can change the colour of their irises with bits of coloured plastic, but they cannot paint over what lies within, I think. Perhaps in the future there will be aura spray for sale? Or soul de-mister? Until then, there is Catholicism, of course, with forgiveness on tap—the ideal stain-remover.)

I make my face blank, to mask my curiosity.

I cannot help wishing I will unmask *someone like me*. But I am alone, as usual.

44

OVER TIME, I SUPPOSE, Jasper's accent slipped, then faded. There were the odd mannerisms still left, verbal tics: the occasional 'Mighty fine!', the 'ma'am', the 'miss'. And, similarly, his fishy odour weakened—or I got used to it. (Worst of all, lately, was the overpowering stench of Californian Poppy—slathered on, perhaps, in a futile attempt to mask the stink of unstirred swamp weed emitted by his hair? Clouds of Californian Poppy, that lingered when he left the room. And then an after-odour of something else . . .)

Some nights, he even did the dishes! But that didn't make him human. He was like a zombie—undead, rather than living. Unnatural. With his skin so damp and slimy, corpse-pale, as if he had spent his life in a cave, and pitted; and his eyes changing like the sea, but glazed, and filmy—and something that he tried to hide, *behind* his eyes.

There were shadows behind his eyes, running about. Didn't Elizabeth notice them? Didn't she notice anything?

Where had he come from, and what was he doing here, Jasper Pease—wafting his strange scents about?

I think I insulted the fishmonger, the way I sniffed at the packets, after purchase, trying to get a hint.

'Is off?' he said to me the other day, his face screwed up in disbelief.

(The fishmonger's at Lemonhurst Mall is really one of the best. I think that's indisputable. Quality fish for Catholics living in hell.)

'No, no!' I said. 'I was just . . .'

How could I explain to him that I was trying to place the lodger?

How many hours did I spend wondering—the smell like a forgotten word rising onto the tip, the tip, of my consciousness?

Then nothing. Nothing. No answers.

∞

'How was Mass today?' he said, this morning.

Elizabeth had bustled ahead into the kitchen, to prepare our usual Sunday brunch: croissants, cold meats for her and Jasper, assorted cheeses, and a bowl of summer fruits.

'Oh,' I said. 'Good. Thank you.'

'Take Communion?' he said.

'Of course,' I said, blushing.

'Oh?' he said, and stared at me—a hard little smile spreading across his face.

I felt cold all over, suddenly.

The moment broke, and he was wearing his usual lopsided grin.

'Thought you didn't eat meat, Eleanora,' he said, and winked at me.

'Oh!' I said, overcome by his oiliness. 'I see what you mean, Jasper.'

'Transubstantiation,' he said, rolling it about in his mouth. 'A lovely word. But do you believe in it, Eleanora?'

'Of course,' I said shortly.

I cannot bear it when ignorant outsiders mock our beliefs.

'I can see the advantage of consuming one's leader,' Jasper mused.

He stretched in his chair, and smirked at me.

'Consuming the leader's superior attributes. Cannibalism, in a word,' he said. 'So primitive.'

'If you like,' I said.

'You belong to one of the longest-surviving death cults,' he said, smiling with his teeth bared.

'Why Jasper Pease!' Elizabeth said, in high good spirits. 'You and your little jokes!'

She plonked a bowl of cherries onto the table.

'So sarky,' she said.

'You must come to Mass with us some day,' she said.

'I couldn't,' Jasper murmured.

'At Christmas, perhaps?' she said, her eyes swivelling to rest fondly on the Baby Jesus, lying in his manger on the mantelpiece.

I stared at the spot where the television used to be.

'Or Easter,' she said enticingly. 'The paschal celebrations are *so* moving.'

'Certainly, ma'am,' he said.

'Death cult!' she said. 'My stars! Wait till I tell Marlene.'

And, although it was unclear with what he had agreed, Elizabeth smiled and hummed as she left the room to put on the kettle for our tea.

Jasper cleared his throat and continued.

'Did the disciples steal and eat the body, after the crucifixion?' he hissed.

'I don't think——' I said.

'I don't think you think at all,' he said.

'On the other hand,' he said, smiling winsomely, 'there are elements of the Roman Bacchanalia, what with the emphasis on wine——'

'Wine?' I said. 'A little sip at Communion. I hardly think——'

'The wedding at Cana. The Last Supper,' he said, holding my gaze with his wet sea-eyes. 'The first and last miracles dealing with wine. Surely you see the significance?'

'Oh,' I said. 'Put like that . . .'

It is always better not to argue about these things. Not to mention them at all.

'I don't drink wine, however,' I said. 'It makes me breathless.'

'Never?' Jasper said. 'What a pity.'

'But you eat the body?' he said.

'Yes,' I said.

'Think about it,' he said.

'It's not something you think about,' I said. 'Faith is something you have.'

'But you don't have it,' he said neatly, and left the room.

Moments later, Elizabeth reappeared, bearing the tray of tea things.

'You might help!' she said.

'I've been entertaining the lodger,' I said.

'Have you?' she jeered. 'Then where is he?'

'Ah, Mrs Bird!' he cried, returning—as if on cue. 'I have a little offering for this morning's supper.'

'Jasper,' she said. 'You kind, considerate man. How did you ever know? We *adore* mangoes. And lovely star fruit! So generous! How ever did you manage it?'

He shopped, Mother.

'I went to the markets in town,' he said modestly. 'While you were at the church.'

'Oh, Jasper! So thoughtful!' Elizabeth cried, clasping the fruit against her chest. 'You're like a son to me!'

∞

Stupidly, later on, I tried to explain some tenets of our faith to Jasper. I don't know why he needles me so much about it. On and on, pushing for details. He is especially fascinated by—or so he claims—the Eucharist.

'But the ghastliness of it!' he cried.

'The mystery,' I said.

'A soggy bit of bread, Christ's flesh, and the red wine, his blood!' he said, sneering unpleasantly.

'I haven't explained it very well,' I said, moving my chair back, hoping to escape his . . . what was it? Aftershave?

I noticed then that even his sideburns were pomaded.

'Transubstantiation,' Jasper said, smacking his lips—in love with the word.

'Yes,' I said, wishing he'd be done with it.

'All right,' he said, fixing me with his deep green eyes. 'Aside from this gory snack, what's on offer, Eleanora? The life hereafter?'

'Naturally,' I said. I felt a tumbling in my stomach. Fear.

'Survival of the individual consciousness? A new disembodied existence? A bit of a yawn, don't you think?' he sneered. 'As if one lifetime wasn't enough.'

'God made us to know Him, to love Him, to serve Him in this world and to be happy with Him in the next,' I said. 'It's——'

'Heaven! It sounds far-fetched, but better than oblivion, I suppose,' Jasper drawled. 'Even atheists yearn to find life on Mars . . .'

'Still, limbo sounds particularly unappealing,' he said.

'Forget I mentioned limbo,' I said.

'Then, *this* behaviour or *that* manner of thinking will land you in hell,' he said, sneering happily, 'and that behaviour and/or those thoughts will grant you a reprieve and—what else?'

'It's not that simple,' I said.

'By the look of him,' he said, nodding at the crucified Christ figure hanging on the wall, 'hideous suffering will guarantee heaven?'

'It's not——' I said.

'I know, I know,' he said. 'I've been down at the library, reading the lives of the saints——'

'Oh, you've been researching us, have you?' I said.

'It's just all so interesting,' he said. 'Some of those saints were sick as sailors, if you catch my drift. St Veronica! St Emiliana! Agatha!——'

'Oh, yes, the martyrs,' I said. 'Not all saints are martyrs.'

'Not all martyrs are saints,' he said, and smirked. 'St Appollonia! St Lucy! Silly Maria Goretti——'

'Oh!' I said. 'Virginity is precious . . .'

'For traffickers in child-flesh, perhaps,' said Jasper.

'It isn't all meant to be literal, anyway,' I said.

'But the message is clear. Suffering is good. And for what? A place close to God. Fabulous!' he said insolently. 'Presupposing God is the best of company, which I very much doubt.'

'It's his *love*,' I said.

'What do you know about love?' Jasper snorted.

'Don't you have a religion, Jasper?' I said.

'No,' he said edgily. 'Do you have a problem with that?'

'Of course not,' I said.

'But,' he said. 'But you can't imagine how I can exist, can you? You know, Eleanora, sometimes I do think I'm really missing out. My parents were atheists. Staunch, staunch atheists, you understand. Then again, sometimes I think the only reason to ram religion down one's offsprings' throats is so that they can reject it later on—handily averting the embarrassment of having a cult attender in the family.'

'What do you mean?' I said, too sharply.

'What I said,' he said, staring at me.

'Tell me about the Trinity again,' he said, then.

'Oh, Jasper,' I said. 'Please. I can't.'

'Just say their names,' he said.

'The Father, the Son, and the Holy Spirit,' I said impatiently.

'Another reference to alcohol, you see,' he said.

I said nothing. There is simply no point in discussing these things with such a creature.

'All very mysterious,' he said.

'It is a mystery, precisely,' I said. 'Even Catholics have trouble understanding.'

'It's hard to imagine grown people swallowing such nonsense,' he said. 'No offence meant.'

'What do you believe in then?' I said, furious.

'Oh, I believe in Elvis,' he said lightly.

'He's dead,' I said.

'So's Jesus,' said Jasper. He smiled, turned sharply on his heels, and stalked out of the room.

He is a beastly fellow. A real beast.

45

SATURDAY. JASPER, FOR ONCE, had an engagement. While Elizabeth was out, I searched the house. I was looking for the doll-room key.

And where did I finally find it? It was in a green glass lidded jar, on Elizabeth's bedside table. Beside her bed . . .

The room reeked of Blue Grass—although there is nothing in it of cut or uncut lawns, blue or otherwise, that I can detect—Elizabeth's signature scent.

My God! I thought. She outpongs Jasper, almost.

While there, I noted various ramshackle piles of clothing, balls of dust, and clumps of loose haircombings.

Well! I thought, amazed. It's perfectly squalid in here! For all her cries of *my* room's air of base neglect!

Think, I told myself.

But I could not remember what direction I'd heard his footsteps coming from, that night.

Then, my heart leaping into my mouth, I heard her heavy tread coming up the driveway.

I scampered guiltily down, and positioned myself in the dining room, by the ironing—which I had abandoned hours before.

'Well!' said Elizabeth, throwing her hat off and fluffing out her hair. 'That was an extraordinarily draining visitation!'

'It's fiendishly hot out there!' she said.

'What?' she said. '*What*? Is it my hair?'

'No,' I mumbled.

'You seem to have forgotten how to talk,' Elizabeth said dismissively.

She plugged the iron back in, and began to vigorously work through the pile of tea-towels beside me.

'Well,' she said, at last. 'You made the right decision in staying behind.'

'Our Josephine,' she said, 'is in very poor condition. Of course, I saw to all her neglected needs. Iris is never up to much at the best of times. And the house! The house is in a state of constant cluttered mess and turmoil. I found the kitchen in an appalling pickle. And, of course, there was no food in the fridge. I don't know what they planned to give us all for lunch!'

'Dymphna helped out. Reluctantly, as usual,' she said. 'The ninny.'

She turned the iron towards me and pressed the steam button, and it hissed *Hell* at me.

I passed her another tea-towel.

'I asked Dymphna to pop down to the Mall to pick up a few provisions, and a cake, which of course I'd pay for—such an expense, which I can ill afford. Well!' she cried. 'The nuisance! Said she couldn't stand the bright lights in the supermarket! Said they made her head ache! "Don't be ridiculous," I said. Of course, she put on an act, and got her own way.'

'I tell you,' she said, glowering. 'I'm fed up to the neck with the wretched woman.'

'So,' she went on, 'I left her to do the dishes—make a few vague passes at them, as usual—and I went off to the Mall. My feet! And, needless to say, when I returned I found everything simply left! She is completely undisciplined!'

'"Oh?" I said to her. "I thought you were going to handle things here, Dymphna?" I said. And do you know what she said to me?'

She turned, the iron in her hand. *Hell*, it hissed.

'"Oh," she said. "You are so much better at that sort of thing, Elizabeth. I've been telling Josephine stories to entertain her,"' Elizabeth recounted, lipless with derision.

'Well! You know as well as I that Dymphna cannot entertain herself!' she cried. '"Have you done *anything* towards our lunch?" I said. "Oh yes," she said. "The table is set, I think."'

'She thinks! Of course, it was not done as I would have done it. And after lunch, which I fixed entirely, I was left with all the dishes!' she said, delivering a resentful stare at the same time as another hiss of the iron. 'Well! I fully expected Dymphna to sneak out of doing the clearing up—which she did, in a very devious manner.'

'I only said,' Elizabeth said, 'in a very resigned tone, I might add, "Oh, all right. I'll do all the work. As usual." Off she went!

Raving like a madwoman at me about I don't know what. Running about and slamming doors!'

She turned and fixed me with her bright blue eyes.

'She's not in her right mind,' she said.

'Perhaps she just needs a rest,' I said uneasily.

'Dymphna?' she laughed. 'Oh, a leopard never changes its spots!'

I stared at the floor, feeling sick.

Elizabeth ironed with furious motions. The only sound, the hiss of steam.

'And what about you?' she said abruptly, so that I jumped. 'Have you finished hemming your new curtains?'

'No,' I said. 'I haven't started yet, actually.'

'Oh,' she said, her voice stiffening. 'That was ostensibly the reason for your not coming.'

'I had . . . a pain,' I said.

'I can't understand why you are so unreliable,' she said, ironing sadly.

'I'll do the curtains later,' I said. 'They're very nice.'

Although, really, I would have preferred to choose my own. I would have liked lemon and pale blue, with lavender trim, or lilac and white, with ice-green piping . . .

But Elizabeth chooses all my furnishings. After all, as she says, she pays for them. Although I do offer, I do . . .

'Later,' she said. 'Later! Indeed.'

'Oh, well,' she sighed. 'I can't make you, can I? As per usual, you are determined to do as you wish.'

'Honestly, Mother,' I said. 'I'll get them done before I go to bed.'

She rolled her eyes and sighed mightily, and hissed her iron at me again.

But I did not finish the curtains, because I was thinking: If someone's 'not in their right mind'—where are they?

In their wrong mind? Is there such a place? What constitutes it? Is it the left mind, the sinister mind? The unconscious mind? The *hell* mind?

And, how do they ever get back again?

46

'DARL?' OTTO SAID, TODAY. 'Whip over to the Church of McDonald's and throw some money on the plate for me. I'll have my usual and a Coke. *And* I'll have fries with that.'

'Oh, Otto,' I said. 'You're a shocker!'

'El,' he said back. 'You need the therapy.'

But before I left he changed his mind—thinking about his waistline, I expect.

I wandered through the Mall before I picked up our lunches. (Clarry the Chemist's sale is on this week.)

On the door of the stall of the ladies' toilet, there was some new graffiti: 'Whoever had written these shits, must be a hore.'

I was still pondering this afterwards when I saw him. He was like some third-rate James Dean, slouching against the tiled wall of Lemonhurst Mall, right outside Mrs Bean's Ice Creams (101 flavours)—staring at me, right through me. (Into the men's toilets? How strange.) Jasper! Wearing sunglasses, his hair greased back in a pompadour—reeking as usual, even at this distance, of too much Californian Poppy.

'Fancy dress day, Jasper?' I said.

'What would you know about it?' he said, his mouth set in an insolent sneer.

'Going somewhere?' I said.

'It's my half-day off. I'm just having a bit of a relax,' he said.

(One of Otto's phrases!)

'Oh,' I said. 'It's Thursday, isn't it?'

His eyes were narrowed and derisive—glinting behind the murky lenses of his dark glasses, now and then, like a flash of silver-green carp glimpsed in an overgrown pond.

'Meeting someone special?' I said, nodding at his outfit.

He wore black jeans, tight against his thighs, a black silk shirt, with a pink T-shirt underneath, and high black Cuban-heeled boots with chiselled toes.

I mean, Jasper is a clerk! Jasper is a clerk who dresses like a clerk, normally. Or rather, a clerk from a comic movie: brown polyester trousers, pastel or paisley nylon shirts, hideous mismatched ties, thick 'walk' socks and grey vinyl slip-on shoes, moccasins, or sandals, and a hand-knitted cable cardigan on the odd cool evening to keep his kidneys warm—'Lovely!' Elizabeth says.

I'd never given it much thought. But now it struck me that Jasper had been dressing up for us. All part of the impersonation.

'What's it to you?' he said.

'Just asking,' I said.

'You never know,' he said, and sneered.

'You get changed in a telephone booth?' I said.

'Ha ha,' he said. 'You know, you shouldn't judge someone by their appearance, Eleanora. You ought to know better. I have to look straight, you know, for the job.'

'And your mother,' he added slyly.

'Oh,' I said. 'Is that so?'

But I knew what he meant.

'Pays to be cautious,' he said. 'Why? You think she'd like me better like this?'

'Well, you know she's only interested in your soul,' I said.

'Yeah, you're right. But what's a soul without an outfit?' he said.

I laughed—briefly.

'That's good, Jasper,' I said. 'I didn't know you had a sense of humour.'

'Yeah?' he said. 'Well, I knew you didn't, Eleanora.'

'What do you know?' I said, feeling uncomfortable.

'Oh-ho!' he said. 'You'd be surprised.'

We stood there for a moment, watching each other.

'Haven't you something important to hurry off to?' I said.

'I revel in my idleness,' Jasper drawled.

Then suddenly his face broke into a smile. He was smiling at me, his head bent towards me, and I was enveloped in his warmth, as if—it sounds crazy—as if he was Jesus.

As if he was Jesus, all lit up with love.

'Your eyes are beautiful,' he said, then, startling me. 'You know that?'

My eyes. Well. One is the colour of gooseberries, and the other the colour of the Lemonhurst swimming pool, well-chlorinated.

'Don't be silly!' I said, blushing stupidly.

He stretched and yawned, and rubbed his forehead, which was damp with sweat, or something.

'I'd best be letting you get back to your business,' he said. 'Got a soft boss, have you, Eleanora?'

'I can come and go,' I said. 'I was just picking up some sandwiches.'

'I'll see you back at the ranch,' he said.

'All right,' I said.

'Tonight,' he said.

'Well, of course,' I said.

'Dinner,' he said.

'Don't be late,' he said, and made a little sign with his fingers as if they were a gun. A friendly gun.

∞

At dinner, Jasper's hair was parted on the side again, a bit of lank silver-black fringe clinging in ribbons to his forehead. He was back in his polyester trousers and his favourite short-sleeved shirt.

'Evening, miss,' he said. 'Ma'am.'

'Isn't it a delightful night!' said Elizabeth.

'Yeah, evening, Jasper,' I said, with the beginnings of a conspiratorial smile.

He glanced up at me—distant, diffident—his mouth wearing its lopsided smile, his eyes cold again. He was back in his role of pleasant stranger.

Maybe he swaps eyes, along with the outfits?

47

MY RIGHT EYE IS blue. When I write right, I mean both right-side, and correct. My good eye, I could write. My *good* eye is blue—the right colour, according to Elizabeth. Bright blue, with a hint of grey. My left eye, my green eye, is aberrant. It shows, Elizabeth says, my double-sidedness. The evil, I suppose she means, that's in my nature.

Sometimes I imagine that my green eye is where my soul has lodged, and that its colour is my poor soul's stain.

I wonder, do some sins merely stain and others scar the soul? I suppose it depends on whether the soul is a separate entity from the self, or spirit—which may, in itself, be a separate entity from the self.

Is the soul merely the inner self? The self below the layers of personality, I mean. The deep unconscious. The self behind the self that the world is allowed to meet. The self rarely seen, and hardly known.

Can one live in ignorance of one's inner self? And is the soul this self—or is it something other? Merely a white slate, where sin is recorded and petty vileness known. A floating white oval that picks up stains. A white bin, where daily evil pools. A repository for sin.

Do other people tend their souls these days? Do others *worry*? I doubt it. People, by and large, I think, have lost interest in good and evil. Success—or the appearance of it—is the only virtue they are interested in acquiring. They go about their business as if it's all old superstition. I envy them. How pleasant, to not fear death, having denied its meaning . . .

Maybe they are right. Maybe the soul really is the unconscious—recording not the wrongs done, but the wrongs that have been done to one.

Or maybe the soul is the spirit, the spark of a person—the starlight, if you like, within. But where does it reside in the body? And where does it go at death? Back into the stars?

Maybe it is that simple. Maybe there's an end to it, there.

Do you know, book? Sometimes I have no faith. No faith at all.

No faith, but so much fear.

What am I frightened of? Everything. Anxious and guilty, always—monotonously so—as if it was my natural state, as if I was born to it. As if . . .

What am I saying?

But then the fear. The fear sweeps up on me, catches me unawares. It sweeps up out of the specks of dirt between the cupboards. Just when I have forgotten fear and am padding about, almost a normal human being—mindless, content—the fear grabs me, snakes onto me, is suddenly upon me.

Oh, it's a strong fear, a Catholic fear, a fear as all-encompassing as our God. I am small, suddenly. Above me, the hidden bodies in their monstrous rustling black, with their wrath, their perfect knowing. And my stomach churns, and the fear takes root . . .

The fear grabs me and shakes me and hisses in my ear: *Never forget to fear*.

And then it is all rolled out, the heavenly imprint—for heaven is a place of tax collectors and health inspectors, stampers and decreers, and mean-mouthed government officials. Every thought and word and deed on record. Even the deeds undone.

Fear me, it says. And its mouth is the bottomless pit.

What shall I do now? What shall I do?

Keep breathing. Act normal. It's getting harder every day.

Keep breathing. Keep breathing . . .

48

LATE THIS AFTERNOON, I came across Jasper in the dining room, studying the nativity figures on the mantle.

Jasper was dressed in his clerk's clothes. But it was Thursday. Had he been out and changed, and changed again? And where did he go, and who did he see? And why did he want us to think he was this other man?

'Baby Jesus never grows up, does he?' he said, turning towards me. 'What's this little bit of stuff wrapped round his middle?'

'That's his nappy,' I said foolishly.

'But he's made of plaster, isn't he?' said Jasper. 'Doesn't really need it.'

'You'd never have Christ *nude*,' I said.

'Precisely why he's not my sort of guy,' said Jasper dryly.

'I don't know why religious people go on and on about Jesus,' he said then. 'He never has impressed me.'

'Oh,' I said nervously. 'I suppose it takes all types.'

'Can't stand a man with a beard, myself,' he said.

Well, it's true. Jesus, in our pictures and our statues, is unromantically bearded.

Of course, I can imagine him without a beard.

Joseph, on the other hand, is such a total bore that I do not bother imagining him. He is like some uncle, silent at the family party. His nativity statue (which stands always at the rear of the group—protectively, I suppose) has an awful beard.

I expect he *did* have one. A dark beard. And black eyebrows that met at the centre. And frightening, rarely glimpsed, over-large teeth.

And then, of course, there's God, with his beard of greyish white. And the Holy Spirit, with its beard of fire!

Jasper was staring at me, smiling faintly.

I swallowed, then said piously: 'Jesus gave his life to save us.'

'From your sins,' said Jasper. 'I know.'

'Hasn't saved me,' he said, and gave a hollow laugh. 'Never mind. God loves a sinner, doesn't he?'

'Perhaps he'll do better next time round,' I said daringly.

'Well said, Eleanora!' Jasper cried, and smiled at me—his strange, lopsided grin.

'Now, Mary Magdalene I find rather more interesting than Jesus,' he said. 'The Whore with the Hair. That's my favourite part of the Bible.'

'I didn't know you read the Bible, Jasper,' I said.

'I don't,' he said. 'Do you?'

'Well,' I said. 'No . . .'

'Using her hair as a mop to wipe Jesus's feet free of the salve,' he continued, 'that he should have sold to help the poor, in my opinion.'

'Of course, there's not enough about her,' he sighed.

'I would like the Bible rather better,' I said, 'if—if—if Jesus fell in love with and married someone. Say Mary Magdalene.'

'Mmm? I'd rather they lived in sin,' said Jasper.

'Mind you, living with Jesus wouldn't have been fun,' he added. '"Where's the casserole I cooked for dinner, Jesus?" "Oh, I gave it to the poor. You don't mind, do you, darling?" What could you say?'

'Actually,' I said, 'being married to Jesus would have been a bit of a joke, with his disciples hanging round night and day.'

'Mmm,' said Jasper. 'So true.'

'Perhaps Our Lord was gay?' he drawled. 'Must remember to suggest same to our dear Elizabeth. No, consider it. All those disciples trailing around, and jealous old Judas Iscariot. It's a possibility. There's no mention of marriage, is there?'

'But who's to say he didn't marry?' I said hurriedly. 'I mean, if virtually his entire childhood could be left out of the records, who's to say a marriage wasn't omitted, for want of interest.'

'Yes, I take your point,' he said. 'It's a man's book, isn't it? Full of the sort of things that interest manly men. A sort of Hemingway in sack-cloths story. Needless to say, romantic or *sexual* love comes a low second to brotherly love. And domesticity, well! Nil interest! Nil!'

'You do read Hemingway!' I cried.

'No!' he snorted.

'There is that recipe section,' I added. 'In the Old Test——'

'Women and children being of note only insofar as they can be worked upon with miracles, brought back to life, or otherwise saved—seven devils, wasn't it?' he winked, 'like good old whorey Mary Magdalene.'

'Or,' he said, smiling wickedly, 'for a quick jig-a-jig with the lamps blown out. The women *and* children, that is.'

I blushed and swallowed.

'Women and children,' he said smoothly, 'being merely pictorial. The women lumped in with the children. And the children, herded and slaughtered like animals. Herod, and all that. You have heard of Herod?'

'For all the talk of being like little children . . .' I said.

'Poor women and children,' Jasper said. 'I'm glad I've never been either.'

I frowned, and would have followed this up, but Elizabeth was ploughing up Glass Street and rounding our gate—both arms weighed down with shopping.

'Anyway,' Jasper said dismissively, placing the Baby Jesus back in its manger, 'whatever some obscure bits of the Bible purport to say, I would think it's perfectly clear that *he* isn't coming back again.'

∞

Our house is full of holy stuff. Holy this, holy that. Now that the TV set is gone—and the clock-radio—there is nothing much else to do, from the look of the place, except sit and eat and pray.

Not that there are shrines, or anything. Not that we actually pray to the holy pictures or the statues or the other sacramentals. That would be idolatry.

Why are they there? For purposes of religious meditation? Or for display?

Jesus, Mary, and Joseph. The Pope, and various saints. (None of Mary Magdalene.)

No statues, paintings, or other representations of God in our house. He's a jealous and angry God, who won't allow his picture to be taken.

I imagine him, on a cloud, grumpy and disconsolate, and overweight. I imagine him looking like Ron, only bigger, wearing a cottonwool beard. Like Ron, wearing a long white Santa Claus suit.

The funny thing was—I realised, as I scanned the room—that we did not own a copy of the Bible. We'd never owned a copy.

Elizabeth, however, was always quoting from the Bible at me, but only from the Gospels, and only from the boring bits—the sort of thing that Father Flynn rehashed every Sunday. There was plenty there to give her pause, but she glided over it. 'Love, and charity,' she said, assuming her pious expression.

She never quoted anything that made me stop and think, though, like the weird stuff Brother Raymund dug up from the Old Testament and Revelations.

Her eyes glowed as she talked of God and his heavenly designs, and her voice softened as she prattled on and on—while her mouth told its own story, immediately returning to its melancholy folds when she fell silent. You might be excused for thinking God had disappointed, despite her claims to the contrary.

After Jasper left, I stood and stared up at the picture of Mary, Our Lady of the Rosary, and sighed. It's not a bad reproduction, but it's a lousy painting. I would never have painted her with such a simpering face.

Mary is far more mysterious in my mind. She is dark, in my mind. Her eyes are lovely, deep blue and sparkling as the night. Her skin is a light olive, with rosy cheeks—you could almost swear roses bloomed on them, the way they do in fairytales.

Her mouth is grave. Her expression serious. She has soft white feet. In my mind, she never grows older. Incredibly, as her son becomes a man, and ages, she remains as she was: untouched fifteen.

She is clean and sweet-smelling. She bathes often, in scented waters. Nothing happens to her. Or what happens leaves no stain.

An angel comes to her. Fascinating to think of her, head inclined to the queer news. Would one offer refreshments to an angel?

She bears the Son of God. And it is as if she is a slate wiped clean, a cipher. It is as if she never woke that morning.

Imagine! Bearing the Son of God, and that's it. That's all that ever happens in your life. You can't count Joseph. And then her son dies, horribly. (Of course, she got to stand at the foot of his cross, beside a prostitute. Well, I bet that made up for everything!)

I can't help but think *her* presence there, beside Jasper's Mary Magdalene, is emblematic—the Madonna and the Whore. That it is just a clever part in the book.

I can't help thinking that she was never there at all. That she is, like all women, a bearer of sons—and other than that, merely symbolic.

49

AND THEN IT HAPPENED, book. Finally. At least, I think it happened.

Last night, we were eating dinner—oyster soup, followed by butterfly prawns, with potato rosti and braised snow peas. Elizabeth had outdone herself. The meal was going swimmingly—and then Jasper ruined it.

More than ruined it.

'There's an awful odour coming from the cellar,' he said.

Smiling in a gloating kind of way?

'Pardon?' I said.

'An awful odour,' he repeated. 'It seems to be coming from the cellar region.'

'I've had a look down there,' he said, 'but I couldn't see a cause for it.'

Elizabeth blenched.

'Rats,' I said, too quickly.

'Rrrats,' I said. (Was I hysterical?) 'You remember, Mother? We put down bait, last spring. Perhaps they crawled in there to die.'

'They go outside,' Jasper said coldly—regarding me with his glassy eyes. 'Rat poison is hydrophobic, these days. It makes them thirsty.'

'Really? Perhaps they lost their way, looking for the water, and congregated there instead,' I said, and giggled.

'Last prayer before dying,' I said, laughing highly.

Elizabeth stared hard at me.

'Sorry,' I said, and burped.

'Well,' she said coolly, rising and stacking the plates. 'At table!'

'Please excuse us, Jasper,' she said. 'We are not normally so ill-behaved.'

'Not at all, ma'am,' he said, the oily boy.

'Think nothing of it, Eleanora,' he said, bowing his head graciously. 'It's only natural, after all.'

'Most unnatural, I would say,' Elizabeth said.

'I am,' Elizabeth said, returning with a dessert cake of marscapone and pear, 'so terribly sorry if our home has for you an unappealing odour, Jasper.'

Crikey, I thought. It's really the pot calling the kettle black, anyway.

'Oh, no!' he said. 'Mrs Bird! I'm, ah . . . absolutely, definitely . . . That is *not* what I meant, Mrs Bird. I do assure you. It's only . . .' he trailed off, swinging his eyes about the room.

'It's only rats, I'm sure, Jasper,' I said smoothly and firmly. 'Don't worry about it. They will rot away eventually and then there will be no more smell.'

'It could be,' said Elizabeth, suddenly, as if inspired, 'compost!'

We had no compost heap.

'Compost, on a breeze. From'—she flapped her hands about delicately here and there—'neighbouring gardens.'

'The Jumpers,' she said eagerly, 'are keen gardeners.'

'Or the lilies. Those lilies do exude a powerful aroma,' she said.

'It's more likely rotting rat carcasses,' I said, frowning.

'Yes,' she said. 'You're probably right.'

Even Jasper raised his eyebrows in surprise.

We ate our cake in silence. From time to time Elizabeth looked across at me, her eyes anxious and overbright—giving her a loony air that reminded me of Darlene.

'Jasper? More cake?' she said.

'Not for me,' he said. 'Though it's delicious. I've had so much to eat today. An unusually heavy luncheon.'

'I'm sorry,' said Elizabeth. 'The conversation.'

'Hell, no. I mean, I beg your pardon, ma'am,' he simpered. 'It's been inspiring. Two ladies on their own, braving a bit of rodent extermination. If you have any more, ah, pest problems, you must let me know. I'm quite good with the chemical combinations.'

'Oh, really?' I said. 'A science whiz?'

'No,' he said, with great deliberation. 'Just poisons. An interest in poisons.'

'Oh,' said Elizabeth.

'Oh,' I said.

And we all stared at the table.

50

OUR HOUSE IS GLOOMY. 'Shady,' Elizabeth says. 'Cool in summer.' But it is a dark place. Some parts of it are dank.

A woman once visited who had an allergy to fungi, and she sneezed and sneezed until her eyes ran, and then she had to leave.

'I'm afraid,' said Elizabeth to Ron—who was alive then, 'that Mrs Percy is not a very satisfactory guest, in any case. She did not display one jot of interest in the dolls, or our travels.'

I can't remember what Ron said back . . .

∞

After Jasper's comments, I waited.

He *knows*.

I know he knows about us.

How long has he known? How long has he known, saying *nothing*?

Elizabeth, since, has avoided my eyes, and intensified her house cleaning.

'I'm so embarrassed!' she said, this morning.

'Oh, Mrs B,' said Jasper. 'It is I who should be ashamed. My rudeness! I only wanted to alert you girls to a possible plumbing problem.'

'How thoughtful!' cried Elizabeth.

But she did not cease her efforts: soon every room sported an air-freshener, or an aromatic plant.

∞

Most evenings, since the rat conversation, Jasper and I have talked—as if something was decided?—while Elizabeth was in the kitchen, stirring, sifting, adding salt or cream. (Or was I imagining this? Perhaps it was my religious instruction that had brought us, finally, somewhat closer. Or time . . . just time.)

He'd had two brothers, he said, last night. Twins, who'd died at birth: Roger and Randy. (Americans?)

'How sad!' I said, wondering whether or not to believe his disarming confidences. Or if it mattered.

'Like Elvis,' said Jasper.

'Only Elvis lived,' I said.

'Lives,' he said smirking.

'Elvis lives,' he repeated.

'Don't be silly,' I said.

'He rose again,' he said. 'I've a book of photos to prove it, if you want to see. There's more evidence to prove Elvis rose from the dead than there is to indicate your God ever walked this earth.'

'I'm teasing you, Eleanora,' he said.

'Well, I sort of knew that,' I said.

'You *are* a liar,' he said lightly.

Then Elizabeth entered, swinging the door with her backside, hands encased in the giant lobster mitts, and the conversation became general again.

I waited for I don't know what, watching him carefully, flirting—yes, that is what I was doing. Flirting with Jasper Pease!

Strangely, I found I began to enjoy myself. I am quite good at flirting, I have discovered.

∞

'Elvis colours,' Jasper whispered, tonight, when Elizabeth was back in the kitchen.

'I'm sorry?' I said.

He gestured at my clothes.

I wasn't wearing anything new or different. A plain black skirt I wear for work, and a blossom-pink blouse with a Peter Pan collar.

'Elizabeth made it,' I said. 'Elizabeth makes almost all my clothes.'

She sews my clothes and trims my hair. It's not always what I had in mind for myself.

'If she had the time, I swear she'd sew your underwear for you,' he said smoothly, as if he'd read my mind.

'Pardon me?' I said.

But Jasper merely smiled and tapped his teeth.

'How old are you, Jasper?' I said, over the stewed peaches.

'Older than time itself,' he whispered.

Elizabeth chuckled. She was a master of the musical chuckle.

'The young have no idea,' she said. 'No idea at all.'

'Youth is wasted on them, isn't it?' he said.

They both laughed merrily.

'Still, in a culture that fears death, youth will always be admired,' he drawled.

'Yes, but——' I said.

'I told you,' he said. 'Older than Father Time.'

'I don't believe you're lying,' I said.

He winked at me.

Well, I am not a teenager myself. I would say—in earth terms—that Jasper is five or seven or possibly nine years older than me. That would make him, at most, thirty-eight or nine.

Appearances can be deceiving. His skin is so moist. A sort of slick lies on it. It is lined, but not very lined. Sometimes it looks quite cratered, from old acne scars, I expect. Sometimes it simply gleams.

Perhaps he uses some special cream on it? Perhaps it is accountable for that faint but lingering smell? Perhaps his age-defying cream is made of *fish eggs*?

∞

It is strange. In the day I am calm, but at night—when the others are asleep, and I am alone in my room, in the darkness—I am full of fear.

My heart beats in the cage of my body, and I am buried alive with fear.

51

'OTTO,' I SAID, YESTERDAY. 'You know how you said . . .'
  'Said,' he said. 'Yes. Said a lot of things.'
  'Oh,' I said. 'You know.'
  'Said what?' he said.
  'Oh, about models, and everything,' I said.
  'God, El,' he said. 'Are you still on about that?'
  'No,' I said. 'Not really.'
  'You have a distinctive look, El,' he said, 'but not a look that lends itself to the two-dimensional form of the photograph.'
  'Oh,' I said.
  'Can I put it any plainer?' he said, exasperated.
  'Oh,' I said. 'I remember. Irregular.'
  'This is not a bad thing, not a bad thing of itself at all,' he said.
  'You don't *want* to look bland, do you?' he said.
  'No, of course not,' I said.
  But I went to the hairdresser's after work—a real hairdresser! a thin and supercilious person, but still——and had my hair washed and trimmed, anyway.

∞

'Do I look . . . nice?' I said, that night—my hair, for once, not in tight plaits.
  'What?' said Jasper vaguely. 'Of course, you do, Eleanora. You always look very nice.'
  'Niceness is, I think, an attitude, Ellen,' said Elizabeth neatly. 'An indication of one's state of mind.'
  'Oh, well, in that case,' I said.

'Quite,' said Elizabeth.

'Jasper?' I said. 'I do look nice? My hair?'

Had anyone even noticed?

'Nice enough,' he said, and winked.

'Thank you, Jasper,' I said quietly.

'It's not *nice* to talk so much when your dinner's getting cold,' said Elizabeth.

'My apologies, ma'am,' said Jasper, and dug back in.

'Oh, that's quite all right, Jasper. Of course, I didn't mean . . .' she said.

'Yes, sorry, Mother,' I mumbled.

How easy it is to say sorry. I'm sorry, so sorry, I'll never do it again. Take ten Our Fathers and three Hail Marys . . .

∞

'Heavens!' said Otto, today. 'Will you stop moping, El. I paid you a compliment.'

'I know that,' I said.

'Do you?' he said.

'Of course,' I said. Although I didn't.

'Good,' he said.

'As if I want my photo taken standing next to a lot of mouldy mince pies,' I said.

'Or tampons,' he said. 'Or floral toilet soaps.'

'Or hideous old joints of lamb,' I said.

'Exactly,' he said. 'That's the spirit, El.'

'Our culture,' he said, sighing, 'is so shallow.'

'It worships youth, and such,' he said.

'I'm young,' I said.

'Yes, but . . .' he said.

Then we were quiet.

'So few young people realise that their youth is valuable. That they can sell it,' he said airily then. 'And then it's too late . . .'

'It's sad, isn't it?' he said, smiling. 'The world.'

'Oh, yes,' I said.

And we were quiet.

'Otto?' I said.

'What now?' he said.

'I was just wondering,' I said. 'How much of me is, well, on display?'

'Good Lord!' he said.

'You know,' I said.

'Know what?' he said.

'Does *something* show?' I said.

'Oh, El,' he cried. 'We're not sending out distress signals, are we, love?'

'Don't be silly,' I said. 'I just want to know.'

'Well,' he said, shrugging.

'Does my character show in my eyes?' I said.

'Oh!' he said. 'Heaps. It's really scary. Sometimes I wonder if I should call the police.'

'Don't banter with me when I'm being serious, Otto,' I said.

'If I don't,' he said, 'who will?'

'Jasper might,' I said slyly.

'Old fish-breath!' Otto shouted. 'The Californian Poppy! You must be joking!'

'He is,' I said, 'quite . . .'

'Smelly?' Otto suggested. 'Odiferous?'

'Quite discerning, actually,' I said.

Otto doubled over, spluttering with laughter.

'Oh, ex-*squeeze* me,' he said, recovering.

'For heaven's sake, El!' he said. 'I doubt he's your type.'

'What are you saying?' I said.

'You know what I'm saying,' he said. 'I thought you told me he struck you as distinctly gay.'

'I'm not so sure of that, after all,' I said. 'In fact, I've changed my mind.'

'Oh, spare me!' he cried.

'*You've* changed *your* mind, and he's obligingly changed his sexual orientation? I don't think so,' Otto said.

'You know what your problem is, El? You're surrounded by women. Females, rather,' he said. 'They're a little too disembodied to be women.'

'There are too many females in your life,' he said, throwing his hands on his hips and staring at me.

'Well!' I said. 'I don't think that's quite right. There's you, and Father Flynn, and there was Brother Raymund——'

'Who?' he said.

'And Sylvester, and now Jasper,' I said quickly.

'Precisely,' said Otto.

52

I CAME HOME FROM work this afternoon, and found Jasper metamorphosed into the rebel again, sitting at the dining table with a handsome, blond-haired man.

It was Thursday, and Elizabeth was spending the day with Marlene, dictating the lay-out of the parish jumble sale. I wonder if he knew this?

(Thursdays are definitely the days to look out for. On Thursday mornings he goes out looking like Clark Kent, after retirement. Thursday night, the look's the same. But somewhere in between he slips his skins.)

'Eleanora? This is my brother,' Jasper said, with a flourish.

'Oh, Jasper, you're such a hoot!' cried the handsome—the overly handsome—blond man. 'You're a walking witty art statement.'

'Isn't Jesse just like a Greek god,' Jasper said. 'Isn't he angelic?'

But I was looking at *him*. His greasy lank hair was combed back and quiffed—elaborately arranged. One strand casually dripped over his forehead. It was an Elvis hairdo. A pompadour?

Hair parted to the side is middle-aged and reliable. In the middle is tragi-comic. Forward is youthful. Long is sexy, isn't it? Combed back is sophisticated, unless the head is lumpy. And back with a quiff and a duck's tail is loutish and rebellious. It's code.

Who was he really? This lewd drawling creature, dressed all in black like some inversion of a priest?

It struck me then that, in my attempt to allay his suspicions, I had almost forgotten my suspicions of him.

'We're brothers, Eleanora,' Jasper said. 'Isn't that grand. Jesse here is my little brother.'

The blond man gave an hysterical high-pitched titter.

'Goodness!' I said, startled from my reverie. 'I didn't—— You don't look anything alike.'

'Oh, we're not blood brothers!' Jasper cried.

'Not?' I said.

'We're *twins*,' he semi-shouted.

The man was obsessed.

'Yes,' the blond man simpered. 'On paper at any rate.'

They both giggled hysterically.

Was this that drug I'd read about, this ECT?

'That's lovely,' I said politely.

'You hear that, Jesse?' cried Jasper.

'Have you offered Jesse some tea?' I said. 'Please make yourselves at home. There are biscuits in the tin labelled——'

'Biscuits!' shouted Jasper.

'I'll put the kettle on,' I said, moving stiffly from the room.

I have been kept on such a tight lead—I have barely surfaced to knowing anyone, really. Outside family. And then Otto. Who is, of course, a very old friend now. (Perhaps I am too formal? Or old-fashioned?)

Jasper soon followed me out.

'Will your brother stay for dinner?' I said.

'My brother of blood,' said Jasper peculiarly. 'No, unfortunately.'

'He's quite unearthly in his beauty, isn't he?' he said.

'Not my type,' I said shortly.

'I shouldn't think a girl as innocent as you would have a type,' said Jasper.

'I'm not innocent!' I cried.

'Only teasing, Eleanora,' he said.

'Well!' I said. 'I have some work to do——'

'Needlework,' he said. 'Most pressing, I assume.'

'Excuse me,' I said.

'I'm pleased to meet you, Jesse,' I said, as I passed through the dining room.

'Pleasure's all mine, ma'am,' said Jesse, and exploded with laughter.

'Shh,' said Jasper.

I looked over my shoulder as I climbed the stairs. They were both lying on their backs, rolling about on the floor, and shrieking like five-year-olds.

∞

'Well!' said Elizabeth, on her return. 'The usual busy day.'

There was no sign of Jasper or his brother.

'Marlene, as always, was most insistent,' she said. 'I finally talked her around to the idea of enlisting the aid of some of the others. They may be daft, but they are at least tractable and, as work horses, will be of enormous assistance.'

'Count your lucky stars you're not living with Marlene, dear,' she said, shuddering dramatically.

'Poor Frank!' she said. 'She has him on toast!'

'He's a nice fellow, really,' she said. 'Always cheerful and obliging. But useless . . .'

'Then Dymphna arrived, looking frazzled,' she said. 'Well. It's not surprising. She is nearly driven mad by all those boys and has not a clue as to how to control them.'

'She really is a most hopelessly incompetent mother,' Elizabeth added, with some satisfaction.

'Well,' she said, 'as you can imagine, knowing Dymphna, who is incapable of doing anything sensible or constructive, and is *such* a dithering nong, I had to work very hard. Very, very hard. But I soon had them sorted. Oh, yes, I did. I think it will be an utter corker of a fete!'

'But I'm ravenous. Ravenous! Marlene cooked a lunch for us. Dry meat,' she said vaguely. 'Then Iris arrived, unannounced, the nuisance. She is always boring me with her health problems, banging on and on. Still, she was duly impressed with my work on the stall plans, and so on. Really, a very productive day! So nice to be in the bosom of the family!'

How suffocating, I thought. Then started at my own horridness.

'And your day, Ellen?' she said, then, staring.

'Oh, work,' I said. 'I took the skirts you wanted to the dry-cleaners.'

'Oh, that was a nice little outing for you, wasn't it?' she said.

Well, really.

'Mother,' I said. 'Did you know . . .'

'What?' she said. 'I hope you remembered to take them to the right place. I'm always the thrifty one, aren't I?'

'Yes, Mother,' I said. 'Don't worry.'

'What was it?' she said.

'Oh, nothing,' I said.

'Mother?' I said, my voice like a squeak, as I pushed the magazine in front of her. 'I've seen a lovely colour scheme for a bedroom.'

After Jasper had teased me about my clothes I'd done some

thinking: Elizabeth chose all the furniture and coverings in my room. Everything, really, is to Elizabeth's taste. My tapestry wool, my watercolour paints. All the stay-in-your-tower stuffs were bought by Mother.

'Mmph,' she sniffed. 'What of it?'

'Well,' I said. 'I thought——'

'Don't be ridiculous!' she said. 'Redo your room? After all the work I've done on it?'

'Absolutely not,' she spluttered. 'Of all the ingratitude! I would feel a positive *foreigner* in my own home.'

'All right, Mother,' I said, closing the magazine.

'And throw that trash away,' she said.

'It's Otto's,' I said.

'Oh,' she said, rolling her eyes.

'And where is Jasper, pray tell?' she said.

'At work,' I said, blinking. 'I suppose.'

53

'SAW YOUR FRIEND JASPER at the Alphabet Bar the other night,' said Otto, this morning, as I was fixing our instant coffees.

'Oh?' I said. 'What sort of place is that?'

'*The* most notorious pick-up bar,' he said, eying me meaningfully.

'Oh?' I said. 'You go there often?'

'Well, I'm not a fixture,' he snapped.

He stared at me crossly, then sighed.

'Actually, I don't go to these places often at all,' he said. 'Fingal wouldn't like it.'

'Fingal?' I said brightly. 'Is that your cat?'

'My lover,' he said. 'Really, El.'

'You never said,' I said, embarrassed.

'You never asked,' he said smoothly.

'How long?' I said. 'Have you been together, I mean?'

'Twenty-five years,' he said proudly.

'Good God,' I said.

'Watch that tongue!' he said. 'Thought we were all toms, out on the prowl, did you?'

'Fingal sounds like a suitable name for a large tabby,' I said, to hide my embarrassment.

'I'll tell him that,' he said. 'He'll like that. He'll purr.'

'So . . .' I said. 'Was Fingal with you, that night?'

'What night?' he said, stirring his coffee and smiling fondly into his mug.

'The night you saw Jasper,' I said.

'Oh, right,' he said. 'No, he wasn't. He was watching a cup final.'

'God!' I said.

'Watch that profanity, Eleanora, or I'll have to inform your mother,' Otto said waggishly. 'Didn't think our sort watched sport, either? My dear, you really have lived a sheltered life.'

'We haven't even got a TV any more,' I blurted.

'Well, that is deprivation,' he said. 'I shall alert the authorities.'

'Child abuse,' he said gaily. 'My poor dear.'

'But that night?' I said.

'Oh, well,' he said. 'I met a friend for a few drinks and a harmless squiz at what's about. We ended up, after a long night of sightseeing, at the Alphabet.'

'And?' I said.

'And that,' he said dramatically, 'is where I saw your lodger.'

'Jasper Pease? You're sure?' I said.

'The allegedly odiferous Jasper, indeed,' he said. 'Why so anxious, little one?'

'Was he . . .' I said. 'Who was he . . .'

'Darling, he was *anyone's*,' Otto said.

'Oh,' I said blankly.

'He certainly is a tart,' Otto said.

'With *men*?' I said.

'Well, yes, El,' he said. 'You don't go to a gay men's bar to pick up women.'

'Oh,' I said. 'Of course.'

'How can you be so sure it was him?' I said. 'I mean——'

'He introduced himself,' Otto said.

'Oh!' I said. 'How odd. Did he remember you from somewhere?'

'Where, darling? The social pages?' Otto cried. 'I have never met the man before in my life. He just bowled up to me, introduced himself, and then we had quite a chat, let me tell you.'

'Did you smell him?' I said. 'That fishy——'

'Californian Poppy,' Otto said. 'Quite over-powering. And a dreadful case of nightclub pallor. Otherwise——'

'What did you talk about?' I said.

'Well, you, naturally,' he said.

'Me?' I said. 'What did he say?'

'Oh, that your home situation was rather strange. Well, I knew that,' sighed Otto. 'Let me think: "I'm living with Victoria and Albert," he said. "It's most amusing." "Victoria's a surprisingly good cook, too," he said. "A woman of many alarming talents." Or something equally ambiguous.'

I felt a blush rise up my neck.

'You think I'm making this up, pulling your leg, don't you?' he said. 'Think I'm having a jolly wheeze?'

I was going to ask him if he knew Jasper's brother. Because a man who looked quite like him was leaving the studio as I came back from lunch. Of course, he might have been anyone, really. It was just the hair. The unnatural gleam. ('Isn't he angelic?' Jasper said.)

'No,' I said. 'I believe you. But——'

'But,' Otto said. 'Beware of buts, Eleanora.'

'So he's definitely——' I said.

'Well, unless he was there as a roving reporter,' said Otto. 'In that case, he should win an award. He was certainly throwing himself into his research.'

'Oh,' I said. 'What else did he say?'

'Said he'd heard so much about me. Said you loved your work,' he smiled. 'Made a pass at my companion. Then disappeared into the gents.'

'Was in there a long time,' he added, winking.

'Oh!' I said.

'Probably having a toot,' he said kindly.

'A ——?' I said

'Snort of coke,' he said. 'Cocaine.'

'Oh!' I said. 'Really!'

'Oh, El, you don't want to hear about this sort of thing,' he said.

'Yes, I do,' I said. 'I do.'

'Not from me,' he said, and his mouth clamped shut.

He barely spoke for the rest of the day. (But was he smiling to himself, secretly smiling? Were he . . . Did he . . . Were he and Jasper *friends?*)

54

YOU CAN IMAGINE MY amusement, this afternoon, when Elizabeth suggested I ask Jasper to the St Clare's social.

'I don't need a date,' I said, and tried to change the subject.

'Jasper's a very nice man. You don't know where these things might lead,' she said, her blue eyes bulging.

'Jasper's gay, Mother,' I said flatly. 'I don't think a dance with me at the social's going to change his bias.'

'What did you say?' she trumpeted.

'I said, Jasper's gay,' I said.

'That's a bald-faced lie!' she cried. 'Why in the name of heaven would you make up such a pointless dreadful lie?'

'Pff!' she sniffed. 'I know otherwise.'

'It's not a lie, and it isn't dreadful. Not to him,' I said. 'Or me. Otto's gay. I like gay men. All the men I meet are gay.'

'Even Jasper's brother is gay,' I babbled on. 'Though maybe they're just blood brothers—not *blood* brothers, if you know what I mean.'

'What nonsense are you talking now?' she said, and laughed—her laugh like a bark. 'You've been eating too much cheese, my girl. Why, Jasper's an only child. He's the only child of two only children. There isn't even a second cousin about, he told me. Which is why he appreciates our family atmosphere.'

She smiled and clucked her tongue affectionately at this. Then she peered up at me curiously, and sighed, as if she was now certain she had hatched an idiot child.

'And as for Otto Horsefield. Well, dear,' she sighed again, and shook her head. 'As a woman of the world, I can tell you he is a *little* asexual—and what in blazes is wrong with that? There's something of a relief in knowing one's employer has other things on his mind, I can tell you. Why, I had to fend off several of the interns with a knife! There's nothing wrong with a low sex drive.'

'Mother!' I said. 'You should see the calendar in Otto's toilet!'

'Enough,' she said, and held her hand up like a traffic cop.

Must buy white gloves, I thought.

'I don't want to talk about toilets over the evening meal,' she said, her lips curled with distaste. 'You'll kindly change the subject and do the vegetables.'

'Of course,' I said.

Best to leave her on simmer.

'But don't go getting ideas about Jasper and me,' I said.

'A little dance!' she said. 'A little dance at the church social. There's no harm in it! Even Father Flynn will be doing his bit.'

'Next you'll be telling me Father Flynn's a fairy. Ha ha ha,' she said.

'Well, no,' I said. 'Not precisely. I think it's more small boys with him, although he tries to keep a lid on it.'

'I didn't hear that,' she said. 'I did not hear that.'

'You really are the limit,' she said.

'In my day, in my day,' she said, her voice rising, 'you could be jailed for exhibiting such a perverted sense of humour. And before you treat me to some more of it, there's nothing funny about jokes like that, nothing funny at all, unless you mean peculiar.'

She turned and faced me, her lips pursed and her furrowed face scrunched down onto her neck.

'Well, I don't think——' I said.

'*I* think! *I* don't think! Who do you think you are with all your opinions? Your *filth*,' she said. 'Nobody thinks this way, and nobody wants to hear this sort of thing.'

She gazed at me levelly, her mouth thin with disgust, then she spat out a sigh.

'I don't know where we went wrong with you,' she said. 'I swear I don't. Sometimes I think it's the devil himself who gets into you. Sometimes . . .'

She sighed again and turned away, busying herself by the sink.

'Yes?' I said.

'It doesn't matter,' she said.

'No, go on,' I said. 'Don't hold back on my account.'

'Some things are better left unsaid. You'd do well to remember that,' she said. 'Now check the potatoes.'

'Done,' I said, putting them to drain, then adding a dollop of butter and putting them back in the pot again.

We stood and stared at one another.

'I know!' she said. 'Let's say the rosary, to clear the air of this perversion.'

'Oh, Mother!' I said. But her face was suddenly so sadly frog-like that I gave in.

We sat at the dining table with our rosary beads—mine silver and pearl and Mother's ebony—and, at speed, we muttered our Hail Marys and Glory Bes.

As we were nearing the end, Jasper came home.

'What a beautiful scene!' he said. 'Mother and daughter in prayer. Such powerful harmony! So rare these days. You don't know how lucky you are, Mrs Bird.'

'Oh, yes,' she said modestly. 'But, please. Don't be so formal. You're with friends here, Jasper, you're with family now. Please, do call me Elizabeth. And won't you join us?'

'Well, now, I can't do that, ma'am,' he said. 'Meaning no disrespect and all. But thank you. Thank you both.'

'Thank you for *being* here,' he said, oily as a car salesman, and slipped upstairs.

We finished the rosary, and Jasper rejoined us. Then we carried the plates in, together—warm, beautiful people that we were—Elizabeth beaming, Jasper in full clerk costume.

From time to time I glanced over at him. Not once did he let the mask slip.

'Eleanora,' he said, after dessert.

Elizabeth winced.

'Eleanora,' he repeated. 'Allow me to offer you the wisdom of my greater years. Be always kind to your darling mother, Eleanora! We never know when our loved ones might be snatched from us.'

'Oh! Indeed!' cried Elizabeth. 'That is *so* true!'

'Mm,' I said. 'No, sit down, Mother, Jasper. *I'll* do the dishes.'

'She's a good girl,' I heard him say.

'She tries,' said Elizabeth, sounding unconvinced.

Well! I have no intention of asking Jasper to the church social. Zero. In fact, I very much doubt I'll go myself.

What is the point? Pimply boys and girls with eager faces. Father Flynn clicking his fingers out of time to the music and drinking too much Brandivino. Simon and Garfunkel and early Kylie Minogue. Everyone wearing crucifixes beneath their shirts . . .

∞

Once there was a boy—long, long ago—and he and I were the same, I thought. He and I were the same: rebels, but in a quiet way.

He was blond and aethereal and alabaster-skinned with a fine, fine nose. He was everything fair. He was beautiful, as I will never be.

He asked me to the St Clare's social. He asked me! Or at least I thought he asked me. And then we danced together for hours, laughing now and then at the others—but not meanly, just laughing at the absurdity (for it is absurd, isn't it, book? Why—everything!). We danced and danced, and he chose me. Or at least I thought he did.

But then I saw him, in the shadows out by the toilets, passionately kissing someone else. (We had talked and talked and we had danced, but he had never kissed me. No boy had ever kissed me. Maybe no-one ever will——) He paused in kissing this someone else and turned and saw me seeing him—and he laughed, he *laughed* at me—and I saw that he was kissing Tony Desmond.

They laughed at me and I went back in, and for the rest of the night he did not speak to me, only sneered when he looked my way, and I did not speak to him.

Well, I had never drunk before, and someone always spikes the social's punch, so I drank copiously then, and woke up on the wooden floor to the sound of muted snickering, and found my dress up round my waist and my big white knickers sticking out, among other things—and beside me on the floor, like a horrid blood-red omelette, was a pool of half-dried vomit.

Jane O'Shea fetched Father Flynn to drive me home. All the way home she sat beside me, with her arm around my waist.

'It's all right, Ellie,' she whispered, her blonde curls tickling my face.

I saw that boy around about Lemonhurst and at St Clare's, but he never spoke to me again, and I never spoke to him.

Then he went to Canberra to the university to study law, and he never came back again.

And I hope he never comes back. I hope I never see him.

Well, then I agreed to marry Sylvester, didn't I, and the date was set. Elizabeth was so happy! She'd been pushing me for months and months to consider Sylvester's offer. (Anything to have a man about the house again.)

Well, I married him. It never occurred to me that Sylvester Clack would want to *kiss* me. Or the rest . . . Ha! He took his clothes off and I screamed. I screamed and ran outside and hid under a bush, dressed only in my nightie.

Still, since that time I have not had a problem with impure thoughts, book. (Count those blessings!)

55

AND THEN, LAST NIGHT—Wednesday, Circle night—Jasper came home from one of his walks. Everyone had left. Elizabeth was long gone—snoring, upstairs in her bed.

'Jesus did marry,' I said, giving the dining table a final wipe. 'I've thought it out.'

'Who?' Jasper drawled, pulling up a chair. 'Do tell.'

'Well, nuns,' I said, sitting down beside him.

'Oh?' he said.

'Well, nuns marry Jesus,' I said.

'Do they?' he said. 'How bizarre.'

'So he's had, he's still got, hundreds of thousands of wives,' I said.

'All married to a phantom,' said Jasper.

'Sad,' he said, pouring us both a glass of Elizabeth's sweet sherry.

I have never been a drinker. (In fact, I've never drunk since . . . well, *then*.) But soon we were knocking them back, he and I. Not looking at each other as we spoke vaguely of this and that, circling around the important questions.

It seemed odd to be sitting with Jasper like this, after everything that had gone before.

I looked at him—his chair tipped back, his silver-black hair gleaming with odorous pomade, his eyes half-shut, his mouth half-smiling. Who was he tonight?

It is hard to say how many different characters Jasper contains.

If someone can be so many people, I thought, haven't I the possibility of change? Why not? Become a new person, my own person, and make a new life.

Yes! I thought. I will go to see the elephants wearing their jewels. I shall ride on their backs and see all there is to see! I shall travel the world, fearlessly. And I shall not collect dolls, or tea-towels . . .

'I'll give you a dollar,' he said. 'Make that two.'

'What?' I said.

'A penny's too cheap,' he said.

'This stuff's not bad, is it?' I said, holding my glass so that the light streamed through it like honey.

'Bit sweet,' said Jasper.

'Oh, we need all the sweetness we can get, here at Chez Devil,' I said.

'What's this Chez Devil thing?' he said.

'It's French, sort of,' I said.

'I guessed that,' he said. 'Who's the devil?'

'I'm the devil here,' I said.

'You wish,' he said, laughing through his teeth.

'Hey, Eleanora? Remember Nam?' he said weirdly, some time after midnight.

'What?' I said.

'Forget it,' he said, sighing. 'You're just a baby.'

'Were you——?' I said.

'Nah, I don't remember it, either,' he said. 'Just footage on TV.'

I turned and stared at him. His skin was suffused with light—a trick of the sherry?

He laughed—a thin high whinny, his mouth stretched tightly over his teeth.

'I'm not as old as you think, Eleanora,' he said, leaning abruptly closer.

'I don't think you're so old, Jasper,' I said.

But close up I could see his face was covered with a network of fine expression lines—of sorrow, of cunning, of kindness?

'Of course you do,' he said, leaning back in his chair and laughing softly to himself.

'Ever *watch* TV?' he said. 'Or you two just sit around your whole lives, clicking your rosary beads?'

'Oh, I've watched it,' I said. 'A long time ago.'

'But you grew out of it,' he said.

'Mother sold it,' I said.

'Shame,' he said.

'It was my only pleasure,' I said. My words came out like spit.

'Shame,' he repeated. 'A girl needs her pleasures.'

'I have lived here all my life,' I said then, thickly. 'In this fucking house.'

'I didn't know you swore, Eleanora,' he said. 'I didn't know you drank and swore.'

'I didn't either,' I said. 'I don't.'

'I think I might just be the slightest bit inebriated,' I said. 'God! Mother would *die*!'

'Darling,' said Jasper, 'you're pissed.'

And he poured us both another one.

'Did you ever stone a toad?' he said lazily.

'No, of course not!' I said, alarmed and disappointed. 'Were you such a cruel little boy?'

'I never stoned a toad, Eleanora,' he sighed. 'My father did, though. More than once. He'd kill anything alive.'

'Spiteful bastard,' he said.

'I don't like seeing a bird shot down, or a rabbit caught in a snare,' he said, leaning closer and fixing me with his sea-coloured eyes. They were more blue than green tonight. Aqua. Aquamarine . . .

'It's been terrible watching the pair of you,' he said quietly then. 'Like watching a snake fascinate a bird. You ever see that, Eleanora?'

'I am a Bird,' I said foolishly—although I felt as if my heart had stopped.

'Silly,' he said. 'Silly little Eleanora.'

I felt a sob shudder through my body.

'Was he kind to you?' I said.

'I don't see much of my father,' Jasper said. 'Let's put it that way. In fact, I've avoided the prick for twenty years.'

He turned away, and poured the sherry higher in our glasses.

'Still,' he said. 'I'm not proud of some of the things I've done, either.'

'What sort of things?' I said.

'Oh, things,' he said. 'Better forgotten.'

'Oh,' I said.

'Yeah,' he said, grinning, and clinking his glass to mine.

'Eleanora?' he said, then, slyly.

'Yes, Jasper?' I said.

'What's the most dreadful thing you've ever done?' he said.

Was he pushing me to confess to him?

Was I going to?

'Come to bed,' I said, instead, surprising myself—and he followed me up the stairs, and into my room.

'Never had a girlfriend,' he said softly, standing at the foot of my bed.

'Not ever,' he said.

He flashed me a look.

'Oh, it's nothing like that,' he said. 'What you're thinking.'

His sea-eyes gleamed at me, the irises almost totally submerged by the dark pool of the pupils. His skin was shining.

'Never felt I had a body,' he said. 'Never felt I had one of my own.'

'Not flesh and bones,' he said, unbuttoning his shirt and trousers, and slipping himself free of them.

'Never done this, never done anything like this,' he kept repeating, as he edged his way towards the bed.

Like a merman dragging himself out of the depths of a pond, he climbed over the bedbase, crawled along the length of the bed, the length of my body.

∞

I woke this morning with a fluttering feeling of expectancy behind my breastbone. Jasper was gone.

I sniffed the air experimentally. My nose was blocked, my mouth was dry, my tongue was thick. All I could smell was the sweet sick liquory scent of my own breath. My head——

I lay there for some time, and gradually pieces of the night before filtered back to me. My heart began to pound as I remembered.

Then Elizabeth shrieked: 'Your eggs are getting cold!'

My stomach lurched at the thought of breakfast.

I knew I should get up and wash and dress. But I stayed in bed, and ran my hands over my naked flesh, and tried to recall exactly what we'd done—what he'd done to me.

We were like two fish, darting at and sliding over one another.

Perhaps *this* was the meaning of his smell? Perhaps it was never the smell of the swamp. Perhaps it was *this* I sensed? Perhaps the odour he carried with him, that only seemed apparent to me, was a sign that I was meant for *this*, and only this.

I went into the bathroom and stared into the mirror.

I seemed to be swimming up to myself. Up out of the pool of mirror, to meet my own reflection. Was that what I was—standing pale and naked in the bathroom—somebody's reflection?

I went downstairs, eventually.

Elizabeth was at the sink.

'They're cold!' she said, incredulous. 'What's got into you?'
'I'm not hungry,' I said, and floated off.
'Sorry,' I added, as I passed the kitchen window.
As I reached the gate and turned towards the bus stop, I saw her watching me, her face screwed up with disbelief.

56

ALL DAY, I FELT strange and fluttery. It was as if hope was a fine glass box that I was holding at my chest. Or in it.

'What, have you got a weasel up your bum?' said Otto, in exasperation.

'Sorry,' I said.

'Sorry, sorry,' he said.

'How do I look?' I said, turning to face him.

'Fine,' he said. 'Coming down with something?'

'Do I look *different*?' I said.

'No, El,' he said. 'What's gotten into you anyway?'

'I don't know,' I said.

'I hope you're not overdoing the prayers,' Otto muttered.

∞

That night, again, Jasper came to me.

He came to me, then, after midnight—his eyes glittering, almost glassy, as if he was drugged.

I could feel him coming towards me, edging towards me, moving softly so as not to wake Elizabeth.

I could smell him. He was . . . fragrant!

Then he stood at the end of my bed, his eyes glittering.

∞

In front of Elizabeth, everything was as always. The terrible jokes, the banter, the flattery. And Elizabeth lapping it up, as usual.

I gazed at Jasper's pallid, waxen skin, and sighed. Now and again I felt his eyes graze mine.

She never guessed that everything had changed. That everything she saw was merely pantomime—mirage—a recreation of the life before. Before Jasper and I became lovers.

We were lovers!

How could she not see?

Even at the dinner table—ploughing my way dutifully through my greens—there was a glaze of happiness upon me like a dew.

I looked at myself in mirrors. At Otto's. In my lunch hour, in the walkways and stores of Lemonhurst Mall.

There I was: thin, pale, and palely freckled, and glowing. Bright red frizzy hair. My one eye blue, my one eye green. I stared and stared, trying to understand the change that had come over me.

How could Elizabeth not see?

Whenever I was away from him, wherever I was, I remembered. I could not stop my mind from telling over the details of the night before. Over and over.

At his approach I felt my heart beat faster. My cheeks were filled with heat.

It was an odd collection of feelings I had bundled up inside of me: nervousness, panic, joy, desire, and still a shadow of dislike. (Fear, was it? Like no fear I'd ever known.) But then I would think of us lying naked together, and imagine never getting up again.

I was his. Everything else was just waiting for him.

And every night he came to me.

(Every night, for weeks, he has come to me! Forgive me for abandoning you, book.)

Softly, he came into my room, slipping his clothing to the floor. Gently, he slid into my bed.

And then I felt his skin on mine—moist, and pale and shiny as a pearl. And his lips were sea anemones. And his fingers caressed my skin like fronds of seaweed. And we were rocking, rocking, and the night was soft and dark and immense as the sea.

57

AND THEN ONE DAY—a Tuesday, a *nothing* day—everything turned upside-down and back-to-front again.

Jasper came home from work, washed for dinner, then sat in his usual place at the table. But he was not the Jasper of the night before—of all the nights before. He held himself apart, and played his role.

What was it? How did I know?

It was his eyes. His *eyes*, book, cold as the sea. He had folded in on himself, like a starfish.

Oh, he played his part beautifully. And yet nothing was the same.

The scallops St Jacques finished, we continued on with cherry flummery. Indescribably hard to swallow.

When Elizabeth left the room, I turned to him, flustered. I searched him out with my eyes—but he remained closed to me.

I felt all my happiness turn then, and rise up in my throat like vomit.

Still I hoped, and wondered, and waited for a sign from him. (Perhaps it was a zombie who had visited my bedroom? A phantom, or a wraith?)

'Jasper?' I said.

And his eyes glazed over.

Elizabeth and I did the dishes.

Then I went to my room, early, and lay awake until four am, my heart thudding. But he did not come to me.

I lay and wondered if I should go to him.

I did nothing.

Finally, the morning came.

∞

All that day, all that night, and all the following days and nights I waited. How different things are when you reach that place of small sorrows.

I waited and waited. Still, I am waiting. But Jasper has withdrawn, like a mollusc, back into his shell.

So must Eve have felt, straining at the terrible locked gates of Paradise.

We were Adam and Eve, Jasper and I. (Eve and the Snake, don't you mean? says a dry little voice in the back of my brain.)

Part of me is pleased and pinch-mouthed. Part of me is glad my impurity is being punished. Part of me yearns, like Eve, to go back—to before the staining. Oh, but it's not the greater part of me, book.

What have I done? How has this happened? Who has come between us?

Once—somewhere in the haze of the last twenty-eight nights—I remember thinking: She can't share *this* with him. The thought flicked into my mind, and I flushed with the brazenness of it. Then, as suddenly, another thought slithered in: Or *does* she?

I remembered the key to the doll-room, on her bedside table, and the direction of Jasper's footsteps, some nights, and their laughter, their glances, their intimate strolls. All sorts of suspicions . . . No! It is unthinkable. I cannot think it, now. Not now, when everything is——

Sometimes my thoughts appal me—they cannot be simply *trusted*. For instance, how silly was I, a few short months ago, imagining that Jasper had been planted in our house to spy on us? I think all these outlandish things, and yet I cannot think this through . . . I cannot!

Think, I tell myself.

Had I, in some way, unwittingly, repulsed him? (But how can I tell if I've said or done something to repulse, when I cannot imagine what I've ever done to attract?)

Oh, book, all I can think is . . . too horrible, too crazy . . . but——

He came to me, that first night, the day after my bleeding stopped.

Tuesday was the day that my bleeding was to begin again, and he did not come to me that night. Nor the next night, nor the next.

He did not come to me again, and my bleeding did not come. Had he known this?

How had he known?

Could he have—why would he have?—studied my box of tampons at the back of the bathroom cabinet? How excruciating——

I cannot bring it up now, with so much already left unsaid—or rather, made unsaid between us.

'Jasper?' I say, when I can take him aside—for he avoids me now, emerging only for meals, then whisking himself off to work or sleep. 'Jasper, please?'

And he peers at me, as if I am something at the far end of a well.

58

AND THEN MY BREASTS began to swell.

Naturally, I told Elizabeth nothing. I waited and watched my body. Then today I went to a doctor, away from our house and away from the Mall.

All the while I felt watched. Was it me, watching myself, or something other? A flash of a black pants leg around a hedge, a blurred face . . . Nothing.

It's your mind, I said to myself.

When the doctor told me, I felt like laughing. It was as if I had known this all along.

I had known this, I told myself.

In fact, I am sure that I felt the moment of conception. A ping of light. A terrible sweetness and sadness. Something irrevocable—that's what it felt like.

I hugged my belly, and said: 'Of course, I will be needing an abortion.'

The doctor did not blink.

'Yes,' she said. 'I understand.'

She handed me a card with details printed on it: the name and address of the place, and lists of all its services.

'Thank you,' I said. 'Very comprehensive.'

'Yes,' she said. 'Don't leave it too long, will you, Lenore?'

'Eleanora,' I said.

'Right,' she said, smiling twitchily, looking back down at her desk and its papers.

I almost expected to meet Elizabeth at the doctor's door.

But there was no-one there I knew, and I went back to work.

'A little late,' said Otto, who was bent over the light box, squinting at transparencies. 'Did you remember to get me a Wagon Wheel?'

'I had the test done in my lunch break,' I said.

'I'm pregnant, Otto,' I said.

'Eugh!' said Otto, his face wrinkling involuntarily with disgust. 'Oh, my dear. My poor dear girl. What is to be done with you?'

He stared at my belly, which was no larger.

'Well, you can't hang round the darkroom with that. I can't be responsible for any damage the fumes might do,' he said.

'But I'm getting rid of it,' I said.

'Good job, El,' he said. 'Still, darling. I'm very sorry, but I'll have to let you go.'

'But, Otto,' I said, 'I'm not having it.'

'I know, I know,' he said, holding up both hands. 'But I can't take any risks in this litigious climate. You come back when you've had the op. Mind you, I don't like your chances with all those crazy women in your ear.'

'But, Otto,' I said.

'No, darling,' he said. 'I'm sorry, El. You'll simply have to go.'

'But——' I said.

'I'll wait three weeks. All right?' he said. 'You sort yourself out, and have a rest.'

'Does it take three weeks?' he said, frowning and puckering his lips. 'Never mind. Have a little holiday. Go to Bali.'

'Get out of that dreadful house,' he said. 'Don't worry, I'll handle things here. But after that, if you're not back—well, good luck, and send us a snap of the sprog.'

'But Otto——' I said.

'You'll thank me then, I'm sure, for not letting you hang around my fumes. They're noxious, you know. Three weeks, and then I'll have to get another girl. Okay?' he said.

'I'll be back way before then, Otto,' I said.

'Of course you will, darling,' he said.

He kissed me twice on each cheek, then sent me home.

'Don't forget your Snoopy mug,' he said.

'But I'll be back,' I said.

'Of course you will,' he said. 'Sooner or later.'

∞

When I got home, Jasper was there, sitting at the dining table.

Strange. It wasn't Thursday.

'Early mark?' he said offhandedly.

'I'm having a little holiday,' I said.

'Quel jolly surprise!' he said. 'Lucky you, Eleanora!'

He looked at me more closely.

'Why aren't you at work?' I said.

'Oh,' he said. 'Thought I'd take a sickie.'

'Things to do,' he said.

'I'm off to bed,' I said.

'Good idea, resting up before dinner,' he said. 'I might follow you.'

I turned and stared at him, hope welling up.

'Might follow your idea,' he said, sneering slightly. 'Take a nap. In my bed.'

'What have I done?' I cried. 'Why have you changed?'

He stood and smirked at me, his mouth twisted, his eyes narrowed and twinkling.

'It must be tiring being such a nasty little twerp,' I said.

'It is,' he said. 'I'm totally fagged out with the effort.'

He winked, then leered.

I ran upstairs and flung myself onto my bed, and tried to think. But it was so hot. The walls themselves were sweating.

∞

Elizabeth's voice broke into my sleep.

'Dinner's on the table,' she said. 'Tuna casserole with rosemary and new potatoes.'

I suddenly felt queer and sick.

'Lovely,' I said. 'Just the thing.'

'Jasper said you were having a holiday from that little job of yours,' she said.

'Yes,' I said. 'Just a few weeks.'

'You didn't tell me,' she said.

'I only found out today,' I said. 'A sort of bonus.'

'Bonus?' she said, raising an eyebrow.

'Yes,' I said. 'Otto thought I needed a break.'

'Oh, indeed,' she said, sounding dubious. 'More likely he wants to save himself your wages.'

'Most probably he's using this so-called holiday to ease you out,' she said.

'Otto isn't like that!' I cried. 'He's a good man. He's good to me.'

'Well,' she said. 'It isn't *usual*——'

'I love Otto!' I cried. 'He's a wonderful boss.'

At this she simply stared.

'What perfect timing, anyway,' she said. 'I was just about to turn all the cupboards out and give the sheets a good bleaching. Really shake this house apart. You can give me a hand.'

'You don't seem overly enthusiastic,' she said, staring at me. 'So many other vital things to do, I imagine.'

'Lovely,' I said, finally, turning away to spit out a mouthful of bile.

But Elizabeth had already left the room.

59

WELL, BOOK, NOW I have no job—although I must remember, it's only temporary—and a baby I don't want. Well, that's temporary, too.

I don't want it. I don't care that it's a sin. I don't want it. A fetid little baby. All pink and white, feet encased in tiny woollen booties. Everything pastel. Little bonnet over its cradlecap . . . I will not keep this abomination in my stomach! This oily weedy thing that Jasper left behind. Of course, it's a sin to do away with it. I know I shall sin——

Go on, put on the nun-suit, voice in my head, and scold me for thinking my sinful thoughts, for keeping my dirty secrets—any secrets being dirty to you, voice in my head.

Oh, they got me when I was good and young, those crow-robed women. What evil those nuns wreaked in the name of good, in the name of God! What stains they left in me. But then, they were only emissaries, gotten good themselves, no doubt.

That's no excuse, is it? For what they did, for what we've done . . . What stain of blood have they—we—spread? Right across Europe, Africa, the East, the Americas? And here, and on all the forgotten islands?

They came, and they conquered. And then they seemed to disappear. But I can see them even if you can't, book. Their numbers are dwindling. They are old now and dying off, or falling away into marriage. The clergy is crumbling, along with the churches—back into the dust from whence they came. But who will fight evil? *Who will fight me?*

Oh, God. They got me so good I am almost one of them! I can hear them winging about me now—ink-black, their stern white faces creased with trouble. I am trouble, they say. Their skin so soft, beneath their stiff white wimples and their billowing black veils—their voices so harsh.

They are with me now, flapping their wings, peering over my shoulder and into my head. They scrape at my heart with bony fingers, and weigh up the whiteness of my soul—the relative greyness. (The blackness! they say. The blackness!)

Oh, book! God! Save me! Hell is one thing, but I don't want a baby. Growing of its own accord like a weed in my belly. I know I shall sin, but Father Flynn will hear my confession and absolve me. I——

I don't care what Our Holy Father says—does the world need one more baby? Does it? *Does* it? I don't think so. You and your nasty thoughts, Elizabeth would say. You and your selfish, selfish——

Why, I'd never get away if I had it, little milky millstone. Not that I know where I'm going. But I must, I *must* get away. I can see that clearly now. So that's one good thing.

First, I shall get rid of it, and then I shall look into getting a place of my own. Yes! A small flat, perhaps a room. Even a tiny room that will be all my own. And I shall paint it whatever colour I like. And then I shall save some money—I shan't need a frightful lot—and I shall go to—to India!

In India, I shall travel by elephant! And I shall wear jewels in my hair, and saris—in glorious cyclamens and turquoises and vivid shades of lime . . .

And . . . and . . . I shall have curried vegetables!

I shall go, at last. I shall turn the key on Glass Street, and Lemonhurst. I shall leave.

Will Elizabeth fall apart? No, of course not, you fool. She'll just sulk, and then she'll pray. The family will gather round. The Circle will say a novena, and then they'll all forget about it. I shall be the black sheep that got away!

I should have done it years ago. How stupid I am, what a stupid idiot . . . Never mind, I shall do it. I shall do it now. I shall have my own life, at last. At last.

How many years have I spent? Wasted—everything *her* way.

What it will be . . . I don't know what it will be, this new life of mine. But not *this*. I don't want *this*.

I shall get away! Right away! As soon as I have gotten rid of this horrible thing, I shall pack my bags and go.

And I shall punch them if they try to stop me, and I shall scream and I shall say: Call the police, I am over twenty-one.

60

TWO DAYS AGO, WHILE Elizabeth vacuumed, I phoned the abortion clinic. It was, discreetly, called The Clinic, and was run by women, the card said. They fitted me in for 'a chat' later on that afternoon.

A burly woman doctor took my details and felt inside me and another woman tested me with questions, to make sure I didn't want to change my mind, and then it was all set for me to have it out on Thursday.

'Friday would be better,' I said, thinking of Jasper lurking about the house.

'That would mean waiting another week,' the receptionist said, glancing at my card, 'and that would not be recommended.'

∞

This morning, I arrived at The Clinic with my nightdress and underpants, and a stack of heavy-duty pads, as I'd been told.

Strange to be a woman, I was thinking, with the body always seemingly preparing for the arrival of a baby, even after doing away with one——

There by the gate, with a placard, was Jasper.

He was dressed in black and his face was contorted and mean.

'Murderer, murderers,' he chanted, as several other women lowered their heads and hurried in.

'What are you doing here?' I said, feeling strange and light, as if I was rising out of my body.

'I am here to stop a dreadful crime,' he said.

He dropped his placard and grabbed my arm and started to

drag me away. The smell of him, so close to me, suddenly, like a tray of day-old fish . . .

Dizzy and nauseated, I pulled away. My wrist stinging, I ran and stumbled up the stairs to The Clinic. Just as I reached the doorway I fainted.

When I came round there was Jasper with my head in his lap.

'Call us a cab,' he ordered.

A circle of women's faces were peering down at me, confused and anxious.

'I'll take care of her,' he said.

'I'm the father,' he said.

And the women retreated. Glad, perhaps to have the embarrassment of me, sprawled with my knickers showing, removed.

'I knew you wouldn't go through with it. Couldn't,' he said, scooping me up and thrusting me into the back of the waiting taxi.

A boy pedalled past on a bicycle, his tongue pressed between his teeth.

I watched The Clinic merge into the other terrace houses in the distance.

All the way home, I stared out the window, with my head against the glass—mute and limp as a doll made of cloth and sawdust.

The taxi pulled up. The driver said, 'She okay? Maybe she need a doctor?'

'Leave it with me, mate,' said Jasper. 'She has these little turns.'

He pushed me inside and sat me down at the hall table. I did not struggle or make a move to leave, but sat as if stupefied.

Then I heard them muttering in the dining room.

'Elizabeth,' I heard him say.

'Now listen,' he said.

'Jesus wept!' she cried. 'How can you expect me to be calm?'

They muttered again, or he spoke to her.

Then I heard him say: 'Mother. May I call you Mother?'

I strained to hear.

'Oh, Mother!' cried Jasper. 'Anything at all I can do to help. Only say the word.'

Say but the word and my soul will be healed . . .

And then a silence. I imagined they were clasping hands rapturously. But at no point, *at no point*, did he say it was his.

Elizabeth came out to me in the hallway then and stood over me. I was sitting limply, like someone waiting for a doctor.

'Well! This is a fine state of affairs,' she said, her lips thin with disapproval.

'Jasper has told me everything,' she said, her voice edged with fury.

'The thieving scoundrel!' she cried.

'And he dismissed you like that!' she cried. 'That's love for you, Eleanor. I warned you about that man.'

'Sent you home!' she cried, with a certain relish. 'Just like that. How dare he!'

I stared at the floor sullenly.

'What's he going to do about it, eh?' said Elizabeth. 'Well?'

'Nothing,' she spat. 'So typical. Why do you think we have such a thing as our virginity, Eleanor? Why do you think we guard it? I cannot believe your perfidy, you stupid, stupid girl. Well? What do you say to me?'

I said nothing.

'I've a good mind to go and have it out with him myself,' she cried. 'The seedy old devil. And I suppose he's put you up to *this*?'

Still, I sat in sullen silence.

'Heh?' she said. 'He put you up to it, did he? I might have guessed.'

'Lapsed,' she spat. 'Yes, indeed.'

'Have it your way, my girl. But don't for one minute think that I am going to let you go ahead with this abomination,' she cried, her eyes bulging and bright.

'It's murder, and you know it!' she cried.

'Murder,' I said weakly.

'That's right,' she said, bending down and pushing her face up close to mine, red and furious, her blue eyes blazing—so close I could see her teeth, beyond the bared lips, covered with spittle, and jumbled together like a lot of gravestones in her mouth.

'You have a think about that,' she spat. And went back into the dining room to talk some more to Jasper.

'I can't thank you enough for helping us out like this, Jasper,' she said. 'You are such a boon to me. Such a decent, thoughtful man.'

'It's nothing,' he said. 'Really. I hate to see a young lady ruining her life.'

'She always was a wilful, stubborn, headstrong girl,' Elizabeth said. 'Even as a little thing.'

I sat there dumbly—as if my body belonged to someone else.

'Don't worry, Mother. I will bring the child up as if it were my own,' Jasper said.

'Of course, marriage should come first,' she said slowly, in a low voice. 'I'll speak to Father Flynn.'

'No!' I shrieked.

I ran outside. I ran and ran, holding my belly which seemed to swell. Two blocks down, on the main road, I flagged a taxi. But as my vehicle reached The Clinic and I stepped out, I saw another cab approaching. It stopped, and they were coming towards me, their arms held out like two descending crows.

'Wait!' I said. 'Wait!' But my driver and his cab had disappeared, and the two were upon me.

'I'm not letting this one go,' Elizabeth said. Her face was fixed and grim.

Jasper gripped my wrists and began dragging me again.

Where were the women—all for one and one for all? Where was the burly doctor? My kindly cross-examiner? The smart receptionist? My sisters in suffering?

Jasper gave me a small smile, full of secret satisfaction.

'We'll *all* stay with you forever, Mother,' he said. 'One happy little family.'

'God bless you, Jasper!' said Elizabeth.

'And as for *you*,' she said, and glowered.

They bundled me into the back of their cab, and sat on either side of me, wedging me in, gripping my wrists like rope burn. The driver's eyes met mine in the mirror for a moment, then slid away. And the taxi drove us home and they took me to my room and they turned the key.

'You look done in, Mother,' said Jasper as they walked away, and down the stairs. 'I'll make you a good strong cuppa.'

Was he a space alien, the way he trotted out these things?

And then I couldn't hear them any more.

I sat on the bed and then I lay down, and my mind was thick, stuffed tight as a pillow with cottondown.

And then they came for me, some time later, and led me downstairs, and put me inside the doll-room.

'But?' I said.

They pushed me roughly inside, their faces fixed and determined, until I banged up against the narrow bed that filled the centre of the room. Then they closed the door slowly, Elizabeth's face watching me all the time, one bright blue eye fixed on me as the door pulled shut. And then the sound of the lock, and the removal of the key, and I was standing hard up against a narrow bed—surrounded by row upon row of costumed dolls.

II

61

I'M STARTING TO FEEL as if I am invisible.

'It's hot,' says Elizabeth, slamming the tray down, slamming the door shut behind her.

Well, a lot like any other breakfast before my imprisonment, I think.

My slops are removed. This should be the hardest part. Instead, I relish the moment when—her nose averted—Elizabeth removes the chamber pot.

But then, she is the woman, or so she says, who changed my nappies.

'Mind,' she says, carrying the pail, passing.

'One move,' she says. 'One move! He's out there in the hall, holding a syringe full of knock-out.'

'Jasper?' I say.

But he says nothing—merely shuffles about.

I am warm enough. Not unpleasantly overheated. Changes of clothing are brought in now and then. A small basin of warm water and a cloth and soap are carried in. A towel.

I have a narrow, but not too hard, bed. I recognise it as my childhood bed, dragged down from the attic. (I was a tall, unfortunate child—even so, my feet protrude from the end now.)

The room is long, oblong. Close.

Ron and Elizabeth bricked up the window years ago, to make room for another cabinet, to house more dolls. There are three cabinets, effectively lining the walls. Three walls of dolls and then the door, and just this slit of glass at the back wall, high high up.

It must be double glazing or armoured glass. I don't know. I tried to smash my way out of it, that first day. I stood on the narrow bed and belted it with my chamber pot. Not so much as a scratch appeared—not a scratch or a crack.

Behind the wall of dolls and the high impassable window is Miss Carew's. Miss Carew is ninety-three and deaf as a post and legally blind, to boot. Although she can see light and shapes with a small part of one eye, she told me.

I could scream all day and Miss Carew would not hear me—would not come to save me, battering down the door with her walking frame.

I have a pillow and a blanket and a quilt. And every few days I am given fresh sheets. I change them, then I lie on my thin bed, in the centre of the narrow space, with my feet towards the door.

At the foot of the bed is my chamber pot.

There is not much room for anything else. Just me, the dolls, and my ordure.

∞

In the mornings and in the evenings, I can hear them. Elizabeth and Jasper, sitting in their usual places in the dining room, talking in their normal way over their meals—as if nothing has changed.

'Mm, these eggs are good,' Jasper says.

'Tarragon,' says Elizabeth. 'Just a hint.'

'I hope you'll pass your recipe books onto Eleanora when we're married,' he says, then, in a perfectly serious voice.

'She hasn't my touch,' says Elizabeth, and sighs.

Doesn't follow up his marriage talk—takes it for granted!

'Now that shirt is an unusual shade,' she says.

'Mm,' he says. 'Glad you like it, Mother.'

Christ! Jesus!

It is one thing to lock me in here, to think they can force the baby from me. But this! This casual appropriation of my entire life.

What could they be thinking? Were they going to drag me to the altar? Were they going to *drug* me? Was Father Flynn in on this too? Would *no-one* notice such a state?

And I thought families were for protection.

'Nobody will ever care for you like family,' Elizabeth used to say. How many times did she say that?

'When the chips are down,' she used to say, 'there's only family.'

If I time it right, I think, I could really scream.

But no-one ever comes to this house, except for Circle meetings. And last Wednesday evening, two nights ago, Elizabeth tied and gagged me! And no-one comes to ask after me. Nobody.

62

'YOU'VE LET IT GO cold,' said Elizabeth, this morning, removing my breakfast tray and sighing. 'I'll have to heat it up again.'

'Yes,' I said. 'It doesn't matter.'

I don't have a weight problem, you know. I'm not weird about food. (There were girls at my school who spent the whole day spewing. The toilets stank of vomit.) But lately I have been noticing that everything I eat is dead.

I mean, long dead. I can smell the death of the fish fillets that Elizabeth brings me for my dinner. Even the vegetables are dead: deceased carrots, snapped beans, peas raped from their pods. Ancient, mortal spinach. Even a salad is just dead leaves.

Body of Christ, my mind goes, as I chew on some cardboardy antique biscuit. Amen, my mind says, as I swallow, trying not to bring the dead stuff back up.

'I'll reheat it,' she sighed.

'Don't bother,' I said.

'Well, I won't say it's no trouble,' she said.

'Hello, Jasper,' I said.

A shuffling of feet. Silence.

Silent as God.

'Why don't you speak to me?' I said.

Nobody speaks to me. Nobody engages me in conversation.

'Don't be daft,' Elizabeth said.

'No-one speaks to me!' I cried.

'Well, what is there to say?' she said.

'I said I'll heat it up again,' she said, and left, slamming the door.

And that was it.

And I am stuck in here. This fusty room, stuffed with dolls—like perfect babies, in frilly clothes. I can see no-one, and no-one can see me, except this horrible array of beady-eyed plastic dolls. And nobody, *nobody* speaks to me that I may answer them. There are no day-to-day observations. No jokes—as if! No dull anecdotes. Nothing said just for the sake of it.

Oh, I miss Otto! I miss my boring little life. All the dull interchanges, the routines, my *life*.

Here, my physical needs are attended to. (My captors are not precisely cruel.) There is food—whatever I would be having normally, more or less, plus gallons of milk and too-sweet tea, and such a lot of fish. (Protein, book.)

Elizabeth is tight-lipped. Jasper is silent. He does not enter my room to bring or take away my tray. Just stands there in the hallway, dumbly.

I expect he is too full of shame . . . Does he feel shame? Remorse? Pity? Do either of them? Apparently not.

'Is it a nice day?' I asked Elizabeth yesterday.

She pointed upwards, and said, 'See for yourself.'

'It looks nice,' I said.

'Pff!' she said, leaving.

Of course, I can see a little of the sky. From the tiny almost ceiling-high window on the wall above the head of my bed, I can see blues and shades of grey. I can imagine the heat, or the wind. I can trace the pathway of the scudding clouds. If I wanted to I could climb up precariously and press the tips of my fingers against the glass, and feel the rain. It's not a weather report I want, though.

63

'I SHOULD LIKE TO go to Mass,' I said, this evening.
 What day was it? All the days had melded.
 'You!' she said.
 'I should like to pray,' I said desperately.
 'You'll stay here,' she said. 'Until you come to your senses.'
 'I've come to my senses,' I said, and began to weep.
 'I'm doing this for your own good,' Elizabeth said. 'You and the baby.'
 'There is no baby!' I shouted. 'The devil's spawn won't take in me. There is no baby!'
 'See what I mean?' she said, sighing and closing the door.
 Oh, the sound of that lock.
 'How is she?' said Jasper, later.
 'Very restive,' said Elizabeth.
 I could even hear their cutlery clinking as they ate. (Salmon with dill and sour cream sauce and tarragon potatoes, and a mound of iron-rich greens.)
 'Oh, Jasper, I am finding it horrendously wearing having her locked up in there, day in day out,' she said.
 'I can quite see that,' he said.
 'She will change, in there,' he said oracularly.
 'Well,' Elizabeth said.
 'She is such a difficult girl!' she cried. 'Always has been. Ron and I were really quite sure at one point that she was a schizophrenic.'
 'Oh?' said Jasper.
 Oh? Indeed. First I'd heard of it.
 'Yes,' said Elizabeth. 'Yes, yes. Always a disruptive element.

Always slightly a problem child. She was more tractable after we sent her to St Ursula's, however.'

'A hospital?' said Jasper, sounding professionally concerned.

'No, no!' cried Elizabeth. 'Tough as an old boot! Never had a day's sickness in her life! The local school. A lovely convent school, with good, old-fashioned values.'

'Ah,' he said. 'So important, the school.'

'Yes,' said Elizabeth, 'for training. They can achieve in a few short weeks what would take *years* in an ordinary home environment.'

Through the locked door I could hear her: sharp-voiced, bullying. Just like the nuns, I realised.

'Ah,' said Jasper. 'Quite.'

'We got to her in the nick of time,' said Elizabeth. 'Still, it is always my fear that Ellen will succumb to the strain of madness that afflicts certain individuals in our family . . .'

'Surely not?' said Jasper. 'After all this time?'

'One worries,' said Elizabeth.

'Dear, dear,' said Jasper. 'My poor Mrs Bird!'

'Now, Jasper,' she said.

'Sorry, Mother,' he said.

Oh, the pair of them!

'Still,' said Elizabeth. 'Even so . . . Even with all this terrible worry and such . . . It was really so pleasant last week without Ellen at Circle.'

'There!' cried Jasper. 'You've found your silver lining, Mother!'

'Oh, Jasper,' she said.

Exchange of silky glances?

'It rained last night, did you know?' she said, adding meaningfully: 'According to Ellen.'

Well, of course, it had! Bang, bang, bang against my window. Drops the size of marbles.

'I wasn't aware,' said Jasper smoothly.

'So *fanciful*,' sighed Elizabeth. 'Always was.'

'Oh, dear,' she said.

'It is for the best, Mother,' he said. 'In the long run. You must not worry yourself.'

How he trotted it out!

'Yes, yes. I suppose it's true. I must bear in mind how moody and unco-operative she is, in general,' Elizabeth said.

'Exactly,' he said. 'Always better not to particularise.'

'I only hope she is not going to drive us silly with sulks and whinges,' she muttered.

'A bit of firm handling, that's the ticket, Mother,' he said.

'She was always a very hard child to handle, Jasper,' Elizabeth said. 'A terrible grizzler. Sulking and whinging . . . Still has a constant chip on her shoulder, just like——'

'Pardon?' said Jasper.

'Oh!' cried Elizabeth. 'We all have our faults, don't we? I shouldn't sit here picking out Eleanor's, when I have a plank in my own eye, so to speak!'

Her chair was shoved out from the table hastily—think of the skid marks on the polished parquet.

'Dessert?' she said. The old standby.

I'd already sampled mine: prune syllabub with marsala cream, topped with a maraschino cherry.

64

I HAVEN'T MUCH APPETITE—I think sometimes I'm going to starve this thing out of me—and when I do eat, I eat so slowly, I've barely started when Elizabeth comes back to get the tray.

She comes in and out in the mornings, before Jasper goes to work, and she comes in again when he returns. (They are inflicting poverty, chastity, and obedience on me. Not to mention monotony. They want, I suppose, to break me.) In between, I am alone. With a thermos of tea and some sandwiches, and a thousand doll's eyes watching me.

'Morning sickness?' Elizabeth said, today.
'No,' I said. 'None at all. Perhaps it is a phantom pregnancy?'
'Don't be ridiculous,' she said.
'Isn't it lucky you weren't the mother of Mary,' I said.
'Pff!' she said, and left the room. Slam!

I pray to the Blessed Virgin, who has such a kindly temperament.

Merciful Mother, I pray. Oh, Virgin most powerful, Refuge of Sinners, Queen of Heaven, Tower of Ivory, Mystical Rose! Release me from this prison, and intercede for God's forgiveness, for what I am about to do . . .

I even prayed to God the other day. But God has turned his back on me—is gone from me—is dead? Is, in any case, entirely silent.

(What if God is *literally* dead? What if, at some point in recent history—WWI, perhaps—God actually died? What if the devil has not just been leased this century for his own, but has in fact gained control—God being dead and unable to rise. And what if the second coming—which surely must be soon?—is the coming of the son of Satan? It is at times like these that I would like to talk with Brother Raymund . . .)

Mary, I pray. Oh, clement and mild. Wipe this child from me. Return it to its native nothingness.

Take it, quickly. Thank you, Mother Mary, I pray.

Every night and every morning and often in between. And then I stare at the ceiling, stare at the dolls. I am so bored, stuck in this room.

Elizabeth won't let me read. (Poverty, chastity, obedience.)

'You've read quite enough books already,' she said, refusing with relish.

'Not even the Bible?' I said.

'Don't give me your lip, girlie,' she said.

'It will do her good to reflect on the error of her ways,' she said, shortly after, to Jasper.

Ah, Jasper. Ever ready with the back-up.

'Quiet meditation on the nature of her wrongs will hasten her redemption,' he said.

Last week I said: Could I have my tapestry stuffs? Or perhaps I could do some crochet work? Or, better still, would she buy some knitting needles, so I could knit some clothes for baby?

'Oh!' said Elizabeth. 'That's a——'

Then she remembered that I can't knit.

'You vile, evil girl!' she said, flinging herself from the room.

65

WHEN ELIZABETH BROUGHT MY dinner tray tonight, I pleaded with her.

'I am ready to be reasonable,' I said.

She eyed me. Then she sighed and said, 'We'll see.'

After a while, she came back in, with a grim face and a cup of over-sugared tea.

She sat on the edge of the narrow bed, and folded her hands on her lap, looking as if she was about to explain at last about the birds and the bees.

'Of course, I shall be whatever help I can be, Ellen,' she said, finally.

'I know you will, Mother,' I said.

She was using my name again (surely a good sign?), albeit the wrong one.

'Mother. Let me be quite clear,' I said—nicely. 'I do not want to go through with this pregnancy. And if you force me to go ahead and have it, I will give it up as soon as it is out of me.'

'Adoption!' cried Elizabeth, aghast. 'You wouldn't!'

'I most certainly would,' I said.

'Actually,' I said, 'I think it would be best if you allowed me to get on with what I was doing. I'm sure it's not too late to be fitted in tomorrow——'

'Don't be ridiculous!' she said. 'Allow you to murder this soul!'

'But I do not *want* this baby, Mother,' I said. 'You must try to understand.'

'What Miss wants and what she doesn't!' Elizabeth cried.

'It is not right,' I said. 'I cannot have this baby.'

'Not right!' she said. 'I'll say it's not. You should have thought of this, before.'

'You can forget this baby, Mother. I'm not having it, whatever way,' I said firmly. 'And *you're* not getting it, either.'

'I shall forget you said that,' Elizabeth said.

'You are not in your right mind,' she said.

'Oh, Mother,' I said.

'I wanted to put it out of its misery, but you stopped me,' I said.

'A mortal sin!' she thundered. 'I *saved* you!'

'It is not too late for that now,' I said calmly. 'But if you insist on it, I shall have to adopt it out.'

Her lips were puckered in bitterness, and her eyes bulged from their sockets—sky-blue and furious.

'I shan't keep it, and I shan't marry Jasper,' I said.

'Do you hear me, Mother?' I said.

'You can't make me,' I said.

She thrust her jaw at me, stood up, and stared down the length of her nose.

'I shall adopt it out,' I said shakily.

'Give it away!' she sneered. 'You foolish girl! You can't just pass a baby on and forget about it.'

'Can't I?' I said.

'You, Eleanor, are a preposterous child,' she said, slamming the door, leaving. Locking the door behind her.

∞

Some hours later she returned, with another cup of heavily sweetened tea.

Was she using condensed milk? Was it *drugged*? Tranquillisers? No, she would never do anything to harm the baby. Surely.

She fussed about, ignoring me, and then she fixed me with her bluest eye and said: 'Listen hard.'

'Having a baby and giving it up, Ellen,' she said. 'That is not something that you can just tuck away. I know. I dealt with that sort of thing all the time in my nursing career——'

'But, Mother,' I said. 'You must listen——'

'No, *you* listen, dear,' she said sweetly. 'You don't know what you've missed until you've tried it.'

'I can guess,' I said. 'Besides, someone else would be thrilled to have it.'

She gasped.

'A baby's not some toy to be handed round,' she said frostily. She sighed, and tried again.

'Adopting a baby out is not something you can just put behind you, Ellen—like a parking ticket or a broken engagement,' she said, sounding delicately aggrieved.

'You can't give birth, and then forget it,' she said.

'Which is why——' I said.

'It is something that will haunt you forever,' she shouted.

'Forever,' I said dully. 'What about now? What about *my* life?'

'You are a selfish, evil, foul-minded girl,' she shouted.

'Bad genes,' I said. 'Bad for baby.'

'We will have no further discussion of this matter,' she said. 'You will come to see that I am right. Your instincts will agree with me. You'll see.'

'So it will have to come to that,' I said.

She stared at me coldly, and left the room, locking the door, removing the key.

66

I FIND I SWING between apathy and rage.

Since our conversation, Elizabeth refuses to talk to me. She replies to my questions with snippy little one-word answers, or leaves the room.

She is a castrator, I think, but not of men. (All the men in her life have castrated themselves. Even Jasper responds, plays the tame old tabby. Oh, she *knows* he is the father. She knows, but she is not letting on. Well, I'm not giving her the satisfaction, book. Let her pretend to guess. Let her pretend to think it's Otto's! *Otto!* Next it will be—who?—Harry Jumper?)

What do you call a woman who castrates other women? Jealous?

She has deformed me. And, because I am a dutiful daughter, I deform myself.

There is nowhere I can go. Nowhere, really.

India! Ridiculous! I will always come back, like a dog to his vomit, like a prisoner to his cell.

But still, in my mind the arguments circle, and I return to them, again and again.

Still, although I am only fighting with myself.

What is it we are fighting about now? Life. Life itself. We are fighting about what life is. And I am fighting for my basic rights. My own version of what life is. My right to life.

Frankly, Mrs Bird, I want to shout. Frankly, I do not believe what you say about life. Life is not what you say it is. I have seen life and I have lived life, but now that you have me locked in your cage—oh, when was I ever not?—you expect me to lie. You expect me to say that *here* is life and life is *here*. Never.

To keep my circulation going, I pace around the spaces in the room. Left, right, left, turn—left right, turn—left, right, left, turn.

All this arguing, I think. All this arguing and answering back. Yet I never said the thing that needed to be said—whatever it might be.

Never said it, never say it. No longer know what it is.

67

IT BEATS ME, THESE days, how anyone can be bothered doing anything.

I think of Otto, slaving away without me. I think of everything, as if from a great distance.

Jasper comes and goes, as if nothing has happened, at his usual times. Elizabeth keeps up her industrious routine: church, house, church, house. (I think she gives herself particular chores to do as penance.) Cleaning, straightening, placing everything in its correct order. Ordering everybody about.

I hear her singing as she works about the house—has my situation cheered her up so greatly?—psalms, and old hymns. Occasionally, self-consciously, in her warbling soprano, she breaks into one of the 'rock' hymns from the heyday of the folk mass: 'Eat his body, drink his blood, Gather round the table of the Lord, Allelu, allelu, allelu, allelu-u-ya!'

She is happy. Happy!

Jasper comes and goes. No-one comes for me. The Circle meets.

I can hear the front door as they arrive, and then a buzz of voices.

I lie there, gagged, my wrists and ankles elaborately tied, as a hum of familiar voices rises and falls in prayer.

What does she think will happen? Does she think I'll scream for help? Does she think anyone would answer me? She has a vivid imagination.

All this time here and not one person has called, or wondered at my whereabouts. Not even Otto, which is hurtful. I could literally disappear, like Brother Raymund, and no-one would be wiser.

Hours pass. The front door again. Then silence.

Another night. Another day. Elizabeth and Jasper have breakfast. Jasper goes to work.

Elizabeth sings as she cleans and recleans the house. Occasionally, she is joined by the mournful tones of the touchphone—Marlene or Darlene asking about me? Iris? Even Josephine?

As for the baby. My prayers remain unanswered, so far. And the spiteful thing has resisted all my efforts to dislodge it. I shall have another go later with the head of this pen . . .

To be on the safe side, I call on Mary again. I have nothing better to do, except count dolls. (If only she would send me a sign!) Well over a thousand: one thousand, one hundred and thirty-one, at last count.

I pray and count dolls, sleep and stare at the sky . . .

At least I have you, book. At least I had the wits to stuff you and this old pen down my underpants, that dreadful day.

Do not worry. I hide you well.

68

THEN, YESTERDAY, AT THE start of another endless evening, it came to me: This room must be airconditioned, or surely I would stifle? How could I breathe, in this box, with only the air from the keyhole coming in?

If I thought about it for too long—more than a moment—I heaved with panic. And then I held my breath, until my breathing had slowed, so that I did not use up what was left. Silly, in retrospect.

I crawled around peering below the doll-cases for some time, and then I located it: a series of grids screwed into the wall. Where there's an in there's an out, I thought.

I lay back down on my narrow bed, and breathed easy for the first time in weeks.

After dinner, I hid my cutlery. While Elizabeth was trying to coax the knife out of me and then crowing in her victory as she wheedled the fork from my hand, she seemed to forget the teaspoon.

When upstairs was silent except for the odd bed-creak (from Elizabeth's room?), and the occasional snort, I turned my light on and fiddled with the screws on the grille with the end of my spoon.

It was hard going. The spoon slipped, and slipped, but I worked away at it for half an hour at a time. I know how noise carries in this house.

All night I fiddled away with my teaspoon. The screws were jammed tight. A little before dawn, I gently removed the grille.

Well! It was impossible. There was no airconditioner, only a hole into the hall closet. Only a narrow hole.

So! I thought. I can see anything that happens, at floor level. Not that much happens in the hall closet.

I fixed the grille back in place and screwed it up again. I turned out the light.

The sun was up. High in my window, the sky was a silvery shim. While I lay there the sky turned to aluminium.

I lay on my bed and examined the dolls in my direct line of sight: Miss Belgium's ruffles, Miss Scotland's kilt, and the moss-green velvet jacket on Miss Wales. Their tiny eyes uniformly watched me—as steady as the eye of God . . .

Soon Elizabeth will come with my tray, I thought. And the endless day will begin.

69

NOTHING EVER HAPPENS IN here. Only the sky, high up, changing slightly, clouding or brightening or filling with rain. Only day turning to night, night turning to day.

To break the monotony, I think about where I am. I do it like that kid's joke, circling out, wider and wider: Eleanora Bird, 13 Glass Street, Lemonhurst, Sydney, NSW, Australia, The Southern Hemisphere, Earth, The Universe. Well, it's not very funny, I know, but it passes the time.

I think: Eleanora Bird, in my body with an uninvited lodger in my southern portion, inside the doll-room, inside my mother's house.

I think about the rooms outside me, their shape and the look of them. It makes me feel less claustrophobic.

Well, Elizabeth's house. It was a dark brick house, last time I saw it, the colour of fruit cake, and the inside walls and woodwork were painted pistachio, marzipan, and icing-white. Pretty.

There were two storeys, although the top storey was mainly for sleeping in—was an almost forgotten storey—and seemed smaller and less real than the floor below. That is, until—— Forget that.

On the ground floor there was the kitchen, the dining room, the doll-room, the never-used living room ('The Parlour' as Elizabeth called it), and a downstairs toilet.

Upstairs, three bedrooms and a full bathroom. Above again, the attic, that no-one entered. The attic was filled with stuff from the past, relegated there for being too depressing—too sad to sort through, but impossible to throw out—like this bed I'm lying on, left-over from my childhood.

Below the house was the cellar, that no-one entered either, now—too dark and damp and foul-smelling, too thronged with unseen presences.

There it was: Hell, the cellar. Purgatory, the 'living' part of the house. Limbo, the sleep-rooms. Heaven, a dusty attic where no-one ever went.

On the verandah, by the front door, was an old brass plaque that said 'Lilydale' in moulded letters.

The garden had withered in our time, as Ron and Elizabeth and I were never interested in gardening. And Jasper was good for mowing and weeds, but hadn't got a clue about growing things—not long-term. Still, there were banks of lilies left.

Once, they decorated the altar for the Latin Masses. Once, they scented the fetid cellar. In the hot months, even now in June, and especially at night, their languid scent drifts into the house, penetrates even this sterile little confining room, this cell . . .

The house, last time I saw it, was well-shaded with beech and pine. It, and the few bungalows surrounding it, provided a pocket of greenery in the greater brick and concrete glare of Lemonhurst.

Glass Street was a good street. People walked their dogs there, and let them foul our pavements and grasses, and complained as they walked of the amounts of water wasted on keeping our lawns and verges green.

It was restful there, on Glass Street, which is one of the reasons why I never properly left—as if I had been born an invalid, in limitless need of rest.

I was born there, and I shall die there, I expect.

Although I speak of it in the past tense, it still stands. And I, unmistakably, lie within it.

70

BOOK, I HAVE BEEN neglecting you. Almost a month, and I have made no entries. Well. Nothing has happened. Except sky. And I have been concerned about running out of ink. However. However . . . This morning I asked Elizabeth for my carved wood box.

'Why?' she said sharply.

'Memories,' I said.

'Your father was a good man,' said Elizabeth.

She locked the door and went upstairs, and returned with the box, her face sour with suspicion.

'There are things in it,' she said.

'Just memories,' I said.

'What's all this, then?' she said.

'Think of it as a birthday present for last week,' I said, when indeed no mention of my birthday had been made. 'It's just a little notebook and some old coloured pens and pencils. I thought I might sketch a few things, note down my thoughts. You know, occupy my mind.'

'I suppose there's no real harm in it,' she said, sounding dubious.

No harm at all—it was too late to terminate the abomination now.

Surely, if I behaved, they would let me out soon?

What more could they want from me? What more could I do?

'No idea why you'd want to record your thoughts,' she said huffily, handing me the box.

'Displaying your filthy mind,' she muttered, leaving. Leaving me with the box—and all its pens.

My birthday present to you, book.

I took out two of the best and laid them under my pillow.

Then the door opened suddenly, and Elizabeth reappeared, her cheeks flaming, and her hair frizzing out around her face, gold and silver, like the Holy Ghost's beard.

She looked younger, somehow. (She was a fine figure of a woman once: stocky as a barrel, and bulging-eyed, but with a good skin, a high colour, and that fiery hair.)

'Give it back to me,' she said. 'I've changed my mind.'

'Oh,' I said.

'Perhaps you should be setting *your* mind to how you might make amends for your recent bad behaviour,' she said, holding her hand out for the box.

'But,' I said. 'I promise it's only——'

'Your promises count for nothing,' she said, and heaved a great sigh. 'That much is clear, now.'

'I really quite expected it,' she said, staring up at my patch of sky, which was a steely grey. 'First, you insisted on working for that Lothario.'

God! Was she still going on about Otto?

'I should have known you had vested interests,' she sighed. 'And now, in your usual impetuous way, *this*.'

'No concessions,' she said, moving to the door.

'I can't see what that has to do with my birthday, and everyone forgetting it,' I said.

'Oh!' she said. 'If you're going to be like that I can't do anything for you.'

'Let me go,' I said. 'Mother? *Jasper?*'

Silence.

'Let me go!' I shouted. 'I'll sort it out on my own.'

'You're being quite silly, now, aren't you?' she said. 'No job, no income, and all the extra expense involved in raising a child!'

'What are you planning to do? Live under a bush?' she shouted. 'I suppose you're silly enough to think a baby can sleep in a *drawer*?'

'Oh, shut up,' I said.

'How dare you!' she said.

'You're not having it,' I said.

'Oh, and you think you'll provide a good example?' she snarled. 'You with your rank ingratitude and your surly ways?'

'As for your birthday,' she said quietly, enunciating each word. 'Well. I have had several days of constant, exhausting work trying to clean up your room yet again, and to find a place for all the books, clothes, music, and belongings you've accumulated—some of which do not please me at all, and some of which are suitable only for burning——'

'Oh, Mother, you didn't——' I said.

'The place was left in such a state of indescribable squalor,' she said. 'I don't see how you will be able to care for a baby when that is the best you can do for a bedroom——'

'Oh, Mother!' I said.

'Your ingratitude is really quite extraordinary!' she said. 'I work just constantly, and *all* for you and the baby——'

'You're not planning on keeping me in here till the baby is due, surely?' I said, horrified. 'But that's another—that's months away.'

'Mother?' I said.

'Mother? You can't mean it?' I said.

'It's for the best,' she said, lowering her eyes.

'Don't go drowning in your own self-pity, now,' she said. 'It's unwanted by all of us, if you want to know. We don't want it. Don't think *we* want it. We're merely stepping in to save you from the terrible pickle you've created for yourself.'

And with that she left the room.

'So temperamental,' she said to Jasper as she locked the door.

'Don't let her get to you,' he said soothingly.

'Yes,' she sighed. 'Dear Jasper! I must remember. She has always thrown tantrums about nothing at all!'

I stared at the door, the lock, the keyhole. So small.

71

I APPEAR TO HAVE dropped off the face of the world, as far as the family is concerned.

Does *anyone* notice I am gone?

Does Otto phone for me?

I do not know. What do I know?

Eat, drink. Crap, piss. Wash, sleep.

Wait for Mother. Dull as a baby.

I can see and feel my body, my fleshly solidity. But if I close my eyes and lie on my bed, my hands face-down at either side, I am not there.

I am just a worry, whirling about in darkness.

I am alone.

I am boring me.

72

OH, BOOK! I HAVE so much time. And nothing to do but lie about and remember—and misremember, or so it seems.

Of course, in a way, everything is past tense for me here—with only the dolls, manufactured and collected so long ago, for company. (It strikes me that these dolls were never intended for anyone's children. There is nothing appealing to a child in them, except their collectibility, I suppose.)

I was not always like this, surely? Although I *was* slow, and timid, afraid to engage in life.

I see now how the small decisions I made, and the tentative actions I took, created ripples in the flatness of the lake that was my life—viewed from here, they seem like mountainous waves. I lie on my narrow child's bed, and watch them crash around me.

I remember how, as a child, I would bury my head in the lilly pilly tree, imagining there was a door to another world I could enter there, if I could only remember what was the key.

I remember my childhood—myself a distasteful doll, soiling its pretty clothes. How still and silent I was, even as a tiny thing.

Don't touch! they shouted. Sit still. Be quiet.

Quiet? I was mute as a tomb.

I tried to obliterate myself in study. Even in kindergarten, perfecting my circles and squares . . .

Oh, God!

I should be thinking of the future—but the future recedes like a tide going endlessly out. And then it roars towards me, like a tidal wave of fire, and it tugs at my blood until I cannot sleep.

And so I must lie and rest and wait it out, and meanwhile the past sifts and shifts through my mind—and I can find no shape to it, nor hold it still.

All I have is the changing light and the tenuousness. These are my days. These are my nights . . .

∞

All my life was leading me here, I see. All my illnesses, to this hospitalisation. All my cowardliness and capitulation to this confinement. All the silence into this great silence.

All my efforts to grow, turned back on themselves, and revealed as this shrinkage into a second childhood—mute, ignored, despised—exactly mirroring the first.

I should fight, I think. I should think this thing through, and find a way out.

But my mind is filled with pattern-making. Filled as if with light, and then emptied—as if something elemental was breathing in my brain.

You cannot fight the universal breath, I think. You cannot fight the breath of life.

It is so painful, this.

Of course, I am being punished——

Meanwhile, murmurings throng the walls, hummings fill the plaster. If I lie flat on the floor and press my ear to the grille, I can hear a surprising amount: the babble of pipes, the ticking of nameless beetles. Termites?

When I can stand no more of my own mind, I do this, and am entertained and diverted for *minutes*, and have much to think about after—until the patterns begin their ceaseless movements of draping and redraping, and I am captured by the conversations and the hidden communications of the past again—played over and over, like the start of a song, only the opening bars remembered.

73

SOME TIME TODAY—MIDDAY?—I heard a rattle at the door.

Oh, at last! I thought. *At last!*

'Eleanora?' someone whispered.

'Yes!' I hissed back.

'It's Darlene,' she whispered. She rattled the knob again, then pressed her mouth up to the keyhole. 'You're in there, aren't you?'

'Darlene,' I said carefully. 'Get me out of here.'

'Oh!' she gasped. 'Oh!'

'Go to the police, Darlene,' I said firmly, as if I was talking to a dog.

'Oh, dear,' she said weakly.

'Fetch someone,' I said. 'Father Flynn. Harry. Anyone.'

'Oh,' she said—a long slow moan.

'No-one will hurt you, Darlene,' I said.

'Is this my ugly sister's doing?' she cried, her voice quavering.

'What do you think?' I said.

There was silence from the other side. I shouldn't have asked her to think.

'Darlene, please——' I said.

'She will not get away with this!' Darlene shouted.

'Darlene, shh. Please,' I said. 'Go now, and get some help.'

'My poor dear child,' she said, her voice drifting away.

'Darlene?' I cried, my face pressed to the jamb. 'Darlene?'

But she had gone.

And nothing happened. And no help came.

74

TONIGHT, ELIZABETH SANG AGAIN as she swept: 'Brothers, sisters, we are one——'

Then Jasper's footfall in the hallway.

'Oh, Jasper,' she said. 'Hard day?'

'Always, Mother,' he said smarmily. 'I'm a man who thrives on difficulty.'

'Young Miss has been up to her tricks again,' she said, sighing loudly.

They were standing right outside my doorway. What a charade!

'Never mind, Mother,' Jasper said. 'We'll keep her on the straight and narrow, you and I.'

Him! The sleaze. The unholy father.

(How could she not know? Why was she so easily satisfied with silence? She couldn't really believe it was Otto's? Could she? Well, why not, I suppose—since, according to her, Otto wasn't gay. And Jasper, according to my experience, wasn't either.)

If Ron was here . . .

Oh, he was a shrivelled little man, a bad-tempered spite-bag, a real buzzard, let's face it. If Ron was here, what? Nothing? Worse? Who knew which way his temper would turn.

If only someone . . . Iris, perhaps? Iris was always my favourite. My godmother, for God's sake!

Why did no-one come asking after me? Not even a ghost.

'It won't be long, now, Mother,' Jasper said, extra-loud, right outside my door. 'The way time's flying.'

Flying!

'No!' Elizabeth said. 'I'm quite excited.'

'Your grandchild,' he said warmly. 'Just think!'

'I only hope the little darling doesn't inherit his mother's temperament,' she said.

'Ha, ha,' he said. 'What's for dinner?'

'Fish pie and peas,' she said.

Essence of Jasper.

'None for me,' I shouted. 'I've had quite enough for one lifetime.'

I will kill him, I thought. I will strangle that bastard . . . But then he could come back in the child. Of course he could come back . . . But then he is in the child already. Oh, God, book.

'See what I mean?' Elizabeth said. 'She's in her usual self-pitying state. Always thinking about herself. Never thinking about our baby.'

Our baby?

'She's a tease,' he said.

'It's worse than that, Jasper, I'm afraid,' she said grimly—standing right beside my door.

'Eleanor Bird is an evil, wayward girl,' she shouted. Hollering into the keyhole?

She was never daft enough to leave the key in it.

'Oh, Mother,' Jasper said. 'Come, now, it's not that bad.'

But I can tell he's lapping it up.

'No, if it's blasphemy to say it, then God help me, but say it I must,' Elizabeth said, her voice warm and excited. 'Sometimes I think that child has no spark of the divine within her!'

'No spark,' she repeated triumphantly. 'Not even a flicker.'

'It's probably her hormones,' Jasper said.

'Oh, dear dear Jasper!' she said. 'Trust you to put a charitable slant on it! What a blessing you are to me.'

'Ha, ha,' she said, moving away from the door. 'Hormones. God help us when she hits the change.'

75

MY HAIR APPEARS TO be growing at an extraordinary rate. Of course, there *could* be something hormonal going on. Or I could be a saint.

I could, couldn't I?

Some saints' hair keeps growing in their coffins, once they're dead. Hair, and fingernails, also. And I am encoffined here. I try not to think about how small the room is. How airless. How narrow its sides.

There are so many things to not think about——

I tend my hair and trim my nails, and save the clippings, for interest's sake. First class relics. I comb my hair out, then clean the comb, and drop the hairs into the lining of my pillow. There is quite a bundle of them, and still it grows and grows. And I can almost sit on it!

Hair is a strange thing. Always too much, or too little, or growing in the wrong place.

Ron's hair was like a merino's fleece: thick, waving, a sparkling pale blond shade. And then of course it thinned, and instead of an over-abundance of waves there were just a few stray strands greased back—which stood about his head when he was angry. Almost all the time.

Elizabeth's hair is like home-brand steel wool, tightly frizzed, a dehydrated ginger-grey. But every now and then it glints palely with the orange lights that once lit it up—how I imagine the flaming tree would look, if you came upon it in a dingy twilight.

My hair is red, not orange. It ripples down, over my shoulders, and tickles below my waist.

Once a week, Elizabeth brings me in a bucket and I wash it, roughly. (It really needs a proper rinse.)

On other days I have a bowl of warm water and a wash cloth and a towel. Slowly, I clean my body and face.

I look forward to my wash days. The water like a caress—and after, the room scented lightly with rose soap. The soap of saints.

When I am clean, I feel I can stand my seclusion. Just another day, I think. And the dolls watch, approving, their eyes gleaming—but still, behind their glass.

Perhaps that is the secret joy of the doll-room. Always silent, acquiescent—they never answer back.

But I am not a doll. Am I?

76

I NEVER THINK ABOUT the baby. If I do, I think about it dead. Dead, and shrivelled, rotting inside me.

I imagine it growing backwards. The size of an orange, I say to myself. And now it's the size of a pea. You can't take seriously something the size of a pumpkin seed, can you?

Elizabeth does.

'Eat your spinach,' she said tonight. 'Folic acid.'

'Like I care,' I said.

'Pardon?' she said.

'I'm not hungry,' I said.

'You must think of your baby, now, Ellen,' she said primly.

'Why?' I said. 'It's got nothing to do with me.'

'Oh, Mother of God!' she said. 'It never ends.'

'I never wanted it,' I said.

'No-one *wants* these things to happen,' she said. 'These things are heaven-sent.'

'As penance?' I said.

'God has implanted this baby in you, a life with a soul of its own, and you must nurture it, Ellen,' she said, speaking slowly, as if I was an idiot.

'God didn't do it,' I said.

'God willed it,' she said, through clenched teeth.

'What about free will?' I said. 'Ever heard of that?'

'Oh, Eleanor! If you had your way all the time, there'd have been no need to create the devil,' she sighed.

What did she mean, saying things like that to me?

'I won't have it,' I cried.

'Fine,' she said. 'See if I care.'

'I won't have no rotten baby,' I said. 'You can't make me.'

'What bad grammar!' she said. 'You're being silly and childish, Eleanor, and most unpleasant.'

'I won't have it, and I won't give it up, either,' I quavered.

'Have it your own way,' she said.

'I don't want to talk about it any more,' she said.

'Fine. I've made my bed,' I said.

'Yes,' she said. 'Precisely. And, no matter what silly discourse you choose to engage in, now, my girl, you'll lie in it.'

'Don't think I'm happy about this,' she said.

'Do you think this is my ideal situation?' she sniffed, fiddling with her horrid hair.

Why didn't I pick the tray up, and smash her on the head? Why didn't I take my knife, and stab her and her vile lodger? Why didn't I stab them both and grab the key and make a run for it?

Why did I lie there like a . . . like a *ninny*, pretending I couldn't see my swollen belly, pretending that I wasn't pregnant? My whole life—lying there.

77

AND THEN, OUT OF the grey, a plan: If I riled her up enough, perhaps Elizabeth would lock the door—and forget to take away the key! Once Jasper had left for work, and Elizabeth was on her rounds, I could wiggle the key out with the end of my teaspoon, and catch it with my pillowcase, or an edge of sheet, slipped beneath the door. I could set myself free!

I commenced then, to be truly offensive.

'I'm not having it, you know,' I said snakily, when Elizabeth brought in my breakfast tray.

'I won't keep it,' I said. 'Christ knows, I never wanted it.'

'Must every second word you utter be profane?' she cried.

'Oh, that's an exaggeration,' I said. 'And skirting the issue.'

But that was all we ever did: skirt the issues.

'Must you always talk back to me, Eleanor?' she said.

'Must I be deaf, dumb, and blind to satisfy you?' I said.

'Oh, don't be so silly,' she said.

'My God!' I said. 'Jesus H. Christ!'

'See?' she said.

I thrust my jaw at her and glared.

'Why didn't you stick to your bloody dolls?' I said.

She jumped, her eyes bugging, then recomposed herself, stroking down her hair.

'There,' she sighed. 'You see? What did I say before?'

'Your bloody buggery dolls,' I said loudly.

'This conversation is terminated,' she said, swiftly exiting, locking the door and removing the key.

'Yeah, back into your box, Eleanora,' I shouted.

'Pardon?' she said frostily, from the hall.

'Back in your box. You heard me. And the name's Eleanora. Got it? I'm the only doll you couldn't return,' I shouted.

'Such . . . vitriol,' she said, amazed.

'Tip of the iceberg,' I shouted.

∞

Returning to pick up my untouched tray, before Jasper left, Elizabeth stood at the foot of the bed—staring at my chamber pot—and said icily: 'When did we last evacuate our bowels?'

'We?' I said. 'There is no we. I'm here on my own, against my will——'

'Well,' she snapped, turning as if to leave. 'I should have known better than to ask. You can live on air, for all I care, Eleanor.'

'I should have known better than to reply,' I said.

'You dwell in darkness, Eleanor,' she said. 'Apparently beyond my prayers. I comfort myself with thoughts of St Augustine.'

Good. She was spoiling for a fight.

'That heretic?' I said. 'You're fond of heretics, aren't you? You were *very* fond of Brother Raymund——'

'Must you?' she snapped. 'I come in here and ask a perfectly normal question——'

'Jesus bloody Christ,' I said. 'I was only——'

'How dare you!' she cried. 'How *dare* you!'

'Profanity, blasphemy. You'd think you were raised in a circus!' she said. 'You'd think you'd never seen the inside of a decent school.'

'Wish I hadn't,' I said.

'Oh, now,' she said. 'Now I'm to be blamed for that. Don't start. Don't start.'

'I can't do a thing right, can I?' she said, her jaw jutting, her eyes blazing. 'I can't put one foot in the right place.'

'Well,' she said, spitefully, her whole face flushed with fury. 'We'll see.'

'Oh!' I said. 'Oh, Mother! You're kidding me, aren't you? Judgement Day?'

'We must be held responsible for our actions, Eleanor,' she said.

'I was going to take responsibility for what I'd done and for what had been done to me, but you stopped me,' I said.

'You were going to murder a living soul!' she cried.

'That's debatable,' I said.

'Oh, very egg-headed, I'm sure,' she said.

'Murder is not abstract,' she said. 'There is life, and there is death.'

'There's life and there's life,' I said. 'This isn't living.'

'You've made your bed,' she said. 'We agree on that.'

'I've dug my own grave,' I said.

At this she stared.

'I do not want the baby, Mother,' I said, while I had her full attention. 'I never wanted it. A baby is not and never has been and probably never will be a part of my plans.'

'Your plans!' she said. 'Oh, it's a modern world, all right. What about God's plans for you, Eleanor?'

She tilted her head back and glared at me.

'Every normal woman wants a baby,' she said.

'Oh, excuse me,' I said. 'This is too surreal on an empty stomach.'

'Well, eat your scrambled eggs,' she said, and sighed heavily. 'I *could* reheat them.'

'I'm not that hungry,' I said.

'Typical!' she snapped. 'Typical selfishness and ingratitude.'

'You're so mealy-mouthed,' I shouted. 'You want me to be grateful for your kitchen martyrdom, Mother? Go find a cross to nail yourself to, and then I'll be fucking grateful.'

Her lips narrowed and her eyes glittered.

'Remember, you're eating for two now, dear,' she said.

She turned and left, slamming the door.

And then, her movements more restrained, she turned the key in the lock, and removed it.

∞

'Don't you want to know who the father is?' I said, when she brought in my dinner tray.

'No, I don't,' she snapped.

'Well,' I said meaningfully. 'It wasn't Otto.'

She stared at me, blinked.

'Who,' she said. She swallowed, then folded her lips with distaste. 'Whose . . .'

'The Holy Spirit came into me,' I said.

'Oh, for goodness sake!' she snapped. 'Can't you ever be serious, Eleanor?'

'Well,' I said. 'I'll give you a hint, shall I? Maybe you should ask Jasper what he——'

'Jasper,' she said quickly, 'has offered to bring up this poor unwanted child.'

'Oh, isn't he a saint,' I said. 'Saint Slime of . . . where did he say he was from?'

'You could learn a lot from him,' she said crisply, moving to the door.

'I won't marry that oil-bag!' I cried. 'You marry him, you're the one who wants to.'

'Daughter of the devil,' she hissed, turning. 'Strumpet.'

'I thought Ron was my father,' I said. Sounding reasonable.

'Eugh,' she said, and left the room.

Locking the door, taking the key.

78

DID I SAY RON was small? A small man? Oh, but he was big, my father. I was only a little girl, and Ron was big, a powerful giant of a man. A big man with small man's complex, thundering around the house.

The house shook with anger: Elizabeth and I, tiptoeing on egg-shells. Every shell broken. The whole charade, played out to the same house every night. An empty house—just Elizabeth and me. And nothing said of the demoralising prison state in which we lived, nothing spoken between us—no word of disapprobation or commiseration.

Did I say small man? Small man? Oh, how I lied. As I am prone to do.

My father was big. *Huge.* My father was a gigantic man. In the beginning was the word and the word roared and the word was God and his name was Ron Bird. And he made me in his image and I was . . .

Unsatisfactory. I was always unsatisfactory . . . No matter. He would beat me into shape.

Of course we didn't have any pictures of God in the house! We knew what he looked like.

Oh, book! Did I say I wept by his grave? I was glad when Ron died. He was my jailer. Ranting, screaming Ron. My personal dictator.

He was kind to animals. He was never kind to me. I was nothing, nothing to him. I was less than an animal.

And now Elizabeth is carrying on his rule, with several new twists of her own. She's got me where she wants me, where she can always hiss—her eyes snakelike, her head thrown back, her voice filling the room like steam, then absorbed by the walls: You're in *my* house, and you'll do as *I* say.

She is my jailer, my soul's jailer. And I am nothing to her. Silent, malleable, as a doll. Thing to be bent, thing to broken.

But you listen to me, don't you, book? You incline your papery ear to me. You devour my words, don't you?

You soak my inked words into your white pages—your fine white pages stain with my black inked words, and there you are, soiled as a soul with sins, as a white glove soaked with blood. Guilty! Guilty! But you don't care. No, you don't care, do you book? Kind, kind book—you absolve me.

So let thing speak, while it can. Let thing tell the truth.

First, I was glad—palely glad—when Ron died. And then the grief. Flood of grief. And then someone hurt my heart and, in my sorrow, I married Sylvester Clack. Grabbed him, fresh and ancient from the choir. (How Elizabeth sang his praises! How happy we would be!) I ran into Sylvester's arms for safety—I married him, and then I lay there, thinking I was sheltered. He didn't know what hit him, poor old bag of sticks.

I could have felled him with a single blow. I could have crushed him in my palm, like a nest of twigs. Poor old, sad old thing. *My* thing, I thought.

Oh, no! How wrong could I have been? Frail old fragile Sylvester Clack—his bowels rumbling all through Mass, farting involuntarily on the high notes. He was just another petty tyrant. 'Eleanora!' he shrieked. (At least he got the name right.) 'Eleanora! My soup's too hot! My back is sore! You haven't brought my mail in! Eleanora!'

I was glad when Sylvester died, also. Glad! And then lonely—which was surprising.

Even after the annulment there were ties between us. Tiny shoots that sprang up underground and linked us as we slept.

I made a mistake in marrying Sylvester, I admit it. But a greater mistake to think it could so easily be undone. Although I hated him, although there was no love between us—only him ordering me about, and me the dog's body, the devil of the house, the *thing*.

Three streets from Glass Street, and a new life away—and nothing between them, the old and the new. Ha!

Well. At least I had the sense to get out then. And then . . .

Oh, book, there is no relief in going over this. In this cell, there is only you and me and my wretched conscience.

And no matter how I press my trouble into you, you cannot soak the stains I bear away.

I am beginning to think it will always be like this: thing gets what it deserves. Always, for ever, and ever . . .

I don't want Him to put me in the fire. I don't want to go into the fire for all eternity . . .

79

'WHAT ON EARTH ARE you doing?' Elizabeth cried this morning, when she came to take out my breakfast tray.

'Looking after the baby, like you told me to,' I said.

'Give it to me,' she said, making a move to snatch the sailor-suited doll away from me.

I had made a mess of him, spooning my mashed egg yolk all over his face. Quite fun, really.

'But Mother,' I said. 'I have to feed my little baby, don't I?'

'Ellen! You are too old for such silly games,' she said. 'Give him to me. You're ruining him, Ellen. Look at those stains on his clothes!'

'No,' I said. 'He's *my* baby.'

'You're being utterly silly,' she said.

'Ellen,' she said, staring at me strangely. 'You do know this is only a doll?'

'Yes, of course, I know it's a doll!' I cried. 'What do you think I am, crazy?'

Then I gave her a cunning glance, and said: 'But I'm not sorry I did it. If I hadn't he might have got malnutrition and we'd have had to take him to the doll hospital, wouldn't we?'

She stared at me hard for some time—weighing me up, measuring . . .

'Give him to me!' she snapped. 'You are the limit. I shall have to soak his little shirt in bleach and hope it doesn't yellow.'

At the door she turned and said: 'I make the rules here. Don't forget that.'

Yes. And she had the key.

80

I HAD ONE MORE card left to play. The obvious one. The joker. I would call her little bluff.

Tonight, when Elizabeth brought in my dinner tray, I seized the moment.

'You never actually asked me who the father was,' I said. 'Not directly. Don't you think that's strange, Mother?'

'Oh, Ellen!' she said. 'It's not the first time a silly young girl has gotten herself into trouble with an older man.'

'It wasn't Otto,' I said. 'Otto's gay.'

'You know that, don't you, Mother?' I said calmly.

She stared at me, her mouth curling. Oh really? it said.

Her bulbous eyes were disdainful. Yet how they gleamed.

'Otto is not the father,' I repeated.

I raised my eyebrows and stared back at her.

A great wind blew up then, and shook the birds out of the trees, like shreds of cobweb from a mop. We both looked up at the window as branches clattered against it.

'I . . .' Elizabeth said, at last.

'I didn't——' she said, turning her face away.

'Want to know?' I said, my voice rising. 'You know, don't you, Mother? You've known all along.'

'What nonsense! You are the limit,' she said.

'I will stay here only if you guarantee to keep control of your filthy temper,' she said.

'Jasper is the father,' I said, staring her levelly in the eye.

'You're crazy!' she cried. 'Why, Jasper would have told me! He is not the surreptitious, deceitful sort.'

Her mouth shrivelled and she glared at me, deciding.

'How could you?' she cried.

'What a thoroughly unpleasant suggestion,' she said.

'Utter nonsense,' she snorted, glaring.

'He's quite another creature with his clothes off, isn't he?' I said.

'How . . . how . . .' she stuttered.

'Don't you *dare* go emptying the wastebin of your mind in my ear, young lady,' she said.

'The sort of sick fantasy . . .' she said.

'How . . . how . . . could you!' She spluttered to a halt and stood muttering, her hands clenched and her face crimson, her eyes glazed and distant.

I said nothing.

Oh, I am good thing, good doll! Stiff and silent and clean in my glass case.

'Regardless,' she said, finally, in a strange, high voice, 'of your slanderous allegations, Jasper Pease has shown unselfishness of spirit and goodness of heart in offering to do the decent thing.'

She was staring at the dolls, her eyes wide open. Staring, so queerly. I thought for a moment that her face would break.

'What decent thing?' I said.

'He's offered to *marry* you, Eleanor!' she said, as if I was an imbecile. 'To provide a father for this . . . fatherless baby.'

And all the while he stood there, listening—silently waiting for her outside my door.

'Oh, I see,' I said loudly. 'Gosh! Thanks, Jasper! First the indecent thing, then the decent thing. I thought it was supposed to be the other way around.'

'Don't make a joke of this, Eleanor,' she said, back to her usual dismissive self. 'Jasper is only trying to help you out of your trouble. He is a chivalrous and decent man. Beyond the call of all kindness, he is willing to sacrifice himself for your mistake. So let us not have any more nonsense. And let us be quite clear who has created this situation. You, young lady, and no-one else.'

'Me?' I said. 'On my own——'

'I'm sure you're quite aware of what is right,' Elizabeth said icily.

'In your view,' I said.

'My name is Eleanora,' I said, for good measure.

'What is *right*,' she said emphatically, glaring at my one green eye.

'There is such a thing as grace,' she said. 'But those who throw themselves into an attitude of sinful pride will never find it. They are abominations in God's eyes.'

'But I am watching you,' she said. 'I am watching you, Ellen. And if you think, for one moment, that I intend abandoning my moral duty, that I intend to let you flounder in your sinful mire, then you underestimate my watchfulness and my determination. Evil will out, they say. But not if I can get to it first.'

'So much for free will,' I said.

'The flippantness!' she said. 'The terrible light touch of evil!'

'You're blind to your own fall, always have been,' she said. 'You were the stubbornest, most mulish little girl.'

'You will,' she said, staring hard, 'be going to do the right thing, Eleanor?'

'Marry Jasper?' I said. 'The lodger! Aren't you going to make me, Mother?'

'Don't be ridiculous, Eleanor,' she said. 'Jasper and I are only keeping you here to save you from doing . . . things, that you will later regret terribly.'

'For all eternity,' she added in a pious undertone.

'Oh, yes. The life hereafter,' I said. 'Hell today and hell tomorrow and never any heaven.'

'I'm not having the filthy baby,' I said.

'Aren't you?' she said, glancing pointedly at my swollen belly, then left the room.

81

OH, GOD. IT'S NOT just that some things, that so many important things, aren't said—it's that when they are said they are discounted, and denied. Minimised, wiped over, derided. They are made unsaid.

The said can be brushed under the carpet as much as the unsaid. The said can be unsaid by refusing to hear it. By pretending it has not been said. Or, hearing it, refusing to believe it.

Why wouldn't you believe someone? Because they'd proved themselves an hysteric, or a liar?

Or because it would be more convenient for you to not believe them? (Because if you believed, you'd have to *do* something about it?)

I told her, and she unsaid it.

How?

And how has she commanded me to keep my silence on so many things, for all these years?

How is this done without words?

A gesture? A glance? By an effort of will?

It is in the very air I breathe.

Oh, how willing I have been to remain mute . . .

Oh, Mother of Mercy!

What is the point of being brave, or honest? What is the point of speaking at all? Knowing that if, by some miracle, an acknowledgment of what has been said is made—that *this* is indeed so, and *that* also—that things will be twisted, so that I am to blame——

Wait!

The creak of a floorboard outside my door . . .

I have to be careful when I write.

I think perhaps they watch me through the keyhole now and then. Or is it the feeling of the dolls' eyes, crawling across my skin?

Well. So I am. So I am, of course, to blame.

82

SOME VERY DEPRESSING THINGS have happened recently.

First, a visit, and some news.

It was, I suppose, Monday, about midday. (There is breakfast. There is dinner. And, in between, there is midday.) The sky in my bit of window was clear bright blue. And then the doorbell went. Silence. Footsteps. (Elizabeth's. I even know what shoes she was wearing.) The front door opening. More foreboding silence. Footsteps. And I could hear them: Marlene and Darlene, in the dining room.

For once, not gagged, I shouted and thumped against my door.

'Oh, hello, Eleanor,' said Marlene tiredly.

'You calm down, now, you wicked girl,' Elizabeth said. 'Or you'll upset the baby.'

That did it. I screamed and shouted to be let out.

'Shush!' Darlene cried, in a high reedy voice.

'Now, Darlene, you calm down, too,' said Marlene.

At last, I stopped, exhausted.

There was a pause, a silence, then they resumed their desultory chat about the parish newsletter, the church flowers . . .

A lot of talk of flowers.

Then Marlene said loudly: 'Shall I tell her?'

'I think so,' said Elizabeth.

'Eleanora?' Marlene barked, rapping at my door. 'I've come to tell you Josephine has passed away.'

'Oh, no!' I said. 'Oh, dear! Poor Josephine——'

'It was probably the shock of hearing about you,' Marlene shouted. 'Broke her tired old heart.'

'Shattered it in two,' Elizabeth agreed.

Well. So much for Marlene.

∞

Josephine's funeral was held yesterday.

Afterwards, the sisters gathered in Elizabeth's dining room.

The men and children were all at work or school—or did not want to come, or else were not invited. (It lifts my heart a little to think the men are in the dark. Perhaps Harry, or Frank will think of me? And then . . .)

I could hear them talking. And they could hear me. Again, Elizabeth did not bother to tie my limbs or gag me. All in the family, I suppose.

Iris will see that something is not right, I thought. Iris will set me free. Iris, my godmother . . .

'Please, can I come out now?' I cried—trying to sound reasonable.

'Marlene! Darlene! Please!' I called. 'Iris?'

Iris? Did Iris know? Iris always liked me . . .

'Please!' I shouted. 'Please, let me come out! I'm very calm. Just for an hour——'

'Now you want consideration,' said Marlene harshly. 'After what you've gone and done.'

'Your mother's very upset with you,' said loopy Darlene.

'Iris?' I begged. 'Please, Iris, talk to them. Let me come out, just for half an hour? I'll be quiet, I'll be good.'

'I don't think so,' said Marlene frostily.

And they carried on, saying pass the ham, and what did you think of the eulogy, a bit sparse wasn't it, and how do you get your scones so *light*, Elizabeth?

'Please!' I shouted. 'Let me out for a minute.'

There was silence, a frozen kind of silence. Then:

'Shut your trap,' Elizabeth shouted, her voice sounding queer and tight.

'There, now,' said Marlene and Darlene.

'Don't let her upset you,' quavered Iris.

Even Iris.

They are all in on it.

∞

And then, today—with no disrespect to Josephine—the most depressing thing.

It was late afternoon, I suppose, and I was sleeping when the telephone rang. I listened in a daze. A stupor.

'Oh?' said Elizabeth. 'Too kind of you to call. Yes, yes. Terribly sad. But what can one do? Life goes on, indeed.'

Mildred Cleghorn, or Mavis Purley . . . Elizabeth's lieutenants.

By beating my head against the bed I'd managed to set up a rocking motion that made quite a clatter during last week's Circle.

'Take no notice,' Elizabeth said loudly.

And no-one did.

Not one of the Circle had remarked on my absence in weeks, so I suppose they all know. Know while pretending they don't—that seems to be how things are done around here.

'Yes,' Elizabeth said. 'Yes.'

Then, 'No, no!'

'Oh!' she said. 'How thoughtful of you to enquire. Yes, unfortunately. No, sadly. Oh, didn't I mention it before? Well, making oneself scarce seems to be de rigeur nowadays. Yes, yes! Always gadding about! She was to leave again on Sunday—take the time to say a few fond farewells, which I'm sure would have included you—but suddenly she changed her mind and left on Friday instead. What a strange, unpredictable creature she is! Yes, back yet again to Byron Bay. Indefinitely. How sad and yet how *typical* for her to miss the funeral, Father——'

'Father Flynn!' I shouted.

Idiot! Too late.

'Too, too kind,' she said. 'Must fly.'

And she hung up. Severing my hope.

I think, book, I am utterly alone in this.

83

THE FRONT DOOR. FOOTSTEPS. Jasper's clerk's shoes.

'Oh! Thank God!' cried Elizabeth.

'What is it Mother? The——' he cried back.

'That Ellen,' she said. 'I'm at my wit's end. She is getting pretty hard to take, I tell you.'

'Oh, dear, Mother,' sighed Jasper. 'What has she said to you now?'

'Well,' she said. 'She's gone mad again.'

'Again!' he said. 'How tedious.'

'Yes!' she cried. 'All week she's been icy and angry with me over her enforced seclusion—as she calls it—as if I chose this situation!'

'I know, I know,' said Jasper. 'It's ridiculous.'

'Yes,' said Elizabeth. 'It is.'

'This morning,' Elizabeth said, 'she gave me a very vicious look when I removed her tray. Well! My heart sank, I can tell you. I am always looking for signs that she is becoming somewhat more co-operative, as you know. However, in her usual cranky way, she has been brooding. Well! I tell myself I should be used to her periods of sullenness, after all these years. But still it hurts me, Jasper.'

'Dear, dear,' he sighed.

'My cranky daughter! I tell myself. It's only Ellen being her natural cranky self. It doesn't pay to take this sort of wilful nonsense personally,' she said. 'But then she shouted at me! She *shouted* at me—and with a demon's voice, Jasper! A ghastly voice, vibrating with something awful, more than rage——'

'Hatred?' he suggested, ever-helpful.

'Something like,' she said sadly.

'That it should come to this! My own daughter, abusing me in this manner,' she cried. 'A tirade of abuse!'

'Tell all, Mother,' said Jasper eagerly.

'Oh!' Elizabeth sighed. 'She said all the most insane things, Jasper. Said I wanted to control her! Said I wanted to keep her tame, and for myself. Well! I can tell you she is not my idea of a pleasant pet!'

'Said I dressed her like a doll,' Elizabeth grieved. '"A missionary doll, " the little ninny said. The nerve! All my work! All that lovely material!'

'I *was* mindful of putting the goods out of the way of temptation—that obscene, thrusting chest—with the nicest possible taste, I might add, and all at my own expense,' she said thinly. 'And just as well! We've seen where her wilfulness gets her.'

'She's always talked the most deluded rot,' she muttered.

'After all we've done for her! After all the lovely things we've bought her! "What things," she said. "Why, all these lovely dolls!" I said. I must show you one day, in happier circumstances, Jasper . . . And do you know what she did then?' Elizabeth cried. 'She *spat* at me! Voice of a devil, Jasper, and then she spits! Can you stomach that? Well! I gave her a piece of my mind, after that, don't you worry.'

'Dear, dear,' said Jasper. 'Gracious!'

'Then, to top it off, all afternoon,' Elizabeth sighed, 'she indulged herself in crying. So uninhibited! I'm sure she has a mental problem, Jasper. Whatever it is was way beyond the nuns and I can't see what more I'm supposed to do about it.'

'You have done everything that can be done, Mother,' he said. 'You have exceeded your earthly duties.'

'That's what I tell myself, Jasper,' she said. 'But it helps to hear you say it. And I pray for her. Of course. She is constantly in my prayers . . .'

'And then,' she cried, 'the limit! She told me, Jasper, that she would sue me over this! Sue me! For holding her in the house! Ridiculous! Who would believe her, anyway?'

'It's all talk,' he said. 'Don't worry, Mother. Her condition. We must not forget. We must make allowances.'

'Well . . .' she said. 'I suppose.'

'Soon, Mother! It won't be long. Our happy threesome will be a happy foursome!' Jasper cried, scout that he is.

'Oh, bless you, Jasper!' Elizabeth cried back. 'You're like a son to me! More than a son! You always know the perfect thing to say to cheer me up.'

I said nothing. Merely listened sourly.

I was trapped, as a zoo animal is trapped, with no-one to plead my case. And Jasper—who I once imagined my ally!—so eager to betray, in order to better his position.

When would she see through his mask of politeness, and he through her mask of piety?

Oh, God. Am I dead, and gone to hell?

This ghastly confinement, this premature burial . . .

Here I lie, book. Entombed, in a glass-sided coffin, surrounded by the symbols of a world I've never understood—a suffocating world of plastic people in multifarious pointless costumes.

Oh, I must not think about it——

Meanwhile, as in some nightmare, my belly is undeniably swollen. My body is growing bigger and bigger, I have to admit. I have to avert my gaze. My breasts are blowing up—I am being engulfed by my own flesh.

What am I saying? As if it was ever *my* body.

Oh, God.

There is no baby, surely? Only foul gases. Water. Swamp water.

84

THE TRUTH SHALL SET you free. That's what the Bible says, doesn't it? Funny, it never occurred to me to tell the truth in my confessions, my formal confessions, I mean—in the darkened box, with blushing Father Flynn or bat-eared Father Dougherty. (Oh, the relief when St Clare's switched to Reconciliation, with no-one but God to hear my lies.)

I shall tell my truth, now. Here, where no-one can spy it—unless they creep in and tear you from under my mattress as I sleep.

I am careful, now. Very careful. Don't you worry. For truth is dangerous. Murders occur, to keep truth silent. I know. I *know*. All sorts of terrible black threads tug and weave about me—begging, insisting on, a conspiracy of silence.

But what if I were to snip those threads with the scissors of my words, my truth?

Why not? *Why not?* Surely it is time . . .

There is a time for keeping quiet.

Thing keeps very still.

And then, a time comes when it is safe enough for it to speak.

Yes. It is time to get it out——

And it must be got out, for I can hardly breathe for the smell of it. There is no hiding from the stench.

But when it is written in you, book, and I have pressed closed your pages, it will be gone from me, won't it?

Oh, book! I am faithful to you, and you are true to me. You keep my secrets. You are the truer part of me. And when I am gone and all but rotted away, you will hold the record better than my bones, my hair, my teeth.

When was my last confession? Let this be my last confession!

∞

It was on a Wednesday evening—years ago, now—quite early, and still light. We were making our usual preparations for the Latin Mass. I was behind Elizabeth, descending the stairs, when I saw them.

At first I thought it was a game. A mock scene, set up for our amusement. But we arrived unnoticed, and they continued with what was not—by the sound of it—mere play.

Elizabeth glided across the cellar like a nun. Brother Raymund had time to see her, at the last, but not time enough to recompose his face.

I shall never forget his face: the gloating, lewd triumph on it. Or the sight of his body, scrawny beneath his vestments, which he wore flung over his nakedness like a cloak.

Suddenly, Elizabeth cracked him across the back of the head with one of the heavy brass candlesticks (knocked to the floor by Brother Raymund, I suppose, in his haste to bed Darlene—who was lying on her back, smiling loopily, spread-eagled across the altar).

Brother Raymund gave a shriek—the sort of noise a goat would make if threatened—and fell heavily to the floor.

'Wolves,' Elizabeth gasped. 'Ravening wolves.'

She wept for a while and muttered incoherently, then turned her head and stared down at Brother Raymund, who was lying face-down on the cellar floor, motionless now, and silent.

'Oh my God!' she breathed. 'I've killed him.'

Then she wailed and slid to the ground beside him. Her head rolled back on her neck and her eyes bulged.

'Jesus,' she groaned. 'Merciful Jesus! I've killed our Brother Raymund!'

I pulled her over and propped her up against the wall.

'I've murdered him!' she shrilled. 'My darling Raymund . . .'

Her head dropped forward onto her chest, and she wept—eyes screwed up and open-mouthed, like a baby.

He lay there, stunned by the blow, his nakedness projecting from his fallen robe.

I checked his pulse. It was weak, weakening.

'Why, Brother Raymund?' I whispered. 'How could you go against your teachings?'

'Brother Raymund?' I said, and shook him lightly.

'Were *all* your teachings bogus, too?' I hissed.

Still he stayed silent, and still she wept and moaned.

'Oh, Mother Mary, pray for me!' Elizabeth cried out. 'What have I done? What have I done . . .'

'Brother Raymund,' I whispered urgently. 'Everything you taught us is a lie?'

'Yes,' he said, his voice barely a croak.

'But why?' I hissed. 'Why did you do this to us?'

'To offend the Catholic Church,' he said, and smiled. So faintly I may have imagined it.

Elizabeth, meanwhile, was weeping inconsolably.

'Stay here, Mother,' I said. 'I'll be right back.'

I ran up the stairs and into the kitchen—in the cupboard, it was, I knew, in the cupboard—and back again, grabbing the sherry from the dining room on my way.

'Here,' I said, pressing the bottle to her lips.

She took a deep swig, and again her head dropped backwards and her mouth hung open. I remembered the stupid look on Darlene's face as Brother Raymund pounded away at her.

'Oh God,' Elizabeth muttered. 'Oh, God help me. Oh, Mother of God, come to me.'

'Save me!' she cried.

'Not now,' I said. 'We haven't got time for a miracle.'

I took the rat poison and mixed it with some altar wine in the chalice.

'What are you doing?' Elizabeth said, suddenly sharp.

I lifted Brother Raymund's bloody head and poured the poisoned wine into his mouth—and wine spilt down his chest and pooled onto the cellar floor.

'Blood of Christ,' I said.

What was in his eyes? Horror, awe, laughter? Forgiveness?

'There,' I said, when he had seemed to swallow some. 'There. We both did it.'

I watched the puzzle of this slowly clearing on her face.

All this time, Darlene lay on her back, smiling strangely.

'Do you think he's drugged her?' I whispered.

'Oh, she's always like this when they get her knickers down,' said Elizabeth. She straightened her clothing and her back and stood up slowly, swaying.

'You'd better go upstairs and head the others off,' she said. 'Make up something. Say we've had a leaking gas pipe . . . Say that Brother Raymund's taken off. No, don't mention Brother Raymund.'

'Quickly,' she said.

'I'll say that Darlene's had a turn,' I said, moving towards the stairs.

'Yes,' Elizabeth said, taking over. 'That's it. We'll have to get her out of the house, and there's no disguising she's in some sort of state.'

Already I could hear Marlene's voice in the dining room. She had no qualms about letting herself in.

'Get rid of them, and I'll dress her,' Elizabeth said.

'Give her some sherry,' I suggested. 'If anyone sees her leaving we'll say she's drunk.'

'Quickly,' Elizabeth said.

I ran then to the stairs.

'I'll lock you in,' I said.

'Yes, that's best,' she whispered. 'Quickly.'

∞

We killed him. We killed Brother Raymund.

Did he deserve it? Well, it must have appeared so at the time. But now, and ever since, it has seemed like an over-reaction.

But what can we do? What mitigating circumstances could we possibly plead to any judge, earthly or celestial? Having a bad day? Possession by devil? PMT?

I mean, what did Raymund Allan do? He rooted Darlene, on the mock altar in our cellar, while partially wearing his priestly vestments. (How his scrawny nakedness haunts. And something else—a strange tattoo, high on his thigh. Twins? One dark, one fair. The zodiac sign of Gemini?)

Well, I always said our Latin Masses were a farce. They weren't sacred, for heaven's sake.

Darlene was forty-something. Forty-four or five? She struck me as a willing participant: smiling gaily, drool running out the side of her mouth, and that weird glassy gleam to her yap-dog eyes.

All right, she's not all there. All right. But you can't expect a man to notice that. Look at Harry. He's been married to her for years. (Some men are so blind that they cannot tell that a woman is ugly beneath her makeup. They cannot tell the difference between a nun and a whore, unless she dresses for the part.)

It is possible that Brother Raymund, despite his mystic gifts, had simply never noticed that Darlene was a few sandwiches short of the picnic—'A whole lunchbox,' as Elizabeth says. (Even so, what was he intending to penetrate? Her mind? Her crazy, perfect mind?)

And, as for the altar. It was handy. (Well, perhaps an added frisson from the altar, I would guess. *That* would have turned Elizabeth's mind, *that* would have twisted her sense of what was right.)

And it was Darlene laid out on that altar, lest we forget. Dymphna. Elizabeth's little sister, who she is careful to protect . . . Yes, it was Darlene on that altar, not her. God.

All these things, compounded. But it is too late for understanding.

And I? I pitied her. I felt a red stain of compassion—a glowing red, like a spurt of blood, spreading from my heart across my chest. For one brief moment—door after door unlocking in all directions, so that it was at once instantaneous and all time, eternity, past and forward—my heart, my chest, my mind, was lit by that soft red glow of compassion. Oh, my poor poor darling. Poor, poor Elizabeth.

There was just that moment—minutes?—in her fury, and then her helplessness, when she went limp and hopeless. I wanted to protect her. I *would* protect her. I would save Mother!

Truly. That was my imperative.

And then it left me. The red glow left me, and I was cold again. Intolerant, and full of contempt for my fellow creatures.

Oh, God. Oh, God!

All right, while we are being truthful: I have no faith. I am not grateful. Nor can I praise God. There.

And, furthermore, I cannot imagine . . . I can only believe in a horrid God. I *hate* him.

∞

That evening, having locked the cellar door, I wiped my hands on my skirt and went to tell the others Mass was cancelled.

'It's Darlene, I'm afraid,' I said.

Marlene took it in her stride.

'Not drunk again, is she?' she said.

'Likes a nip or two, does she?' said Gladys Gilmour, her yellow eyes bright with interest.

'Well——' I said.

'Oh, dear,' Marlene said. 'The woman's sent to try us.'

'What is it?' said Mildred Cleghorn, arriving.

'A little family drama,' said Marlene.

Gladys winked at Mildred. I could see her tucking away the information, already anticipating the pleasure of spreading it around.

'She sleeping it off?' Marlene said to me, out the side of her mouth.

I nodded.

'Come on, dear,' she said to Mildred, pressing her towards the door.

'Gladys?' she said. 'I'll give you a lift, shall I?'

'Oh, that's not necessary,' said Gladys, sprinting down the drive.

'Elizabeth with her?' Marlene said to me, over her shoulder, as she left.

'She's a saint,' she said. 'Give her my best.'

'Oh,' she said then, stopping. 'What about Brother Raymund. I should hate to put him out——'

'I've rung him,' I said quickly.

'Marvellous,' she said. 'You're more capable than you look.'

I stood at the door and watched as Mildred tottered off and Marlene met the others, one by one, and sent them home again.

After they'd all left, bewildered and put-out, I went back into the cellar.

Elizabeth was mobile now, although her face was white and stiff.

I let Darlene drink the rest of the sherry, then hauled her to her feet. She staggered, and seemed happy to lean on me, planting sloppy kisses on my face.

'Oh . . .' said Elizabeth.

'I'll handle it, Mother,' I said.

'We're pals, me and Eleanora,' said Darlene, her mouth wet against my neck.

'Go and lie down, Mother,' I said.

'Oh,' Elizabeth said. 'All right.'

Together, Darlene and I shuffled upstairs. I phoned a taxi, and gave her some cherry liqueur. There wasn't much else left. Then I sat in the back of the cab with her.

We travelled the few miles in silence. The taxi waited, racking up dollars, while I put her to bed.

I gave her some brandy I found in the back of her fridge.

'It's cold,' she said, sounding more upset than she had at any other time during the long evening.

'I found it in the fridge,' I said.

'What's it doing there?' she said.

'Darlene,' I said abruptly, a chill running down my neck. 'Where's Harry and the boys?'

I'd forgotten all about them—until I'd suddenly realised the house was far too silent. I could hear the taxi's engine ticking over outside.

Christ! I thought. Concentrate!

I told myself that she was so drunk, anyway, there would have been no need of explanation. Still . . .

'They've gone fishing,' she said. 'Somewhere near Newcastle. Some Heads place. Fish Heads?'

She started to do her rising, rocking laugh, but did not seem to have the energy for it, and petered out.

'Can you sleep, do you think?' I said.

'Mm,' she said. 'Thanks for coming over.'

'I get bored,' she said. 'But that was some party.'

I took the cab back home.

'Family stuff?' said the driver. He mimed a glugging motion with a bottle. 'Yeh, yeh. Tell me about it. My sister-in-law, the stories I could tell you.' He smacked his lips and shook his head.

Elizabeth was sitting in the dining room, her hands folded on her lap, her back rod-straight.

She turned her head and stared at me.

'Well?' she said, one eyebrow raised.

'I think she'll be all right,' I said uneasily. 'I don't think . . . I don't think——'

'What?' she interrupted.

'Well, I don't think she remembers being here,' I said.

'She'd better not,' said Elizabeth grimly, staring straight ahead.

I comfort myself now with the thought that Darlene's mind was not on the job, that night. Or if it was, the alcohol wiped the memories out. Or something.

Later, we gave her ample opportunity to discuss the matter, Elizabeth and I. Not openly, but with subtle hints and reminders and timely pauses. But Darlene remained closed, as if a veil had been drawn over the events.

We killed him. We did kill him, and right in front of her. And she did not bat an eye. Merely continued to lie on her back, her legs apart, eyes glazed—mouth grinning as if it did not belong to her.

'Mother, what shall we do now?' I said.

Elizabeth turned her head and looked at me. Her eyes were bright, and blank behind the brightness.

'I'll lock the cellar door again,' I said.

'Yes,' she said, and shuddered. 'We'll clean that mess up in the morning.'

This notion seemed to cheer her. She stood up and, smiling wanly, went to bed.

Mother is right. We must clean up this mess, somehow, I thought.

Which, of course, eventually, we did.

∞

There now, it's out. I feel much better now it's out. Not that it's entirely gone from me.

Not that it will ever go away . . .

But a substantial portion of the stain has been lifted from me—and placed in you, dear book, in black and white. Well, in black, really. And that is fitting, isn't it? Of course, that doesn't mean my soul is any less grey.

But the burden of it, layered over with silence—silence and omission, thick with conspiracy, sweet and deadly as a sentimental lie—this, I give to you, book. It is yours, too, now. Ours. Make of it what you will.

85

OH, GOD, BOOK. OH, God. What is this darkness in me?

It is fear, hell-fear. The fear is so dark in me. I can feel dark flames licking away at my entrails.

For ever and ever, they say.

For ever and ever.

The blame—the apportioning of it—impossible. Our guilt mixed, as inseparably as the poison with the altar wine, as the poisoned wine with Brother Raymund's blood.

And where do these things begin and end?

It seems guilt is a thread that winds on forever in either direction, back to the past, and forward into the future, round and round us, binding us tightly, binding us together, for better or worse. Forever.

The thought of an eternity with Elizabeth by my side . . .

Oh, God. Keep breathing.

∞

The next morning, Elizabeth was hiding behind her usual carapace. And all the days and nights after that.

She never betrayed a moment of remorse. After the murder, she continued as before, weighing up my petty errors.

(Nothing could ever just *be*. She wanted to put her personal stamp on everyone and everything: the right thing to say, the right time to say it, the right way to behave, the right place to do it in, the right way to live—the only way.)

It was as if she believed he deserved it, and so absolved herself.

As if, like Darlene, she had a sliding screen in her mind which sealed him—and our act—off thoroughly.

Oh, for the gift of forgetfulness!

I was not like her. Nothing obscured the memory of his crumpled body from me. Over and over it I went.

In the end, I stopped berating myself for my part in the murder—which had seemed so logical and necessary at the time. In the end, even guilt, even grief, grow wearisome. Then I began to worry about being found out.

I swing from one to the other still: from remorse to fear, from horror to terror. It is a toss-up which is worse: being caught in this world—exposed and shamed, and bringing shame upon the family—being tried, and jailed in a tiny cell. Or eternal damnation. Hellfire.

Never mind, I tell myself. You're going there anyway, aren't you? But this thought is not so very comforting.

We both killed him, didn't we?

She more than I, because she went first?

I more than she, because I murdered coldly?

There is some relief in remembering that it is not for me to decide, not for me to apportion either punishment or blame.

Until the final moment, there is always hope of a reprieve, I tell myself. But who will argue my case in heaven, outside heaven's gates? Ron? Sylvester? Brother Raymund? Josephine? Elizabeth?

God, but how we hammer at each other! It's *this* way, it's *that* way. And since we bumped off Brother Raymund it's been worse.

There can be no difference, when all between us is different. It is as if an allowance of difference would split us apart—two halves of a whole—and reveal the rot within us.

Every petty detail, tugged and pulled, and rearranged. Every word, redefined. Every tiny fact of life tugged and tugged between us—and it's a deadly serious tug-of-war. It's a war, I tell you, not a game. But never, *never*, did we talk about the thing that we had done.

Had we done it the right way? What did she think? Was it the right thing to do?

Nothing seemed to touch her. Even this killing.

Had we done the right thing, in her eyes? After all, Brother Raymund was clearly in the wrong. In her eyes . . .

Nothing. Silence. Only her blue eyes bulging at me, scrutinising, silencing.

I had woven the sticky weave connecting us tighter. Ever tighter.

And what did I think? Was it right he should die for his sad little sin?

I no longer knew what I thought. Only what I had done, what we did.

Meanwhile, ever since (for ever and ever), her eyes watching mine, fishing for secrets—warning, forbidding, but serene in their righteous judgement.

∞

What happened then? The police called by. The Circle was disillusioned. But there were further disappointments in store for Elizabeth and me.

Elizabeth got Brother Raymund's address from Father Flynn.

'Strange he never gave it to us,' I said.

She silenced me with a look.

A day or so after the police came around, we went there.

'Why?' I said, shuffling along.

'To see,' said Elizabeth. 'Evidence.'

'Something that might implicate us,' she said.

'Some article of Darlene's?' I said.

'Quite,' she said, her mouth clamping shut.

It was a shabby house on a run-down block, a half a mile away from Glass Street.

'Not at all what I expected,' I said, as we picked our way up the cracked path.

'Is anything?' she said coldly.

'Shh. Let me handle this,' she said, as we neared the door.

'Hell-yoo,' she said.

'Hullo?' a voice croaked back.

She was a blowzy middle-aged woman, with crookedly applied lipstick and a gaping cleavage.

'I don't suppose you're after a room?' she said, momentarily brightening.

Elizabeth stared narrowly at the woman's dyed blonde hair, and explained her mission: she wished to pick up something of ours that Raymund Allan had borrowed. A missal, she said.

The woman sighed, eyed her suspiciously, then motioned us inside.

We followed her up two flights of stairs.

'Keeps me sprightly,' she said—although her middle had spread so much she could have been eight months pregnant.

We reached a door, and she felt around in her capacious blouse for a key.

The room was small and dusty, and dominated by a giant TV. We both stood, our mouths open, staring at it.

'I'll be selling that,' the landlady said defiantly, as if she suspected we'd come to claim it.

'Although it won't bring much, not these days,' she sniffed.

She thrust her raddled face at us and almost shouted: 'Won't put a dint into what he owes me.'

'Really!' said Elizabeth. 'Quite!'

'Don't think your missal's here,' the woman said. 'But have a poke if you want.'

She stood with her hands on her heavy hips, waiting. Clearly she was not going to leave us alone in there.

While Elizabeth picked gingerly about beside the rumpled bed, I examined the dresser and lowboy, still full of his soiled underwear and other clothes.

'Didn't take much with him,' I said.

Elizabeth turned and glared at me.

'Left quickly,' the woman sniffed. 'I might have known he was the type.'

'But he had a job,' I said. 'He was a salesman, wasn't he?'

'Coffins,' said Elizabeth. 'He was in coffins. Wholesale, I believe.'

'Oh, no,' said the woman. 'Not that. He was a cleaner of some sort. Janitor, he said. But I think he was just being fancy. Janitor's like me saying I'm a concierge, isn't it? When all I do is take the rent.'

'When the bastards pay it,' she growled.

'Where,' said Elizabeth icily, 'does he do this *cleaning*?'

Handling the word with tongs.

'At some place, some hospital place,' the woman said, scratching her scalp with the door-key. 'Oh, don't worry. I rang them, all right. He gave me the number when he first arrived, and I had it, in my book. I rang 'em, all right. Not been in, they said. Most inconvenient, they said. You're telling me, I said.'

'I'm sure,' said Elizabeth.

'Now what was the name of the blasted place?' said the woman. 'Bloody hell! It's on the tip of my tongue.'

She screwed her face up, while Elizabeth and I stared at her bosoms.

'I know! I remember!' she said brightly. 'It's called The Clinic! The Clinic, that's it. Knew I knew it. They're not very helpful, but.'

'Really,' said Elizabeth. 'How good of you to rack your brains for us.'

'St Vincent's Private Clinic, perhaps,' she said, out the side of her teeth, as we left.

∞

Oh, God, book.

The *Clinic*, she said.

But, of course. The Clinic, where I had meant to go to be relieved of *this*.

The Clinic. Women's services. All our staff pleasant and direct. No cheques, please.

Of course, Elizabeth had no way of knowing what sort of clinic that was, until recently. Would she have so admired him, knowing this?

And then I thought—the flesh.

The pure flesh of little children . . .

All his talk of purity, and chastity, and temples.

The bastard!

And then I thought—the *meat*—the white meat in the communion cakes. ('Is it chicken, or pork?' 'Oh, it's pure, don't you worry.') And vomited violently, missing my chamber pot.

86

WELL. HERE I AM, with all my secrets—the past—tucked away, harmlessly out of sight. Here I am, listening to rust forming in that lock. Me, the dolls, the milk-blue sky.

I think I have told you everything, book. It strikes me that the things I haven't told are hardly worth remembering. I have already forgotten them. Almost——

You will not forget, though. Your ink and paper are my evidence, as much as flesh and bones.

Dear, dear book. You have set me free from my lonely incarceration. I should have gone mad—should go mad—in this doll-infested glass asylum.

Book, do you realise, in all this world there is only you and me . . .

But imagine if Elizabeth read you! With my confession, and her confession thrown in for free! She'd murder me, book! Well, thank God for family.

No-one loves you like your family, as Elizabeth so much likes to tell me. In times of trouble, there's only family to rely on . . .

And I am one of them. Or so they say. Appearances to the contrary.

Still, it won't be long. As soon as I am shot of it, I shall get out of here. When she's got what she wants . . . And Jasper. The snake. They're welcome to it and each other.

Elizabeth says the baby will come at Christmas.

'A Christmas child!' she said, this morning.

'Our very own manger scene,' I replied.

Every day now, it seems, she takes my pulse. She pushes and prods around, feeling my belly, as if I am a cow—poking around, modestly, beneath the sheltering tent of the huge maternity smocks she has made me wear since July.

I suppose I am not a person, any more. I am a breeder, a sort of human test-tube, housing her baby. Her little lodger.

Oh, well. It will be over soon. It will all be over.

In fact, we won't have to wait long for the end of any of this nonsense. Only two and a half popes to go, didn't Brother Raymund say? God, what fools we were!

I imagine the months ahead—had we not killed him, and exposed his fraudulence: Katoomba!

We'll go up there in the New Year, as planned. In 1999, we'll be in the mountains, breathing mountain air—waiting for the tsunami to turn the mountain valley into a swaying seabed.

Ah, but we'll be ready, with our lifejackets and our flares. The attics of the cottages we've bought or rented—high on the highest hills—will be stacked with food and water. Torches, inflatable boats, oxygen tanks, masks, and warm, woolly underwear—all ready and waiting.

March, April, May. Then winter comes.

Then . . . nothing. The trickster. God! How could he do it?

Why didn't you stop him, God? Why didn't you pause my hand——

Oh, God, book, if Brother Raymund *was* right there are only seven months left . . .

Oh, God. God, God, *God*.

I don't know what to believe.

Damn you, God.

There! More blasphemy. That can be added to the list of small acts and thoughts engendering dismay that I tell each night like endless dreary decades of the rosary.

I accuse myself of deceit, vanity, delusion. Hypocrisy, malice, resentment. Self-pity, self-righteousness, and spite.

I accuse myself of countless mistruths of convenience. Sins of mind, of speech, of actions. And, of course, murder. Oh, by the way, *murder*.

There is no reparation.

Oh, when will it end?

When will it begin?

Eternity . . .

If only I could rid my mind of those dark-robed women. Their muttering forms, clustered about my neck. (If I strip away their costumes—the hooded capes, the wimples—I see that they are just doughy old Irish women. Virgins, propagating misconceptions.

Malicious? Simple-minded? Addled?) And I am not a child. I am not a virgin. I have seen Brother Raymund naked, without his cloak . . . And Jasper——

No, don't think about it.

And yet the dark winged things, their fluttering vestments, descend and cling to me, and press me close—and I can neither breathe nor see, the stink of earth in my nostrils.

This lies before you, they whisper. This is all there is for you, all there will ever be.

∞

Oh, book. Why do I trouble myself with imagined scenes of hell, when I will have so much time to see and experience it for myself when I finally die?

And purgatory? Purgatory will be like a piece of filter paper that I tear through in my downward plunge . . .

Still, I lie on my bed and think about death—who could be lurking, anywhere, waiting to take me. I think about the blackness of it.

In with faith, out with doubt, I breathe.

The night sky is a starless sable—high, high in my narrow window—with only a shred of moon.

I think about the coffin, lid closed. The earth on top of me. The cold dampness of the earth, deep down. The depth.

Then I remember Brother Raymund and the shallow bed we made for him on the floor of the cellar. How we covered him with concrete.

We put him in the earth like a bag of seed, and then we covered him with a thin skin of concrete—heavy on him, no doubt.

'We could burn the house down,' I said, that day.

'What if the concrete cracked in the heat? There is nothing covering him then,' Elizabeth said.

Her mouth was contorted in a grimace of fear, all of her teeth showing, uneven.

What a pity. I should so like to burn those dolls, I thought. (But, of course, I didn't say it.)

I imagine Raymund waking up from wherever he'd been, coming to in the darkness and feeling the weight of it on top of him—closed as a coffin lid.

I sit up from these thoughts and gulp for air, but there are no windows in this room that I can open—only the glass doors of the cabinets glinting in the occasional flash of moonlight, as the trees strip their leaves back and forth in the wind across the moon's half-face.

I stumble to the door and feel for the light switch, and cannot find it, and I am breathing darkness.

Hail Mary full of grace, Hail Mary full of grace, I pray, my breath coming in thick gasps.

Finally, I find the switch. I snap the light on, then lie back on my narrow bed, in a sea of dolls, gasping.

Oh, save me, book. I am so afraid.

87

IT WAS BORN SOME hours ago. Elizabeth delivered it. (I don't know where she got it from, but she gave me a shot of morphine afterwards—which was, I must say, quite delicious.)

I screamed my head off during the birth. It went on for hours. Days? The labour, I suppose I mean. The birth went on for all eternity.

My face reflected back to me from the glass, swollen and distorted, as thousands of doll-eyes watched.

And then I split.

'Go on, scream away,' said Elizabeth. 'No-one will hear you.'

How did she say it? Cheerily? Jeering? Triumphant?

'Scream away,' she said, crouched over me like a bug.

'Jesus!' I shrieked. 'Oh, Je-sus!'

'God will forgive you,' said Elizabeth. 'Mother Mary will intercede.'

'Fucking Christ!' I shouted.

'Let it out,' Elizabeth said, tight-lipped.

'Drugs,' I said.

'I'm sorry,' said Elizabeth, smiling sweetly.

'No, you're not!' I screamed.

'Pain is perfectly normal at this juncture,' she said, lips like wire. 'We must simply bear it.'

'You bloody bitch,' I said.

I closed my eyes and grunted.

'It's happening now,' she said. 'And nothing and no-one can stop it.'

She was hovering over me like a nun, or a spider, so totally absorbed and serious.

This was her work, I realised. How forbidding she must have been as a nurse.

Some time passed and I looked up and—was I hallucinating?—there were Marlene and Darlene, grinning at me, and bending over, her bearded face between my legs, was Mildred Cleghorn.

'What is this, open day?' I shouted. 'What's *she* doing here?'

'She's a midwife,' said Elizabeth.

'Bullshit,' I said.

'Getting salty, isn't she,' said Mildred. 'That's a good sign.'

'I don't like it,' said Elizabeth.

'What?' I said sharply.

'Nothing,' she said.

'Get—them—out—of here,' I shouted.

'I want them out!' I screamed. 'Right out of the house.'

Mildred sighed and clicked her tongue.

'It's all right. I'll manage,' said Elizabeth.

Martyr.

'Going, going,' said Marlene, waving snidely.

And the three of them trooped out together, Darlene looking more than usually dazed.

∞

After the thing was out of me, Elizabeth was busy, frowning, down at the end of the bed. Two heads, I thought, flatly. Everything was draining out of me.

It crossed my mind that she would let me lie there, bleeding. Take the baby and let me die, having got from me what she wanted.

Then she held something up, crushed and purple and wrapped in a towel.

'See?' she said.

I turned my head away.

Then something else cannoned out of me.

'Jesus! What was that?' I shouted.

'Afterbirth,' she said tersely.

Something was rippling out of me.

'Lie still,' she said.

I was struggling to sit up, and something was rippling out of me . . .

Then she gave me the morphine. (As a reward? A thank-you present?)

She stuffed me with what felt like six packets of cotton wool, and swabbed my legs, and expertly changed the sodden sheets. And I lay there, smiling to myself. Daft as Dymphna, I thought. But it was only the lovely morphine.

'Are you going to eat the afterbirth for dinner?' I said dreamily. 'You and Jasper?'

'Don't be disgusting,' Elizabeth said.

I could hear her splashing about. Washing it, I suppose. Then she held it up, and it bleated.

'Look,' she said. 'A boy!'

The beast which comes up from the abyss . . .

'He's a beautiful, beautiful baby,' she said. 'See?'

'I am not bonding with it,' I said.

'Of course you're not bonding with it,' she cried. 'You haven't even held him. You haven't even smelt his delicious head.'

'Oh, God,' I said, and turned away.

She took it out of the room—stopping to carefully lock me in. Ha!

I heard her saying, 'Far better than could have been expected, really.'

Could have been a fish, it's true. Could have been a toad.

'Oh!' I heard Jasper say. 'What a poppet!'

And then I seemed to fade away . . .

Now, every few hours she brings it in and lies it in a bassinet beside me. It howls and howls, and she comes and glares at me and takes it out again.

88

ITS EYES ARE BRIGHT pale blue, round as sixpences. Its lids slide open and closed—and when they open, they seem to stare at me. A tuft of corn-yellow hair stands up around the edges of its head—the rest is bald, as if it has been tonsured. Its face is sickly white, with mottled red spots around its nose and on its cheeks. Most unattractive, I think. And then, to top it off, from time to time, it bleats like a goat or sheep—its mouth open in an absurd little circular pucker.

How strange its eyes are!

∞

'Feed him,' said Elizabeth a moment ago, thrusting it forward. 'He wants you to feed him.'

She's been doing this periodically for days.

'Go on,' she said. 'He's yours.'

Little bright-eyed thing.

'Get it away from me!' I cried. 'The devil's child!'

'Don't be absurd,' she began, then thought better of it.

She unwrapped its shawl, then beckoned me closer.

'Look,' she said temptingly.

It was long, with long pale legs and arms, and drooping, tadpole hands and feet.

'Pale,' I said.

'Fair,' she said.

'Isn't he lovely?' she said.

I stared and stared. I saw a spindly naked boy baby, pale and pathetically mottled, lying in a puddle of familiar red.

'Jesus!' I said, realising.

'Don't blaspheme, Ellen,' she said wearily.

'You've wrapped him in the altar cloth, Mother!' I said. 'Look at that! That's sick.'

'Don't be ridiculous! It's only a cut-off from the same material, you silly girl,' she said.

'I haven't had time to get him any proper things,' she said.

Liar, I thought.

'How much time do you need to buy a couple of nappies and a shawl?' I said.

'There's a lot more to it than that,' she said smartly.

She darted me a look.

'You've no idea, the strain I've been under,' she said.

'No,' I said dully. 'Of course I don't.'

'I simply haven't had time to think straight, let alone buy nappies,' she sighed.

'But *you* could,' she added, her voice thick with hinting.

'I could,' I said slowly, 'go out now? Now that it's over?'

'And shop,' she said, her voice thick and sweet, 'for baby.'

'Ye-es,' I said. 'Yes, I could . . .'

'We'll take a taxi,' she said quickly.

'Oh, together,' I said.

'Well, of course, together,' she said, her blue eyes bulging innocently.

'You don't trust me,' I said flatly. 'No, of course, you don't. Or else you wouldn't have locked me in here, would you? And you wouldn't still have me locked up in this stinking room, would you, now that you've got what you wanted——'

'What I wanted!' she shouted. 'You've forgotten a thing or two, young misery.'

She clamped her mouth shut, as if over a mosquito.

Then, her voice calmly moderated, she said: 'You show me you can be trusted, young lady, and I'll learn to trust you. But don't you forget what you've put me through.'

'Put you through, put you through,' I muttered. 'It's always all about you.'

'What's that?' she said.

'Forget it,' I said sullenly.

'If you're going to malign me to my face,' she said, drawing herself up and thrusting her jaw imposingly, 'at least let me hear it.'

I stayed silent, staring at my feet.

'I have had quite enough of your moods and your accusations,' she said.

'Oh, it's nothing, nothing,' I said.

And it was nothing. It was just another little truth that would crumble to dust later on, for lack of any evidence.

'And who will mind it?' I said. 'When we go shopping. Together.'

'The *baby*,' she said, in this oily holy voice. 'Jasper will mind the baby.'

'Oh, you trust him,' I said. 'That's interesting.'

'Jasper,' she said, in the same oily voice, her eyes glazing, 'has been a marvellous support for me. In this special time. He's even taken a week off work!'

'Probably a paedophile,' I said.

And she blinked twice, and turned her head away.

All the while, it lay on its red cloth, gazing at us benignly with its peculiar bright pale eyes.

'Look!' I said. 'It's got eyes like Brother Raymund! See?'

'You don't know where to stop, do you?' Elizabeth snarled.

She scooped it up, and went to leave the room. At the door she slowed, and turned back.

'So lovely,' she said, her voice thick and sweet again, 'when you can think of a suitable name for baby . . .'

I rolled my eyes.

'I'll bring your clothes down,' she said, leaving—closing and locking the door.

Already, the room smelt of it. Pale and milky, and the slightest trace of urine.

89

WE SHOPPED FOR SEVERAL hours. Nappies, pilchers, jumpsuits, singlets, bootees, a summer shawl, and several bibs. Everything tiny as doll's clothes. Everything pastel: lemon, blue, pearl, and mint green. Nothing pink.

After so long in my room, the shops seemed strangely glaring. The people, the endless array of supplies, the boundlessness of it—like an hallucination. I was glad, almost, when we returned.

It was crying, as usual.

Elizabeth installed me back in the doll-room, then raced off to see to it.

'Jasper! Jasper?' her voice fluted as she rushed up the stairs.

I could hear her moving about, and then the baby stopped its noise.

I was tired after my expedition. I lay on my bed and went to sleep.

∞

Some time later, Elizabeth unlocked my door. She stood in the doorway and stared at me blankly.

'He's late,' she said. 'I'm scared.'

'What?' I said, struggling to sit up.

'A little worried,' she amended.

By the amount of light in the room, I could see it was not yet night—but then the summer days went on and on, and night did not fall until well after dinner.

'What time is it?' I said, yawning.

'Eight,' she said tragically. 'Dinner time, and he's not back.'

'Perhaps he's *gone*,' she said.
'Who?' I said.
'Jasper,' she snapped.
'Oh, Jasper,' I said.
'He went out for some milk,' she said.
'Well?' I said.
'It's been hours!' she cried.
'Oh,' I said. 'I see. Did he take it with him?'
She stared at me.
'Oh, well,' I said. 'You have to admit, it would be handy. Still, if it's just that greaseball gone, that's a blessing. Must be thankful for small mercies, mustn't we?'

She continued to stare at me, her mouth slack with disbelief. Then she began to cry, slow glass-bright tears.

Upstairs, the baby began to cry also. Louder, and louder, a terrible wail.

'Oh, you wicked girl,' she said.
'See what you've done?' she cried, and ran from the room.
Not so disturbed that she forgot to stop and lock me in.

What did she want from me, now that she had what she wanted? My milk? (Horrible business. My breasts engorged, and leaking. Things—just other things, that did not belong to me.)

The baby stopped wailing, at last. And I dozed off again.

Of course, Jasper showed up. No doubt, he'd felt the need to change his clothes—to slip his skins—to escape the tension in the house. God, the air was thick with it.

Tearful reunion between old mother and prospective son-in-law played out loudly in the dining room: Elizabeth, weeping tears of relief. Jasper, all apologies.

'So silly of me,' said Elizabeth. 'But then, we've had a very unsettled day.'

'And our little man, how is he?' said Jasper.

'Charming, utterly charming,' she cried, 'with occasional bouts of screaming. All quite normal, under the circumstances.'

'But let's not worry about any of this!' she cried. 'Our boy is sleeping, all's well in the world, and I've got you, Jasper, all to myself!'

'Oh, Mother!' he said.
All ooze and slime.

90

ELIZABETH STOPPED PRESSING ME for names after I suggested we call it Baby Jesus, and began presenting her own to the room at large.

'Francis Xavier,' she said.

'No, it's too fussy,' she muttered. 'John? *John*? Too short.'

'John-Paul . . . No, something plainer. Peter,' she said, sighing happily.

'After your grandfather?' I said idly.

'No!' she snapped. 'After Peter the rock.'

'Call it Rock,' I said. 'That's plain enough.'

'Childish,' she said. 'Always so keen to irritate, aren't you, Eleanor?'

'What about Mark?' she said, then, her blue eyes wide.

'Mark. Or Mathew. No, then he'd get called Matt, like something the cat sleeps on,' she muttered.

'Luke?' she said. 'What do we think of Luke?'

We? Perhaps she thought the dolls were listening.

'Christopher? *Christopher*? It has a lovely ring to it,' she said. 'So nearly a Christmas child, too.'

'Three syllables, though,' she muttered. 'A man needs a manly name. George? James? Andrew! That's not so bad . . .'

'Yes!' she cried. 'I think that's it, Ellen! Andrew. My angel, my pet. Dear, sweet, little, baby Andrew!'

'Lucifer would be more appropriate,' I said. '*Little* Lucifer.'

What a pleasure to see her face.

91

I AM SLEEPY, SO sleepy. I doze on and off all day, and sleep like a lump of wood at night.

Today, I had the strangest dream. I hardly ever dream these days—not so as to remember them, at any rate.

I dreamt the doors of the cabinets flew open, and the dolls all turned to stare at me. Thousands of tiny, solemn faces . . .

Pray for me, they said as one—with quite a pleasant voice.

Suddenly, each and every one of them commenced to weep, and they were weeping tears of blood.

Pray for me, they said, again. And the tears of blood slowly fell.

And I woke up and looked up above me, and it was raining. That was all. I can't say I wasn't disappointed.

∞

After dinner, Elizabeth brought it in, decked out in more new clothes. (Every few hours, since the birth, she brings it in.)

It is getting used to me, I think. Horrid little thing. It doesn't howl and bray as often as it used to. Just lies there, damply, like a little rollmop.

Though my breasts threaten to burst and shower the wretched dolls with milk, I will not feed it.

It lies then, forlornly, in its travel-cot, smelling vaguely of her perfume, until she comes back to take it out again.

'I'll leave you two to get acquainted,' she said tonight. Not for the first time.

'Oh, lovely,' I said, rolling my eyes.

As soon as she'd left the room, I bent and sniffed its head. The sharp, soapy smell of her perfume, yes. And . . . Just as I thought. And worse in the neck region. The stink of fish!

'Get it out of here!' I shouted.

I shout and shout, and still it lies there and—I don't know—it watches me. Its pale cold eyes . . .

'Mother,' I screamed then. 'Take it away from me.'

'Oh, dear,' she said, returning. 'Has the little darling filled his nappy?'

She handles it with swift efficiency, every action saying: See? He's mine!

'Not a maternal bone in her body!' said Elizabeth, in the dining room, her voice rising in a crow of triumph.

'Lucky our little man has you, Mother,' said Jasper.

'Isn't it,' she said, with satisfaction.

Well. Let them have it. It is *theirs*. Good riddance to it.

'And to think I thought that having him would soften her stubborn heart,' she sighed.

'Well!' she said happily. 'Some things never change.'

I can hear you, I said to myself. I can hear, I can hear, I can hear you. What do you think: I'm deaf as well as mute? Deaf as a corpse in this tomb of a room, and dumb as a painted dolly?

∞

I could take it on. I could. If only to wipe that smile of satisfaction from her face.

What is it to her, anyway? A pawn. A *symbol*.

If I am not careful, I can feel sorry for it.

92

JASPER WENT BACK TO work, Christmas came and went, and we settled into a routine: our fractured family.

I remained quarantined in the doll-room. Further punishment? And then . . . And then . . .

One night, a few weeks after it was born, I heard the rattle of the key being inserted in the lock, then slowly turned.

I lay rigid on my single bed, listening, as Jasper's footsteps moved towards me in the darkness.

He stopped beside me and breathed for a while. Then he bent down and slid into the bed, cradling me from behind.

I said nothing.

I felt his breath on my neck and cheek. Then he stroked my belly and whispered, 'Ah! You're back.'

I was back?

'I've missed you,' he whispered. 'Eleanora.'

I said nothing.

'We're twins, you and I,' he whispered.

'Twins, Eleanora,' he whispered, stroking my thighs. 'No-one can separate us. Do you understand? Not even the baby.'

Still I said nothing.

'Thank heavens it's gone from you,' he whispered then.

'I thought,' I said in a voice that sounded stiff from disuse, 'the baby was what you wanted? Part of your plan.'

'Plan?' he whispered, kissing my neck. 'How could you think that of me?'

'I thought you wanted it. Used me,' I said bitterly, 'to procreate. A handmade family——'

'Hush,' he said, covering my mouth. 'It was you I wanted.'

'Me?' I said.

'Oh, my Eleanora,' he said, pulling me closer, caressing my neck.

'Really?' I said.

But my body had already made the move, half-turning towards him.

'Let me come closer,' he whispered.

'Oh, Jasper,' I said. 'Why did you go from me? Why did you leave me alone?'

'Hush,' he said. 'Hush, now. We don't want to wake the little bastard.'

'And Mother?' I said.

'Don't worry,' he said, chuckling softly. 'The old gorgon's out like a light. Popped a few pills in her coffee!'

He began to stroke the length of my body.

'Oh, my darling,' he whispered.

'We will go away together, you and I,' he said.

'But my mother——' I said.

'She's a tartar,' said Jasper. 'She rides you bareback, my poor Eleanora. How I'd hate to be God when her time comes!'

'You seem to like her,' I said.

To lap her up, I thought.

'That is my charm, silly,' he said. 'I use it to ward off dragons and hack my way through thorns.'

'Oh, my poor darling,' he said, hugging me closer. 'She's nothing! A piranha in a goldfish bowl!'

'Don't be afraid, Eleanora,' he said. 'I will take care of you.'

'And . . . ?' I said. 'What about *it*?'

'We shall give it to the poor,' he said airily—though his hands which had been caressing my body ceaselessly were suddenly still.

'You don't think I'd leave it here!' he said. 'No chance.'

'We can't just give it away,' I said. 'Can we?'

'Adoption,' he said. 'Or a basket with a note. There are ways. You'd be surprised what some people's birth certificates reveal.'

I remembered his job. How silly. To forget, I mean. And how silly to ever think he'd taken that job to spy on Elizabeth and me!

'Leave it at a church?' I said, warming to the theme. After all, it was never my intention to keep it. Never my intention to *have* it.

'Not a church,' he said quickly. 'A hospital, or a police station.'

'Or maybe,' he said, 'a telephone box. The weather's mild enough.'

'Wouldn't you wonder?' I said. 'If it was——'

'Oh, life is too short, sweet Eleanora,' he said.

'I'd wonder,' I said.

Then I stiffened and pulled away.

'Why did you stop me?' I said. 'None of this need have happened. Now it's a *baby*, with a life of its own. If only——'

'Hush,' he said. 'Don't want to wake it.'

'Oh, God,' I said.

'What if you'd died?' he whispered. 'They're butchers, those people.'

'What if I'd died giving birth?' I said.

'My mother,' he sighed, 'died like that.'

'But I thought you said——' I said.

'My step-mother. My father married again,' he said. 'My real mother died giving birth.'

Oh, pull the other one, I wanted to say. But he was convincing—his body rigid, his face turned stiffly aside.

'Under the anaesthetic,' he said, his voice small as a child's.

'Having an abortion?' I said.

'No, you idiot, it wasn't legal in those days. She died, in a hospital, under the anaesthetic. She died giving birth to me,' he spat.

'Oh, Jasper,' I said. 'I am sorry.'

Hang on, I thought.

'Giving birth?' I whispered furiously. '*I* might have died giving birth. Elizabeth's not a doctor. She hasn't even nursed in thirty years! I might have died, too!'

'Not under anaesthetic,' he said cunningly. 'She doesn't have any, does she?'

'Oh, Jesus, Jasper,' I said. 'Go away.'

I pushed him, but he clung to me on the narrow bed.

'It's too complicated to explain,' he said. 'The unconscious mind is very strange. You must trust me, Eleanora. We're together now, aren't we, Eleanora?'

'Aren't we together, my darling?' he wheedled.

I waited, feeling his breath against my neck in the dark like the fanning of tiny wings.

'When will we go?' I said.

'Soon,' he said. 'Soon, my sweet.'

'How soon?' I said.

'Soon, my darling, soon,' he said.

'Be patient,' he said, stroking my hair.

'Oh, she's red as a rose,' he said, burying his face in it. 'And she will be mine.'

'Won't she?' he said.
'Yes,' I said, all thought vacated.

∞

Later, he whispered, so softly I could have been dreaming it: 'Eleanora? The most amazing thing! You had twins.'

'What?' I whispered back.

'You had *twins*,' he hissed.

'Don't be silly,' I said, and slapped him lightly on the thigh.

He was twined around me, stroking my face. His breath smelt of rock pools, sea anemones . . .

'Mother delivered two babies,' he sang.

'Of course she didn't want to tell you. The first died. Just like Elvis. Another boy,' he said, stroking my ear.

I went rigid. I flicked his hand away.

'Don't be silly,' I repeated. 'Why would she hide such a thing from me?'

'Oh, Mother hides a lot from you,' he said quietly, and slid backwards off the bed.

'Night, night, darling,' he said.

'Darling?' he whispered, pausing. 'You're not upset, are you, my sweet Eleanora?'

He was padding softly away.

'I'm sorry, sweetest,' he whispered as he reached the door.

'Just thought you should know,' he said.

'It's part of the synchronicity, you see,' he said, while I stared stupidly at the outline of his departing form.

And the door closed, and then slowly, slowly, with an elaborate series of clicks and rattles and shoves, the lock clicked into place.

93

LAST NIGHT, FINALLY—SEVEN or eight weeks after the birth—I was allowed out of my cell to eat dinner in the dining room.

Was this a sudden decision? A whim? A *reward*?

Elizabeth led me to my place. There was Jasper, already at the table, beaming wildly.

My heart began to pound.

'Ah, Eleanora! So nice,' he said, formally, half-rising—as if it had been a long time since he'd seen me.

When every night . . . Every night . . .

'Please, Jasper, sit,' said Elizabeth.

And he sat back down, obedient as a dog.

We spoke little. We had a kind of shepherd's pie, made with salmon and chives, and potatoes mashed with sour cream. Delicious! There were half a dozen vegetables, in butter, on the side.

'Mother,' Jasper said. 'You have surpassed yourself!'

Any old chestnut, he'd crank it out.

I suppressed a giggle. How long it had taken me to realise it was all an act!

I looked up. They were both staring hard at me.

'Excuse me,' I said. 'The excitement . . . So glad . . .'

'Well, of course, dear,' said Elizabeth, smiling tolerantly.

Halfway through the main course, it began to wail upstairs.

'God!' I said, screwing up my face.

Elizabeth for once did not chastise me.

'I'll go,' she said, throwing down her napkin with a little sigh.

'It would be easier to leave it down here with me, wouldn't it?' I said. 'I could look after it.'

Little thing. I could almost warm to it, now that I knew I was going to get away.

Elizabeth's face softened. She glanced solemnly at Jasper, as if a breakthrough had been made.

'I'll see to him for now,' said Jasper swiftly.

He went upstairs and was gone for quite a time.

Elizabeth smiled at me, her eyes so bright with hope I thought they would pop right out and land in her mashed potatoes. I grimaced a facsimile of a smile back, and we ate.

The crying had stopped and we had finished our main courses, and were waiting for Jasper before beginning our dessert of cherry pie with clotted cream.

'That's fixed him,' said Jasper, sliding back into his seat. 'I think he's down for the night.'

'He's a good sleeper,' said Elizabeth, beaming proudly. 'Our little Andrew.'

After dinner, Jasper made his familiar limp offer with the dishes.

'No, no, no!' said Elizabeth gaily. 'You stay and rest after your hard day's work.'

'Ellen, here, will help me,' she said.

'Of course,' I said meekly.

'It's Eleanora,' he whispered to me out the side of his mouth, as Elizabeth headed into the kitchen.

He flicked me gently on the behind.

I turned and smiled at him.

I had never felt happier, it seemed to me then. All the pain of those long months, gone—wiped away with one flick of his fingers.

'Tell you what,' he said. 'You ladies see to the kitchen area and I'll just whip upstairs and check on our young man again.'

'You're a gem, Jasper,' cried Elizabeth. 'Isn't he?'

I smiled, and followed her.

∞

I suppose it was while we were doing the dishes that Jasper let himself out. I thought I heard the front door softly clicking closed. (But of course all sounds in the house had shifted, after my time in that room, and I could as easily have heard another door pulled to on the upper floor—misheard it, that is. Mentally misplaced the sound.)

Well, I know now it was Jasper slipping out, bags and all.

That night, after the dishes, I went to bed in my cell, as usual. Elizabeth locked me in, as usual. But she was wearing a hopeful, pop-eyed smile.

Things were working out at last, she must have thought.

And so, in my own way, did I.

∞

I was roused from my sleep by her scream. On and on it went. Then her feet were tearing down the stairs and my door was unlocked and she was standing there in a floor-length sheer white nightgown—a ghostly vision—her face pale grey and twitching, her eyes bugged out with fright.

'What is it?' I said.

'Ah!' she shrieked, glancing round wildly.

'God takes, and he takes,' she gasped, and began to cry.

Her fingers raked at the air, and her arms waved about helplessly, and her mouth hung open, and she cried and cried.

She reminded me of *it*, flailing about in its carry-cot.

'Mother,' I said. 'What is it?'

'The baby's dead!' she shouted. 'Dead!'

'My little baby,' she moaned, clasping and unclasping her hands.

'What?' I said. 'How——'

'And *he's* gone!' she shrieked, in a rising voice.

'Jasper?' I said, my throat tight.

'Who do you think?' she shouted.

'I don't believe you,' I said.

I felt as if the blood had stopped moving in my body.

'Dead, and gone,' she moaned. 'Oh, my baby . . .'

And then she began to scream. On and on and on.

'Mother,' I said sharply. 'Mother? Where is the syringe?'

'Mother?' I said. Receiving no response, I slapped her briskly across the cheeks. She stopped her hideous shrieking, and stared at me, blank-faced.

'Where is the hypodermic, Mother?' I said, shaking her. 'The knock-out drug? Remember?'

'I don't know what you're talking about,' she said.

'But——' I said.

'Oh, that was just to keep you from getting any silly ideas,' she said, momentarily bright. 'Jasper wasn't even in the hallway half the time——'

'Oh, God,' she said, her face collapsing, her eyes filling again with tears.

She slumped onto my bed then, rocking back and forth and wailing.

'He takes and he takes,' she sobbed.

Her blue eyes were bulging and glazed.

'Who?' I said.

'My son,' she wailed. 'He's taken my only son.'

'I had the baby,' I said.

'No,' she said.

As if I'd forget that!

'Who takes?' I said.

'God!' she screamed, clenching her fists and thumping her thighs with them.

'It was my baby,' I said blankly.

My baby . . .

I remembered Jasper saying to me: 'All flesh is like grass to God, Eleanora. He has such an appetite. He chomps and chomps on us, and still he's not satisfied . . .'

I remembered him at the dining table earlier that night, smiling, smirking. The Last Supper. How he must have laughed at us, at me.

'It was my baby,' I repeated.

'You don't understand,' she said. 'Oh, Jesus!'

'Show me the baby, Mother,' I said coldly.

'It's a terrible, terrible thing,' she wailed. 'You don't want to see that. No!'

'I've seen terrible things,' I said. 'Take me to the baby.'

∞

It was in my old bedroom, in a white bassinet.

It was cold and still, mouth fixed open.

I gazed at it blankly, for quite some time, it seemed. Then I mouthed one word:

'Piranha,' I said.

Elizabeth took no heed.

'And the poor mite's not been baptised!' she wailed. 'Oh, what a web we've woven for ourselves, what a noose!'

'I was going to take him,' she spluttered. 'I was going to——'

'Don't worry, Mother,' I said. 'I'll baptise it.'

I looked down at the little thing, all mottled mauve and blue.

'He's set me up,' I said.

'What?' shrieked Elizabeth. 'What are you talking about?'

'We did it,' I said. 'We killed him.'
'Oh, don't get all metaphysical with me, my girl,' she said.
'Jasper,' I sighed.
'Jasper?' she croaked, and began to sob soundlessly.
'That evil snake,' I hissed.
'What?' she said, as if startled awake.
'Perhaps he's ill?' she said. 'Out of his mind, in some peculiar way . . .'
'He won't have gotten far,' she cried. 'I'll call the police.'
'What for? The baby doesn't exist. It never existed officially,' I said.

She stared at me, her mouth agape.
'And now it's dead. We killed him, Jasper and I,' I said.
'But you were in there!' she said. 'You couldn't have.'
'Even so, my hands aren't clean,' I said.
'You can't call the police, and he knows it,' I said.
'What are you talking about?' she spluttered.
'The *cellar*,' I said.
'Oh!' she said. 'You're sure?'
'Oh, yes,' I said.
And for once she did not disbelieve me.
'Show me Jasper's room,' I said.
She opened her eyes wide like a madwoman. Like Darlene.
'He's gone, I tell you,' she said.
'I want to see for myself,' I said.
'Gone,' she sobbed. 'Gone like a ghost.'

The wardrobe door swung open. Only hangers. The desk was empty. There was only a balled-up piece of paper in the bin, and a lingering smell—just a faint fish smell on his pillow.

'I'm not surprised,' I said. 'Not surprised. The signs were all there, from the first. If only . . .'
'You know who he is, don't you?' I said.
'You *know*?' she said incredulously.
I nodded.
'But——' she said.
'I smelt him,' I said.
She looked at me strangely.
'I swear to God I never knew, until recently,' she said.
She rolled her eyes and wrung her hands.
'Of course I know,' I said. 'I've known since the day he came.'
'But——' she said.
'It was foretold,' I said, 'in the Book of Revelations.'
'Don't be ridiculous, Ellen!' she said.

'Look,' I said. 'It's simple, really. Jasper is the Antichrist.'
'But this is silly,' she said. 'You're hysterical——'
'He's the Antichrist!' I shouted. 'I knew it the moment he entered the house. Can't you see? I thought you could see everything, Mother.'
'No!' she cried. 'Stop this. Stop this at once.'
I stood in the centre of Jasper's empty room, heaving.
'This is no time for joking, Eleanor,' she said.
'Eleanora,' I said quietly.
'Oh, for Christ's sake!' she spat.
'It's my name,' I said.

She clenched her fists and thumped herself about the head. She stood there, with her eyes screwed shut and her mouth pursed horribly, and her face quite scarlet. Then she made an effort to regain her composure—breathing deeply in and out, so that her waist moved beneath the sheer white gown like a fleshy pair of bellows.

'I am his mother,' she said flatly.
'I had the baby,' I said. 'You seem to keep forgetting——'
'Jasper,' she said. 'I am Jasper's mother.'
I laughed.
'Oh, that's going too far,' I said.
'Do you understand what I'm telling you, you silly girl?' she said. 'Jasper is my son.'
I stared at her for a while.
'Well!' I said. 'He would want you to think that, wouldn't he? It's his pleasure to twist your mind. He's the King of Confusion. The Prince of Lies. The——'
'Look at these,' she said.
She handed me some papers.
'Well,' I said. 'That's easy——'
'No,' she said.
She began to cry.

His actions, so confusing—deliberately so—bore all the hallmarks of the devil. Surely she could see that?

'He's, well, slippery,' I said. 'Just because——'
'He's my son,' she said flatly.
She turned and left the room.

∞

He worked there. He knew this. He *knew*.
And Otto? Was Otto in on this, too? Was no-one what they said they were?

I waited for a moment, then followed her. She was in the doll-room, sitting on my narrow bed, stroking one of her dolls. (It was the boy in the sailor suit, that I had smeared with food. Indeed, his collar had yellowed.)

'I found the papers when I was vacuuming his room,' Elizabeth said dully.

'They were just lying about,' she said.

'When?' I said.

'Weeks ago,' she said. 'They were there, on his desk, in plain view.'

'Beneath a stack of books,' she added, looking away.

'Oh,' I said. 'What did he say?'

'Nothing,' she said.

'I couldn't talk about it,' she said.

'How many weeks ago?' I said. 'Mother?'

But she ignored me.

'How long have you known this?' I shouted. 'Mother? How long?'

'Weeks. Months,' she said whitely.

Poor Elizabeth. Aghast at her holy family unravelling.

'My only son!' she said. 'Found after all these years, and now he's gone.'

'Gone,' she said. 'And the baby——'

'That doesn't rule him out from being the Antichrist,' I said slyly.

'Enough!' she shouted, thrusting her red face at me. 'You never know when to give up, do you?'

We sat together in horrible silence.

'Why didn't you tell me when you found out?' I said quietly then. 'It might have made a difference to me——'

'I'm telling you now,' she shouted.

I was calm. It was the only thing to be.

'He must have counted on your silence . . .' I said.

She had nothing to say to that either.

'It's just as well he's killed the baby then. He's the baby's father, after all,' I said.

'Mother,' I said, 'Mother, are you listening? It's true, what I said. It's Jasper who fathered that baby.'

Silence.

'My brother,' I said.

'I believe you,' she said flatly.

'You do?' I said. 'I'm surprised. I thought you *knew* it was Otto's. Are you sure I'm not telling you more of my devious lies?'

'Don't,' she said, her eyes immeasurably weary.

'I take it he's killed the baby?' I said. 'I take it it wasn't you?'

'Oh, Jesus!' she screamed, her eyes bulging. 'Jesus Christ. You *filthy* slut.'

She slammed the door, leaving me with the papers.

For once she did not lock the door, and yet I lay there.

94

I WOKE UP. MY arms were bandaged. Elizabeth was babbling outside my door.

'Why she had to cut herself with the glass I don't know,' she said. 'She said she had to get the evil out of her. That's what she said——'

'Well, she's *had* the baby,' said Marlene. 'Could it be something to do with that?'

'No,' Elizabeth snapped. 'He's sleeping.'

'Oh,' said Marlene. 'I meant——'

'I saw the red flowing under the door, rolling towards me. Like a red sea, Marlene,' Elizabeth said plaintively, her voice beginning to quaver. 'Blood pouring out like water . . .'

'*Waves* of blood,' she said.

I did not want to die—only to end what I could not bear. Well.

'I opened the door,' she said, 'and there was glass and blood—she'd smashed the glass from the cabinets—and blood, and blood . . .'

Her voice was rising.

'But you've sewn her up, haven't you?' said Marlene in her brisk way. 'No harm done, really?'

'Oh, but Marlene,' moaned Elizabeth.

'It's all sorted, Lizzie,' said Marlene.

Their crow voices!

'Just as well you had your sewing skills,' she added.

'She never listens to me,' muttered Elizabeth. 'She *never* listens to me.'

'The blood, Marlene!' she said. 'I tell you, I nearly fainted . . .'

'After all your training,' said Marlene sternly.

And I just lay there.
Eventually, they left, and I fell back into a deep, drugged sleep.

∞

I woke up, finally. Had she given me more of the morphine? Or some drug similar? If only I could remember it. What is the point of pleasure if you have no memory? When there is no gap that is not pain.

All the glass had been removed as I slept. Even the stuck shards, that had protruded from the framework, even the smallest splinters had been removed, and the floor most thoroughly swept.

Who did it? Frank? Harry?

Harry and Frank. Usually, they're both interchangeably useless, in Elizabeth's view. I'd like to say they are something different to me—a nod, a warmth, a wink. But I can't even remember what colour their eyes are.

Harry, Frank. They're all in on it, I expect.

All the blood whisked away . . . *My* blood. The rags already burnt. All the shattered pieces, parcelled up, disposed.

Where do the pieces of shattered souls go? Do they fly out, and imbed themselves in others? Yes, I think that's how it goes. One day, my soul will filter down, like sprinkled confetti, like glass confetti, over all humankind . . .

But you, book, kept safe and warm through it all!

When I woke up, at last, I felt beneath the mattress. (My first thought was for you, book.)

There you were! Oh, the joy of seeing your familiar cover!

As long as you are safe and well, so am I. More or less.

∞

I closed my eyes. And then I opened them again, and no time had passed at all.

I could hear them, in the dining room, still having their tea.

'The blood,' Elizabeth kept saying. 'So horrible——'

'Are you sure,' Marlene said, her voice sharp, 'you don't want to call the doctor?'

'No,' said Elizabeth quickly.

'All right,' said Marlene. 'Are you sure, then, that you won't have one of these pills?'

'No, thank you,' said Elizabeth. 'It's just——'

'I know,' snapped Marlene. 'The blood, the blood.'

95

THE FOLLOWING MORNING, ELIZABETH brought in my tray. She set it down, and sat at the foot of my bed, and said: 'I never wanted to call him Jasper.'

Her eyes shone like synthetic sapphires.

'It's not a name I'd ever call a boy,' she said. 'Mark or Peter or Stephen, now they're nice names. But Jasper . . .'

She looked up and stared right into my eyes. I flinched.

'I have something to say to you, Eleanor,' she said.

Her mouth became obstinate.

'Jasper's not your brother,' she said.

'But, Mother——' I said.

'Don't interrupt,' she said. 'Don't make this any more difficult than it's going to be.'

'Mother,' I said gently. 'He's your son. Jasper is your son. This proves it.'

She stared at the birth certificate disdainfully.

'Are you saying he forged it?' I said, my spirits rising. 'Well, of course, he could have, couldn't he, working there——'

'Jasper's not your brother because you, Ellen, are not my daughter,' she said abruptly.

'Dymphna's your mother. Your birth mother, I think they say,' she said, in a rush.

'Darlene . . .' I breathed. 'You can't mean it.'

Elizabeth stared at me unwaveringly.

'*Darlene?*' I said. 'Darlene . . .'

She nodded.

'It was easy enough,' she said. 'Dymphna signed into the hospital under my name. Ron went along with it. He knew how unhappy I'd been. He was the father, as far as the paperwork was concerned, you understand.'

'Ron's not my father, either?' I said.

'No,' she said, and lowered her eyes again.

'Not my father?' I said.

'No,' she repeated softly.

We sat in silence for a moment.

'Then who is?' I said.

'Nobody is,' she said.

'What do you mean?' I said.

'She'd never say,' Elizabeth said. 'We didn't like to push it. Dymphna's always been soft in the head.'

'I doubt you'd get it out of her now,' she said warningly. 'You've seen the state she's in.'

'Does anyone else know that I'm not your daughter?' I said.

She stared into my eyes again. Crank by crank, down into my well.

'Mother?' I said.

'You still call me that?' she said, her eyes filling with tears.

'Marlene, Iris, the men,' she said slowly. 'The whole family knew—but of course, most of them are dead. We all knew. There was no hiding it. I've never seen a woman so enormous in pregnancy. But, then,' she said quietly, 'she was only a child.'

'So you signed the papers, and you adopted me?' I said.

'No. Never,' she said. 'It was never made official. Dymphna impersonated me, you understand. Everything was in my name. They didn't know me, or Dymphna, or any of us in that hospital. Private. Ron paid. She could have said she was Mahatma Gandhi for all they cared.'

'*Prodistants*,' she said.

'Dymphna said she was Elizabeth Bird, and Ron played the proud father, and when it was time to leave the hospital they came straight here, Dymph and Ron, and handed you over to me,' she said.

'Poor little thing with no hair,' she sighed. 'And those startled eyes. Always on edge, you were, as if you knew something was up. I put it down to Dymphna's bad blood at the time.'

'If you'll forgive me,' she said, seeing my face.

'Are you sure you're up to this?' she said.

'Aunty Darlene's my mother?' I said. 'Darlene? Loopy Darlene?'

'Well, yes,' Elizabeth said. 'There's no getting round it.'

'And whoever my father is, is worse,' I said.

'I never said that,' she said quickly. 'Some things are better left uncovered.'

'The father from whom you are is the devil,' I quoted.

'What?' said Elizabeth.

'Nothing,' I said. 'Just something Brother Raymund said once. It's from John's Gospel——'

'Oh, him,' she snorted dismissively. I suppose she meant Brother Raymund.

'Here,' she said. 'I'd better have a drink. I know it's early in the day——'

'Sherry,' I said. 'Bring the bottle.'

'Yes,' she said, slowly, staring at me. 'All right then.'

She returned with the bottle and glasses, and settled herself down again at the foot of my bed.

'She was terribly young, you know,' she said, after we had both swallowed a large amount of drink.

Then she fixed me with her eyes and said: 'You must never say anything of this to her, Eleanor. God knows what damage you'd do, bringing it all up. I don't think what's left of her mind would stand the strain.'

'All these years, and you've never talked about me with her?' I said.

'No,' she said. 'Not since the day she handed you over. There's never been any sort of sign.'

'Was that when she changed her name?' I said.

'It was around that time,' she said vaguely.

'Perhaps it was losing me . . . her baby that sent her crazy,' I said. 'She . . . she . . .'

Elizabeth looked straight at me and said, 'She was always strange.'

I smoothed the slightly crumpled certificate between my fingers.

'And so, Jasper is not my brother,' I said.

'No!' she said. 'That's a happy thought for you.'

'He's just my creepy slimy cousin,' I said.

'At any rate,' she said cheerily, 'you don't have to worry about having committed a particularly offensive sin, as Jasper is only your first cousin. And, while that's not recommended, it's not forbidden either.'

'I don't think,' she said, anxiously, frowning.

'Don't you remember, Mother? Consanguinity is one of the twelve impediments to marriage that can lead to annulment,' I said.

'I'll just get us some tea, shall I?' she said brightly, slipping from the room.

'Or would you rather I went down the road and got a drop more sherry?' she said.

'Sherry,' I said.

'Sweet or dry?' she said.

'Both,' I said. 'Either. Aren't you going to lock me in?'

'Oh, you're not going anywhere, are you?' she said.

∞

'I am, of course, disappointed that you've had intercourse out of wedlock,' she said stiffly, on her return.

As if she'd just remembered who she was.

'Oh, but the baby's dead,' I said. 'So, that's fine then. No *evidence* of sin.'

'Ellen, please,' she said, lowering her eyes.

We sat in silence, and poured ourselves another drink each.

'Perhaps Jasper has that plague. You know, the AIDS. Perhaps he has infected me,' I mumbled. 'Perhaps that is why he——'

'And Andrew!' cried Elizabeth. 'Why——'

'The baby's dead, Mother,' I said again.

'His name was never Andrew,' I said quietly. 'He wasn't yours. He never was. Not your bloody doll——'

'Your spitefulness about the collection has always saddened me, Eleanor,' she said. 'I abhor jealousy.'

'Even so, he wasn't real,' I said bleakly.

'Hush,' she said. 'We must forget about him.'

Time seemed to be sitting very still, as we sat neatly side by side on that child's bed, politely sipping our sherries, surrounded by the posing dolls—like a pair of social outcasts at some outlandish party.

'Anyway, it's better he's dead, really,' I said, then.

'Who?' she said.

Was she drunk? Was I?

'The *baby*,' I said. 'How were you going to explain him?'

'Oh,' she said. 'It's a modern world, Ellen. Many babies are born before a wedding these days. The pregnancy is a sort of engagement period, you might say. Once you and Jasper had done the right thing, there wouldn't have needed to *be* any explaining.'

Good Lord! I thought. I turned to check her face for irony. But she was smiling benignly into her golden sherry. Shock, I suppose.

I sat and thought about all she'd told me.

'What a tissue of lies,' I murmured, then.
'What?' she said.
She turned and gave me a dirty look, all the way down the length of her nose—and it was like soot. I contrasted it with those burning stares that travelled down in pursuit of my soul, that singed.
'Omissions, then,' I said.
'Lies? Is that what you call it?' she cried. 'I was only protecting you, looking out for your best interests.'
'Well, you have to admit——' I said.
'Have to admit!' she shouted. 'It would have been fine if you hadn't led him on. You asked for it! Thrusting your breasts about. How dare you place the blame on me for what you've done. Oh, you know what you've done, all right.'
'And?' I said.
'That was different,' she said.
'I didn't want you to go through what I went through,' she said thinly.
'Now don't start,' she said.
It's one thing to assume the blame, another to be ascribed it. She was watching me, beadily.
'If you say,' I said mildly.
'Oh, Lord,' she said, and took a great swig from her glass.
'I'm sorry,' she mumbled.
'But why did he do it?' she cried. 'Why did he come here, and ingratiate himself into our lives?'
'Revenge?' I said. 'To make his mark?'
'He obviously meant for us to find this,' I said waving the birth certificate. 'You, particularly.'
'I don't know,' she said.
'He must have hated you, for leaving him,' I said.
'Yes,' she said, in a voice like a sigh.
'He must have hated me, for having what he hadn't,' I said.
She nodded.
Was he happy now he'd got what he wanted: this mockery, this travesty?
'But good can come from evil,' she said.
'Oh, Mother,' I said. 'The baby is *dead*.'
'Another one lost, and another one dead,' she said strangely.
Her mouth was shaped like a groan. She watched me with her bright blue eyes.
'He was my son,' she said bleakly. 'I had him for such a short time.'

'Twice, now . . . for such a short time,' she said, her eyes full of pleading.

'You don't see, do you? I only had him for a moment,' she said. 'After he was born, I saw him, with his thatch of black hair. That was a mistake, of course. I wasn't supposed to see him . . . Not my mistake, theirs. Or perhaps it was mine.'

'They took him away so quickly,' she said. 'And now this . . .'

She looked up at me and her eyes were terrible. I looked away.

I poured her another sherry, topping up my own.

Again, we sat in silence.

'And you were young, also?' I said. 'Like Darlene?'

'Not so young, but yes,' she sighed, 'young enough, and foolish.'

'Sixteen,' she said.

'Sixteen,' I sighed. 'But then Jasper . . . My God! He did hold his age well, didn't he?'

Silence. The two of us grimacing into our sherry . . .

'Poor Granny,' I said. 'With the two of you——'

'She took it in her stride,' she snapped. 'Said I must do what I had to do. Sent me away.'

'I gave birth to my baby, and then came back and went on with my schooling as if nothing had happened,' she said.

'And then Darlene,' I said.

'That was many years later,' she sighed. 'We were good Catholic girls. *Ignorant*. It would have happened to Marlene, too, except that she was so bossy no boy would ever go out with her.'

'I always thought there was something about you,' I said slowly.

'And I, you,' she said, staring into her sherry.

'You weren't him,' she said flatly. 'That was it, although I didn't like to say it to myself.'

She sighed and plucked at the bedclothes, then looked up and stared me horribly in the eye.

'I took you to make up for him,' she said. 'It didn't seem wrong. There weren't any babies for Ron and me. I thought I was being punished for what I'd done earlier. And then Dymphna had her trouble, and it was your father—Ron—he always thought of himself as your father, you know. It was Ron who said, "Why don't we, Liz?" "What?" I said. "Why don't *we* take the baby?" I was well over thirty then. Middle-aged. It wasn't unheard of, but it was different in those days. Still, Dymphna was a change-of-life baby herself. She was only thirteen, you know. Twelve, when he got to her.'

'*Who?*' I said. 'Please.'

'Oh, leave it, Eleanor,' Elizabeth snapped.

'Why don't you like my name? You've never liked my name,' I said petulantly.

'It's not a real name, you know,' she said. 'Dymphna made it up. I think she read something like it somewhere—and got it all wrong, as she does.'

She sighed, and clicked her tongue.

'"If you're good enough to take my baby, you're good enough to take the name I've chosen for her," she said, and I had to go along with it. If it had been up to me, though, I would have chosen a nice plain name like Susan or Mary,' she said, gazing at me appealingly—as if she was sure I would, improbably, after all this time, agree.

'I tried to get you to shorten it,' she said. 'When you were little, remember? Ellen, Nora. You were stubborn as a mule, even as a girl of two or three.'

'You won't tell me who my father was?' I said.

'It's better I don't,' she said. 'You can rest assured though. At least he wasn't family.'

'At least,' I repeated dully.

'God,' I said. 'Let's have another one.'

How many was that? Elizabeth held her glass out, and I poured unsteadily.

'And Jasper's father?' I said.

'Oh, him. Nobody,' she said impatiently, lowering her eyes.

'It wasn't Ron?' I said.

'No,' she said, and hung her head. 'I'd rather not say, really.'

'He was already married?' I said.

No answer. Then:

'He was not free,' she said.

'He's long gone, Eleanor,' she said. 'He came back and then he went away again . . .'

'But good old Ron put his hand up for that one, too,' I said. 'I mean, he's on the bit of paper.'

'It's all on computers now, as well, isn't it?' she said listlessly. 'I'd known Ron since I was a little girl. He'd lived three doors down from me all my life. I always knew I would marry him. He was a decent man. Kind. Not that it was obvious . . .'

'But *both* birth certificates,' I said.

'I told you. He loved me,' said Elizabeth. 'It was all in the family.'

'Right,' I said.

'So, on paper, at least, Jasper's my brother,' I said.
'Yes,' she sighed.
'And Ron's our father,' I said.
'I never said——' she said.
'Our paper father, then,' I said.
'Mother?' I said. 'Please. Who is he really?'
'Who's who?' she said.
'I know,' I said, laughing sharply. 'It's Elvis!'
'Don't be ridiculous,' she said. 'I don't know what's gotten into you. You changed, you know, when you went off the rails.'
She stared at me hard, favouring my green eye.
'What about Father Dougherty, or Father Flynn?' I said. 'Or better still, Brother Raymund!'
She glanced up quickly, then lowered her eyes.
'You're drunk,' she said.
'Father Flynn?' I said. *'Brother Raymund?'*
Good old Elizabeth, planter of the seed of doubt.
'I never said,' she said. But she would not raise her eyes.
Omissions, the holes in the webbing of untruth . . .
Oh. There is more. I am sure of it.
What did I know? What did I *know*? Only what Elizabeth had told me.

She'd exposed areas of truth, then covered them up again. Caught out—or having backed herself into a corner—she exposed another 'truth' (supposedly more palatable). She reminded me of herself, flicking through her recipe files, waiting for inspiration.
'So that's what Jasper thought was true,' I said.
'About Ron?' she said.
'That I was his sister,' I said.
'Well——' she said.
'He worked for the Registry,' I said. 'He thought he knew the truth.'
She sat there, her mouth gaping.
'He did it deliberately!' I said. 'Cold-bloodedly. He . . . he seduced me, he made me pregnant, he let me imagine——'
'I can't believe——' she said.
'Anyway,' I said bitterly. 'It's *all in the family*, isn't it? So that's okay.'
'Eleanor, *please*,' she said.
'You still call me that?' I said dryly.
'Don't make this worse,' Elizabeth said.
'How can it be worse than it is?' I said.
And we both sat, slumped, staring at the floor.

'Mother,' I said, then. 'What name did you give your baby?'

Was she my mother? My aunt? A person of no blood relationship? My grandmother? My *sister*?

It makes little difference now. She has so totally mothered me, and I have become what I have become. And the matter of blood ... Well. The baby *is* dead, isn't it?

'I called him Raymund,' she said, and looked up at me, her blue eyes frightened and full of tears.

'Raymund?' I said. 'With a U?'

My whole universe tilted.

III

96

WHEN YOU ARE BORN you are pushed out of your world, your red room, your plush nest—pushed out, expelled, contractions gripping you like great shoving hands—pushed up, as if you are convulsed—vomited up from the bowels of the earth—pushed out, into the over-bright light, towards faces with masks and knives in their hands.

And when you die you are shoved from your perch on this earth, into the over-darkness.

And this earth, a testing ground? A way-station? A waiting room, merely?

Or are we being punished, for sins we have forgotten?

I think about the baby . . . rushing into infinity. What will it find there? Will it stay in heaven—or limbo? Did I baptise sufficiently? Will it rest? Or have I damned it, like me, for all eternity?

I see it twirling into a bottomless pit of darkness, flecked with what might be stars, but are only other white shapes twirling slowly down—like snowflakes, or ashes . . .

I think about the baby now, torn from its red room—after so short a stay, it must have seemed—forced tunnelling through clutching darkness towards the light.

What did it make of its new rooms, with their sharp edges? Rows of dolls like rigid frills, lumpen furniture hard against white uprights, and the gnarled old faces bent towards it?

So little time to adjust. And then it met Jasper's pillow, and darkness. Darkness, I suppose? And again the clammy tunnelling, the self thrust forward into the light.

I can only hope it *has* gone into the light—the light that I can only see now as darkness—the darkness that is light. That in dying it has been born, that this life we know is death, is hell—that death *is* life, and that Raymund Allan was right about one thing: that there is nothing, nothing whatsoever to fear. And the faces more welcoming, I hope, on the other side.

OUR HOUSE IS OF the type known as a bungalow. It is dark brick with brisk white trim. Our house, pulsing with enormous anger and unforgiveness.

In Glass Street there are mostly bungalows. Ours is the largest, then Miss Carew's next door.

In the surrounding streets, there are old apartment buildings the colour of offal, and new ones the colour of tripe.

Lemonhurst!

No-one builds houses around here any more. They knock them down and put up blocks of units instead, to squeeze more people in and make more money. Not that it is an especially desirable suburb.

Glass Street is the best street in this part of Lemonhurst: sloping, curved, shady, with lacy handkerchiefs of lawn and flowerbeds, and established European trees. (I expect the apartment-dwellers are envious of our situation.)

Who would think our quiet house on pleasant Glass Street—a shady haven in that Hades known as Lemonhurst—would hold so many secrets? Who would think, to look at it: crisp and clean-lined as a Christmas cake? Who would imagine these things? That its plaster had lapped up all Elizabeth's sadnesses, her sour self-righteousness, all Ron's rants and rages, and all my maudlin murmurings? That its walls had absorbed so many muffled wails? That its foundations were feeding on the blood and bone of several corpses?

∞

The land slopes away beneath our house, towards the front, the street. It is not a tremendous slope, not a remarkable one—a visitor would hardly notice it. But below the house the incline is quite pronounced.

There is an area where you can stand—the cellar proper, where the congregation stood, where we held the Latin Mass—which is mostly floored in concrete now, and then, towards the back, a series of closer and closer spaces.

The air is dank and cloying there. But it is not damp. The floor of the rooms above form a low and cobwebbed ceiling. There are some spots where one can only crawl.

It was to this low-ceilinged, close place that Elizabeth moved that day.

'Here,' she said. 'The ground is quite soft.'

Indeed, it was soft and moist and red. A silken red dirt that clung to itself. With our little hand-spades we dug away.

I was, all the time, expecting to unearth the tiny body of his brother. But that was only a tale of Jasper's! And—supposing it were true—would Elizabeth take me to its burial place, only to unearth it, having taken the trouble to have hidden its existence from me? Of course not! It was nonsense, the sort of pointless nonsense Jasper left about him in a trail.

Even so, something strange occurred yesterday.

I was in the city, rummaging through the department stores and, for the queerest moment, I thought I saw him, reflected in one of the mirrored pillars: Jasper, holding in his arms a baby—gliding from mirror to mirror like a saint. Jasper, his mouth open, his eyes filmed, as if undersea. And the baby, so pale, so fair, and with a tuft of hair as bright and red as mine!

The twin, I thought. *My* twin.

I ran towards them—pushed my way through stolid shoppers.

'Excuse me,' I said, shouted.

'Jasper, wait!' I shrieked.

Faces turned to stare at me. But they were gone, the man and the red-haired infant, as if they were never there.

Well, of course they *weren't*. Not our Jasper, not my child. You can't bring the dead back to life. Can you?

But the twin. Would that child be Jasper's half-brother, both brother and son to him—or do I mean cousin and son? Both nephew and son to me?

But this is ridiculous. How could a second child have survived, and I not known? Upstairs, in my room, two in the crib . . . Surely Elizabeth could not be so perverse as to allow it? What reason could there possibly be? But, then, God in his wisdom is mysterious and perverse, isn't he?

When we had hollowed out a suitable resting place, we took the baby from the laundry basket—where Elizabeth had lain him, wrapped in towels.

We placed him in the hole. We covered him with the soft red dirt—that clung to our fingers.

Suddenly, I could not bear to think of it covering his face.

'Mother! He cannot breathe!' I cried.

I steadied myself, after a dreadful look from Elizabeth.

We shovelled on with our tiny spades, until we had him fully covered.

'Tea?' she said then, as if we had merely been doing a spot of gardening.

∞

How strange to see her, now—her hands quietly clasped, her eyes bright and fervent—and know what she has done.

What we have done.

Her hands, then, tight on the shovel, her face red and contorted, her eyes diamond bright.

'*Pace Aeterna*,' I'd said. Eternal peace.

'What?' she said now, staring at me across the table.

Had I spoken out loud?

'Oh, I was remembering,' I said.

'You!' she said. 'That's a laugh!'

I would have thought after all this—after all this time—that there would have been a softening of the heart: understanding, acceptance. The wisdom of forgiveness.

But there is no forgiveness. Our life is as much a pretence as it ever was. Watching, watching one another—bumping up against each other's peculiarities, our lips withered with disapproval—hoping to catch each other out.

My heart is as empty of love, as cavernous, as dark as it ever was. And I can only assume that we are alike in this.

98

I CAUGHT THE BUS up to the Mall today for the first time in ages—it's odd, I haven't wanted to leave the house—and I ventured over to the studio, half-expecting Otto to have vacated (and what, run off with Jasper?)

Well, in short, book—I got my old job back!

The new girl was a real drifter, Otto said. And then he had some teenager, on some government scheme.

'It's a joy to have you back, El,' he said.

'It won't be forever, Otto,' I warned him.

'For however long,' he said. And then he blushed.

'I thought it best to keep away,' he said. 'Your mother——'

'It's okay,' I said.

'Oh, but I did ring! Months and months ago,' he assured me. 'I rang to enquire after your health. Your mother—I expect it was your mother—answered. "There is no-one here by that name," she said, and plonked the receiver down in my ear.'

'Sounds like Elizabeth,' I said. 'Oh, God! I suppose she didn't want to lose me.'

Or her baby. Her *babies*. Her little family . . .

'Thought I was going to carry you away, did she?' Otto twinkled. 'Deduced my inner knight?'

'And . . . the infant?' he said.

I sighed and shook my head.

'Some things are better . . .' he said. 'I'm sorry, El, dear——'

'How well do you know Jasper?' I said abruptly.

'Jasper Pease?' he said, looking genuinely surprised. 'Only what I told you. God, El. I'm no club-bunny!'

'Fingal and I,' he said. 'We like quiet things.'

'Actually...' he mumbled, his eyes lowered. 'There *was* something.'

'Yes?' I said.

'Oh, it was most awkward,' Otto said.

'*Yes*?' I said.

'He came to the studio one day,' he muttered. 'After the Alphabet—the night we met there, I told you?'

'I remember, Otto,' I said.

'He wanted...' Otto stopped, and sighed heavily. 'He wanted me to take some photos of his friend——'

'A blond man?' I said.

'*Yes*,' Otto shuddered. 'I explained I didn't do that sort of work. Oh, it was peculiar, El! He seemed to know an awful lot about me.'

'I don't do that sort of thing any more!' Otto cried. His face was lined and anxious. 'I do... dogfood tins and well, *you* know, and I'm proud of it.'

'Yes, Otto, and you do beautiful work,' I said.

The poor man stood there panting shallowly.

'Don't worry, Otto,' I said. 'He just thinks he knows things.'

'Ye-es,' he said, and laughed. 'Yes, the old pongster. What would *he* know?'

'He's just a creep,' I said. 'A sad old twisted lonely creep.'

'Not *entirely* bad-looking, though,' Otto said.

'Not entirely,' I agreed.

∞

Then, this evening, I walked to St Clare's in the last of the pastel twilight.

I was still looking for an answer.

I caught Father Flynn, looking disconsolate.

'Father!' I said. 'Am I too late?'

'Late, early. I'm not exactly rushed off my feet either way,' he said.

'It's been a long time since we've spoken, Eleanora,' he said sadly.

'Yes,' I said. 'I'm sorry. I've been... so busy.'

'And you were in Byron Bay, for a time?' he said.

'For a time,' I said.

'But you did not get a tan,' he said. 'Ah.'

He looked at me quizzically, then said, gesturing: 'Shall we?'

'You *have* come for reconciliation?' he said, when I hesitated.

'I think so,' I said.

'Would you prefer it the old way?' he said, indicating the confessional box.

'I don't think the light's good enough in there,' I said, thrusting my book at him.

Again he looked at me, his face soft with puzzlement and patience.

'I have sinned terribly, Father,' I said.

'Well, never mind,' he said. 'I don't know about you, but my God does not turn away in disgust from sinners.'

No, I thought, he *burns* them.

'It's all in there,' I said.

'Please,' I said helplessly.

I sat in silence while he read you.

A long, long silence.

When he had finished, he closed the book and laid it slowly on the pew beside him, and looked across at me.

'There,' I said bleakly. 'You know it all.'

'And I shall never forget, Eleanora,' he said, taking both my hands between his. 'Never, never, never. But I am not the one you seek.'

Then I began to cry.

So few tears . . .

'Forgive me, Father,' I said.

'You have my absolution,' he said. 'Your Father in Heaven forgives you, my child, even before you can *think* of the sin . . .'

Was it so? I was already redeemed, already forgiven?

Could it be?

Perhaps the rustling I heard was in fact the settling of the feathers of my guardian angel's wings!

'Do you know, Eleanora,' Father Flynn said excitedly, 'the Hebrew word for repent means *to remember*?'

'Yes?' I said.

I noticed he was sweating.

'And sin,' he went on. 'Listen to this. I hope I've got it right. Sin, now. Sin has its root in the Hebrew word for *forgetting*. Isn't that marvellous? Mind you, in Greek the meaning is *missing the mark*. Which we as humans tend to do, somewhat.'

'Yes, murder,' I said.

'Murderers, thieves, prostitutes! My God excludes no-one, Eleanora. No-one!' he cried earnestly.

'So you see . . .' he said. 'So you see?'

'Repent, my darling, *repent*,' he said. He flung his hands out, gazing into my eyes. 'And I shall repent with you.'

'But, Father——' I said, my eyes filling with tears.

'Forgiveness,' he said. 'It's a matter of simultaneously remembering, but . . . cultivating the ability to forget, I think.'

'It's easy,' he said. 'Well, no. Actually. Actually, I tell a lie . . .'

'Actually, I don't know, really,' he muttered. 'Actually, Eleanora, you see. The truth is, I've never had a murderer. A murder. *Adultery*, yes . . . But. A hundred Our Fathers? What do *you* think? It's a formality, really . . . Yes, a hundred. That should do the trick. Now, let's get down to business.'

He concluded the rite, blessed me, then handed you back. His sad brown eyes were soft with kindness.

'Is that it?' I said, trying not to cry again.

He shrugged, and smiled nervously.

'That's my best,' he said simply. 'Go in peace, Eleanora.'

I sat, staring at the pew.

The weight of it, the weight of it!

'Father, what shall I do with this?' I cried, waving you about. 'Burn it?'

'Burn it? You must be joking!' he said. 'We live in a modern age, Eleanora, and must behave accordingly.'

'Publish it,' he said.

∞

I had one answer. But still so many questions.

If Ron was not my father, what gave him the right to beat me? Did he beat me because I was *not* his child? Is that why Elizabeth allowed it?

And my *real* father . . .

He's long-gone, she said. He went away, and then he came back again . . .

Not in the family, she said.

Who knew when she lied?

He was not free, she said. That meant married or in the clergy . . . or in the family.

Well. They were all long dead.

It could have been Father Flannery, or any visiting priest . . .

But why call her baby Raymund? It was not a common spelling of a common name, or plain, or even short, the way she liked them.

And if Raymund *was* Jasper's father, possibly—could he have been also mine?

She was so jealous of him, and so queer with Darlene. And then, his eyes. The way he followed me with his strange pale eyes. The way he always knew where I was, in any room . . .

If Raymund *was* our father, then he was the baby's grandfather, both paternal and maternal . . .

Had I—had we—had Elizabeth and I, in killing Brother Raymund killed my—what should I call him? My *sperm*-father?

Had I—had we?

If I had known then what I know now . . .

But perhaps I would never have known anything, without these events occurring?

What do I know, anyway?

Truth? The truth? Ha! Because of the lies—so many lies—because of the cover-ups, the burials . . . Truth—the actual truth—is gone. Dust, or ash. Unknowable.

And absolution? How?

How can a heart so black and cavernous as mine make that conversion? If I am truly contrite, I am already forgiven, Father Flynn says. So it goes. Before the sin—the sins—have been confessed. Before the impulse to commit them.

But, am I truly contrite? Am I?

WELL. THAT IS THAT. I have spoken. Or rather you, book, have spoken for me. But there is something else that must be told.

He did not die that night.

No. He did not die that night. Nor the next day, nor the next. On the third day . . .

Well. Let me begin with that first morning.

I went downstairs early, unlocking the cellar door. Elizabeth was still asleep.

Virtuously, I sped down into the cellar, thinking—what? That I would tidy up this mess for her?

He was not dead, book.

I touched his clammy neck, and felt a pulse. (He was cold, yes. But it had been a cool night, and cooler I'm sure, down there.) He lived! He breathed!

The horror of it! There was blood soaked into the earth around his head, blood spreading in a halo . . .

I expected—what? Eyes flung open? Accusations? A chill hand clutching at my throat? But he just lay there. Brother Raymund lay there, breathing shallowly.

'Oh God,' I groaned.

Elizabeth took the news calmly. Coldly.

'Well,' she said. 'He's not coming into any house of mine.'

'But, Mother——' I said.

'He can stay there,' she sniffed. 'Make him comfortable. The spare quilt.'

'Mother——' I said.

'Give him,' she said, fixing me with a sharp blue eye, 'a drink, why don't you, Ellen? Give him some of your special wine.'

I stared.

'I'm not touching him,' she said.

'You tend to him,' she said. 'It won't be long.'

But Brother Raymund was our guest for several days. Days, book, in that awful state. Our *captive*.

After a while, he would take no more of the wine.

I left him alone then, in the cellar, for hours on end. For days . . .

On the third day, I went down to him. His eyes were closed and motionless—they never opened. I knelt beside him and touched his neck again. Still, he breathed!

I sat with him a while. And then I noticed something strange. Tears of blood were forming slowly, and running down his face.

'Mother!' I shouted. 'Come quick. I think a sign——'

As Elizabeth clattered down the stairs, he jerked his head up and sharply vomited—his mouth open in a grimace or a roar—a massive jet of blood that sprayed the dirt around him, that clung in droplets to my hair.

And then he sank down into death.

'Well, that's done,' Elizabeth said.

I slid the quilt from his body then, thinking I would soak it—but Elizabeth ordered it burnt.

I waited a while, then went down and checked his pulse. Nothing moved. No blood, no breath.

I touched his neck again, and shivered.

He was dead.

(Who knows? Perhaps he had already absolved us of our actions, and was, at that particular moment—as I stood in the cellar contemplating how to dispose of his stiffening body—putting in a good word for us, and including us in his prayers.)

I took—I cannot explain this—the opportunity to inspect Brother Raymund's penis. Awful, awful. Just as awful as Sylvester's.

I stared again at the tattoo on his thigh. Two gods? Two warrior gods? One dark, one fair . . . The twins, of course—one dark, one light!

Of course, it all makes sense when seen like that—Hiroshima, the Holocaust. This century . . .

Two gods, not one. And my God weak, not up to it.

It all makes sense if everything that I've been taught is an invention designed to deny, or hide from, or obscure this central fact. But not a deliberate lie. No, surely?

100

WHAT IF EVERYTHING I think I know is . . . *inverted*?
  What if my strangest perceptions are correct?
  If I am mad, then I am not alone in this. I've been to the library and looked up Brother Raymund's twins. I've been reading books on Gnosticism and dualism, and short entries, mostly—the greater knowledge having been burnt, or buried, or hidden?—on the practices and beliefs of the Manichees.
  There are two gods, they say. A god of matter and a god of spirit. A God of Darkness, who created earth and rules it, and his co-equal, creator of heaven and God of Light. (This is my God, in another guise. Less powerful than he's been presented to me all my life. Oh, book, I pity him!)
  Good/Evil, Spirit/Flesh, Light/Dark. Or—and this is most interesting, I think—Truth and Lie. The two principles, forever in combat, and fighting for our souls. (The dark god—the flood-causing, jealous, vengeful God of the Old Testament?—or something darker, hungrier?)
  These were *his* beliefs, book. The more I read, the more I'm sure of it. What he did, what was done, is more understandable now—but how could he have perpetrated that disgusting Eucharistic sacrilege upon us?
  In these old books I have read of others with my belief: that we, trapped in our bodies—our luminous spirits engulfed in matter—caught in this material world, are now in hell. (There! There! There! I am not alone!) That we dwell, on earth, in hell. That we are the damned.
  If we are indeed in hell, then are we fallen angels? Imprisoned here, incarcerated in our bodies, yet driven by the ache of like

desiring to return to like—Light calling to the light that is our spirit?

How to release the captive spirit? Forgiveness, Father Flynn said. Far harder than following Brother Raymund's, or the Manichees' rigid diet.

The Albigenses, the Vaudois, the Catari (of whom St Francis of Assisi was a suspected member, because of his commitment to poverty!), and the Bogomils—all Manichaean offshoots—were persecuted, were *roasted*, by the Church during the Inquisition. The Church——

Was Brother Raymund enacting some sort of belated payback for this slaughter and suppression?

Had he come into our lives to find me, and then stayed to pay the Church back—Elizabeth being incidental? As, inversely, Jasper came to pay back Elizabeth, and found me. (And could not resist the urge to add a little spice of corruption to his task? Oh, book—and could not resist *me*?)

If we are fallen angels, then am I, in my night-time horrors of the abyss, not looking into my future, but my past—our terrible Fall?

Are we the angels who fell?

Are we *angels*, book?

Did we fall to earth? Have we fallen into these awful bodies? Buried alive, in these tombs of flesh. Endlessly struggling to be freed, cannon fodder in this infernal war. Then——

I, too, am at war, within myself. The good self, who stays at home and goes to church and is helpful and industrious, no matter what my mother, what Elizabeth says. (And I don't care what she says about my parentage, I cannot embrace Darlene and call her Mother, now. I would rather a fury than a fool.) The good self, and its evil twin, who wrote this journal, or much of it, who thinks bad things—or makes accurate observations, I've come to recognise.

And then, the Church. Where does it stand within this war? Is it of the Light—or is it, as Brother Raymund said, corrupt, 'a stinking corpse'; itself, the Beast?

Most peculiar of all this knowledge I've been scanning is this small item regarding smell. One strange entry, in a fusty book with peculiar blood-brown print and curious typeface, spoke of the gods as twins: one fair and sweet-smelling—fragrant!—and the other dark of colouring and evil-odoured.

Did Jasper know of this, with all his talk of twins? *Could* Jasper have known of this? Jasper, who was as beautiful in the end to me as, it is said, Lucifer can appear. What was he? Who was he? A ghoul? A chameleon? A mirage?—as this God I have been taught so much about now seems to be.

Did he *know*? Did he know Raymund was our father? Did he know we killed him? *Did he know about the two gods*? Did he know about the war between them, between us, inside us, between the splitting parts of me?

Or was he just a vicious drifter, toying with us, keen on Elvis, knowing nothing real about any of us, or anything at all?

He was here, so briefly, and now he's gone . . . But even Jasper brought his gifts.

Didn't he say: God loves a sinner. Well, my old God *did* love St Augustine—who believed in his youth in the Manichean heresies, in the *two*. Or Light blessed light, looked at another way, when light, all but extinguished in the darkness of the flesh, divined the true essential state of things . . .

And Christ loved Mary Magdalene——

Oh, book, this is all hopelessly jumbled, I know.

I do not understand. I do not understand Elizabeth, or Jasper, or Brother Raymund—only inklings . . .

But I cannot forget his words, that day, when I sat outside in some despair. There is light beyond the darkness, he said. The darkness *is* light. If we could only see it . . . but it blinds us.

Is *everything* inverted?

Is . . .

Oh, book! We *can* be freed! There is hope for all of us! In the not knowing, there is hope.

To hell with certainty. I shall keep . . . no, more than just breathing. I shall keep tunnelling into the light.

101

I AM SLEEPING, ONCE again, in my old bedroom upstairs. Where the baby died, and so much with it. I lie down quietly, every night. I expect that is where I am supposed to be, for now?

We did it. We both did it. All of it.

What else?

Oh, say it, won't you?

That morning, book. The argument at breakfast—soft eggs, toast, and ruby grapefruit—when I had answered back, and Elizabeth laughed uncharacteristically, and Ron's face swelled and rose above the table like an angry sun.

That morning. You see. It was the day his heart exploded . . .

We killed him.

There.

After the first, the rest were easy.

∞

I cannot go just now. Though I will go. Soon. I cannot leave Elizabeth here, in this house—her house—with so many layers of truth buried below her. And she will never leave, now.

If only she would go *before* me. Then I would take my matches to every curtain. And, last, the doll-room. I would lie down on the floor and watch their eyes pop, their smug little faces curling in the heat . . .

No. Not that.

Soon I shall go, up to the mountains. I shall flee to the mountains! (There *are* mountains near Byron Bay, aren't there?)

Soon, soon, I shall put down my pen, book. I shall close you, and let who will find you do with you as they will.

No. No, that is not right.

When I leave, I will bury you with them, book, deep in the dank earth of the cellar. I will leave all my secrets behind, to commune with one another. And the waters ... No. And then *time* will corrupt you, as it does memory, as it does flesh.

But, no. That is not right, either.

Soon, I shall put down my pen and I shall rise and I shall walk from this house.

Soon. Slowly, at first, then faster, surer, I shall walk away, and towards the world.

This is the way it will be. Yes. Soon.